Hallowed Grounds

Hallowed Grounds

PATRICK J. O'BRIAN

ISBN: 978-1-60414-921-0

PRINTED IN THE UNITED STATES OF AMERICA

Thanks to Wayne Loudy, Becky Tolbert, Troy Lobosky, Kevin Sommers, Brent Mundy, Brian Tolbert, Jim Hathaway, Whitley Tolbert, Frank Stapleton, Dave Blackford, Barbara Caster, Brad Wiemer, Jason Chafin, and Korby Sommers for their participation in this project.

Special thanks to Kendrick Shadoan at KLS Digital for creating the cover, handling photography, and doing a great job as always.

Visit www.klsdigital.com

Other novels by Patrick J. O'Brian include:

The Fallen
Reaper: Book One of the West Baden Murders Series
The Brotherhood
Retribution: Book Two of the West Baden Murders Series
Stolen Time
Sins of the Father: Book Three of the West Baden Murders Series
Six Days
Dysfunction
The Sleeping Phoenix
Snowbound: Book Four of the West Baden Murders Series
Sawmill Road
Ghosts of West Baden: Book Five of the West Baden Murders Series
Red Rain
Sin Killer
The Doomsday Clock: Book Six of the West Baden Murders Series

Non-fiction projects by Patrick J. O'Brian include:
Risen from the Ashes: The History of the West Baden Springs Hotel
Pluto in the Valley: The History of the French Lick Springs Hotel

Check out the author's other projects at
www.pjobooks.com
or look him up on Facebook.

Chapter 1

Jeffrey Lancaster couldn't believe life as he knew it was truly coming to an end. He supposed in truth it already *had* ended, but his mind wasn't registering the events from the past few hours as factual quite yet. Images from the courtroom still flashed through his mind, along with the finality of the verdict. Months of preparation, negotiation, and finally arbitration left him emotionally drained, weakened, and virtually flat broke.

After fifteen years of marriage he never expected to navigate through divorce proceedings, particularly since he wasn't the party that filed.

Making matters worse, he heard rumors that his now ex-wife had slept with one of his colleagues at work. Under ordinary circumstances such an act of treason was unforgivable, but considering he worked for the sheriff's department in Lawrence County, it only compounded the problem. How was he supposed to back up a fellow deputy he now knew slept in *his* bed with *his* wife while he patrolled local Indiana roads?

Currently driving toward his temporary home directly from the courtroom proceedings, Lancaster still couldn't believe his luck. Not only had Candice filed for divorce, but she came away with almost everything he owned. He retained his pension at the expense of his house, his boat, and what stocks they once shared. Left with an old truck, the family dog, and a few minor bills, Lancaster felt a pang in the pit of his stomach that just wouldn't leave. She also saddled him with the horse they bought a year ago for the farm she now possessed. They intended to buy a second horse for weekend rides together before Candice decided to end their marriage.

Seeing a familiar stop ahead, he decided to pull in for some dinner even though he wasn't particularly hungry.

Although they had never shot pool or attended cookouts together, Lancaster considered Roy Daugherty a friend. The man owned a Marathon gas station on Highway 37 that Lancaster frequented in uniform, and sometimes after work. He supposed right now he just needed to see a friendly, familiar face before heading home for the night.

Pulling his marked police car into a vacant slot, Lancaster stepped out to find the early August weather muggy and stiflingly warm. Still wearing dress slacks, along with a nice shirt and tie, Lancaster found the cloth sticking beneath his armpits because he hadn't stopped sweating all day. His perspiration originated more from nerves inside the courtroom than the unforgiving weather.

At least the settlement took place with hardly any audience.

"Jeff!" Daugherty called out in a friendly manner from behind the counter when he spotted Lancaster entering his establishment. "You're dressed a bit fancy today."

"Divorce court," Lancaster said wearily.

Daugherty's broad smile immediately diminished to a frown.

"Sorry to hear that, brother. How did it go?"

"It's over."

Nodding his head upward, the gas station owner seemed to understand that Lancaster wasn't quite ready to talk about the details.

"I've got some pizzas ready if you're hungry."

Daugherty always gave him half price, regardless of whether Lancaster was in uniform or not. In some ways the man was like an uncle, but the two men never met outside the gas station, short of an accidental run-in at the grocery store, or walking the streets during the town's annual festival.

With a thick mane of gray hair, the owner stood four inches over six feet, built like a football player with a gut that hid his belt buckle. He wore a shirt with the company logo each day he worked, which was often because he didn't trust the help to leave all of the cash in the register. From what Lancaster understood the man didn't need to work at all because the store thrived either way. Daugherty liked getting his hands dirty, though, so he often came in to make certain the store was stocked and clean.

Sauntering around the store, trying to decide what he wanted, Lancaster knew deep down he was simply killing time. Going home to an empty house hadn't suited him the past few months, but he wasn't about to stoop to the level of his ex-wife and jump into bed with the next woman he saw. He knew of local officers and state troopers who did just that, and their reputations quickly became tarnished beyond belief.

Daugherty waited on a few customers who walked inside to pay for gas and buy cigarettes. Lancaster decided on a personal supreme pizza and a Pepsi in the meantime, taking them up to the counter once the other customers were finished. He set them on the counter as the owner rang them through, deducting fifty percent as usual.

"That'll be three-seventy-six," Daugherty said as Lancaster handed him a five.

The gas station owner started to get the change out of the drawer, stopping suddenly to point at the state lottery tally.

"It's over one-hundred-million tonight," he stated as though everyone should buy a ticket.

Lancaster never understood the craze of people buying numerous tickets when the lottery reached record levels. He figure a million was enough to keep him perfectly content and financially safe for life. Taking a look into his wallet, he saw no other monetary bills, thinking he probably wanted the single back in case he needed it later. Deciding a dollar really didn't help him much in the scheme of things, he motioned with a nonchalant wave for Daugherty to run him an instant ticket.

"Can't win if you don't have a horse in the race," the man spoke his sagely advice, probably learned from fortune cookies at a Chinese restaurant down the road.

He handed Lancaster the ticket and his loose change, which the deputy pocketed while staring at the ticket. Though the lottery was a completely random drawing, the sequence of numbers didn't look very appealing to him.

01 02 04 08 15 28

Considering the numbers ranged into the high forties, Lancaster wrote the ticket off as a loser right away while slipping it into his shirt pocket. With no reason to linger inside the store, he was once again re-minded about his terrible day and the fact that he was destined to return to an empty house.

After thanking Daugherty for the discount, as he customarily did, Lancaster gave a quick wave before exiting as another customer walked inside. He set the Pepsi in the cup holder and the pizza beside him in the passenger seat. Most of the drive home didn't register in his memory be-cause Lancaster continued to dwell upon the new chapter of his life. Only a few years away from turning forty, he didn't feel like playing the field again or trying to find love on one of the many dating websites. Maybe that would change over time, but without much of anything to his name, Lancaster simply wanted to re-establish his life and his finances.

After living in virtual isolation on a country farm, Lancaster detested living in town where everyone seemed to know everyone else's business. His neighbors acted enthused about a county police officer living right next door, but he didn't like parking his car along the street. Between youthful vandals who liked defacing property, and the town police who avoided him as though *he* had committed the heinous offenses that ended his marriage, Lancaster hated being stuck within city limits.

The population in Mitchell, Indiana, never wavered much from around four-thousand people. Located along a highway, it offered several gas stations and fast food chain restaurants to travelers and locals alike, but most of the industry had shriveled up over the years. When one of the nation's largest school bus producers up and left, the town took hits in population and tax revenue. Other manufacturing businesses constantly came and went, often within the same tired old buildings.

Downtown contained a few churches, second-hand stores, and eater-ies, which didn't seem the least bit busy during the late afternoon. Lancaster turned on Eighth Street, one of the most traveled streets in town, and host to some of the nicest Victorian homes in the county. Well-maintained, and painted in a variety of colors, the residences were the envy of people who lived in other neighborhoods. Despite his hatred for living in town, Lancaster couldn't make too much of a stink because he lived in one of the nicest homes on the street.

Fortunate that his brother had yet to sell the place, because he was moving into his custom-built house in the county, Lancaster paid nothing to stay there, despite offering his brother every other paycheck as rent. His brother simply asked him to monitor the property, help him pack and move, and eventually clean and paint the house as payment.

Lancaster parked his patrol car along the street because his personal truck occupied the driveway while the two-stall garage was full of loaded boxes and his brother's tools, including a few lawn mowers. Stepping out, he looked at the two-story house, complete with balcony on the second story, wishing he could transport it to a rural road and keep it. In another month it would be listed with a realtor, likely sold before winter, while Lancaster contemplated where he was destined to live next.

Taking up his pizza and Pepsi, Lancaster trudged toward the house to begin his first official night of bachelorhood in fifteen years.

***

Because he wasn't working the next morning, Lancaster switched from Pepsi to beer within the first hour of being home. Too restless to accomplish anything productive, and unwilling to leave the house after consuming alcohol, he finally plopped on his couch to pass the time with some television.

Every sound echoed throughout the house because very little furniture remained from his brother's tenure, and Lancaster didn't have much to bring with him when he and Candice first separated. If he threw some white sheets over the few remaining items the house might look borderline haunted, he decided.

He eventually drifted off to the sounds of the air conditioning unit sending cool air through the living room vent and music from a local weather channel on the television. It wasn't until a few hours later that he awoke with stiffness and slight pain in his neck from sleeping awkwardly on the couch. Lancaster tried stretching his arms, but even that hurt his neck and he cursed himself for falling asleep before it even grew dark outside. Standing to move his muscles and force his body into an awakened state, he flipped through the channels to see what was on television, finding commercials on virtually every channel until he reached one of the lowest channels possible in the guide.

Finally able to stretch away some of the pain from his neck, Lancaster plopped down into the couch as the state lottery draw appeared live on Channel 4. He flipped the top of the pizza box to discover nothing except a few crusts remained, which he wasn't going to eat. His stomach didn't particularly agree with food at the moment anyway, so he closed the box and lifted each of the beer cans, finding each of the four empty beside the plastic Pepsi bottle.

Grumbling to himself, Lancaster stood again. His footsteps sounded like those of a giant stomping down a path because no carpeting or furniture dampened the sound, and though his feet felt a bit heavy, they weren't crushing the natural wood floors of his brother's living room. The noise dissipated substantially when he reached the tile floor of the kitchen, opening the refrigerator to snag another beer from the bottom shelf.

He lingered in the kitchen, popping the can's top as the numbers announced in the next room circled around his ears like a basketball atop a rim, never truly entering his mind. Carrying his beer, Lancaster ensured that both main doors were locked because thoughts of heading to bed early crept into his mind.

When he returned to the living room, his ears perked up when the numbers were reread because the jackpot was now a record high. A man dressed in a suit stated the numbers emphatically, but Lancaster only caught the last few.

"Fifteen and twenty-eight," ended his second calling of the numbers with a booming voice that indicated it might be someone's lucky night.

Wrinkling his face in confusion because something about those two numbers sounded familiar, Lancaster quickly shook off the notion even as he reached for the ticket in his shirt pocket. His eyes glanced between the numbers on the screen, memorizing them before he dared look at the ticket for a comparison. He constantly played mental games, often testing his short-term memory by studying numbers or phrases before attempting to recall them after a few minutes. In his line of work, it helped to remember details because accurate police reports made testifying in court far easier.

Even with his trained memory, Lancaster couldn't believe his eyes were revealing a true event to him. It had to be some kind of dream, as though he hadn't awoken at all.

01 02 04 08 15 28

"You've got to be fucking kidding me," he muttered, still not believing what he saw.

Chapter 2

Saturday, September 25
One Month Later

"You sure this is what you want to do?" Lancaster's older brother asked him while they both stood at the edge of a long since abandoned property.

David Lancaster had stood by him through the divorce, providing him with a place to stay when he otherwise had none. Of course his brother was an attorney, so money wasn't much of an issue for him. Lancaster never forgot his brother's selflessness, even after the two-hundred million dollar lottery win changed his life. Of course the government took only about a third of that because David was able to minimize the damage through some crafty, but lawful tricks.

His brother inherited dark brown hair from their father, standing nearly as tall as the man who raised them. About the only time the family ever saw David not donning a suit was around the holidays, when he hunted in the fall, or when he found time to attend sporting events. Even then he often wore business casual, as though he didn't own a pair of blue jeans.

"I've always dreamed of this," Lancaster admitted. "Now I don't have anything holding me back."

Lancaster and his brother worked hard during their youth and teenage years, both for family businesses, and other families who hired them during the summer months to work on farms and mow yards. During those times Lancaster loved the few family vacations they took together, often to theme parks. He remembered riding the water log rides, whatever roller coasters he was brave enough to tackle each year, and entering his first haunted house.

He knew exactly what his ideal theme park looked like, with a strange combination of traditional roller coasters and family rides, and the stuff out of horror movies like the ones he grew up watching on weekends when his parents weren't around. People flocked to local haunted houses every fall, and he didn't see a reason to restrain such entertainment to a month or two. People craved a controlled, safe, scary environment like a haunted house much the way they did roller coasters or bungee jumping.

Of course his idea could fall completely flat, and people would say how stupid such a hybrid concept was from the beginning, but Lancaster believed the things he relished were the same things many teenagers and adults enjoyed.

Belief in such a grand project meant gambling his entire new fortune on it, and Lancaster possessed incredible faith that his concept would not fail.

Staring across the flat field that was almost the county fairgrounds decades earlier, Lancaster saw the ruins of a failed theme park hadn't changed much since his childhood. The outbuildings were in disrepair, all faded and in some cases collapsed into heaps. A few carnival style rides remained ahead of him, rusted to the point that their original colors were almost indecipherable. One was a spinning ride with a central post that gave way at some point, sending one rounded edge and several spinning cars into the ground.

Slabs of concrete dotted the otherwise overgrown ground that looked like a domesticated jungle at best. Only a summertime drought and cooling fall temperatures kept it from growing out of control. Behind the crumbling buildings and smaller rides, partially obscured by the morning fog, loomed a wooden roller coaster that stood more out of habit than structural stability. Its wooden structure, covered with moss and rotting from the inside, wasn't destined to stand many more years. Trees and shrubs that cared not for the grand structure simply grew through the track's rungs and between the support beams.

Lancaster knew his brother simply saw something equivalent to the city dump before them, but Lancaster envisioned something far grander. What failed decades before could now be realized because he possessed the finances, the desire, a solid plan, and an attorney who couldn't avoid him. While he didn't know much about running his own business, Lancaster felt confident enough to learn. His brother wasn't going to steer him wrong once he tired of trying to talk the new millionaire out of buying the property in the first place.

"You are one lucky bastard," David said, shaking his head. "Who wins the lottery the day their divorce is finalized?"

"Makes it all the sweeter," Lancaster said, smiling at his brother. "I guess it's because of her that I even bought a ticket that day, and it's even better that she'll never see a dime of it."

Lancaster questioned part of his judgment because of the rural location and family friendly competition just over an hour away. He was also reaching the age where rides hurt the body and the head was left spinning or aching the rest of the day after riding anything that spun. Deep down it was a love for such places from childhood because their family vacations always took them somewhere away from their little town. If a theme park wasn't their destination, it was certainly a stop on the way to any number of thriving businesses in that part of the state.

David was two years older, and usually wiser in most everything, so Lancaster never felt reluctant about asking for his brother's advice. Their father once owned a local hardware store in downtown Mitchell, and never planned on having a second child because business wasn't always good, particularly when some of the factories closed up shop and moved south. Both boys learned the ins and outs of running a business from their father, instilling confidence within them for the future.

While David attended college and pursued a degree, Lancaster worked in the store with his father. He stocked shelves, waited on customers, and even learned how to keep the books in a time before computers did absolutely everything for a business. The work didn't particularly interest him, and he made his mind up early that he wanted to pursue a career in law enforcement. He knew about the stigma of being a local boy going to work for a police agency. Gaining respect in a small town as a police officer wasn't easy in the first place, but knowing the area residents made it that much tougher.

Joining the state police at the time meant getting shipped far north for at least a year, which made little sense to Lancaster. He opted to stay local and work as a dispatcher and a reserve until he passed the test to join the county police department. During this entire period of time his father was supportive, and Lancaster never thought his informal education in business would ever come in handy.

Until now.

"I don't mean to sound like a broken record, but even the farmers passed on this place, Jeff."

"That's because they're too cheap to remove a few heavy objects out of the way."

"Like the four tons of wooden roller coaster in the distance? What the hell are you going to do with that thing anyway?"

Lancaster felt a sense of pride when his brother asked the question, because the preservationist in him wanted to somehow save the structure. Roller coaster enthusiasts tend to fall in love with their rides, seeking to avoid seeing them torn down at almost any cost. He hoped that kind of devotion might fuel the means to save a roller coaster that hadn't provided a ride in over forty years.

"I'm going to start a webpage and write some foundations to save the thing," he informed his brother proudly. "Tearing it down doesn't do a lick of good, but if it can be saved, even piece by piece, people will chip in."

"That's either a flash of brilliance or the dumbest thing I've ever heard."

"I may have millions, but I've still got to watch the bottom dollar if I'm going to make this place work."

"I'll check into some foundations," David said, taking a deep breath through his nostrils as he stared at the long since abandoned park. "I think the bank is practically ready to give this place away since the farms and county won't even buy it."

Mesh wire fence surrounded the general area where the downed rides and concrete remained. Numerous signs warning against trespassing surrounded the grounds, but the lawyer obtained permission from the bank to step foot on the property once he explained that he represented a potential buyer. The bank wanted to keep potential trespassers from getting injured and suing, but they certainly didn't want to chase away someone who might purchase the property and carry out the work no one else dared attempt.

"We have a shit ton of things to do," David declared, still wincing as he stared at the mess before them.

"Then let's get to it," Lancaster said, unwavering in his dream to own the best theme park in all of Indiana.

"I'll get some inspectors out here so there's no surprises. In the meantime you'll probably want to hire a crew for some cleanup, and maybe an industrial contractor or two. Man, I can't even imagine where you're going to find a park manager and people to maintain all the stuff you want to put out here."

"It shouldn't take much to lure some people with experience away from their current positions," Lancaster replied with a devilish smirk.

"Now you're thinking like a lawyer."

Chapter 3

Thursday, September 20
Two Years Later

One might have mistaken Vivian Weatherly for the retired grandmother who simply baked goods all day for her grandchildren before settling into a rocking chair in the evening, but they would be dead wrong.

Granted, she was currently baking some treats in the kitchen, but even they were created with an ulterior motive. For the past five years she had won ribbons in the Novelty Dessert Contest during the week of her town's annual festival. Lasting one week every September, the Persimmon Festival in Mitchell not only hosted a car show, a photo contest, and all kinds of charitable dinners, but it also drew families from around the state for the huge Saturday afternoon parade. Carnival rides remained set up in town all week, much to the delight of children and chagrin of their parents.

Sunlight brightened her kitchen in the late morning hour since the brief rains had moved east, towing a cold front behind them. After watching some of the morning news, Vivian set to making her famous persimmon pudding and frosting-topped brownies. She decided to make some pies for her daughter since the grandchildren were visiting later that afternoon. An alluring scent of pumpkin bread traveled through the house as it neared completion within the oven.

In the background a newscaster talked about the new theme park opening locally that weekend, and its owner who had won the lottery a few years back.

What a travesty, she thought as she carefully shaped the edge of the piecrust with her fingers. Back in her day people worked hard to get ahead in life, but now undeserving people won contests and lotteries that made them richer than people who worked for a living. Like a virtual slap in the face, the man who owned the park bought the land she made a power play to obtain decades earlier.

The days of her making investments and embedding herself in the political scene remained only in her memory. With her husband buried in the cemetery at the edge of town, Vivian remained one of the few testaments to how the town thrived for decades. Now eighty-three, she counted each day as a blessing, often attending church more for the social interaction than for worship purposes. She supposed she had religion in her heart and mind, but she never felt overly sentimental about anything. Even when Harold passed away, she never shed one tear. Perhaps the fact that he lay dying for three months from pancreatic cancer prepared her for the inevitable, but Vivian doubted she would have openly wept regardless of how he met his maker.

Left in the largest house within city limits to her own devices, Vivian could have downsized, but with two children and five grandchildren, she opted to keep the spacious dwelling. She closed off much of the upstairs after selling off and donating her husband's belongings a few years prior. The family took care of small matters for her, and she could easily afford to hire professionals for the larger household problems that emerged.

Curio cabinets and custom-built display cases showed off her expensive dishes and antiques throughout the four-bedroom home. Original wood trim lined the walls along the ceilings and acted as trim along the darkly stained, completely wooden staircase. Even the large dining room table remained set, as though an impromptu dinner might transpire on a whim. In truth, it grew lonely eating alone on a nightly basis, though Vivian often turned down offers to eat with her extended family.

Currently rolling a piecrust along one edge of her large kitchen island, Vivian kept a thin layer of flour on her hands to prevent the dough from clumping between her fingers when she worked it by hand. All of the ingredients lined the island's flat surface, and the pie was intended for her grandchildren, and not the contest downtown. She planned to make a day of baking while the oven was warm, getting everything done in one fell swoop.

A dog barking outside distracted her from the pie crust momentarily. The neighbor's dog seldom made a peep unless someone unfamiliar approached one of the nearby properties. She walked to a nearby window, peering outside to find no one in the direction that the collie was barking incessantly. Fighting back the urge to yell at the canine for fear she might ruin her good neighbor status, Vivian simply returned her attention to rolling the dough before carefully placing it into the ceramic pie plate. A hot bath sounded delightful in the early afternoon hours after she finished in the kitchen. Her joints often ached after working in the garden or preparing food for hours on end, and she had little else to occupy her time before the grandchildren came for a visit.

Carefully placing the pie crust into the dish, Vivian was just about to begin shaping it when she heard the front door creak. Positive she had never unlocked it that morning, she slowly walked toward the foyer that formally divided the kitchen from the other areas of the house. Stepping around the doorway she found no one there, and no one standing outside. A gentle breeze rustled the leaves along her front yard, still clinging to the trees. Southern Indiana leaves didn't change colors until late October, and seldom fell before the end of the month.

"Is anyone there?" Vivian decided to ask aloud, figuring the wind somehow caught the door and pushed it open.

She walked up to the doorway, peering outside both ways to make certain no one was playing a prank on her. Satisfied she and the neighbor dog were simply paranoid on this particular morning, Vivian angled herself to bump the door shut with her posterior to avoid getting flour all over the knob.

Shaking her head, she grunted under her breath, wondering how the normally reliable door suddenly swung open. One look at the doorknob revealed it was in a locked position. On such a beautiful early fall day she had chosen to open several windows throughout the house, but open windows had never caused the door to open before. She supposed she might be asking her son or son-in-law to take a look at the doorframe in the near future. Returning to the kitchen, Vivian looked to the decorative wall-length pantry that held many of her prized dishes and precious photographs. Covered from end to end and top to bottom in glass, the pantry acted more as a display case, affixed permanently to the kitchen wall.

A framed image of her with her colleagues from their heyday had fallen forward, so she wiped her hands clean with a nearby towel before walking briskly across the room to open the section of glass to restore the frame to its rightful place.

She carefully pulled the old photo from the case, holding it steadily in her hands as she thought back to the days when she made her name and stepped on anyone who stood in her way. On the outside her town looked like any small suburbia area because it was quiet, virtually crime-free, and quaint, but politics and lucrative deals built the town into a desired settlement. Vivian alone drew a dozen businesses to the area, some of which had recently departed because local leadership no longer possessed the strength and resolve necessary to close deals.

The photo showed five people standing side by side, all wearing business attire, and by the coloration one could guess it was taken during the early days of color photography. Two men and two other woman displayed serious, if not rather rugged stares instead of smiles for the professional photographer. Vivian believed the occasion was a ground-breaking ceremony for a bank, or perhaps one of the restaurants on the outskirts of town. Though similar occurrences were routine, seldom did all five of the movers and shakers get together at one time. They worked behind the scenes individually to build the town and secure their legacy, often too busy to gather for anything larger than business lunches.

Replacing the framed image to its rightful position, Vivian sensed a presence behind her, invading the sanctity of her kitchen. She turned around quickly, expecting to find an intruder standing there after the door mysteriously swung open. Instead, an unnerved feeling stuck to her like glue as she found only her baking items atop the counter and the window behind the island still open just a crack.

Taking in a nervous, deep breath, Vivian circled her way around the island, prepared to finish her baking before her family came to visit. She tried to settle her nerves by focusing on the task at hand, but a guilty conscience nagged at her, as though living the past thirty years and enjoying the fruits of her labors was a result of borrowed time.

Less than a second after she returned her fingers to the pie crust she heard the front door swing open with a creak before striking the coat rack to the side of it. Sucking in a more panicked breath this time, she cautiously approached the doorway again, peering around the corner to see no one beside the door, and no indication of why the locked door had swung open a second time.

This time she stepped forward to shut the door by hand, wiping off the doorknob with her apron while testing to make certain it was locked. Vivian even tugged at the door, trying to prove the door was faulty instead of the dreadful alternative. Closing businesses and crushing dreams over the years made her a great number of enemies, and any one of them, or their families, might have waited this long to exact revenge.

Trying to put any thoughts of home invasion aside, Vivian approached the threshold into her kitchen, prepared to remove the pumpkin bread from the oven before it burned. Her mouth widened when she spied a haze lingering in the kitchen, indicating the distractions had gotten the better of her, but no pungent odor accompanied the thickening white smoke. Immediately upset with herself for letting the bread get overdone, she huffed before marching forward to start anew.

The second Vivian stepped foot into the kitchen her hands went up to fan the intensifying haze before her, finding it thin and moveable, unlike smoke. Making her way toward the oven, she still detected no smell linked to the foggy substance. When Vivian wondered if the fog emanated from somewhere else completely she felt the back of her head grabbed by a powerful hand. She grasped and clawed at the hand, a mixture of moaning and screaming emitting from her lips, as she was led toward the kitchen's island. As she attempted to look to her left to identify her attacker, he thrust her head downward against the island, a poof of flour rising into the air as her skull bounced off the faux marble top, leaving her on the brink of unconsciousness. If not for the guiding hand, she might have toppled to the floor, or stumbled back against the sink, but he rammed her head downward a second time. Absolutely dizzy and stunned, Vivian remained barely conscious enough to behold what heinous acts her attacker had in store for her during her very limited future.

Chapter 4

Lancaster thought his last day on the job was going to be a cakewalk, but a call shortly after lunch changed his opinion. It seemed a neighbor near Vivian Weatherly's residence had spotted smoke emerging from her kitchen window. Firefighters from the Town of Mitchell and Marion Township arrived to quickly extinguish the flames once they discovered the source of the smoke, and a small fire, inside the kitchen oven. What they discovered in addition to the fire, however, caused them to back out and call in the authorities.

After weighing his options while the theme park was being constructed, Lancaster decided to remain on the sheriff's department for insurance and benefits. His job also occupied him, which kept him from checking on the progress of his new business all day long, which the construction workers surely appreciated. When an opening in the investigative division caught his eye after one of the three detectives retired, Lancaster decided to apply for the position he once held briefly.

"Who would want to kill an old lady?" Jared Thomas asked from the passenger's seat as Lancaster drove them to Mitchell from the county seat in Bedford.

Once Lancaster had decided upon a final day of work and turned in his notice, three other deputies applied for his position. Thomas endured two interviews, which many said were simply for show in the still highly politically driven promotional procedures used by most local agencies. Thomas had an uncle who headed up the street department in Bedford, which gave him the edge. Lancaster received the position, or so he guessed, because the sheriff was hoping for a healthy donation from the now wealthy man around election time.

Lancaster liked the sheriff well enough, but he wasn't going to shovel heaps of money into his campaign chest just yet.

"What do you know about Vivian Weatherly?" Lancaster asked, figuring he personally knew about as much as any typical Mitchell resident.

"I heard she was kind of a bitch back in the day."

Lancaster wasn't certain her gruff personality ever ceased with any particular decade or birthday. He had laid eyes on her several times during the Persimmon Festival, often when she was asked to judge portions of the parade, or when she attended events to watch her grandchildren.

He remembered her as looking younger than her eighty-three years, perhaps because her skin aged well, or because she dyed her hair a reasonably natural shade of black. Her beauty hadn't faded without a fight, and Vivian Weatherly was hardly the type of person to rely upon assistance from others. She walked upright, dignified and purposeful with each stride, never requiring a cane. Most times she barely stole a glance at those around her, as though she were royalty to their commoner status.

Despite her treatment of those outside of her precious family, Vivian was glorified by the locals as a charitable benefactor to numerous charities, her church, and even the two local fire departments that protected her town. Like everyone else in town, Lancaster knew these facts but he wasn't going to be blinded by surface indicators. From what little information he gathered during the phone call from the first responding Mitchell police officer, the homicide in question was gruesome.

"Who would want to kill her?" Thomas questioned.

"Who indeed," Lancaster said just above a whisper.

"That isn't much of an answer."

A veteran of six years on the county police force, Thomas continued to show enthusiasm and broaden his horizons. He was destined to pick up the worst of the investigation shifts because of his lower seniority, but turnover on the department never seemed to ebb, which meant he wouldn't wait long for a better spot. Much of his work before joining the force included patrols as a reserve officer and patrolman in nearby small towns. Any naïve thoughts running through his mind ended soon after he joined the sheriff's department and experienced the highs and lows society had to offer.

Still in his early thirties, Thomas wasn't an especially handsome officer. A football player in high school, he remained stocky and imposing, particularly with a regularly shaved head. Despite any physical imperfections, Thomas knew how to use the uniform to attract police groupies. Unfortunately his reputation was preceding him, which meant any lasting relationship wasn't going to come from within Lawrence County. His sexual prowess aside, Thomas was a reliable officer with good instincts and improving judgment regarding other people.

People often put on facades when confronted by police, and a good number of those individuals can lie with a straight face. Like most cops, Thomas learned to decipher the facts from untruths over time, though he tended to categorize people a little too often for Lancaster's taste.

He often talked about his conquests in the bedroom when he worked around other officers, but Thomas appeared focused on the task ahead of them today. Besides, the new detective knew such talk remained a sore subject for Lancaster.

As he pulled the unmarked car to the edge of the cordoned off scene, Lancaster found three police cars parked near the house and two uniformed officers securing the area with yellow tape. Both the town police chief and one of his officers strung the tape along the property while a uniformed deputy stood watch at the door with a clipboard to monitor who accessed and departed the scene with time logs. About two dozen people surrounded the scene, curious onlookers who stood across the street or on the fringe of the property despite the police chief barking at them to back away.

Slowly shutting the door once he stepped from the car, Lancaster noticed a single fire engine parked down the street, likely standing by in case of additional fire issues. A charred odor lingered in the air, and as Lancaster led the way toward the house, he nodded at the police chief and the Mitchell officer. They both appeared a bit shaken, as though none too anxious to step inside the house for another look at the victim. Lancaster's natural curiosity arose, but he decided to speak with them after viewing the crime scene for himself.

Lancaster took the clipboard from Larry Goodpaster, the deputy keeping watch over the door, to sign both he and Thomas into the log before entering the building. Even an experienced deputy like Goodpaster with more than a few gray hairs atop his head swallowed hard before giving Lancaster a mild shake of the head. Whatever awaited the two investigators inside had shaken all three men who laid eyes upon the scene. Police are naturally curious about any homicide, whether patrolmen or investigators, and often harden themselves to the sight of the deceased. Something far more disturbing than a natural death or a victim mangled from a car accident awaited the duo.

Pulling a pair of latex gloves from the left pocket of his slacks, Lancaster snapped them into place as Thomas followed suit.

After exchanging an uneasy glance with Thomas, Lancaster stepped inside the door that led directly to the kitchen, his eyes immediately spying a blackened stove with a charred trail from the appliance to the ceiling. An island covered in flour and overturned bowls blocked his view of everything else, but Lancaster noticed some blood droplets that piqued his interest. He began circling the island as odors of burned food and charred kitchen walls entered his nostrils. What awaited him around the next corner caused him to freeze in his tracks because it was certainly the most gruesome and cruel crime scene the detective had ever viewed.

"Holy shit," Thomas muttered, almost bumping into Lancaster when he laid eyes upon the corpse behind the island.

Lancaster held a foreboding arm to make certain Thomas didn't step around him for a closer look. They were going to need a forensic team to check for fingerprints and DNA evidence while they questioned neighbors and any potential witnesses. He wondered if they had already stepped inside too far and corrupted potential evidence, though three other police officers and a handful of firefighters were likely guilty of the same faux pas.

A mix of morbid curiosity and nausea tied knots in the detective's stomach. Vivian Weatherly's body was lying face down atop the tile floor, looking like a novelty shop Halloween prop. And though the mechanism of her death wasn't readily apparent, ten thin streaks of blood were in front of her head and shoulders. The intense heat of the fire had baked them into a darkened maroon color atop the floor. They emitted from her severed fingers like tiny reddish-black serpents, her hands sprawled in front of her as though she attempted to crawl to safety. All ten fingertips, cleanly cut at the knuckles, remained only inches from her violated hands at the end of the bloody trails.

"She was tortured before she died," Lancaster said aloud.

"Obviously," Thomas added, "or she wouldn't have bled like that. But why clip off her fingers and risk being heard?"

"He didn't clip," Lancaster replied, pointing to the indention marks scattered along the floor near her fingers. "He chopped them off with something rather sharp and heavy, probably while pinning her down and making her watch."

"She would've screamed, Jeff."

"Not necessarily. The body tends to go into shock rather quickly when parts get lopped off."

Without drawing any closer to the body, Lancaster knelt down for a look at the neck area, trying to determine the mechanism of death. No wounds or significant blood appeared along the clothes on her back, and none of her clothing was torn or disturbed, significantly reducing the chances of sexual assault preluding the homicide. Despite not having foot coverings, Lancaster wanted a closer look at the body. The forensics team was already going to be unhappy with him for lingering inside with Thomas, but he felt compelled to arm himself with more answers before speaking with family members.

"I thought we weren't getting any closer," Thomas complained in a rather neutral tone because he obviously wanted a better look as well.

"We aren't so far as the technicians know. By the time they know better we'll be long gone."

"I feel like such a degenerate," Thomas replied sarcastically as Lancaster made his way around the body for a better angle.

Though Lancaster had seen his share of corpses over the years, only a few were homicide victims. More often than not he was called to fatal automobile accidents as a patrol deputy, or the occasional open and closed murder or suicide. Very seldom did deaths in little old Lawrence County require much detective work, much less extensive questioning and forensic analysis, but that didn't mean Lancaster was ill-prepared for such measures.

Although he didn't expect his last day of work to include one of the largest cases of his career, the detective planned to work it thoroughly and leave his department with a solid head start toward finding the killer.

Making his way to the side of the body, Lancaster carefully reached for Vivian's shoulders, turning her body halfway over by lifting only the side closest to him. He found her body firm but light as he rotated it on the far shoulder, examining her torso and neck for visible wounds.

Except for the blood near the ten severed fingers, none of the red liquid pooled anywhere else around the body. Lancaster found no blood along Vivian's clothing, though he noticed some purple marks on her arms, particularly around the elbows. He surmised that her attacker may have restrained her by pinning her down, which required incredible strength if the same person began chopping her limbs. It seemed plausible that two people might have carried out such a heinous act, but individually cutting off limbs seemed like overkill to Lancaster.

He knew the fingers were cut one at a time because of the ten gouges in the tile floor. If Vivian Weatherly's murder wasn't some sort of thrill kill, he believed the killer, or killers, might have committed the act for a much more personal reason. In his experience, most people didn't take the risk of staying so intimately close to the victim for so long because the chances of being caught went up with each passing second. He felt reasonably certain this murder occurred because Vivian Weatherly had committed some wrong against the killer or the murderer's family.

Looking from the torso to the neck area, Lancaster found additional purple bruising along the neck and the lower jawline. He took a guess that she was either strangled or the killer snapped her neck once he was contented that enough punishment was dished out for whatever sins Vivian Weatherly may have committed. Her face was frozen in a death mask consisting of bluish lips and hazel eyes that were locked in a partially opened position. She appeared far from the distinguished dignitary the people of Mitchell came to recognize on the rare occasions they spied her in public.

"What have you got?" Thomas asked, now squatting at an angle that provided a very good look at the body.

"No wounds or blood on the body," Lancaster reported. "There's trauma along the neck area though. If one person did all of this, he was strong as an ox."

"Had to be at least two people."

"They said there was no forced entry, Jared. You really think this woman let two strangers into her house?"

"Maybe they offered to mow her lawn or trim her shrubs. Or they asked to fulfill any other needs she might have had."

Lancaster sighed.

"You're one sick motherfucker sometimes."

"At least I didn't imply they were part of some Mexican cartel."

"I'm starting to wonder if you were the best they could do as my replacement."

Thomas scoffed.

"With your millions you could have left a long time ago."

Saying nothing, Lancaster simply gave a cagy smirk. Leaving was certainly an option, but he knew biding his time kept him out of trouble, and from slowing the progress at his new investment.

"And yes," Thomas added, "I was the best they could find."

"You're so humble it's easy to see why," Lancaster kidded, carefully setting Vivian's body to its original spot. "You ready to get down to business before the techs catch us in here?"

"Sure thing."

The two investigators carefully backed out of the crime scene the way they had entered to minimize evidence contamination. Both knew the forensic technicians could decipher various shoeprints by style and size, and they hadn't touched anything without latex gloves, so any damage caused was minimal.

"I'm a little disappointed you didn't ask me to head up your security team at the new theme park," Thomas stated as they walked outside to sign their departure time on the log sheet.

"Yeah, me too," Goodpaster chimed in as he took back the clipboard once they were done signing it. "I heard you got some dude from out west to take the job."

Lancaster gave a disarming grin.

"You mean the guy who's already headed up security at a bank after retiring early as an assistant chief on his department? I got him for a steal because his old job dissolved. Don't worry guys. There'll be lots of security openings next year when I get things up and running for a full season."

"I won't hold my breath," Goodpaster kidded.

"Besides, I couldn't hire you guys full-time and deprive you of your state pensions."

All three couldn't help but laugh because they all knew the pensions were slightly varied versions of what civilians received for teaching and similar jobs. Lancaster would never knock school teachers, but they didn't risk their well-being on quite the level that police officers did. Unfortunately the police pension didn't travel easily with officers, meaning they couldn't necessarily take a job with another county or city and accept an easy transfer.

Lancaster already refused to miss his job and the lack of perks that accompanied it.

***

Lancaster and Thomas had barely started their search for witnesses and interviews with neighbors when Vivian Weatherly's daughter and two grandchildren approached the crime scene.

A Mitchell officer came to tell Lancaster about the family's arrival while he was speaking with a neighbor who seemed more concerned about relaying past stories than providing concrete information. Considering the conversation revealed nothing of use, Lancaster felt somewhat relieved about speaking with his first family member, though breaking the news of someone's death never proved a simple task. Emotions from the family always made his job difficult from the very second he told anyone a family member was deceased.

Lancaster immediately suspected they were already planning to visit because no respectable parent brought children with them to a crime scene. Stories in a small town were often distorted immediately, and perhaps they knew nothing more than a fire had broken out inside their loved one's home.

Wearing a grim expression, he approached the woman, who had already handed the children off to a familiar neighbor. She appeared gravely concerned, though she looked to Lancaster with a longing hope for good news.

He figured she was in her mid to late fifties, though her face was practically free of wrinkles. Dressed for business, she wore a blouse of emerald green that bore a similar shade to her penetrating eyes. This woman was certainly her mother's daughter, but Lancaster wondered why two very young children were accompanying her.

"Detective Jeff Lancaster," he introduced himself, shaking her hand.

"Mary Reagan," she replied. "I was coming to visit my mother but I saw all the police cars and the fire truck outside."

A glance down the street let Lancaster know Thomas was speaking with neighbors, and apparently in no hurry to join him in bearing bad news. Per custom when relaying bad news, Lancaster wanted both of them, though Mary for certain, to be sitting. One of the town's many churches was less than a block away, but he didn't want to walk her that far away from the children.

"Where is my mother?" Mary asked when he didn't immediately say anything.

Lancaster looked around for somewhere private where prying eyes weren't welcome and he could tell her the horrible news before asking a few questions.

"Please, follow me," he said, deciding to take her to the unmarked police car.

"I'm not going anywhere until you tell me what's going on here," Mary insisted.

Lancaster decided if she was going to act tough then he wasn't going to beat around the bush with the information, though he still didn't want a public spectacle, especially with the press beginning to swarm the area. Not wishing to appear on every evening news program, he decided to give one last plea for her cooperation.

"Please," he said, motioning in the direction of a nearby tree just outside of the crime scene tape, away from prying eyes.

After returning an expression that might have burned holes through a lesser hardened man, Mary followed him over to the tree. With only grass and mulch surrounding them, there was no ideal place to sit, so Lancaster decided to just keep them out of sight behind the tree and close to a wooden fence.

"There's no easy way to put this," he began hesitantly, "but your mother was murdered."

"Oh my God," Mary said, cupping her hands over her mouth momentarily. "Someone set fire to her house?"

"No."

She appeared on the verge of tears, fighting to remain strong before the stranger who gave her such terrible news.

"How?"

"The fire came from the stove. It appeared as though she was baking."

"She always does for the Festival contests. So what happened?"

"I can't go into detail, but it wasn't quick. Someone made her suffer."

"My God! Who would do such a thing?"

Lancaster hated revealing such a thing to the woman's daughter, but he needed suspects. He felt uneasy, but remained prepared to step forward if Mary collapsed from the weight of the horrific news. She remained steady and strong, but visibly upset.

"What did they do to my mother?"

"I can't go into details, but the intruder tortured her. Is there anyone who would hold some kind of longstanding grudge against your mother?"

"No," Mary said without hesitation, but the expression of realization quickly crossed her face that indicated something pertinent came to mind. "Back in the day she made lots of deals and signed dozens of huge documents. But that was decades ago."

"I'm aware of that," Lancaster said, leaving the end of his statement hanging to push for additional information.

"People lost their businesses, sometimes their houses," Mary revealed, dabbing her eyes with a tissue from her purse. "Mom didn't talk much about it, but we all knew growing up that she stepped on a lot of locals. There were a lot of people upset with her and her business partners."

Nervously rubbing her face, Mary fell into a bit of despondence for the first time, walking in partial circles around the tree.

"I know this is difficult," Lancaster said sympathetically, "but can you tell me your mother's associates, or help me locate her documents?"

Mary looked to the ground momentarily, possibly in thought, but more than likely entering the initial stages of shock. He feared losing her, but at the same time so many other avenues awaited him, like searching the house, talking to other family members, and helping Thomas with more potential witnesses.

"If you don't find anything in the house, Mom rented space in one of those storage facilities just outside of town."

"Thank you."

"Can you please tell me how she died?" Mary almost pleaded.

"To be perfectly honest I won't know until the medical examiner conducts an autopsy."

"Was it that bad?"

"The scene is just too messy to tell," Lancaster confessed, turning from her as he spoke the words. He tried to draw some of her resolve before speaking again. "I promise, when I get some answers you'll be the first to know."

He realized the moment he spoke the words that they were a complete lie, though Lancaster slipped unintentionally. Reassurance was second nature to him, but it continued to slip his mind that today was his last day as a detective and sheriff's deputy. From now on people would simply know him as the lucky son-of-a-bitch who won the lottery and opened a theme park.

Lancaster wasn't about to correct himself because Mary Reagan already had enough to worry about without him explaining his career change. Instead, he led her back to the neighbor who watched over the two children before resuming his duties. While Thomas interviewed neighbors, he decided to search the house for any evidence of Vivian Weatherly's prior business dealings. While he couldn't absolutely rule out home invasion or any number of contemporary possibilities for her murder, hate and revenge seemed at the forefront of such violence.

The only thing he knew for certain was his last day of work would be memorable and none too short.

Chapter 5

Darkness fell across Indiana before Lancaster's final workday came to an end. He discovered hundreds of pages of vintage documentation, which proved far too much for him to sift through from old case files and newspaper articles. Much of the paperwork fell to Thomas and whatever other investigators took over the investigation.

A lingering suspicion haunted him that hundreds of other documents existed, possibly with other business partners, or lost in some attic, basement, or closet. Perhaps they were burned in a fire pit years prior on some warm summer evening. His gut instinct told him the motive for Vivian's murder stemmed from her past, but countless hours might be wasted reading the documents and interviewing past associates. Such a problem no longer fell to Lancaster, but he felt a strange connection to the case that left him uneasy. Unable to calm his mind and settle down, he took a drive to the venture that cost him virtually every bit of his millions before he decided to take the plunge and quit his job.

Two years passed like centuries because Lancaster began to believe his vision would never become fruition. Basically acting as owner, CEO, and the creative force behind an entirely new theme park required much more of his attention than he ever anticipated, but he made it work. Many long days and sleepless nights wore him down, but Lancaster knew what he wanted and nothing was going to prevent the business he dreamed about from opening.

Even coming up with a name that sounded family friendly but captured the overall theme of the place proved rather challenging. Lancaster finally settled on Hallowed Grounds because it rolled off the tongue and didn't sound entirely ominous to kids. It also made for an incredibly neat entrance sign above the front gate that featured two of the letters randomly blinking off and on like old neon hotel signs as though they were about to burn out at any given moment. Lancaster even had sound experts create a buzzing sound that could be heard over loudspeakers within the vicinity of the gate that mimicked a dying light.

With a soft opening that would last the weekend only a night away, Lancaster felt a bit nervous when he laid eyes upon all of the lights and noises his theme park offered. It provided a distraction from the day's events as his employees conducted a dry run of their duties and tested the rides rather gleefully.

No longer the junkyard from two years prior with broken down rides and faded components, the park looked more like a modern marvel with more lights than a carnival and attractions that were either new or masterfully restored. Buildings were constructed for haunted houses, eateries, and shops, all of which blended into the haunted theme perfectly with their dark paint schemes and low lighting along their exteriors.

Directly ahead, as part of the skyline, Lancaster's greatest achievement towered over the rest of the park. Easily visible from the parking lot, a two-hundred-and-thirty foot steel roller coaster named Sidewinder could also be spotted from the county road that led to the property. An ominously dark green paint scheme left it visible from anywhere in the park during the day, but at night it provided a scary ride because the track became virtually invisible to riders.

"Rough day, boss?" someone with a drawl not native to Indiana asked Lancaster from a few feet away as he stood and admired his own park in its natural environment.

"You could say that," he answered, looking to Danny Schall, his director of security.

Daniel Christopher Schall was a steal with his experience as a police officer, and an assistant director of security at a national bank chain. Born and raised in the Kansas City area, Schall had lost his father to cancer a few years earlier, so he moved his mother to Indiana, allowing him and his wife to be near her parents.

While Lancaster fell in love with the man's résumé immediately, it was Schall's character that won him over. Laid back, the man spoke softly with an accent naturally acquired from his birthplace, not as distinct as those found in the south. He tended to shorten a number of words, sometimes skipping vowels and syllables, and Lancaster had to bite his tongue not to chide the Missouri native sometimes.

So far as payroll went, Lancaster spent as much money hiring Schall as he did the park manager, but he considered the hire a sound investment.

Still five years short of fifty, Schall was one of the lucky police officers hired at a young age that put in twenty years and retired to the private sector. He spent four of his years as an assistant chief until the politics changed following a mayoral race and someone new took his position.

"At least it's over," Lancaster stated with a sigh.

"Feels good, don't it?"

"What's that?"

"Retirement."

He spoke the word more like re-tar-ment.

"It does, but I feel like some things were left unfinished."

Schall assumed a spot beside his employer, also staring at the numerous bright lights inside the park. Wearing his usual slacks with a shirt and tie, the security manager also wore shined black cowboy boots, often saying nothing else felt right on his feet. A Glock rested along the right side of his belt, held in place by a fastened holster. Before leaving the sheriff's department, Lancaster saw fit to get Schall placement as a reserve officer, making it legal for the man to carry a firearm in Indiana and make arrests.

A husky, powerful individual, Schall stood right at six feet tall. His brown hair was little more than a fringe with a thinning patch of hair above his forehead. A thick, almost bushy goatee encircled his lips that would make most bikers envious. More than once Lancaster had seen the man's blue eyes narrow when locking onto something of interest, like a lion spying a gazelle in the distance.

For all of his outward convictions, however, Schall impressed Lancaster more with the burdens he carried. Only after he'd hired the man, Lancaster spotted a tattoo on Schall's left arm when they were quickly changing dress shirts between press conferences. Lancaster had offered his private office because Schall's office was getting a fresh coat of paint. When asked about the body art that carried two dates and a military emblem, Schall revealed that his best friend was killed in Afghanistan during a roadside patrol.

Stating little more than the fact itself, Schall didn't seem to want to talk about it, so Lancaster didn't push. He recalled the pain of losing retired friends from his department, so he couldn't begin to fathom the loss of a lifelong friend.

"I saw the news about the fire and the body," Schall said casually. "Sounds like it was pretty brutal."

Lancaster felt torn between discussing the case with a fellow retired cop, even if the title felt new to him, and protecting the integrity of the investigation. He quickly decided he harbored no issues about sharing the details of his day with Schall but Lancaster felt mentally exhausted. He simply wanted to escape the day and enjoy the fruits of his labor and perhaps take part in a few of the rides and attractions.

"It wasn't pleasant," he finally replied. "That kind of thing just doesn't happen around here."

"Can't say the last time I even heard of something that brutal back home," Schall said, the tone of his voice indicating a willingness to let the conversation drop. "Look, I don't want to hold you up, but I wanted you to know everything looks good for the soft opening tomorrow in my department."

"Thanks, Danny. I'm going to try a few things out before I have to stand in line like everyone else."

Schall chuckled.

"I'm pretty sure we can rustle up some VIP passes for you."

Lancaster returned a smirk and a half wave of his hand before stepping forward to examine the rest of his creation. The fog machines weren't running, so the full effect of the amusement park wasn't visible. He considered any weather conditions good, short of rain. Precipitation was the one element that killed visitation at theme parks, so Lancaster hoped the weekends were reasonably warm and dry. Five weeks remained until Halloween, which would mark the end of his short run for the year, allowing him to make even more improvements in the off-season.

With the park located between Louisville and Indianapolis, Lancaster hoped to capture a bulk of the market. He worried that such a distinctive theme might keep some theme park enthusiasts away, but expansion of both thrill rides and family rides would likely appeal to most families planning a getaway.

Hearing screams of joy and laughter as his employees and their families tried out the rides, he couldn't help but smile to himself, despite the horrible circumstances surrounding his last day working for the county.

Walking up to a food stand to order an ice-cream cone, Lancaster decided he wanted to put the murder behind him. Something about the timing plagued him, not so much because of his personal endeavor, but rather the local festival kicking off and the fact that the killer apparently took *nothing* from Vivian Weatherly's home.

Even worse, a nagging feeling in his guts that he chalked up to experience told him this particular murder wasn't going to be the last.

Chapter 6

Lancaster's alarm clock woke him from an indiscernible dream the next morning with a jolt, immediately forcing him to question his location and the time. A general lack of rest the past few months left him jarred awake from various naps and brief overnight sleeps on numerous occasions. Surrounded by darkness except for the glowing red numbers from his alarm clock across the bedroom, Lancaster blinked frequently while he tried gathering his bearings. While he wished the previous day's events were part of some job-related dream, images from the gruesome murder scene flooded his mind with incredible detail.

As the alarm clock continued to blare, Lancaster swung his feet from the bed and briskly walked across the room to flip the alarm switch to off. Not one to waste time, he hated hitting the snooze button on the alarm clock and didn't want to risk disarming the clock during the night, so he began placing it across the room a few years into his career as a deputy.

One of the first financial moves Lancaster made after winning the lottery was looking for a new residence. He thanked his brother more times than he could count for putting him up in his time of need, but a return to the country definitely provided peace of mind. Considering Lancaster waited two years to give up his regular job he didn't want everyone in town knowing his business.

Lancaster avoided the waiting period required to build a house by finding one only a mile away from the site of his theme park's construction.

Sitting on twenty acres, with lots of trees and scenery, the country home provided him with three extra bedrooms, two full bathrooms, an outdoor pool, and lots of square footage. A reasonably modern home, it provided him with a great basis for expansion in the future, because he certainly didn't plan on moving further away from his new business. The newer house required very little upgrading to meet Lancaster's tastes, but he did add a flagpole, complete with an American flag and a powerful light fixture to illuminate it at night. He flew the American and state flags proudly at his theme park, but security personnel lowered them nightly.

He walked out of the bedroom, greeted by the two Golden Retrievers he had adopted as puppies. A brother and sister pair, the two were now fixed and housetrained, keeping his yard safe from critters and the house protected from would-be criminals. The old dog he kept after the divorce proceedings eventually couldn't stand on his own and Lancaster felt obligated to put him down to end his suffering.

His bedroom was located on the second story, along with the kitchen and a small family room that Lancaster transformed into a home office. A wraparound balcony literally surrounded the entire second level for a complete view of the nearby woods. Lancaster slid a glass door open, allowing the dogs to rush down the exterior stairs and into the yard to relieve their bladders after a night indoors.

After a shower he returned to his spacious bedroom, opening the large walk-in closet to search for the right clothes for the grand opening of his theme park. For years he felt like he wore nothing except a police uniform, making the rare times he got to kick back in blue jeans something special. Not one to make a big affair out of things, Lancaster planned a brief ribbon cutting ceremony to start the day and a press conference he prayed would be equally short.

Even before all of that he opted to shadow his head mechanic who conducted most of the ride inspections. Curious about every facet of his new industry, Lancaster wanted some working knowledge of the most important jobs around the park. In most cases knowledge was power, but in this case it provided leverage when he and his human resources people conducted interviews.

He finally settled on a charcoal gray suit, almost black in color, a white shirt, and a tie with black, white, and red slanted stripes. After eyeballing his favorite black cowboy boots a moment he opted for dress shoes instead. For one day anyway, he would sacrifice comfort for practicality because he didn't want people casting judgment about him with all of the press covering the grand opening. Some people already thought the residents of Lawrence County were a bunch of hillbillies, which wasn't true at all, but he wasn't going to fuel any stereotypes on this day.

After bagging his shoes and covering the entire suit in a garment bag, Lancaster threw on blue jeans and a flannel shirt to shield him from the chilly morning weather. He gathered what few things he needed for the one-mile trek and left the dogs outside to protect his property before heading to the theme park. The dogs never strayed too far from his property, and no neighbors were nearby to complain if the canines did some exploring.

***

By comparison the theme park looked tame during daylight hours, even if dawn didn't provide much light. A pink horizon greeted Lancaster when he walked through the front gates of his property and the top of the sun indicated a nice day ahead. So early in the morning only a few workers occupied the park, but they were the most essential people on his staff.

Without management, security, and the few men who dared ascend anywhere from eighty to two-hundred feet in the air to inspect roller coasters, the park couldn't open on a daily basis. Lancaster needed to secure enough income during the short season to sustain payroll through the winter and hopefully make minor adjustments before the spring opening.

While much of the park guests saw was a façade, behind the scenes the offices were very modern, albeit rather condensed until Lancaster could expand his regular employee roster. Not even bothering to visit his personal office, he marched straight into the sizeable pole barn that housed his mechanics and their equipment. At the moment the interior appeared rather bland with toolboxes lining several walls and very little work actually being done. Luckily that meant the roller coaster cars and other rides remained in excellent working condition.

His footsteps echoed through the primarily vacant building as he walked across the floor to greet a man dressed in navy blue work pants and a lighter blue work shirt already adorned with numerous battle scars from grease and paint. Hank "The Tank" Barwick stood just an inch taller than his employer, but his thick forearms came from years of farming and working on engines. A genuine jack of all trades, Barwick could also weld, do body work on vehicles, and fix electrical, plumbing, and carpentry issues. Lancaster felt blessed that the man gave up a daily bus route and some odd jobs to accept the position for head of maintenance.

"Hank," Lancaster said with a friendly nod as the two men solidly shook hands.

"Boss, you ready to go sky high?"

"As I'll ever be."

Barwick handed him a safety belt, complete with rope and harness, which made Lancaster assume they were checking one of the larger roller coasters. Although there were only three functioning roller coasters in the park, Barwick and the other nine mechanics on staff worked in the overnight hours to test each and every ride, which included numerous family-friendly rides much lower to the ground.

Aside from the gigantic Sidewinder, Lancaster had also purchased a hybrid coaster in the mine train category with a combination wooden and metal track. He received a tip that a theme park in Pennsylvania was about to scrap the roller coaster because they couldn't find a buyer, but he reached the park manager a mere two days before the demolition was scheduled for contractor bidding.

A three-minute ride with only one lift hill and no major downward slopes, the coaster was renamed Nightmare Mine and given some animatronics, a few enclosed wooden chutes to pass through, and a launch station complete with a wooden barn side and a small water tower. Lancaster made certain not to forget the theme when it came to the attractions inside his park. So many theme parks grew lazy after they made their millions, not even bothering with repairs on broken down animatronics or continuing use of the props on their rides like fog and music. As a true enthusiast, he vowed never to follow in their footsteps.

"Where are we heading first?" he asked Barwick.

"Figured I'd give you a taste of the big boy. We saved it special just for you."

"I appreciate that," Lancaster replied sarcastically, wondering if his staff would find their choice as funny when their paychecks ceased after a horrific accident claimed his life.

When he consulted with the company that custom built Sidewinder for him, Lancaster was given the option of a few lift chain styles and methods of scaling the lift hill for maintenance. Some new, larger coasters used a mechanical cart that ascended parallel to its lift hill track, but Lancaster opted against it because Sidewinder was built with a traditional lift chain. Though such chains seldom stranded roller coaster trains along the lift, it *did* occasionally happen. The idea of thirty-two passengers walking down metal stairs from the top of the hill sounded bad, but the idea of bringing them down one at a time in a motorized cart made him cringe.

Barwick drove them in a marked utility truck to the roller coaster entrance, since the access was through the launch station itself. Lancaster bought several small trucks at auction and had them painted with his park logo to save money. He was impressed with the smooth ride they offered, but his stomach turned over when he stepped from the vehicle and looked up to the top of the lift hill, which might as well have been a jagged mountain.

Sighing under his breath, Lancaster strapped on the safety belt before following Barwick through the currently dark station to the base of the stairs where the maintenance man undid the lock on the metal gate to gain access to the green metal stairs. Practically guaranteeing safety and security, Barwick made certain the gate locked behind them before leading the way up the few hundred stairs that awaited them.

Lancaster glanced at the track several times until they reached a height that would certainly kill anyone who fell off the tracks. His right hand kept constant contact with the metal rail on the outside of the stairs because a sizeable gap existed between the steps and the track itself. If Sidewinder's train was present with its flat footing surface and stadium seats the void would be an inch or two instead of several feet. Unfortunately several other areas of inspection existed with rather steep climbs, so Lancaster decided to make the best of the situation and put the dizzying height out of his mind.

Riding to such heights in seconds felt far more enjoyable than trudging up and down stairwells. And while he wasn't highly concerned with being two-hundred feet in the air, the potential fall worried him until he clasped the safety belt into the railing.

When the pair reached the small platform that awaited them after the top step, Barwick prompted his employer to strap in his safety harness. Lancaster looked at the stairs that continued on the other side of the level platform, traveling about twenty feet downward after the crest of the largest hill. A small sign attached to part of the railing provided strictly for employees stated that safety gear needed to be worn beyond that point. He remembered that detail being part of the inspection process during negotiations with Sidewinder's designers. Feeling no desire to step further than the platform's peak, or descend the twenty feet of stairs that gave the optical illusion that nothing tied them to the ride, he watched Barwick carry out his duties.

Between the three roller coasters, several methods were used to inspect them on top, beneath the tracks, and sometimes from the side when it was visible from a traditional vantage point. Climbing stairs or ladders was one method, but sometimes the mechanics required ropes with pulley systems to dangle beneath the coasters for a closer look. Lancaster had also purchased a telescoping boom lift capable of reaching most of the way up Sidewinder's tallest hills. The behind-the-scenes costs, like the fire engine he kept on the grounds, added up to the point that he couldn't add every fun thing he wanted to right away.

He needed some profit before adding the attractions that would create a skyline visible from the highway.

"Sure you don't want to look over the other side with me?" Barwick asked before descending the stairs on the other side of the platform.

"I'm good," Lancaster answered as casually as possible, considering his knees felt a bit wobbly. "I'll just observe from here."

Trying to put aside the fact that nothing except air occupied the space between the railing and the ground, Lancaster discovered new respect for firefighters and utility workers.

Barwick started a brief lecture about what kinds of issues he looked for along the track but Lancaster couldn't have recited one word of it back to him because of the distraction he spied along the ground. More than two-hundred feet below him, staring upward, stood a man with a mop of black hair that obscured much of his face. He wore what appeared to be a costume, tattered and discolored, though Native American in appearance. Complete with leather leggings, a cloth poncho with gray, red, and black tribal designs, and face paint that appeared ghostly white, the person didn't appear to blink, or move. His stare simply burned a hole in the theme park's owner, the white of his face marred with the occasional red streak or speckle.

Like blood stains.

"Hank, didn't I leave orders for the actors to arrive closer to three this afternoon?" Lancaster asked, calling across the platform to his chief mechanic.

"How would I know? I don't get those memos."

"Who is that?" Lancaster persisted, turning to see Barwick climbing the opposite stairs toward him, already slightly winded from their earlier ascent.

"Who?" Barwick asked with slight confusion when his eyes followed Lancaster's stare.

When Lancaster looked down once more, he found no one standing there, answering why his employee acted so perplexed.

"He was right there," Lancaster said under his breath, unable to see anywhere the creepy figure could have slinked off to in such a short time.

Barwick wiped the sweat and dirt from his hands with a rag, giving his employer a cagy stare.

"Save your Halloween shit for the other guys, boss. I'm not one for pranks."

Lancaster started to object, but simply shook his head. Barwick wasn't going to believe anything he said about the pale specter of a man at this point. He wasn't even sure he trusted his own eyes, but his lingering cop instincts told him to take a closer look in case the unidentified man wasn't a valued employee. Undoing his safety restraint, Lancaster felt determined to see if someone was playing an early Halloween prank on *him*.

Barely half a step into his descent, Lancaster heard something power up below him as the lights along the lift hill gleamed to life. He stood frozen momentarily, unsure of whether to continue downward and wait for Barwick's opinion about why a supposedly locked out area was suddenly coming to life.

"What the fuck?" the chief maintenance man asked from genuine surprise, taking Lancaster's side for a better look at the launch station below. "Murphy was supposed to check the seats and operator controls. He knows better than to power anything up."

Next the chain began clanging silently as one of the three trains emerged from the lift station, climbing the lift hill toward them. Certainly in no danger from the roller coaster cars, both men stared with mouths agape, wondering who had disobeyed direct orders and standard protocol.

Lancaster descended the stairs at a rapid pace, skipping a few at a time to discover the source of the trouble. Barwick wasn't far behind him, but the older man couldn't quite keep pace until his boss stopped to look at the empty roller coaster train as it passed them on its ascent, like some ghost ship without a crew. A light tremble vibrated through the metal stairs, intensifying when the train reached and surpassed their location. Both stood paralyzed by the vacant seats, as though expecting some kind of haunting sight to materialize until the train disappeared over the top of the hill, leaving only the grumbling roar of its travel along the tracks in its wake.

Wasting no time, Lancaster ran down the stairs, reaching the station first, looking quickly around him with clenched fists, but finding no culprit in sight.

No one stood along the concrete platform, so he quickly walked a few steps up to the control booth and yanked the door open, finding no one inside, though the control panel lit up like a Christmas tree. Knowing enough to conduct basic ride operations, Lancaster pushed a few buttons to ensure neither of the other two trains went up the hill while monitoring a control panel that indicated where the currently traveling train was located. Stopping it in the middle of the track wasn't a huge issue because they tested its ability to stop and start again daily, but he wanted it back at the station.

While he brought the ride under control, Lancaster overheard Barwick on the radio contacting Bryan Murphy, one of the maintenance men on staff, asking for his whereabouts. Murphy was already working on one of the kiddie rides, and stated he finished with the Sidewinder's trains and control panel an hour prior when Barwick inquired. He said he had followed the lock out procedures the park immediately adopted when installing the rides.

Unconvinced, Barwick marched to the operator's booth where Lancaster remained, turning to a door that might have been mistaken for a storage closet by guests. He went to unlock the door, but it pushed inward without any effort, revealing damage to the door jamb as though someone had kicked the door in forcefully. Inside the tiny room was a small electrical panel that held six different breakers and all were thrown to the powered position. The main breaker, however, still had part of the lock out tag in place, dangling helplessly from the tiny round clasp it once fully embraced. The other pieces of its plastic and metal housing lie in pieces atop the concrete padding, snapped by someone with a fractured sense of humor.

"Maybe it's time to splurge for metal doors and frames," Lancaster said weakly, very much aware of the greater danger lurking over them until they discovered who damaged the door simply to start a ride.

Now more infuriated than ever, Barwick shot his employer a look that indicated whoever started the ride without permission and endangered both of their lives didn't want to be discovered if they valued their own well-being.

Lancaster couldn't say he didn't feel the same way, but his mind flashed back to the strangely-dressed man who stared at him from the ground just before the trouble began.

Chapter 7

When Charles Edwin Stafford learned that his former business partner was murdered in the small town of Mitchell he felt some degree of shock, primarily because such things never happened in the town he helped shape. Nearly a full day later, however, as facts began to emerge, Stafford started questioning the motivation for murdering a woman only two years his senior.

As a former bank president, he pushed through dozens of deals that built the town he grew to call home, also putting thousands of dollars in his pocket over time. Intelligent, timely investments turned thousands into millions before he retired a few years short of traditional retirement age. Not burdened with children or grandchildren like his deceased counterpart, Stafford divorced and married a second time, residing with his wife just outside of town. Surrounded by numerous large trees in his large, mainly wooden villa, he knew in a matter of months the leaves would transform into gorgeous fall colors, but his primary concern was learning about Vivian Weatherly's demise.

The news made it sound less and less like the perpetrator was a sexual predator or interested in robbery. While the police weren't forthcoming with answers, simply stating the murder was still under investigation, what they didn't say concerned Stafford the most. After watching four different newscasts that morning with similar reports, he decided to call the police chief in Mitchell for a more personal account of the murder. What Chief Nathan Fields told him about the murder gave Stafford a completely opposite feeling from the reassurance he expected. The chief wouldn't ordinarily volunteer such information to a private citizen, but Stafford assisted the man's church and his department with *very* charitable donations annually.

Learning that Vivian's fingers were individually lopped off with an axe or hatchet sent chills through his spine. A flood of memories entered his mind, mostly of an unpleasant nature because creating a thriving town required sacrifices by people who weren't prepared to make them.

Shortly after hanging up with the chief, Stafford began fixing a light lunch in the form of bologna on white bread. He layered the bread slices with thin coats of mayonnaise, sticking to his childhood staple although so many other aspects of his life had changed. Located in the back of the large residence, the kitchen provided a view of the beautiful yard out back, including the hot tub and guest cottage. Much of the view was provided by the large French doors constructed mostly of glass that led out to a short deck. Currently they were swung inward, but a sliding screen kept any bugs and pests from landing inside.

With his wife still in Bloomington more than half an hour away, shopping with her sister, Stafford bided his time by watching television and contemplating the death of his colleague. The timing seemed odd to him considering the hometown festival began the next day and the new theme park built on land he once acquired was likely thrilling its first guests.

That specific purchase contained a secret that Stafford and his colleagues vowed to take to the grave because the land would never have come up for sale if blood hadn't been shed. Thumbing his bottom lip nervously a moment, he considered checking on his two other remaining partners in crime, not because he truly cared for their well-being, but rather for peace of mind. There was also the question of the once young criminal the group paid to carry out the horrific deed. Stafford lost track of him after he went to prison for unrelated crimes, never uttering one word about how a group of five paid him handsomely. The man certainly wasn't stupid enough to believe his word could outweigh that of five upstanding community members. Besides, they were careful to avoid creating any direct link between themselves and the criminal they hired to carry out the deed, meaning he could never truly finger them as his employers.

Stafford put down his sandwich as something streaked past the screen door overlooking the backyard. He often fed deer and other wildlife, partly for cheap entertainment, and because his wife liked seeing the animals come around. Usually when wildlife visited they sniffed around the area or dared come near the door in search of treats, but seldom did any of them sprint through the yard as though being chased.

Standing for a better look, he walked to the screen door, panning his head from side to side for a look at the vacated backyard. If any critters had run past, they didn't linger in the area, which left Stafford wondering if something scared them away.

Or if something unfriendly lingered behind his residence.

He craned his neck for a better look, finding no living thing beyond the screen door. Wondering if anxiety and panic were setting in, Stafford took a few deep breaths, trying to calm his mind. Returning his attention to the kitchen island, he spotted something beside the small plate that held half of his sandwich.

Two blood droplets of varying diameter sat beside the plate, and he felt certain he wasn't bleeding from any part of his body.

Feeling his chest tighten, Stafford considered exiting through the screen door to clear his head or assess whatever potential danger might have entered his house. He felt almost certain his imagination was getting the better of him, but he spotted a misty haze beginning to smother his backyard, particularly close to the ground.

"It can't be," he thought aloud, seeing a low-lying fog creeping in as a few large water droplets audibly tapped some large nearby leaves, despite the sun already claiming the sky above.

His mind traveled back to a day forty-one years ago when his group eliminated the one obstacle that kept them from making a purchase they believed would change their lives forever. He recalled waking up to a similar misty fog the morning he knew the deed had been done and the county would be taking a major financial step forward.

Unfortunately things didn't work out quite as planned on a few separate fronts.

Hesitantly sliding the screen to one side, Stafford wondered if he dared investigate further when fleeing sounded like a much wiser option. He couldn't imagine the fog represented anything more substantial than a quirky coincidence because he wasn't superstitious. Still, the timing of so many events felt almost cosmic in nature, like some kind of perfect storm was brewing and he was a necessary component.

The moment he took a step through the threshold a line of some sort hooked both of his feet from behind, pulling hard enough that he fell face-down onto his belly. Immediately sensing the danger of an intruder inside his home who meant him harm, Stafford tried clawing at the deck with a limited hope of escaping the predicament. Arthritis and diminished strength in his hands ensured his attacker got the better of him when the rope was tugged with incredible power, dragging him inside. Stafford couldn't even leave fingernail tracks in his wake as he skidded across the kitchen floor while his screams went unheard by any distant neighbors.

Chapter 8

Jean Garrison felt as though her eyes were about to burn out of their sockets from staring at so much paperwork all day. While Vivian Weatherly left behind her two children, neither of them were involved in her family business. As the woman's great-niece, Jean learned to manage money through stocks and bonds, various banks, and other kinds of investments most people never even knew about.

Like a bloodhound, she remained tenacious at given tasks until their completion. Right now, however, she felt virtually brain-dead after searching through her aunt's paperwork for any outstanding business ventures or clues to assist the police in their search for her killer. Vivian kept a good number of documents at her house, but Jean had yet to explore the contents of a rented storage facility and a safe deposit box her aunt leased at the largest bank in town.

Deciding to take a break she texted her daughter, who was just getting out of school, to let her know that she wasn't home. Once Jean received a reply that her daughter was heading to work she took up the key to the safe deposit box. She had an hour before the bank closed and grew weary of reading through paperwork that didn't seem to differ very much. Terms were laid out and signatures applied to the bottom of the last sheet in each case. Jean wondered why her aunt kept so many documents, but she supposed the woman was thorough to a fault.

Rather than marry into money, Jean took the independent route to financial security through an accounting and financial investment business.

Jean felt completely puzzled. Never before had she heard of such a business transaction, either in writing or from Vivian's lips. She flipped through the packet, discovering copies of signed documents and numerous photographs, though she didn't take the time to study each page individually. Despite having no knowledge about the transaction, Jean felt certain it was the most important business deal Vivian had ever completed.

Some of the photos reminded her of the county fairgrounds, but none of the rides, even in the concept photos, looked familiar. Jean wondered if her aunt had helped purchase the fairgrounds, uncertain of when the current location actually opened. Since childhood she remembered the county fair and 4H events taking place at the same grounds.

With her time running out, she reached into her purse and dug out a small notepad with a pen. Already familiar with Vivian's usual associates, Jean flipped to the signed documents inside the packet, writing down every name signed along their bottom lines.

From the corner of her eye she noticed Ellington watching her like a hawk. Several times she had sensed his presence, either from a noise or a shadow creeping across the vault's interior from the door. Jean suspected he could have watched her actions from some remote security monitor but he apparently wanted to hurry her along for some reason. In no position to complain, she finished jotting down the names, folded the sheet of paper, and replaced each of the items to the metal safe deposit box.

Leaving the box atop the table, Jean thanked Ellington on the way out and he finally softened his expression a bit, considering she *had* just lost a loved one. When she stepped onto Main Street, Jean barely gave the numerous antique stores and the police department down the street a glance. If she thought the town police were in charge of the murder investigation she might have checked with the chief for any progress, but she knew the sheriff's department or state police would handle the case.

Along some of the side streets she noticed parked food trailers that would be set up by Sunday evening for the Persimmon Festival that coming week. These were local owners who didn't travel far, but the distant vendors and ride operators wouldn't appear until late Saturday or early Sunday. The ride company that roamed much of the Midwest from week to week came to Mitchell every year. Their rides delighted children, but agonized most adults who had to partake in their spinning and bucking. Jean felt relieved that her daughter had outgrown the rides three or four years ago, now content to meet friends uptown on the nights she wasn't working.

Suddenly feeling like a dunce, Jean wondered why she hadn't assumed the packet inside Vivian's safe deposit box wasn't something *other* than the current fairgrounds. She recalled driving with a friend to some business destination in the country almost a decade ago when she spied what appeared to be faded amusement park rides scattered across a mostly open field. Her friend didn't have much of an answer except that some theme park was supposed to open years earlier but bad luck kept it from seeing the light of day.

"How did I not remember that?" Jean chastised herself aloud.

She needed to look the packet through more thoroughly, but doing so meant finalizing the will and distributing the estate. Her aunt wasn't even in the ground yet, so making any aggressive requests would certainly make her look like a gold digger. Considering she was definitely mentioned in the will, Jean decided to consult Vivian's attorney to see which family member was entitled to the safe deposit box. If the box wasn't mentioned specifically in the estate she foresaw a skirmish amongst her aunt's children to pick and plunder like hyenas over a fresh corpse.

Contacting the police sounded like another viable option, but Jean possessed no proof that the packet had anything to do with Vivian's murder. Something about the information, and the business transaction that never truly materialized, felt like a step in the right direction. Out of *hundreds* of business dealings, Vivian chose to keep that single, personal item inside a locked box and away from prying eyes.

Jean felt more determined than ever to dig deeper, even if she had to interview everyone in town.

***

Lancaster felt sore after being filmed and photographed all morning and afternoon. At least five news channels and half a dozen newspapers sent representatives to his theme park, and that number didn't even compare to the roller coaster enthusiast website managers and bloggers who showed up. While he conducted a formal press conference in the morning, many of the reporters requested he ride some of his own attractions, and he figured there was no better way to display them.

Free publicity in the form of a dozen roller coaster rides left his back slightly sore, though he loved every minute of the experience. Lancaster had never ridden such rides in a suit before, which left him feeling a bit uncomfortable because the cloth didn't give. The weather was a bit too warm and humid for wearing layers of clothing, but he needed revenue if the park was going to remain open beyond the fall, so he was happy to put on a show.

Considering he planned on experiencing only one grand opening of such magnitude, Lancaster bribed most of the photographers for copies of their photos on disc once they were available. He didn't consider himself egocentric, but Lancaster wanted the images for later use and for his personal collection to relive the day occasionally. During the long winter months he sometimes daydreamed about riding roller coasters or getting back to some of his warm weather hobbies.

The entire morning and afternoon went by like a whirlwind, and his head continued to spin, trying to process all of the people he'd met and the thousands of park guests who came to experience his new product. Lancaster watched for reactions to the rides and attractions, pleased to see smiles abound from his guests. So far, even the college kids and local adults he hired to fill hundreds of positions appeared to be enjoying their work. For the first time Lancaster felt somewhat confident his venture might take off and bring some much needed tourism to the area.

Personally, he hadn't blown all of his money, but he spent enough of it that quitting his county job would haunt him if the theme park failed.

Once the press finished with him Lancaster walked through the employee area of the park to his office where he planned on changing into some casual clothes. He wanted to observe more employee and guest interaction while receiving some feedback via eavesdropping about guest opinions of the attractions.

Exhaling a deep sigh as he entered his office and turned on the light, Lancaster took a moment to soak in the day and look at the personal items lining his desk and walls. A few photos of his big lottery win were framed and hanging beside the front page of his divorce decree. At eye level pictures of the theme park's different stages of development were hung in chronological order. He hoped to someday see images depicting the expansion of the park, and while he didn't have room to hang them in the present, Lancaster figured making room was a good problem to have.

A large L-shaped desk created the focal point of the room, giving him plenty of space for work or small, informal meetings. An adjoining conference room allowed him to meet with his park managers or businesspeople from various companies. Lancaster worked closely with the construction company and the designers who helped him create the layout for the park, ensuring room was left for future expansion. He created different areas, based on theme, for the rides and attractions so guests could say out loud which area they wanted to visit first, but he also left room in the employee areas for new buildings or expansion of existing structures.

Feeling somewhat uncertain that his day's activities weren't some kind of dream, Lancaster gently slid one hand across the desk's surface before reaching up to loosen his tie. His fingers had barely touched the red silk when the cell phone clipped to his belt rang for the first time all day. It beeped often with congratulatory text messages throughout the morning but no one had actually called until now.

He barely gave the phone screen a glance before answering it, certain the Lawrence County sheriff was calling him about some unfinished business at his old job. Steve Parsons wasn't usually one for trivial conversation, and the sheriff certainly knew the theme park was opening, which piqued Lancaster's interest.

"Hello, Sheriff," he answered.

"Sorry to bother you on your first day of retirement," Parsons said without hesitation, "but I could use your help."

Lancaster wanted to refuse immediately, but he hadn't made concrete plans. He just desperately wished to stay with his investment and watch the magic unfold. Deciding he was just being selfish and fulfilling his own desires, Lancaster decided to at least hear what the sheriff had to say.

"What have you got?"

"You worked on a lot of our cold cases, Jeff, and we had another murder this morning that might have tied into one of your cases."

"Who?" Lancaster asked, his mind already racing to think of his past cold cases.

"Charles Stafford."

Lancaster struggled to put a face to the name, and his silence over the line apparently caused the sheriff to intervene.

"He was one of Vivian Weatherly's business partners back in the day."

"I'm not sure I can be much help, Steve," Lancaster said honestly. "I don't know anything about Stafford."

Parsons paused a moment.

"It's the crime scene I want you to see."

Lancaster waited for an elaboration that took several uncomfortable seconds to arrive.

"I can't even describe it, Jeff. You need to come out here and see it yourself."

Instead of answering directly, Lancaster groaned hesitantly.

"Jeff, I know you don't need the money, but I can pay you as a consultant. On principle I wouldn't feel right not compensating you."

"Fine, Steve," Lancaster answered, his mind screaming at him all the while to run for the hills and live happily ever after. "I'll have a look at your crime scene, but that's it. I've got a theme park to run."

"Okay," Parsons said, sounding a bit defeated despite getting his way. "I appreciate it, Jeff."

"No problem. Text me the address and I'll be on my way."

Chapter 9

Lancaster felt strangely out of place when he approached the deputy staged at the end of the long rural driveway in his pickup truck. No longer carrying a firearm and a badge, he didn't feel like saying he was consulting on a case, or that the sheriff personally called him. Fortunately he didn't have to speak a word because the deputy simply waved him past, meaning Parsons took the time to ensure he entered the scene without hassle.

He drove up the gravel-covered driveway, surrounded by trees with leaves on the brink of changing colors, for what seemed like several minutes. Thinking such acreage probably required significant funds, Lancaster wondered why someone was targeting the local elders. If robbery wasn't the motive then the killer possibly held a grudge against one or more of them. Lancaster remembered the sheriff telling him Vivian Weatherly and Charles Stafford were likely allies, if not partners, in business during their heyday.

Shade finally gave way to the intense late afternoon sun when the trees thinned out and numerous police cars and yellow tape created the foreground for a murder scene. A rather large, well-kept house stood in a moderate clearing, but behind it Lancaster saw an extension of the wooded area. His eyes didn't blink as he took in the details before him, even though nothing noteworthy was currently occurring.

Stepping from his truck once he parked it short of the crime scene tape to avoid contaminating potential evidence, Lancaster walked toward the house without hesitation. He spotted two uniformed deputies standing near the front door and a state trooper retrieving something from his marked car.

At this point he assumed the forensics people had already combed the area for evidence, so he relaxed a little, but continued to observe the grass and soil below him for any footprints or trace evidence.

Lancaster felt as though he was late to the dance because a lot of the time-consuming activities appeared completed. He found it strange the sheriff even invited him for a few reasons. One, he was technically no longer a county employee, and two, police officers tend to be territorial when investigating cases. While television and movies portray the FBI as a bully that swoops into town and takes over cases in a hostile manner, they're truly more of a resource. Most police agencies that land a case want to see it through to the conclusion unless they're over their heads and require assistance.

"Where's the sheriff?" Lancaster asked one of his former colleagues at the door.

"He was inside," one answered, thumbing behind him.

Lancaster cautiously stepped inside the residence, seeing no personnel and nothing of interest inside the foyer or the living room that followed. He heard voices ahead and made his way across the carpeting, fortunate the living room was spacious because no lighting was turned on and barely any natural light penetrated the windows. Between the woods blocking the sun outside and the closed blinds inside, the living room looked like a carpeted cave with dim lighting coming from only one exterior source behind him.

After allowing his eyes to adjust to the lower lighting, Lancaster took a careful look at the carpeting. Normally he might have continued through the room with little thought, anxious to see the crime scene, but something told him to slow down and look in this particular room. He didn't see the forensic team's crime scene van parked out front, which meant they had already left or parked behind the house. Either way the lack of foot traffic indicated very little time was spent in this particular room. Lancaster returned to the front door momentarily, drawing stares from the two deputies as he looked at the door jamb. Wanting to avoid leaving fingerprints on any surfaces because he didn't have latex gloves with him, Lancaster ran the back of his finger along the jamb, trying to locate any tampering.

The surface of the jamb felt smooth until his finger drew near the latch. Even then he barely detected an indentation that most people would overlook completely as a flaw created during installation. Upon careful examination Lancaster didn't see how such a small crease could have allowed anyone to bypass the lock mechanism to gain access. Even so, something about the minimal damage left him suspicious.

He finally decided to break down and ask one of the deputies outside for some latex gloves and a flashlight. After receiving both and donning the gloves, he touched the door jamb again, still caught between rational thought and experiences with damaged doorways. When he shined the flashlight against the portion of the jamb just beneath the latch, Lancaster discovered more of a smooth groove in the wood. It almost looked as though someone held the side of a smooth metal rod against the jamb and tapped it with a hammer. Strangely, there was no visible paint chipping along the area, and Lancaster noticed several specks about the size of dirt granules within the indentation.

If he didn't think it would sound crazy, Lancaster might have thought someone wedged their finger between the door and the jamb and manipulated the opening.

Without the benefit of a collection canister, he moved on from the door to the inside of the room once again. Shining the light along the floor as he cautiously stepped forward, Lancaster noticed a small object close to the wall just before the living room reached the next area. He knelt down, thinking he'd discovered some kind of partial uncooked pasta noodle that looked like linguine.

Upon picking it up, however, Lancaster felt certain it wasn't decomposing pasta. He gently rubbed it between his thumb and forefinger, finding it hard, but retaining some flexibility. Whether synthetic or natural, the inch-long shard certainly wasn't any sort of food. Lancaster quickly set it down in the exact spot where he discovered it, hearing voices from the next room coming his way.

He stood as Sheriff Steve Parsons walked through the door, offering to shake hands until he noticed Lancaster already wearing latex gloves.

"Old habits die hard," Lancaster said with a shrug.

"I'm glad you're so eager, because you haven't seen the half of it yet."

Lancaster detected the odor of cologne emanating from the sheriff, as though the man had important obligations ahead. Parsons wouldn't have bothered dabbing on any aftershave or cologne for the media, meaning dinner with an important campaign contributor, or a public relations event, was likely postponed.

A decorated war veteran from his time in Iraq and Afghanistan, Parsons made a name for himself when he saved four men from a roadside bomb during a transport mission that injured one of his legs. Rumors spread that the injury cost Parsons his right leg below the knee, but the war veteran remained humble and refused to speak about the injury. Of course conspiracy theorists began stating that he was never truly injured and remained quiet because of a guilty conscience. Naturally his incumbent opponent in the sheriff's race subtly brought up the subject, but the man failed miserably in his quest for a second term.

The former sheriff now worked in the rank and file under Parsons as a patrol sergeant on the afternoon shift.

Lancaster thought briefly of giving the room a final look, but he realized he had already lingered long enough considering the sheriff requested his presence.

A physically imposing man a few inches over six feet in height, Parsons didn't show evidence of a limp, but modern physical therapy and artificial limbs made walking a natural, fluid process. He continued to shave his head, much like he had in the United States Army while a newer addition of a thick, black mustache drooped down past his lips. Though he often sported a suit during business hours, Parsons had taken the time to put on his official uniform, adorned with a gold badge and emblems, anticipating the arrival of television stations. A slightly protruding gut ensured the uniform added ten pounds on television, and Parsons constantly fought to look and sound intelligent when he spoke in public.

Lancaster felt for the man because the sheriff ran a clean election, seeking office for the right reasons. While his predecessor was mired in controversy over the legality of purchasing equipment with department funds and taking it home, Parsons followed the rules impeccably. The deputies seemed to respect him far more than the few previous sheriffs, but he was only forty-three, meaning he didn't possess their experience and expertise.

It also meant he wasn't afraid to swallow his pride and call upon unconventional resources.

Following the sheriff inside the spacious kitchen, Lancaster immediately found his eyes wandering to the floor where several pools of blood appeared to be connected by thinner trails of the substance. Much like the scene within Vivian Weatherly's kitchen, scuff marks and deep etchings covered the tile floor. Whatever happened within this particular room occurred over a period of time and the victim was most likely alive and conscious for much of it based on the amount of blood.

"Where's the body?" Lancaster inquired, kneeling down for a look at the gouges in the floor, possibly created by a sharp bladed object.

The damaged areas looked like wedges created within a log by a lumberjack, powerful and deliberate in nature. Lancaster wasn't so sure he wanted to meet the angry person who wielded an unidentified weapon and created this kind of damage.

At least not without a shotgun handy.

Feeling like the last person invited to the dance, Lancaster knew other investigators and the forensics people had already taken hundreds of photographs, looked for trace evidence, and packed samples of blood and DNA. What could he possibly offer to the investigation at this point?

"The body is outside," Parsons stated. "When you see it, all of this in here will make more sense."

Unsure of what the sheriff meant, Lancaster stood, carefully maneuvering around the kitchen island, following the thinning trail of blood toward the open screen door. Most of the blood appeared dry, but a few of the larger pools still glistened, indicating enough time hadn't passed for them to solidify. Lancaster paid careful attention not to step on any of it, fearing he might contaminate a second look at the crime scene.

When he neared the back entrance, his eyes traced the thinning bloody trail from the tile floor to the wooden deck out back, finally ascending to witness the most gruesome scene he'd ever witnessed.

"Oh, Jesus."

Chapter 10

Lancaster immediately regretted uttering anything the moment he spied the mutilated corpse in the backyard, hating the idea of showing weakness in front of his former colleagues. Even so, he couldn't imagine any of them responding much differently when they discovered an assortment of body parts hung from a tree within a natural fiber rope net.

Unable to break his fixated gaze from the horrific sight before him, Lancaster slowly stepped forward, distancing himself from the sheriff and other nearby officials. Obviously set up for display purposes, the net dangled from a thick branch above, and Lancaster questioned how anyone could scale the tree to hang it. He spotted no marks along the ground from a ladder's square feet, and there were no other trees near this solitary oak. All of the other trees were part of the wooded area beyond the property while this one stood alone to provide shade over the deck during the warmer months.

Like some kind of jigsaw puzzle dumped from the box, the body parts were scattered throughout the net, as though crammed in there to ensure every piece fit. The rope itself was old, made from natural rope and not one of the modern synthetic kinds that were much easier to maneuver. Even more strange, Lancaster felt certain the net was crafted by hand from the rope, and not from some factory. He noticed several types of knots interwoven within the netting, blood still dripping from a few of them.

With an occasional creak, the net spun right or left until it reached the end of its axis, then turned back the other way. Lancaster noticed a left arm and a right leg beside one another, devoid of clothing, sticking straight up and down within the net, almost like doll parts stuffed inside a woven bag. Directly beside them stood Stafford's torso, and more eerily, his face pressed against the constraints of the netting with an agonized look upon it. Lancaster squinted for a better look, positive he wasn't seeing the details quite right. The head was separated from the torso, and actually pressed against the center of the chest about where the sternum was located. Stafford's eyes remained closed, but his lips were swollen and curled, as though he'd spent many a painful minute with his face pressed against some unyielding object before his death.

Like a tile floor, perhaps.

A closer look at the face revealed some scuff marks and a hint of redness that remained, despite the body being virtually drained of blood during the struggle and following dismemberment.

"Where are his clothes?" Lancaster inquired, seeing no shred of clothing in the net.

Perhaps the killer wanted to shred the older gentleman of all dignity during the process of murdering him, giving additional backing to Lancaster's original revenge theory.

"We found them along the side of the house," Parsons answered. "They're already bagged and tagged."

"That's fine. Was there blood on them?"

Parsons didn't immediately answer, so Lancaster turned around.

"No, I guess there wasn't," the sheriff said with a somewhat confused look.

Returning his attention to the corpse, Lancaster envisioned Stafford struggling against a much younger, more powerful assailant, facedown against his own kitchen floor. The attacker took time enough to strip down the old man, robbing his dignity, and possibly giving the implication that sexual assault was in the near future, before settling into his main objective.

Lancaster couldn't quite fathom what kind of sick individual tortured and killed two pillars of the community without obvious motive. His biggest concern at the moment was not knowing where the list of victims ended, or who might be next. If the grotesque nature of the murders escalated, future victims might be burned alive or chopped into even smaller pieces set out for display. Lancaster felt stumped, and if gathered evidence didn't reveal fingerprints or DNA, the investigation was certainly going to grind to a halt.

Part of him wished he'd declined the request to visit the crime scene. A multimillion dollar business required his attention and personal touch, and here he was staring at an assortment of body parts. Natural curiosity overwhelmed his common sense once again, and it seemed leaving a police agency failed to curb his appetite for investigations.

Very little blood pooled beneath the netting, implying most of the carnage was complete before the killer dragged Stafford, or what remained of the man, into the backyard. Like an added effect at his theme park, meant to scare unsuspecting guests, a few smaller body parts were lying in and beside the blood on the ground. Lancaster felt certain he saw part of an ear and parts of various fingers.

"There's nothing we can do for him," he muttered under his breath, realizing Stafford and Vivian Weatherly were victims, but others might be in harm's way.

"What was that?" Parsons asked, stunning Lancaster with his sharp hearing.

He couldn't imagine someone who worked around explosives in the military retaining very good hearing at all.

"Nothing," Lancaster said, turning from the body. "We need to assume this isn't over," he said, addressing the sheriff. "If someone has a beef against the wealthy elite of our quaint little town, it would probably help to know who the other players were back in the day."

"I've already got Thomas working on that. Besides, that's not why I called you out here."

Lancaster felt a bit stunned, if not hurt, that Parsons didn't want him delving into more of the investigation. A minute ago the sheriff was encouraging him to look around the crime scene, or so Lancaster believed.

"This doesn't look at all familiar to you?" Parsons questioned, nodding toward the body parts still entangled within the net, swaying in the breeze.

Taking a moment to ponder the question, Lancaster knew he wanted some answer that referred back to a departmental cold case. Parsons revealed that much during their phone conversation.

Referring to old photographs and information gathered by a long since retired detective wasn't nearly the same experience as viewing a crime scene live. Lancaster had combed through most of his department's cold cases during his investigative tenure, and certainly *all* of the high profile crimes. Murders in Lawrence County seldom occurred, and when they did, residents tended to panic and talk amongst themselves. Most local deaths resulted from traffic accidents, or more recently, the occasional police action shooting with uncooperative suspects.

Lancaster could think of only one unsolved homicide in the area, but it was decades old. A more recent murder was solved during a deathbed confession a few years prior, ending police suspicions that a man killed his ailing mother for a moderate inheritance. Feeling no personal connection to either case, Lancaster recalled looking into both of them with a fresh perspective and optimism as a new detective. After reviewing the facts, conducting new interviews, and examining physical evidence, he found no reason to expend further hours or manpower on either case.

Parsons waited patiently with his hands placed atop his hips for the answer to reach Lancaster, and though the former detective knew what the case *had* to be, he couldn't relate it to their current scenario.

"The Tanksley case?" he finally asked, hazarding his best guess.

Without saying a word the sheriff motioned for Lancaster to follow him. While everyone else continued to keep busy with individual tasks, he wove through yellow tape and natural obstacles, following Parsons to the man's black, unmarked sedan. Shooting him a less than pleased stare with his chocolate-colored eyes for a tense moment, the sheriff held up a wireless remote and unlocked the vehicle. He ducked inside and recovered a moderately thick vintage file that Lancaster immediately recognized as the murder investigation of Michael Tanksley from 1971.

"I assume you remember this?" Parsons asked with a level of irritation that Lancaster couldn't understand.

He suddenly felt as though the sheriff had requested his presence to corner him with information as though he was more of a suspect than an asset.

"I reviewed that case a year ago," Lancaster answered cautiously, looking between the file and the stony face of his former boss. "Michael Tanksley was a weird hermit who was murdered on his own property."

"How was he murdered?" Parsons pressed.

Lancaster recalled the crime scene photos and pages of notes typewritten by detectives that appeared archaic by modern reporting. Tanksley was subdued, tied up and beaten within an inch of his life before the killer hung him by the same kind of natural rope that bound his hands and kept him from escaping the slow asphyxiation that ended his life.

"I know how he died," Lancaster answered, tired of playing games. "What I don't see is how it ties into this murder, even if he was strung up."

"That's not the connection I found," Parsons stated, opening up the file to a certain page.

He pointed to the address related to the scene of the crime, which didn't immediately register with Lancaster because it was an old rural route address. Closer to the new millennium all rural addresses were designated with county road numbers and directions for first responders and the broadening 911 system.

"What's so important about that address?" Lancaster questioned.

"It's the address to your theme park."

A figurative hammer dropped on Lancaster's skull the moment the words reached his ears because he immediately felt both shocked and betrayed. He hadn't put the connection together earlier, and he never visited the property until his brother walked the grounds with him the year he purchased the land.

"How the hell did you find that out, Steve?"

"I got a call right before you arrived from a county employee who looked up the old address for me."

"Why the fuck would you even throw this in my face?" Lancaster asked angrily, inwardly glad the sheriff hadn't simply called him out to cast suspicion his way. "I wasn't even born when Tanksley was murdered."

"Hell, I was still shitting in my diapers, but it strikes me as a major coincidence that your theme park opens and we have two murders in two days."

Lancaster showed his displeasure with a highly audible sigh.

"I've got a business to run, Steve. I'll cooperate with this investigation, and I'll even act as a consultant if you want me to, but I *won't* have you pointing fingers at me."

"I'm not," Parsons said, softening his stance, holding up a slightly defensive hand. "I just needed to reaffirm my faith in you. And now that I know better, I want your help on this case. Actually, I'll probably *need* your help finding this maniac, especially if this has anything to do with the Tanksley murder. You're the one who thought this might be some kind of retaliation, and I'm starting to agree now that we have two dead community elders."

Lancaster shook his head negatively.

"Four decades have passed, Steve. This trail is long since cold."

"Look, we've got the state police helping out, and I've got all of my guys scouring the area. I just want you to look into the past. What happened to Tanksley is eerily similar to what we have here, would you agree?"

"I'm not convinced. Tanksley wasn't hacked into pieces."

"But an old rope was used on him. And his murder wasn't quick and easy."

Nodding, Lancaster credited the sheriff with that much correct information.

"Anything you can find out about Tanksley's property, *your* property, would be valuable to me right now. I think we can handle the rest."

Parsons' eyes didn't appear to be pleading, but they were on the verge of such emotion.

"I'll get the county council to compensate you for your time," he added. "It's only fair."

"Not necessary," Lancaster answered. "I'll find out what I can, but don't be hounding me. I left the department for a reason."

"Understood. Thank you, Jeff."

Lancaster turned to leave, but decided to make one additional demand he didn't consider outlandish considering how Parsons had just ambushed him with new information.

"I also want copies of everything in that file and the current investigations."

Parsons bit his lower lip momentarily in thought, but quickly decided the tradeoff was worthwhile.

"I'll get them to you personally."

It occurred to Lancaster that he could share the strange finds from the living room that some of the detectives and forensics people overlooked, but he wasn't in the mood to speak with the sheriff any longer. He gave a quick nod before heading for his truck.

Chapter 11

Saturday, September 22

Jean Garrison wasted little time asking her aunt, Mary Reagan, for access to the safe deposit box Saturday morning. Although Jean was Vivian's favorite relative in everyday life, she chose her daughter to act as executor to her last will and testament. Mary provided no resistance, particularly when Jean explained that the document might have information useful to police in the murder investigation.

Both had seen the previous evening's news on the television and read the morning newspaper, learning about Charles Stafford's horrific death. With the reading of the will held off until Monday, Jean asked Mary to accompany her to the bank in order to borrow the thick brochure that Vivian considered important enough to secure behind steel and concrete.

Mary looked like a younger version of her mother, the gray only beginning to show in thin streaks along her dark hair. She dressed less formally than Vivian or Jean, but she retained the strong demeanor and upright walk that ran in her family. For this occasion she donned heels and a nice dress, taking a cue from her mother that women needed to look sharp in public when conducting any sort of business.

Because Mary possessed adequate paperwork to prove her position as the head of Vivian's estate, Joe Ellington didn't give either woman an ounce of trouble. Like Jean, Mary appeared intrigued by some of the other items in her mother's safe deposit box, but set everything aside, knowing the lawyers would sort out everything in two days.

"She was a woman of many secrets," Mary noted quietly when they stepped from the bank, wiping a bit of moisture from her eyes.

"Yes, she was," Jean agreed, putting forth a strong front, anxious to read the professional packet from cover to cover.

Considering she had vowed to keep the original safe and return it to the estate rather quickly, Jean wanted to make a copy first.

"Do you know anything about your mother's murder that you didn't tell the police?"

Jean might have expected Mary to appear shocked at such a question, but the older woman remained stoic, saying nothing for a few tense seconds. Vivian harbored numerous secrets, revealing very little to her family in order to protect them. Jean never understood the two distinct sides of her aunt because she learned family values before she discovered the art of mastering finances.

She and Mary had never been particularly close, perhaps because Vivian took Jean under her wing when the rest of her children pursued career paths that didn't specifically involve handling finances. While their relationship certainly wasn't adversarial, an unspoken, invisible layer of unfamiliarity lingered between Jean and Mary, as though they were both friends of a mutual friend and not necessarily one another.

Instead of answering Jean's question, Mary looked away as though she knew something she dared not speak about. Perhaps she felt shame for not knowing *more* about her mother's previous business dealings, as though such knowledge might prove useful in the present.

"Maybe you'll find what you're looking for in there," Mary said, nodding at the packet. "If you or the police think anything else might help, just let me know."

"Thanks," Jean said, treading lightly to ensure she didn't lose her aunt as an ally.

She felt no desire to acquire finances from Vivian's untimely passing, and Jean really didn't have any financial needs other than saving for her daughter's college fund. Fearing alienation from certain family members, Jean planned on acting aloof about the reading of the will, possibly skipping the event altogether. At the moment she simply wanted to learn who brutally murdered her great-aunt and why.

Jean parted ways with Mary a moment later, neither uttering another word.

Clutching her new source of information, she headed straight to the library, where the nearest copy machine awaited her. She felt paranoid about asking the bank personnel to use their copier, because she didn't want to take a chance of anyone else seeing the information on the documents. At this point she trusted no one outside of her family. A professional copy center in nearby Bedford might have made sharper, cheaper copies, but Jean didn't want to waste fifteen minutes driving there because she wanted to dive into the information immediately.

When she walked into the Mitchell Public Library, Jean discovered the place virtually deserted for a Saturday morning. The bustle of setting up the Persimmon Festival went on just down the street, and in the library's basement level where paintings created by local artists were hung for display, sale, and voting. On the main floor she quickly made copies of the brochure, deciding as she did so that a look at the original, in full color, might provide better perspective.

Doing work in the library had always felt quiet and peaceful, stemming back to her high school days. Perhaps the opportunity to spread out her work on a clean workplace free of a teenager's clothes and belongings helped, but Jean never expected to be interrupted in a library when she browsed or read there.

She settled into the Indiana Room for privacy afforded by three solid glass walls. While families looked through the movie selection along the nearby shelves, and children ran through the basement level, Jean took a seat at the large table inside the room, wishing she could shut the single door entrance. Opening the brochure, she began realizing that a huge piece of land went to developing a permanent carnival between the towns of Bedford and Mitchell just after she was born.

"What happened?" she questioned under her breath.

Looking at her watch, Jean realized half an hour had flown by while she carefully read the paperwork, which appeared to be promotional material. Either the conglomerate wanted to hype the new investment to potential advertisers and partner companies, or they were opting to take the theme park public through shares.

Jean felt as though an incredibly large backstory continued to elude her, and for some reason no one talked about the carnival.

Was it sold?

Did it move?

Did it go defunct after opening briefly?

What seemed a surefire local treasure, certain to bring much needed income to Lawrence County apparently vanished without a trace almost forty years earlier. Jean might never have cared why, but her aunt considered the transaction important enough to store, or perhaps conceal, within a vault.

Without any solid answers coming her way, Jean was about to pack up and begin looking for alternate methods of discovering why her aunt's group dedicated so much time and money to a property they apparently abandoned when she overheard a conversation at the front desk.

It sounded as though a male patron was inquiring about archived newspaper articles referring to the property just off the highway where the theme park was located. Gathering her paperwork, Jean carried the brochure and the copies with her just outside the door where she pretended to peruse some new books.

"I'm looking for articles about the property from the time it was originally purchased or the theme park went under," the man told the female librarian waiting on him.

Stealing a glance, she thought he looked like the man on the evening news who owned the new theme park. If that were true, she couldn't imagine why he hadn't researched the property before buying it, and more importantly, what he needed to know about the past. He wasn't as tall as she might have imagined, but he maintained the stern countenance of a cop. Dressed rather casually this morning compared to his press conference and news appearances, Lancaster was mentioned as one of the investigators in Vivian's murder by Mary. Information circulated through small towns like wildfires, and Jean overheard gossip everywhere she'd visited the last two days.

"We only carry the *Mitchell Tribune* archives here," the older red-headed librarian informed him. "You'll have to go to Bedford if you want their paper's older stories, and most of those are still cataloged in microfiche."

Lancaster groaned.

"I don't even have the dates."

Jean decided if she was going to speak with this man a better opportunity wouldn't present itself. Police officers tended to be guarded people, and if he owned the new theme park as she believed he did, access to him wasn't going to prove very easy in the future.

"Maybe I can help," she said, hoping she sounded more confident than she felt as she slapped the professional brochure on the counter.

He stared at it momentarily before his eyes widened with familiarity before slowly drifting in Jean's direction.

"I'm Vivian Weatherly's niece," Jean offered.

"I'm very sorry for your loss," Lancaster said, his eyes drifting downward momentarily, indicating he wished he might have accomplished more in the investigation.

The irony that they stood surrounded by fountains of information, none of it useful toward their objective, wasn't lost on Jean.

"Jeff Lancaster," the former deputy said, offering his hand.

Jean shook it with a friendly grin, despite the dire circumstances that brought them to the same location.

"Jean Garrison. And it's hard not to know who *you* are."

Lancaster returned a sheepish grin that indicated fame, even local fame, remained very new to him.

"I hate to interrupt," the librarian said, "but may I ask exactly what you two are looking for? I've lived in the area all of my life."

Jean and Lancaster looked at one another before Lancaster shrugged.

"I can't speak for Ms. Garrison, but I'm looking for information about the land where the new theme park is located. There was a murder there years ago, and it looked like there was some other theme park, or a carnival, abandoned on the site."

What Lancaster said about the murder was news to Jean, but she found it incredibly hard to believe the murder and the land development didn't have *something* to do with one another.

"I go on break in ten minutes if you both have time to wait," the librarian offered. "I can give you a few definite truths and a lot of conjecture I've heard over the years."

"That sounds better than what we have," Lancaster answered.

Jean agreed with a nod.

Chapter 12

Ten minutes later Lancaster waited with Jean at a table in the children's section of the basement since the conference rooms were being utilized for Persimmon Festival activities. Fortunately no one else occupied the area, or they might have been the subject of scrutinizing eyes. Few options were available for the brief discussion that accompanied an equally short break.

"Again, I'm very sorry about your aunt," he said, finally breaking the tense silence between them.

Neither seemed capable of finding the right words, considering the dark circumstances entering their lives.

"She wasn't a saint by any means," Jean replied slowly, "but she made me everything I am today."

Lancaster rubbed his forehead in frustration with both hands, finding his skin warm and flush from stress that extended beyond opening a theme park.

"I just want to help however I can," Jean said. "Vivian didn't deserve what happened to her."

Nodding in agreement, Lancaster struggled for fitting words.

"You were at the crime scene, weren't you?" Jean asked hesitantly, taking notice of his discomfort.

"Yes," he answered simply.

"I know you can't talk about the case, but do you have any leads?"

"I'm really just a consultant at this point," Lancaster admitted. "It takes time to get forensics results, and we didn't have any immediate suspects."

"You must know something or you wouldn't be checking on your theme park's history all of the sudden."

Lancaster folded his hands atop the table, looking away momentarily.

"I know my theme park was either a carnival or fairgrounds before I bought it," he said after a moment. "I also know the man who owned the land before that was murdered on those very grounds. And it looks as though your aunt and her partners may have been very interested in that land."

If he possessed any inclination that Jean wasn't truthful in her statements about assisting with the case, Lancaster would never have revealed even the slightest detail about the investigation. He immediately regretted speaking the last piece of information about his theme park, almost implying that Vivian Weatherly and her partners were somehow part of a nefarious scheme.

He didn't like speaking untruths about people, knowing that lack of evidence damned police officers in the courtroom. Although the same principles didn't exactly apply to civilian life, Lancaster didn't want to speak badly of anyone who didn't deserve it.

As though on cue to break up their awkward conversation, the librarian emerged through the nearby doorway and drew one of the empty seats at the table. Lancaster remembered her name, Paula, from her nametag, though he hadn't called her by name yet.

"I can't tell you exact dates on these things, but I can get you in the ballpark," she began. "When the murder occurred I was still in college. It made national news for a day, but it was big local news for the longest time. No one around here had ever heard of such a thing, especially the way the man was brutally murdered."

"You mean Michael Tanksley?" Lancaster asked for clarification.

"Yes," the librarian answered tentatively, though he could tell it wasn't from the gruesome depiction of the man's death.

Something else perturbed the woman.

"What do you know about him?" Lancaster pushed with a curious tone.

"I know the man wasn't completely right in the head," the librarian said with a bit of emotional pain for the deceased. "Folks around here said he was odd, but the man didn't have anything left except the land his parents left him."

"Left him?" Jean inquired.

"They were part Indian, like a fractional amount, but they won some kind of settlement with the state years and years ago."

"I thought Indiana didn't have any reservations," Lancaster thought aloud.

"They don't. This was a lawsuit against the state that the family won. And when his parents died young, from natural causes I suppose, he was left with this huge tract of land that would have made farmers or businessmen a lot of revenue. Needless to say, a lot of people weren't very happy about the settlement."

Lancaster questioned how the state could decide to allocate land so easily, but he supposed there wasn't as much red tape back in those days. He also suspected the state or Lawrence County owned the land at the time, which meant giving it away in a settlement bypassed any red tape.

"So what happened to the property when Tanksley died?" he asked.

"It got held up in court again. The only surviving family member was a kid, so a settlement was made to set up a trust fund for him and the land was sold. The only reason I remember all of this is because the news made a big deal about both court cases."

Lancaster couldn't help but give Jean a cagy look.

"What is it?" she asked, her eyes narrowing because she knew his thoughts weren't favorable.

"It would seem your aunt and her people were either extremely lucky, or they manipulated the situation to acquire that land."

Jean didn't seem to like the implications one bit. Good fortune in a land deal was one thing, but making one's own luck, particularly through murder, led down a dark path from which there was no return.

"So the group got the land and obviously tried to make a go of something out there," Lancaster said, trying to prompt Paula to elaborate.

"They tried to open a permanent carnival, or what we call a theme park these days. It was supposed to coincide with the Persimmon Festival, but a series of mishaps kept it from staying open after the first fall season."

"Mishaps?" Jean questioned.

"No one was killed, or even harmed as I recall," Paula answered. "Rides were vandalized and kept breaking down. The owners just kept dumping money into the place, only to see things keep falling apart."

She paused momentarily in thought before continuing.

"I seem to recall the owners were having a roller coaster imported from Europe and the ship bringing it sunk in the Great Lakes. The news made a big deal about that, too, because there weren't any bad storms across the lakes at the time. People called the entire project jinxed, and maybe that's why it sat vacant for so long."

Lancaster doubted anyone's luck ran so badly for so long that they couldn't keep a theme park afloat. He personally anticipated nothing except success for his endeavor, and he personally believed he lacked business savvy compared to anyone in Vivian's group.

Still, he swallowed hard, hoping whatever bad karma affected the land back then didn't carry over to present day.

Paula took out a piece of paper and pen to write down some years and possible months before sliding the list to Lancaster.

"Those are approximate times where you two might find some articles about the theme park, the group, and Michael Tanksley's murder. It might be worthwhile, but you're going to spend a lot of man hours digging through the microfiche."

"Do you have another suggestion?" Jean asked.

"Perhaps you can go directly to the source for some answers."

"Source?" Lancaster questioned with a raised eyebrow.

"Colby McWilliams. He was the only living relative from that entire family after they sued to acquire that land."

"But he was a kid," Lancaster surmised.

"True. But if anyone has family heirlooms, and maybe some answers, it's him."

Lancaster couldn't argue the logic, so he looked to Jean.

"I've got time," she stated.

"Then I guess we're going to pay Mr. McWilliams a visit."

Chapter 13

More tense silence accompanied Jean and Lancaster during the drive to Colby McWilliams' property, starting with the argument about who was going to drive. After a two-minute debate Jean finally wore down the former police officer and Lancaster agreed to let her drive.

"I don't like you inferring that my aunt had some part in Michael Tanksley's murder," she stated about halfway to their destination.

"Can you definitively say she or her partners didn't have something to do with it? I'm just playing devil's advocate here because someone tortured your aunt and Charles Stafford before killing them."

"You've made that abundantly clear, but you haven't provided any details."

"Because you don't want to hear them," Lancaster replied, looking down to his smartphone for an update on their navigation.

Vivid images of the gruesome crime scenes passed through his mind like a slideshow, making him wish he had quit the department a day earlier.

The scenery along Highway 37 changed from small businesses and up-scale houses in the distance to country homes and large fields primed for harvest once Jean turned onto the appropriate county road. Farm houses appeared to stand guard over the tan corn stalks or lush bean plants lining every other field.

"I need to know all of your aunt's business partners," Lancaster said evenly, making an effort to keep the peace.

"Could one of them be behind all of this?"

"Doubtful. I think someone is targeting them, or at least some of them."

"I can probably help with that," Jean revealed, though her tone didn't provide reassurance that she believed he wanted the information for the right reasons.

About half a mile down the road they came upon a two-story renovated house with brick trim along the lower level and newer beige siding above. Lancaster thought the property seemed a bit much for just one person to care for with vast acreage surrounding every side. A fully paved driveway sat beside the house, and a large two-bay garage occupied the opposite side with a large awning hanging toward the road. Several vehicles and tractors lined the yard behind the garage, though the space certainly didn't look like a residential junkyard. Each of the vehicles appeared neatly parked and in running condition, as though they were projects awaiting their turn. Behind everything was an old, large, red barn with slightly faded paint that appeared in otherwise good condition.

Lancaster wasn't sure he expected McWilliams to be home until he spied the rear garage door wide-open. Being a Saturday morning, he didn't figure the man would stray too far because most people were holding garage sales or finishing up yard work before the cold weather moved in. Most area residents tended to stick around when the Persimmon Festival opened because they reconnected with old schoolmates and friends during the week ahead.

Jean pulled into the driveway and while no human beings emerged to greet them, a yellow Labrador wagged its tail along the house's front landing before trotting their way. Lancaster stepped cautiously from the vehicle, quickly discovering the dog wasn't a barking protective kind of pet, but rather a dog that craved attention.

He scratched its head, waiting for it to lead them in one direction or the other, but it simply planted its posterior on the ground and waited for more affection.

"Hello?" Lancaster called, wondering if the property owner was even home.

Jean shrugged when he looked in her direction. About to walk toward the house, Lancaster spied someone emerging from the open garage bay with an old work shirt that contained no name patch. Making direct eye contact with them, the man wiped his hands thoroughly with an already dirtied rag.

"Are you Colby McWilliams?" Lancaster asked in case the man had someone else working on his property.

"I am."

The reply came with a twang that Lancaster typically associated with country singers from Nashville. McWilliams looked to his hands, still smudged with oil and grease.

"I'd offer to shake, but that's probably not a great idea."

Lancaster and Jean introduced themselves, and Jean explained the circumstances leading them to their property as McWilliams listened patiently.

An average-sized man carrying a little extra weight, McWilliams possessed a mostly full head of graying brown hair parted to one side. A thick beard covered the man's face, despite seasonal hunting and steadily cooler temperatures remaining a few weeks away. Glancing at the rag between the man's hands, Lancaster noticed how thick the mechanic's fingers appeared, likely a result of daily tinkering. Lancaster put McWilliams close to fifty years in age, partially based on what history he knew about the man and the time of Michael Tanksley's death.

"I'll answer any questions you might have, but I really don't know much about my cousin," McWilliams said genuinely when Jean finished her explanation. "I was only nine when he died."

He invited them inside, and while Lancaster and Jean seated themselves on a plush chair and a loveseat respectively, he walked into his kitchen for a glass of ice water.

"Can I get either of you anything to drink?" he offered. "I've got water, soda, and beer."

Both declined, so McWilliams returned with his glass of ice water and sat on the loveseat a comfortable distance from Jean.

"Can I ask what you do for a living?" Lancaster inquired as their host took a deep drink from the glass.

"Pretty much what you see out back. I work on tractors, mowers, and just about any kind of vehicle you can imagine. I get enough references from friends that there's always something out there needing fixed."

"You just do engine work?" Lancaster asked.

"I can rebuild engines, I can shape metal, and on occasions I even weld."

"I could use someone like you at the park," Lancaster said with genuine enthusiasm.

Mechanics weren't incredibly difficult to come by, but they were often specialized, forcing him to hire additional people for various jobs. Some didn't like heights, some couldn't take machinery apart and recall how to put it back together correctly, and a few lied during the interview just to get the job. Those people were quickly discovered and terminated, because Lancaster wasn't going to pay dishonest employees.

"I'm pretty happy just doing my own thing," McWilliams admitted. "Being around other people isn't always easy for me."

Lancaster knew the feeling, suspecting the reasons for each of them were quite different. Perhaps McWilliams simply didn't trust people after once having a sizable inheritance, or maybe he liked a life of solitude. He certainly didn't act suspicious or seem the least bit hostile, but Lancaster didn't feel as though he'd removed enough layers of the man's personality to know Colby McWilliams just yet.

"What can you tell us about your cousin?" Jean asked, quite possibly to change the subject because they all felt a little tense.

"I don't know much," McWilliams admitted. "Even though he was murdered, people don't like to talk about him."

He hesitated, as though crafting his next statement carefully.

"It's almost as though there really isn't much good to say."

Lancaster started to press for anything at all, but McWilliams casually held up a hand, indicating he wasn't finished.

"I'm gonna start from the beginning," the man said slowly, openly disturbed by drudging up the past. "My parents died when I was only five in a car accident. They were coming home from some party that had to do with my father's work, and their car skidded off the road and crashed headfirst into a tree."

"I'm so sorry," Jean said earnestly.

"Thank you. After that, I went to live with our family lawyer because he was my godfather. I think he somehow felt partially responsible for what happened to my folks because he was always good to me. He even started a trust fund for me when my cousin passed away."

"Your cousin was brutally murdered," Lancaster stated, not for effect, but to test how much the man knew of the situation.

McWilliams took a drink of water and stared at the floor momentarily.

"He died when I was nine," McWilliams said after a lengthy pause. "They didn't say much to me, except that he was a distant cousin. I remember asking Henry, my godfather, why the casket was closed. He quickly changed the subject and talked to some other people there. I've lived long enough to attend calling hours a dozen times or better, and I now realize my cousin had the most barebones ceremony I've ever seen. Hardly anyone attended, and there weren't any personal touches in that funeral home. Not even a photograph."

McWilliams appeared almost mortified by that fact as he spoke the words.

"Most of the people who attended were probably more curious than anything. I can't imagine going through life and having no true friends or family attend your service."

He seemed to swallow hard after speaking the words. Losing one's last family member, even if he never met the man, probably left him alone in the world, Lancaster supposed. People depended upon family members for emotional support, advice, and perhaps the occasional personal loan. At least McWilliams seemed to have steered his life in a morally upstanding direction.

"What was it like growing up?" Jean inquired.

Lancaster didn't want to hear all of the sappy stories about the man's childhood, but he supposed background information might prove useful. The more he heard, the more he could gauge when the man was being truthful or deceptive with the facts.

"Like I said, Henry Cauldwell was my godfather and very close with my parents before they died. He basically adopted me, and he took good care of me, but he was an older man. It was hard for me to relate to him and his wife, so I found some different outlets. They lived in the country, so it was natural for me to try 4-H after working on their farm. Most of my friends worked on cars, so I learned a lot from them and went to vocational school during my last few years of high school."

"Are your adoptive parents still alive?" Jean asked.

"No," McWilliams said, shaking his head as a solemn expression crossed his face. "Henry died a few years after I graduated high school, and Lilly passed away about five years ago in a nursing home. She didn't even know who I was at the end, but I fulfilled her wishes when she passed."

"I'm so sorry," Jean said just above a whisper, as though regretting the inquiry.

"Don't be," McWilliams said, letting a grin pierce his bearded countenance. "I still have lots of friends around, so I'm never alone."

Lancaster's police instincts kicked in. He wasn't going to be suckered in by a few words and some personal history that appeared genuine. Murderers, rapists, and thieves were able to lie with straight faces during interrogations in his experience, so he wasn't going to trust this stranger just yet.

"If you were the last family member in your bloodline, you stood to inherit something from your cousin," he noted aloud.

"Henry set up a trust fund for me after Michael was killed," McWilliams admitted without hesitation. "I didn't receive any of it until I turned eighteen, and like any kid I wasn't very smart with money. I blew through almost half of it before Lilly talked some sense into me."

"And now?" Lancaster pressed.

McWilliams appeared unhappy for the first time during the reasonably informal talk. No one enjoyed revealing their personal finances, especially if doing so placed them in a negative light. If the man didn't suspect it before, he now understood that Lancaster considered him a person of interest in the murders.

"These days I make a good living working on my own," McWilliams answered a bit testily a few seconds later. "And I invested what money I had left in some good places."

At this point Jean turned to Lancaster with a look of displeasure, realizing his questions were pointed. Although the former detective tended to believe McWilliams in general, she was displaying excessive empathy for a man who admittedly made mistakes in his past. Lancaster remembered why he disliked involving lay people in any kind of investigation. They slowed progress to a crawl and lacked the ability to put emotions aside when judging a person's words and body language.

The fact that she didn't openly apologize to McWilliams showed Lancaster that Jean still wanted answers to her aunt's murder, no matter the cost.

"Do you have pictures of your cousin, or personal effects?" Lancaster asked.

"Why pictures?" McWilliams inquired with a skeptical stare, complete with narrowing eyes.

"I'd like to see how the man lived."

McWilliams didn't appear to entirely buy the answer, even though Lancaster harbored no further motive. When piecing together a puzzle he wanted every shred of information available, no matter how mundane it seemed.

"I actually have a chest full of his stuff," McWilliams answered. "Henry offered to throw it away several times, but I asked him to keep it. I haven't been through it in years though."

Maybe Henry had something to hide, Lancaster thought.

"May we see it?" Jean asked of McWilliams.

"Sure," he said, taking a drink of water before standing. He set down the now empty glass and led them toward the front door. "I keep it in the barn."

Only when they stepped outside did Lancaster notice several familiar rural odors. Perhaps the wind had changed direction, explaining why he failed to notice them before, or perhaps his mind was narrowly focused when he first arrived. A faint smell of manure entered his nostrils, but he detected hay more intensely. He discovered why when he stepped into the barn and found several old bales stacked beside the main door. Although a large, double swinging door existed for tractors and farm equipment to enter, McWilliams took them through the conventional red door with a white X crossing the center on its way to the corners.

Much of the barn appeared vacant, but a tractor occupied part of an open bay. In that same portion of the barn the hayloft access was visible, though the hayloft itself stretched across the tops of the other two sections, leaving a vastly open space between the lower level and the arched rooftop. The center section, by far the narrowest of the three, acted as a storage unit of sorts, loaded with boxes and crates.

Lancaster followed Jean and McWilliams inside, astounded at how much property one man could own, or at least store, inside a barn. Each end of the room contained a grime-covered window that made it nearly impossible to see outside. Cobwebs danced above the trio in the corners, so aged that dust covered their numerous broken strands as they flapped in the breeze.

Strangely enough, and old trunk occupied one corner by itself. Lancaster wondered if an immigrant brought it over from another country because it appeared so old and heavy. A noticeable layer of dust covered the trunk, indicating it hadn't been disturbed in some time. McWilliams headed straight for the storage unit, opening the lid rather easily, though it protested with a loud creak before revealing its contents.

With its top securely propped against the wall, Lancaster peered inside the trunk, noticing several items stacked atop one another. The topmost layer appeared comprised of albums and books. The uppermost items were covered by a thick layer of dust except for an area about the size of a hardcover book. He looked to McWilliams for permission to touch the items inside.

"May I?"

McWilliams nodded affirmatively.

Running his finger across the clean area, Lancaster found very little dust on his finger, indicating the missing item had been somewhat recently removed.

"What was there?" he asked.

"I'm not sure," McWilliams answered. "It's mostly photo albums and documents in there."

Without any prompting, the owner began removing items from the chest and handing them to Jean. Once her arms grew full with books and albums, he handed several more to Lancaster, who examined one in particular. Like the trunk, the book's front cover displayed a layer of dust except for a strange outline with three sides but no distinct angles. Though the imprint appeared partial because another object loomed over it in the trunk, Lancaster felt he should have recognized the shape.

He took out his smart phone to snap a picture of the shape before it was smudged away, drawing curious stares from Jean and McWilliams. Though he noticed, Lancaster tapped the button on his phone to snap the picture anyway. A strong feeling that something about the trunk wasn't quite right plagued him. Someone, quite possibly McWilliams, recently accessed the storage unit and removed a few particular items.

"Did you ever go through the trunk?" Jean asked the mechanic.

"Not really."

"Why not?"

"I guess because I never really knew my cousin. I know it probably seems odd to you with everyone doing genealogy searches these days, but from what I heard it almost felt better not knowing him. It just felt better always having the possibility of knowing him just around the corner."

"It doesn't seem odd at all," Jean said sympathetically. "I have members of my family I barely know and I've seen them all of my life."

Grasping the lid by its clasps, Lancaster slowly lowered it to see if any fingerprints or smudges were evident on the exterior. He found no evidence of recent tampering, so he returned it to an upright position, taking a step back to allow McWilliams to dispense the remainder of the stored items. Lancaster received a few bound folders, likely containing legal documents, a few framed photographs, and a photo album. The vintage album barely clung to its original binder, faded and worn from the burden of protecting family memories.

Momentarily all three carried armfuls of memorabilia and documentation into the house for examination. Lancaster regretted being so forward about considering McWilliams a potential suspect. He feared he might have alienated a potential witness who seemed to be rather helpful so far, but Lancaster wasn't about to cross the man's name off of the suspect list just yet.

It bothered him that McWilliams didn't recall what the two missing items were, and more importantly, why they had disappeared. The man didn't appear particularly fazed about their disappearance, but he barely knew the man who once owned them. Lancaster had noticed a downward spiral in the man's cooperation level after the former detective made it clear McWilliams was on his radar.

McWilliams hadn't verbally objected to anything, but his demeanor changed considerably, and he made it a point to speak to Jean rather than Lancaster. All three rummaged through the belongings collected from the trunk, seldom speaking or glancing at what the other two were examining.

When Lancaster opened the vintage photo album, he discovered dozens of black and white images that might have deteriorated if removed from the sticky backing and yellowed laminate covering. He flipped through the pages, carefully studying each family member and friend captured in time, understanding why no one remained from Michael Tanksley's family. Only one child, the same each time, was ever pictured, and Lancaster suspected the child was indeed Tanksley.

He subconsciously began flipping the pages a bit faster, wanting to see the murdered man as an adult. Around the middle of the album, early color photographs occupied the pages, appearing both flat in contrast and faded. Lancaster dated them to the late 1960s based on the attire family members wore. He spotted images of a happy Michael Tanksley in early adulthood, often holding a can of beer in one hand while making a funny face for the photographer. Several posed family pictures were sprinkled amongst the family vacations and holiday gatherings. Lancaster noticed the number of family members diminishing as grandparents were no longer present in the more recent photographs. The quality of the photos themselves improved with each page in both color and clarity, indicating at least one member of the family upgraded cameras at some point.

Lancaster felt a bit saddened, even though he never met the family, because he understood loss. Investigating murders provided him with a sense of death, loss, and coping through his interactions with others, but he'd also lost close family members in his lifetime.

Just after the middle portion of the album, he discovered the last page that contained any photographs because he suspected no one survived to insert any additional images into the book. The very last photo in the album, likely taken by a loving mother, displayed an adult Michael Tanksley who appeared grossly different from the fun-loving, beer drinking man photographed in earlier years.

Lancaster swallowed hard because the man wore Native American garb, as though consumed by the marginal portion of his bloodline tied to an American tribe. His spunky disposition appeared to be replaced by a serious demeanor, as though the man found a crusade that required his full attention. With a cloth poncho around his shoulders, somewhat like Lancaster recalled seeing from two-hundred feet in the air, the man wore a somber, stoic expression that bordered on mental illness.

What disturbed Lancaster most, however, was that the man looked identical to the person he spotted on the ground from atop his roller coaster. True, the distance made details difficult to make out, but he knew his eyesight was fine, and the color of the clothing in both the image and present day looked identical.

"What's wrong?" Jean asked, taking notice of his stare at the haunting image encased within the book.

"Nothing," he answered, trying his best to act naturally as he closed the book. "Either of you come up with anything?"

Both shook their heads negatively.

"If you didn't take those items out of the trunk," Lancaster asked McWilliams, "do you have any idea who might have?"

"No. Most of my friends who stop by have work for me to do. All of them stay and visit from time to time, but there's no reason for anyone to go in the barn." "Any signs of trespassers recently?"

"I had an issue with someone trying to break into my house last year, but nothing really came of it."

Lancaster knew his former department would have dispatched a deputy to interview the homeowner and fill out a report. He made a mental note to check on that particular front later, because he wanted a third person perspective of McWilliams.

He'd taken time to glance over the rest of the items from the trunk, finding little of interest regarding the case. He suspected someone already found, and stole, anything of interest from the barn, unless McWilliams himself had something to hide and discarded the evidence.

Lancaster found it difficult to concentrate because in the back of his mind he kept reminding himself that he had a multimillion dollar business requiring his attention. He felt a bit selfish about wanting to oversee his affairs personally, but dozens of employees relied upon him for paychecks. Investigating a murder once fueled him, often keeping him up nights in search of answers and clues, but now it felt like a chore.

An unrewarded chore at that.

Within another twenty minutes the trio had finished looking through the last of Michael Tanksley's legacy, discovering nothing useful. Jean and Lancaster both thanked McWilliams for his time before exiting through the front door. It wasn't until they were half a mile down the road in her car before Lancaster spoke.

"It's hard to believe that trunk held everything one man owned, like his entire life story was inside that trunk. Kind of sad, really."

"What had you spooked in that photo album?" Jean asked without bothering to address his smokescreen comments.

"Nothing," he answered, deciding the truth only served to make him appear crazy.

Jean grunted not so subtly, indicating she didn't believe him. Lancaster said nothing, attempting to collect his thoughts and decide where to check next. He needed to tend to his business first and foremost, he decided, figuring the professionals could handle the investigation until Monday when his theme park would be closed for the week. With the Persimmon Festival monopolizing downtown Mitchell he suspected figurative roadblocks would accompany the physical barricades regarding the investigation. People tended to flock to the downtown events daily, or leave the area altogether during the week to escape the crowds and traffic.

"Can I get a copy of that list of your aunt's business partners?" he finally asked once Jean turned onto the highway, taking them back to Mitchell and Lancaster's truck.

"You know, you were awfully tough on Colby back there."

"So you two are on a first name basis already?"

"Maybe being friendly to people just comes easier to me, but you basically implied he was a suspect in my aunt's murder."

"Well, he *is*, Jean. I probably laid it on a bit thick, but you can't investigate these things without testing your suspects. It's all about saying the right things at the right time. You didn't find it a bit convenient that two objects were missing from that trunk?"

"He had no idea we were coming to talk to him," Jean said, turning to Lancaster with an expression that indicated she would fight to prove McWilliams wasn't a murderer. "Why would he wait until now to remove those things?"

"It's funny that he can't remember what those objects were, and if he was involved in foul play, he probably knew better than to leave evidence lying around."

Jean placed both hands tightly upon the steering wheel, looking straight ahead.

"You can't believe everyone you meet is innocent, Jean," Lancaster said honestly, softening his tone a bit. "The world doesn't work like that. I've had stone-cold rapists and killers lie to me without blinking."

"Colby McWilliams is no killer."

"I'm not saying he is. I'm just saying there's the possibility. He's not giving us the entire truth."

Silence filled the car the last five minutes of the trip until Jean pulled into the library parking lot beside Lancaster's truck. He was about to get out without so much as a farewell gesture when she reached behind her and leafed through her paperwork. She whipped out a single sheet of paper so fast he nearly got a paper cut before clasping it by one edge.

"That's your list of names. I suppose now that you have it I won't be hearing from you again."

Lancaster had already made up his mind that their partnership was dissolved the moment he stepped from her car on the trip home.

"We'll see," he lied, not so differently from some of the nefarious types he once interviewed as a cop.

Chapter 14

When Lancaster arrived at his theme park it was already open for business, with screams, cheers, and shouts emanating from every direction. Unfortunately as he looked down to the sheet of paper clutched in his right hand he didn't feel very much like celebrating. Two names on the list didn't mean a thing to him, two others he knew only from the past week's events, but the last one disturbed him on intuition alone.

James Barwick.

As he walked through the thicket of teenagers, children, and adults strolling through his property, Lancaster felt somewhat uneasy because he seemed to recall Hank Barwick talking about his father having already passed away. Based on Barwick's age, it stood to reason his father was approximately the same age as Vivian Weatherly and her other colleagues. Lancaster trusted his head of maintenance enough that he doubted the man had any involvement in the recent murders.

Still, he needed to know for certain.

Barwick typically slept during the daytime, so Lancaster walked directly to his office and did some internet research to find the answers he needed. He used software that assisted with background checks, and within minutes he learned that James Barwick was indeed father to Hank and three other children. After giving Jean a stern lecture about mistrusting people, he decided he needed to know if his employee came to him under false pretenses. And if Barwick wasn't a valid suspect in any wrongdoing, Lancaster definitely feared for the man's safety because someone seemed hell-bent on revenge.

Lancaster spent a few minutes trying a Google search for James Barwick's death date and an obituary, but nothing concrete appeared. He found too many results that contained either a partial name or occurred outside of Indiana. Knowing it might take hours to comb through the barrage of links for useful information, he decided to spend his time more wisely and use a local resource to solve what he assumed was a local mystery.

He picked up his office phone and dialed the number for the library.

"Mitchell Public Library," a woman answered. "This is Paula."

"Paula, this is Jeff Lancaster. I was in there this morning."

"I remember," she said with a neutral tone. "How can I help you?"

"I'm needing some help finding an obituary and any information you could give me about a James Barwick. He would be somewhere around eighty if he was alive today."

"Any idea about when he died?"

"I'm guessing here, but probably around ten years ago. I can probably get you an exact date later today."

"That would certainly help. His birthdate, county of death, or even birthplace would help narrow down the search. It may take a few days, even if you get me more information, but I'm sure I can find something for you. Do you have a contact number?"

Lancaster provided both his office and cell phone numbers. He wondered how difficult it could be to track down information about someone with such an uncommon surname. Then again, he wasn't going to look a gift horse in the mouth since he didn't want to spend time searching through hundreds of records.

He thanked her and hung up the phone only to immediately scoop it up a second time to call his security director's cell phone.

"Schall," the man answered after two rings with lots of audible background noise.

Schall was apparently conducting rounds amongst the park guests.

"Danny, we need to grab lunch."

"That sounds ominous, boss."

"Not for you, it isn't."

"Are we going off-campus?"

"We are *definitely* going off-campus. How does Mexican sound? My treat."

"Then Mexican sounds great," Schall answered, the drawl in his voice indicating he liked the idea of a legal bribe.

Lancaster tapped his fingers atop the desk, hating the idea that his property might be tied in with the recent murders, and wondering if his employee's family somehow tied into the mystery.

"Get to my office as soon as you can," he instructed Schall before hanging up the phone and standing to look out his office window at a skyline comprised of wood and metal.

It looked incredible at dusk with an orange glow behind the twisting metal and perfectly curved wooden rails. Like the rest of the park, it became part of one huge, frightening show once the fog emerged from dozens of giant fog machines and the artificial lighting from lanterns and jack-o-lanterns barely pierced the hazy white substance. People never knew what awaited them, even a few feet ahead, because they couldn't see a thing at times. Lancaster personally loved a controlled scare, which inspired him to create a theme park packed full of thrills and frights.

He once looked forward to the small stresses that owning a theme park brought, but those compounded with the investigation were beginning to wear on him physically. He already regretted agreeing to help the sheriff despite a few pieces of information coming his way that might have been ignored by other investigators. The timing felt so incredibly wrong, yet Lancaster wondered if his park's grand opening, the Persimmon Festival, and the murders were somehow inevitably linked.

Even though Michael Tanksley was marginally Native American, Lancaster wondered if he had unwittingly, and ironically, purchased hallowed grounds. He wished his brother would have done a better background check on the place before giving him a green light to purchase the property.

Swiping the keys to his truck from atop his desk, he decided to get some fresh air by waiting for Schall outside.

✳✳✳

Fifteen minutes later the two sat inside Buena Comida, where Lancaster sometimes ate during his law enforcement days. A rather homey place, the restaurant walls were painted in colorful patterns native to Mexico. Several framed paintings also adorned the wood paneling, and every chair and bench inside the building was constructed of wood and engraved with the restaurant's name. Most of the lighting came from the two large windows toward the front, giving the indication that at night the place looked like an old, authentic restaurant found in the Southwest during the previous century.

After the two received their drinks and placed their orders for lunch, Schall leaned on the table and gave his employer a look of anticipation.

"What's so important that you have to kidnap me from my duties?"

Lancaster appreciated that his security director didn't mince words, often getting down to business in a hurry. He wanted to confide in him as one former cop to another, but the murder investigation took some strange turns that Lancaster considered bad for business if word leaked to the public. Jean could easily make incriminating statements, but she had personal motive to keep any clues to herself. Though Lancaster considered Schall a trustworthy individual, the man was still fairly new to him. He couldn't take any chance of his "cursed" land's legacy getting out to the public, particularly on opening weekend.

"I need you to keep watch over Hank Barwick for me," he answered as neutrally as possible.

Schall's eyes narrowed before a suspicious smirk crossed his lips.

"Does this request mean I'm observing him as a suspect, or I'm his guardian angel?"

Lancaster wasn't completely certain of the answer, but he couldn't picture any of his employees hacking off the limbs of elderly people. He planned on speaking with Barwick later that day for some clarification on a few matters, but for now he felt compelled to trust the man.

"Unless I say otherwise, I want you to personally make certain nothing happens to him."

"You want me to log in some overtime, or change my work hours?" Schall asked, trying too hard to act impartial about the decision.

Both men knew police officers absolutely love overtime, particularly easy gigs like shadowing a single individual.

"Change your schedule, Danny. I can't afford to fork over too much extra money right now. Besides, Hank won't be there much during the week."

Schall dipped a complimentary nacho into the house salsa, taking a small bite before speaking again.

"Why do I have a feeling this has something to do with your murder investigation?"

"Why would you think that?"

"Because you haven't had time to work on anything else the past few days."

"Maybe something came across my desk."

Schall scoffed at the words.

"If something came across your desk, it would be from me. Boss, it's none of my business, so tell me to fuck off if you want to."

"To be honest, Danny, I wouldn't even know where to begin. This case is worse than anything I experienced while I was on the job."

With the usual prompt service, their food arrived on hot plates before the two men truly had their fill of the delicious salsa. Schall divided his burrito with a fork before speaking to his employer with a grim, almost pained expression.

"I mostly worked patrol in Kansas City," he began, "but this one time I had to transport a guy who claimed he'd murdered five women in our state and two in Illinois. He confessed to everything, very slowly, very methodically. And I had to sit behind that mirrored glass and listen to every single word. Worse yet, I had to transport him to and from the jail, and around to different burial spots throughout the day."

"Did they unearth his victims?"

"Oh, yeah," Schall said assuredly, shaking his head negatively. "He definitely wasn't lying. But all day long my mind kept going back to those movies where the insane guys always dislocate a thumb, or get loose from their shackles and kill the cops. This dude was that kind of creepy, and he wouldn't have given it a second thought if the opportunity presented itself."

Schall paused momentarily to fork a few bites of refried beans into his mouth before taking a drink from his glass of soda pop. Lancaster hadn't heard the man speak more than a few sentences at a time since he interviewed him for the security job. Although Schall spoke slower than most people with his native drawl, he certainly wasn't uneducated or stupid. Lancaster felt certain the man moved and talked slowly as a disarming front for people who engaged him in conversation.

Unlike refried beans from a can, the restaurant's version proved somewhat runny. Along with the white shredded cheese coating them, they stuck to the thick hair above Schall's lips, forcing him to dab them off with a napkin before continuing his tale.

"Anyway, he led us to three bodies the day I was chauffeuring him around the county. Not *once* did this guy show remorse or emotion about what he'd done. Personally, I felt relieved the families were getting some closure, but he didn't care one bit about them or the loved ones they lost. He actually got his rocks off by reliving what he'd done and seeing the grave sites again."

Lancaster knew serial killers often acted that way. The entire reason they killed was for personal satisfaction, often reliving some kind of fantasy or past event each time.

"What happened when it went to trial?"

"He was declared mentally competent to stand trial, but in the end they ruled him insane. He'll spend the rest of his days in some mental hospital being medicated, prodded, and studied in the interest of science. Needless to say, the families weren't happy."

"I'll bet not."

Both of them ate silently the next few minutes. Lancaster ultimately decided he wasn't going to reveal the nature of the case to Schall, at least not until he spoke with Hank Barwick. Although he needed to craft his words carefully when he talked to his head of maintenance, Lancaster felt confident he would derive the truth from their talk. Instinct told him Barwick was indeed loyal and truthful, but he needed to know how the man's deceased father played into what appeared to be two revenge murders.

While Barwick was certainly powerful enough to carry out the two brutal slayings, it made little sense for him to target his father's former associates *now* of all times. So far as Lancaster knew, James Barwick died from natural causes, so the revenge theory didn't seem to apply in this particular scenario.

"You still with me, boss?" Schall inquired, disrupting the stream of thoughts flowing through Lancaster's mind.

"Sorry," Lancaster apologized, quickly taking a bite of the virtually untouched food atop his plate. "It's just *not* been my week, Danny."

"I don't know how you're doing it."

"That makes two of us."

Lancaster finished his lunch making minimal small talk with Schall before the check arrived. He sent his credit card with the waiter and turned his attention to his security director.

"I'll call you after I talk with Hank this afternoon. Hopefully he can shed some light on a few of my concerns."

"Whatever you need, boss. I'll plan my schedule accordingly."

Lancaster wasn't looking forward to asking Barwick very personal and possibly loaded questions, but he liked the fact that two murders might be tied into his property even less. He also felt compelled to warn the last two survivors of Vivian Weatherly's group, though he suspected they might already know their lives were in mortal danger. Lancaster also needed to speak with Parsons because he wasn't doing every aspect of the sheriff's job for him.

Unfortunately he didn't know half of what the county sheriff was enduring at the moment.

Chapter 15

Steve Parsons hated his job sometimes.

After proudly serving his country and earning an honorable discharge following his leg injury he joined the Lawrence County Sheriff's Department at age thirty-two. Now eleven years had passed and he found himself at the helm of a department in need of some improvements. He made some headway shortly after his election by working with the county commissioners but criticism never seemed to end. The jail needed improvements, the road officers and jailers wanted raises, and an inmate suicide under the old sheriff's tenure continued to plague him while the state investigated without restraint.

Those kinds of problems he learned to take one day at a time, but homicides on back to back days left him reeling for answers. He wasn't accustomed to the media attention, but the state police deflected most of the questions since they were the agency possessing the most resources. His confidence in his own people waned with unseasoned investigators looking into high profile homicides. He didn't particularly like asking Lancaster to assist in the case, but the man possessed knowledge and experience, and he was the only person with working familiarity about the cold cases.

Parsons lacked investigations experience personally, so he wasn't planning on tackling that aspect of the open cases. He spent two months dabbling in detective work one summer, but that was five years prior and Parsons hadn't kept up with the advances in techniques and forensics because he patrolled. Only current investigators went to state classes and mastered the newest techniques because they obviously needed the information more than road deputies.

Walking through his office area, which desperately needed a makeover from the ragtag carpeting to the yellowed ceiling tiles, he nodded to a few passing deputies and his office manager. Miranda Castle hated being referred to as a receptionist or secretary, so he appeased her by giving her the title of office manager. In truth, his office would be turned upside-down within a day if she ever quit. If there was one gift the former sheriff provided Parsons, accidental as it might have been, it was keeping Miranda around to the very end of his term. He felt thankful she agreed to work a little weekend overtime to keep his head from exploding due to the influx of calls.

"Sheriff, you've had calls from Channel 13 and Channel 8, along with a message from Captain Tullar in Bloomington," Miranda reported as he strode past her desk.

Ken Tullar was a veteran with the state police, likely wanting to touch base with Parsons to exchange information. Considering he hadn't learned anything locally, Parsons decided to postpone speaking with the captain until he touched base with his detectives.

Most sheriffs walked into offices that adjoined conference rooms, or looked like a snapshot from some contemporary home decorating magazine. Parsons didn't count himself among those lucky sheriffs because his office fared no better than the rest of the operating space in the aging building. He added personal touches when he first took office, like a large framed photograph of his old platoon from Iraq that hung behind his desk, but even a fresh coat of eggshell paint did little to mask the stale interior.

The photograph reminded him of the sacrifice his fellow soldiers made, because six of the dozen men frozen in time had since been mourned and buried in their hometowns. Parsons chose not to display any of his medals or commendations within the office, mainly because he didn't want to appear egocentric. In the military he was paid, not overly well, to carry out hazardous duties, but every command he followed was simply part of his job description. Instead, he lined his shelves with technical manuals and books that were part of the police profession.

With no better location or funding for a new jail coming his way, Parsons knew this was his second home for the remainder of his term. He took a seat behind his desk, hearing chatter just outside his open door before a phone rang. Because he often left his door ajar, Parsons grew adept at ignoring everyday noises, but he suspected this particular phone ringing involved him somehow.

When a light on his office phone flashed with successive beeps, Parsons pushed the speaker button to hear what Miranda had to say.

"Pete Thompson for you."

He felt like a psychic, knowing the call was destined for him. He wondered what the Monroe County sheriff just north of him needed. Thompson wasn't typically one to call and exchange pleasantries, though the two men occasionally grabbed lunch to talk about their golf swings and gripe about their hardships.

"I'll take it," Parsons said as he pushed the blinking button on his phone to answer the other line. "Parsons."

"Steve, it's Pete. Hey, I've got someone in my jail who's insisting on talking to you."

"Who is it?"

"Ralph Nichols."

Parsons sighed as he rolled his eyes, picturing the career criminal who constantly ended up in any one of half a dozen local jails. Around sixty years of age, Nichols committed minor crimes to get into jail, often for a roof over his head and three square meals. His rap sheet, if printed, likely caused the demise of at least one small tree for the required paper. The man knew better than to commit crimes that might land him in prison, or he at least hid those crimes very well. Road officers and jailers considered him a nuisance, but Nichols didn't cause them additional trouble when they booked him.

"What's he in for this time?" Parsons asked his fellow sheriff.

"The usual. I was going to ignore him on your behalf, but he says he has some important information about your two homicides."

"You still shouldn't give him the time of day."

"Well, I wasn't planning to, but he told me he knew who your killer is."

Parsons felt his body tense. He never considered Nichols a reliable informant because the man was often drunk or delusional, but even the worst of criminals sometimes found useful information to contribute.

But why talk? And why now?

"Did he provide a name?" Parsons questioned.

"No, but he says he can also close the Tanksley murder for you."

Inhaling through his nose, Parsons contemplated what angle Nichols might be working to his own advantage. Most of the time the man *wanted* to be in jail, so early release or leniency seemed to be out of the question. Nichols was certainly old enough to be around during the Tanksley murder, and the man was an area resident all of his life.

"Did he give you any information about the Tanksley case?" Parsons asked his fellow sheriff.

"Yeah. He said he killed the man. He also said you'd want proof, so he said the right pinkie finger was one of the four he cut off."

Parsons felt as though a frying pan had whacked him upside the head. He needed to look at the case file for confirmation, but he felt certain the right pinkie finger was indeed chopped off, and police never released such details to the public.

"Pete, can I call you right back?"

"Sure thing. I'll be in my office the next hour or so."

Without money for extra manpower or overtime, objectives like converting files into more easily backed up computer files went by the wayside. When a cold case was reopened or reexamined, Parsons asked that the detective enter the file into the computer system for organization and ease of searching. Despite him barking at his investigators several times over, most of the old files remained in paper form only.

Even Lancaster, who once acted obsessive compulsive about organization and following procedure, slacked near the end of his career once his theme park neared completion. And so Parsons walked into the records room, protected by nothing more than a lock and deadbolt during the rare times the room was actually closed. No laser grid, computerized keypad, or steel vault protected the paper case files. Parsons once thought his department was the model of backwoods police agencies, but he'd since visited departments in far worse financial shape. Some of them lacked the equipment he now took for granted in everyday policing.

Unaccustomed to the file organization, and unwilling to swallow his pride and call one of his detectives for help, Parsons searched several file cabinets until he discovered the chronological system held true except for open cases. Those cases, whether new or cold, were stored in a smaller cabinet that required less time to rifle through. Miranda brought him the file the previous day for him to take when he heard about the Stafford murder. He made the mistake of asking an investigator to put it back instead of simply keeping it handy. Now he cursed himself for not knowing the filing system better because he *needed* to find that file immediately.

He ended up locating the Tanksley file, now yellowed and weathered, slightly out of chronological order in one of the main cabinets. Wondering if his people had slipped once again and placed the file and put it in the wrong spot, Parsons flipped open the file and immediately perused some of the photographs. Without forensic evidence back then, investigators relied almost solely upon what they observed, so photographs proved crucial. Unfortunately for Michael Tanksley they hadn't provided much assistance in solving his murder.

Not a complete stranger to the case, Parsons flipped through the documentation trying to find an image or the medical report to confirm or disprove what Ralph Nichols claimed. A few seconds later he found the yellowed paperwork from the medical examiner, using his forefinger as a place marker while he skimmed the wording about Tanksley's gruesome death.

Finally, listed in a separate line like every other detailed injury found during examination, Parsons discovered the words that left him very interested in Nichols' statement.

Right pinkie finger removed via sharp, heavy object while victim was alive. Marks consistent with a hatchet or axe.

Parsons took a deep breath before snatching the cell phone at his side to call Pete Thompson back.

Chapter 16

Lancaster felt like a complete heel bothering any employee at home, but the circumstances that brought him to Hank Barwick's residence made his stomach ache with apprehension.

After parking his truck along the curb he walked through the small front yard, following the concrete walkway that led to the front door. Barwick's 1957 Chevy truck sat in the driveway, so Lancaster knew the man was home, possibly sleeping after a night of inspecting rides. The red truck was a project Barwick neglected for years until a turn of events changed his life and provided him with time to complete a full restoration.

A few years removed from his wife's death, Barwick sometimes talked about downsizing his life, which included selling his old house. His current house lacked a woman's touch like flowers and decorative shrubs, though the lawn appeared manicured. The house, nearly fifty years old like the others in the small, suburban neighborhood, held up well because upgrades were something that came easy to Barwick.

Barwick had said his old house was far too big for one person and the memories of his wife fading from cancer plagued him. Much of the reason he went to work at the theme park was to remain occupied and keep him from thinking about the past.

Looking skyward, perhaps for forgiveness, Lancaster knocked on the man's front door.

He waited almost a minute until Barwick answered the door, not sleepy-eyed the way Lancaster expected him to look.

"Are you here to fire me?" Barwick asked as he opened the door for his employer. "Or give me a raise?"

Lancaster forced a smile.

"Sorry to bother you at home, Hank. You got a few minutes?"

"Sure," Barwick said, glad to have company though he fought inwardly not to show his emotions. "Come on in."

Lancaster followed him inside, choosing one of the two chairs opposite a loveseat where his head of maintenance opted to sit.

"I didn't wake you, did I?" Lancaster asked.

"No. I left the park a little after nine this morning and took a nap. I'm a little surprised you're not riding coasters and mingling with the guests."

Groaning to himself, Lancaster wished he hadn't gotten preoccupied with murder investigations.

"I'm helping my old department with the two homicides, Hank. Vivian Weatherly and Charles Stafford were business partners, and they were part of a conglomerate."

"And that group included my father," Barwick admitted, looking displeased by either the stated fact or his boss questioning him about it.

"What can you tell me about your father and his business dealings?"

"I wasn't that old when he dealt with those people," Barwick answered. "When I was a kid things weren't always good. I knew when my dad had a good week because we'd go out to eat, or drive to Bloomington so my mother could buy something new. It wasn't until I was a teenager that things got good on a regular basis."

"You knew they bought the land where my theme park sits, didn't you?"

Barwick gave a guilty shrug.

"Of course I knew. They had big plans for that place and a string of bad luck kept it from staying open. You would've freaked out if I said anything during the interview."

"Back then I wouldn't have known any different."

"And now?"

"Now I'm just looking for answers. I'm worried about you."

"*Me?*"

Lancaster needed to tread carefully when revealing the nature of his consultation with the sheriff's department. He felt as though he was conducting a full investigation by himself, but he still couldn't go around spouting facts to everyone he interviewed.

"Look, if someone is targeting the people involved in your father's group, they could decide to take out their frustrations on you."

Now Barwick grew openly concerned.

"My mother is still alive."

"I understand, but you're the one working on the property where Michael Tanksley was killed."

A look of realization crossed Barwick's face because he was old enough to remember that murder, much like Colby McWilliams.

"Are you asking me to quit?" he finally questioned with a concerned tone.

"No," Lancaster said empathetically, wishing he could quit being so suspicious of everyone in his life. "I'm just trying to put together a puzzle and I'm missing a lot of the pieces. Can you save me some time and effort by telling me how your dad died?"

"Heart attack while he was driving home one night. It took the whole family by surprise."

Barwick's expression turned increasingly somber just mentioning the details.

"I hate to keep pressing, but did your dad's group piss anyone off in particular who might want retaliation now?"

Shaking his head, Barwick looked incapable of providing an answer.

"He didn't talk about the business. Not even to Mom."

Taking advantage of the uncomfortable moment, Lancaster finally examined the living room, seeing several photographs of Barwick and his deceased wife atop the fireplace mantle. Relegated to living a downsized, more simplistic life, it appeared as though Barwick was slowly preparing for his own inevitable end, making things easier for his family.

Only a few books lined a nearby bookshelf, along with several additional family photos, some of which looked decades old. The furniture wasn't particularly new or aesthetically pleasing, and what few electronic devices Lancaster spotted in the living room were probably bought and installed by Barwick's adult children.

Any concerns about Barwick's possible involvement with the two murders were now crushed because the man was brutally honest and lived a lonely life. While the man certainly hadn't begged him for a job, Barwick certainly appeared happier with each passing day at the theme park. Distracted from his previous issues, he found a reason to get up each day and report to work.

"Do you feel certain those two murders are connected?" Barwick asked almost sheepishly.

"I don't have a doubt," Lancaster answered as images of severed body parts drifted through his mind. "Were your father's business partners involved in all of his dealings?"

"They were always together at meetings and lunches. Sometimes Dad brought me along, and I always saw the same people. I can ask Mom for a list of his friends and associates if you like."

"I got a list of his business partners already, but anything else she can add might be useful."

"Okay."

"Not to bring up bad memories again, but can you tell me when your father died?"

"December of 2003. How does that help?"

"I'm not sure it does," Lancaster replied honestly. "I think at least some of the people in your father's group may have wronged someone in a bad way. And if someone is seeking revenge like I think they are, I'm worried for the last two partners, and for you and your family."

Barwick waved off the notion.

"I doubt my father ever screwed anyone that badly that they'd wait forty years for revenge. Sure, his job included repossessing land from people who couldn't afford it, but I don't remember any bad blood. Most of those people ended up getting their property back anyway."

"Is that a certainty, or is that what he told you?"

Barwick openly didn't like the manner in which Lancaster posed the question.

"Both."

"I'm not here to run down your father's legacy, Hank. I'm just searching for answers before someone else gets hurt."

Or chopped into pieces, he thought.

"My father wasn't perfect," Barwick admitted, "and I don't place him on some pedestal above the rest of us, but I cannot picture him committing an act against anyone that would cause that person to murder him or his friends."

"No one deserves what Vivian and Stafford received, believe me. Anything you can find that might help, I'd appreciate."

"I'll talk to Mom before work today. I still have a job, don't I?"

Lancaster grinned.

"I couldn't replace the best mechanic I've got."

Looking a bit more at ease, Barwick stood to shake his employer's hand.

"Then I'll see you later, if you're not too busy working at your old job."

Hoping to oversee the operations at the theme park at some point during the day, Lancaster knew he needed to contact Paula the librarian and Schall to provide them both with updated information.

He didn't detect any indication of deception from Barwick, but if his father truly was some kind of monster who wrecked lives without regard the man certainly wasn't going to confess to his family about it. Lancaster wondered if the circumstances had been different, and the man knew of his impending death, if the family might have heard a deathbed confession.

Walking away from Barwick's house, he certainly didn't feel any closer to the answers he needed.

Chapter 17

Sunday, September 23

Parsons avoided some red tape by waiting until Sunday morning to travel to Bloomington because Nichols was due to be released from jail. It occurred to him that Nichols might be making up a story to stay in jail on a more permanent basis, but the fact that he knew an undisclosed fact about the Tanksley murder forced the issue.

Although Pete Thompson wasn't present, he'd taken the liberty of instructing his jailers to put a hold on Nichols and hand him directly to a representative from Lawrence County. Struck by the curiosity bug, Parsons decided to pick up Nichols personally and interview him once he drove them both back to his own building.

A light rain on the return trip prompted him to turn on the wipers from the unmarked vehicle borrowed from his fleet. He chose the dark sedan because it provided the metal cage between the front and back seats. Although Nichols wasn't known to cause trouble, and he was technically free to go at will, Parsons knew of cops dying from complacency when known criminals didn't follow their typical patterns.

Very much against his weekend routine, he donned dress pants with a pressed shirt and tie. Wearing his badge clipped to his belt, Parsons looked the part of a sheriff and wasn't delayed by the jail staff who seemed happy to see Nichols leave their facility. Now just minutes away from his office, Parsons realized Nichols hadn't said two words since leaving Bloomington.

Usually a jovial, talkative criminal, the man seemed almost downright despondent and jittery, as though something weighed heavily on his mind.

"You okay back there, Ralph?" Parsons asked when he pulled into the alley behind the jail where most of the county police vehicles parked.

"Yeah."

The tone and the look on the man's face were neutral at best, bordering on meek. He certainly wasn't afraid of the sheriff, but something had Nichols acting the opposite of his normal demeanor. When he wasn't staring blankly out the window, or at the floorboards, Nichols' eyes panned quickly in every direction, like a prairie dog wary of predators.

Parsons had already decided he didn't want to bother any of his investigators, particularly on the weekend, until he knew Nichols was being truthful with something to offer either murder investigation. Although not formally trained in the art of interrogation, Parsons had participated in numerous interviews over the years, certainly enough to know if Nichols spoke the truth or not.

"Come on," he instructed Nichols as he opened the rear door of the sedan, ushering him out with a sweep of his hand.

Complying rather cautiously, the confessed killer stepped out, looking up and down the alley. Parsons wasn't sure who Nichols thought posed a danger to him, but he grew less patient with each passing second as he cupped the prisoner by the elbow and led him toward the rear entrance to the county jail.

Handcuffed in the front, basically as a formality, Nichols diligently followed Parsons to the door where the sheriff typed the correct code into the square keypad to bypass the electronic lock. He took the prisoner up a set of stairs surrounded by painted cinderblock, bypassing the jail section completely, to a small room where he could interview Nichols at length.

Calling Nichols a prisoner felt premature, Parsons decided, until the man provided irrefutable proof that he deserved to remain behind bars.

"You want some coffee?" he offered Nichols, since he planned to grab his pen, a pad of paper, and a recording device from his desk.

"I could use something a little stronger."

A notorious alcoholic, Nichols often used his heavy drinking as a method of getting arrested when he wasn't delivered to a homeless shelter or a hospital.

"I'll get you some coffee," Parsons replied without so much as a blink before heading down the hallway.

Less than five minutes later he returned with his interviewing tools and a cup of coffee for Nichols. He set the Styrofoam cup before the interviewee and twisted the top off a sealed bottle of water before taking a sip. He set the audio recorder on the table for Nichols to see before opening his pad and clicking on the top of his pen. Though the room contained a video camera overhead, recording devices, and a computer, Parsons preferred redundancy in case any of those failed.

Unsure of exactly where to begin, he decided to ask some vague questions to let Nichols elaborate unless the man ventured off the subject.

"Please state your full name for the record," Parsons requested.

"Ralph Emerson Nichols."

Parsons shot him a questioning stare.

"For real," Nichols assured him.

Simply shaking his head, Parsons believed the man because a simple look at his criminal background would reveal any deception.

"Mr. Nichols, can you state for the record why you requested to speak with me today?"

"Because I want to help you solve a murder."

"And what murder is that?"

"The murder of Michael Tanksley in 1971."

Nichols took a slow sip of coffee, looking around the room as though he thought someone might be watching them. Although one wall contained one-way glass, no one was even at the station to watch the interview at the moment. And though Parsons had taken the liberty of switching on the camera mounted in a corner above them, none of the feed monitors were turned on for weekend hours.

Parsons decided to ask his next question a bit more informally.

"Why are you so nervous, Ralph?"

"Because he's watching. He's the reason I have to confess, so I don't have to go free and take my chances."

"Who?" Parsons asked, trying his damnedest not to sound skeptical.

"The man who murdered Vivian and Charles."

If Parsons hadn't thought Nichols warranted attention before, he certainly wanted to take in every word the man uttered now.

"Can you state their last names for the record please?"

"Vivian Weatherly and Charles Stafford."

Parsons felt a tingle of excitement, wondering if the old drunk could possibly hold the keys to three significant murders in Lawrence County. He almost didn't dare proceed with the interview, expecting only disappointment wrapped within the next answer Nichols provided.

He decided, instead, to start from the beginning, to better test the man's honesty.

"Ralph, let's start from the beginning. You claim you murdered Michael Tanksley back in 1971, so please explain how all of that came about."

Nichols sipped on the coffee momentarily, alternating his stare between the wall and the floor when he finally began his tale.

"Back then I didn't have a home, or a job, so when someone offered me ten big ones to off some guy outside of town, I realized I didn't have much of a choice."

"Ten-thousand dollars?" the sheriff asked for clarification.

"Yes."

"Who made this offer, Ralph, and how?"

"I'm not exactly sure. It was a guy who worked for a guy."

Parsons felt frustration creeping in almost immediately. The minute prior the sheriff felt fairly certain he was going to solve at least one murder, but with vague statements flying his way the optimism was replaced by disappointment. Cases were built on facts, figures, and especially names, not hearsay and conjecture.

Attempting to stay the course, Parsons took a deep breath and a swig of water before continuing with his line of questioning.

"Ralph, I need more detail or this interview is over."

"I don't know the guy's name, but he worked for the lawyer."

"What lawyer?"

Nichols hesitated, and for a moment the sheriff wasn't sure if Nichols believed he was dense, or if the name eluded him. A few seconds later he repeatedly snapped his fingers, trying to recall the name of the mysterious attorney.

"The one who worked for Vivian Weatherly and her group," he finally answered, unable to recall the name.

Parsons grimaced, believing the answer resided within at least one of the case files just down the hall. He shut off the electronic recorder and excused himself as he took up the water bottle and exited the small room. Stepping into the hallway, he chugged most of the water before striding into the records room. Now acclimated to the system, Parsons quickly found the old Tanksley file, followed by the printed versions of the two recent slayings. He finished off the water with the files tucked under one arm during his return to the room. Opening the door, he found Nichols sipping coffee and patiently awaiting his return. Parsons stepped inside, flopping the files atop the table before reaching into his back pocket for his canister of Kodiak.

He pinched an appropriate amount and placed the dip between his lower lip and his gums with practiced ease. Parsons immediately tasted the wintergreen flavor when his tongue pressed the tobacco into the nook formed along his lower lip from years of dipping. He then removed the top of the plastic bottle to create a spittoon. Drawing the chair, Parsons took a seat as he flipped through the old Tanksley file, discovering the attorney's name in one of the old newspaper clippings accompanying the initial report and photographs. It spoke of the old Tanksley property being sold at auction to a group of local businesspeople, and their attorney Henry Cauldwell acted as their mouthpiece with the press.

He turned on the recording device before continuing with his questions.

"Does this name ring a bell?" Parsons asked Nichols, turning the article toward the man as his finger highlighted the name in question.

"That's him. He worked for that rich group, and I heard through the grapevine they wanted Tanksley dead for his land."

"Can you prove that?"

"I overheard the lawyer talking to one of them one day about how Tanksley won that land in a state settlement and didn't deserve it."

"That still isn't proof, Ralph. Did you ever have direct contact with anyone from that group, including the lawyer?"

Nichols shook his head negatively.

"You kidding me? They would've had me killed if they thought I knew something."

"Then who paid you?"

"The lawyer's assistant."

Parsons sighed. He hadn't planned on having to conduct a photo lineup to receive solid answers, particularly when forty years had passed since the event in question.

"Do you know for a fact that this man worked for Cauldwell?"

"Yeah. They never told me that, but I checked around because I wanted something to hold over these people in case they double-crossed me. They thought I was just some stupid hick, but I wasn't dumb enough to do the job without no insurance."

Parsons spit tobacco juice into the bottle, prepared to change tactics slightly until he could unearth photographs for identification later. Right now he was more interested in answers and facts, particularly the kinds he could confirm more easily.

"How did this man pay you exactly?"

"Briefcase full of money."

"Would you happen to know where that briefcase is?"

Nichols chuckled.

"What's so funny?" Parsons asked.

"I pawned that thing years ago."

"Again, Ralph, I need physical evidence or some way to corroborate what you're telling me."

Nichols suddenly looked very serious, cupping his hands together as he leaned forward.

"How about I give you the details from the night I killed Mike Tanksley?"

Parsons nodded.

"That would be a start."

"Since my teenage years, that was probably the only night I didn't drink nothing. I wasn't happy about the idea of killing another man, and I definitely didn't want to remember it, but if I screwed up the job I didn't get paid, and I knew I'd wind up in a grave myself."

Spitting into the bottle once again, Parsons listened with great interest, waiting for the moment he knew irrefutably that Ralph Nichols wasn't lying.

"I knew Tanksley wasn't right in the head. Everyone in town said he was crazy, so when I went out to his place and he was holed up inside some teepee I wasn't surprised. There was a perfectly good cabin on the property he was letting fall apart because he went native. Now I'll admit I was scared shitless because he had some Indian spirit shit going on and here I was trespassing on his land, hoping he didn't see me first."

"Did you even have a plan when you went over there?"

"Not a good one, but I came prepared. I bought a good knife, some rope, and a flashlight, but the flashlight didn't work. I remember a full moon that night, so I rode my bicycle out there in plenty of time before it got dark and waited at the edge of the property."

"Your bicycle?"

"I ain't had a car since I was a teenager and wrecked it."

Probably after drinking, Parsons thought as he frowned at Nichols.

"You didn't bring a gun?" he questioned.

"I couldn't afford no car. I couldn't afford no gun. The only reason I even agreed to hit Tanksley was because I had two cents to my name."

"We've never run you in for anything more than theft and drunk and disorderly," Parsons noted. "I'm having trouble picturing you as the killer type."

"I did what I had to," Nichols assured him. "I saw the teepee in a clearing, not far from the cabin, and there was a light coming from inside, so I crept up to it and waited for movement. Tanksley never heard me, because when he stepped outside the teepee to stretch I didn't hesitate. I knew if I waited just one second and didn't commit, I would chicken out."

Nichols drew a deep, emotionally pained breath.

"What did you do?" Parsons pushed, still wondering if his ears were hearing the truth, or this was simply an elaborate scheme to give Nichols an easier life than the one he knew on the streets.

Prison wasn't a good alternative for young men, but senior citizens often got a pass from violent criminals locked away in such facilities.

"He walked out of that teepee carrying a kerosene lantern and some kind of tomahawk like he'd seen trouble out there before. He didn't know I was there, but Tanksley was coming out to get some firewood or something. I was already in motion when I saw the hatchet, so I tackled him and knocked it out of his hand."

Parsons tried to mentally weigh this battle, knowing Nichols was half his victim's age at the time, but the man never possessed much in the way of physical stature. He didn't recall Tanksley being pictured as a stout man in the news clippings and vintage photographs, and he supposed adrenaline might have fueled Nichols during the attack.

"You tackled him from behind?" Parsons inquired, trying to envision the narrative.

"I had to. It all happened so fast, Sheriff. I remember confirming that he dropped the tomahawk, so I wrestled him to the ground, letting go of my rope so I could keep him pinned down while I struck him in the back of the head with my flashlight. It was one of those cheap flashlights so I had to hit him two or three times before he finally went limp.

"There was no way this was going to look accidental like the clients would have preferred, so I went ahead and made it look like a hate crime. Everyone in town thought he was some kind of weirdo anyway, and people weren't happy about his family winning that land in a lawsuit, so I didn't think anyone would really care."

So far the story made sense when compared to the original autopsy, but Parsons wanted more details before committing to an arrest.

"At this point I wasn't real sure of how to finish him off," Nichols confessed. "I thought of strangling him, but that would take forever, especially if he came to, so I decided to use the rope I brought to string him up. My flashlight wasn't working, so I stumbled around in the dark to find a tree big enough to hold his weight.

"By the time I got back to Tanksley, he was starting to come to, so I had to smack him with the flashlight again."

"Where did you strike him this time?" Parsons pushed, wanting details for the official record.

"The head as I recall. From there I dragged him over to the tree I'd found and started kicking him wherever my feet could reach."

Nichols took a sip of coffee, either stalling to continue his work of fiction, or attempting to jog his memory. Parsons couldn't imagine anyone recollecting details from forty years prior, but he supposed murdering someone probably cemented the memories in a killer's mind.

"Where does the severed finger come in?" Parsons decided to ask, since it was the one piece of testimony that might solidify Nichols' claim.

"Even after I pounded him, Tanksley still had some fight left in him, and when I turned my back to study the tree, he clawed his way toward the tomahawk. He hadn't made it halfway when I spotted him and jumped on his back. This time I didn't have the flashlight, so I hit him with my fists in the back of the head and neck to slow him down. He kept reaching for the hatchet, so I reached over and beat him to it. Tanksley had his right arm outstretched, making a last-ditch effort to defend himself but when I grabbed the hatchet his hand clasped into a fist except for his pinky. It acted like it was locked straight or something. I wasn't going to kill him with the thing, but I needed to hurt him, so I aimed the hatchet toward his right hand and missed, except for the pinky."

"Did the finger come off cleanly?"

"Yes. I missed getting more of his hand and struck just above the large knuckle as I recall," Nichols said, pointing to his own pinky finger to clearly identify the area.

Parsons knew from the report that one direct blow from a heavy, sharpened blade removed that exact half of the finger. He suddenly felt with some certainty that Nichols wasn't lying about murdering Michael Tanksley.

"And was the weapon a tomahawk or a hatchet? You've called it both."

"It was a tomahawk with the little feather thing on it. It was definitely Indian, but it's basically the same thing."

"I see."

Nichols smirked a bit, deriving satisfaction from the words he was about to speak.

"He screamed like a little girl when I chopped off his finger, just moaning and screaming forever. I couldn't take much more, so I used the blunt edges of the tomahawk on his skull until he went limp again. I remember hitting and kicking him some more while I wrapped the noose around his neck, just to keep him from struggling. At some point I got sick of him coming to and fighting, so I cut some rope or twine from his teepee and used it to bind his hands."

Parsons considered that statement another piece of concrete proof, because investigators found the teepee collapsed and twine from the dwelling that matched the bindings around Michael's Tanksley's hands behind his back.

"Once he couldn't fight back and I knocked him out for the last time, I used the rope I brought to string him up. He wasn't going anywhere, and I was tired as hell, so I booked without making sure he was dead. The last thing I needed was some family friend or the cops showing up and catching me in the act, so I took it for granted he was going to suffocate."

He did indeed, Parsons thought.

"Anything else you can tell me about that day?" he asked, ready to proceed with the next phase of charging Nichols.

"That morning," the man said thoughtfully with a tremble in his lip. "The weather was almost unholy just before dawn. A low fog spread through the fields, and dew seemed to drop from the sky, even though I couldn't see any clouds. Like even the weather was saying it knew I did a bad thing."

Parsons took note of the last statement, though he couldn't imagine confirming the weather report from that day unless one of the investigators took studious notes. He now felt ready to progress into the interview with more detail to solidify the case. Calling in a detective or two felt like the correct move before he pressed Nichols for details, but the sheriff thought of a solid method of linking Nichols to the murder case aside from the man's confession.

On a Sunday obtaining a DNA sample wasn't going to be easy unless he wanted to call in a crime technician or use an independent lab. His small department didn't currently have anyone certified as a crime scene technician, often relying upon the state police to assist them on major crime scenes. Their post commander wouldn't be the least bit delighted about paying a technician overtime on the weekend, so Parsons decided to phone the lab's on-call number to request a technician. Waiting until Monday seemed more prudent, but he felt reasonably certain Nichols hadn't obtained this information secondhand, so he wanted to start the process of building evidence for an eventual trial.

Parsons had compiled a mental list of questions he wanted to ask Nichols, but he decided to wait for his dayshift detective to arrive. He would call his investigator once he made arrangements with the contracted lab to obtain a DNA sample from Nichols, which meant transporting his new prisoner at some point.

Before he did any of this, however, Parsons decided to ask the most pressing question on his mind.

"Ralph, you said you knew who killed Vivian and Charles."

"I do," Nichols answered with certainly. "It was Michael Tanksley."

Chapter 18

Nearly two hours after Nichols made the seemingly insane statement that a man now dead for forty-one years was murdering the statesmen of Lawrence County, Parsons watched his most seasoned detective conduct a similar interview, seated across from Nichols in the same room.

Although Lancaster appeared to have the pulse of the investigation, Parsons wasn't completely certain the man could be trusted, despite contrary statements to his former detective. Lancaster made no secret about his desire to be near the theme park during its inaugural weekend, so the sheriff decided not to contact him.

By involving Bryan St. Amand, Parsons lost a great deal of time catching his senior detective up on the day's events thus far. He entered the interview room with St. Amand long enough to make Nichols comfortable with a new person interviewing him while providing a transition for the detective. They quickly discovered that Nichols would not elaborate upon his statement about Michael Tanksley carrying out recent murders. The career criminal simply stated he knew Tanksley was going to come back for revenge, but wouldn't give details because certain people remained who might bring harm to him.

"So let me get this straight," Parsons had stated while still seated across from Nichols. "You're afraid Michael Tanksley is going to somehow get to you, which is why you're telling me all of this, but you're equally afraid to give me details because someone else can get to you?"

Nichols nodded slowly, still unwilling to spill any details.

"If what you're telling me is true, these people who put you up to this are basically using wheelchairs and walkers, Ralph. What can they do to you?"

Leaning forward, Nichols put his face within inches of the sheriff's, close enough that the faint remainder of alcoholic fumes wafted into the sheriff's nose, even after the man spent at least the overnight in jail.

"They still have money and power, Sheriff. You of all people should know a little bit about that. And like I said, I never had direct contact with any of them."

Parsons assumed the middle part of Nichols' statement meant the contribution of campaign dollars, which he never received, directly anyway, from any of the elder townsfolk. Sometimes the money came in through businesses, veiled groups, or anonymous donations, which meant even he didn't know everyone who funded his campaign.

"Are you implying that Michael Tanksley didn't really die the night you went to kill him?" St. Amand inquired, his eyebrows arching with skepticism.

"No," Nichols answered evenly, but firmly. "I'm saying he came back."

Parsons felt utterly frustrated because everything he felt so confident about during his interview with Nichols was unraveling like the thread from an unfinished sweater. At this point St. Amand's eyes darted subtly his way, indicating the detective questioned why he was called in to interview a mentally deranged suspect.

"We'll be back right back, Ralph," Parsons stated. "Can I get you anything?"

"Maybe some more coffee."

Parsons nodded affirmatively before leading St. Amand out of the room to the other side of the one-way mirror.

Once the two stood in the unlit room, Parsons decided to assert his authority before his detective even posed a question. Although St. Amand was his senior detective, the man was barely in his mid-forties. During the past five years the department had experienced a major turnover when a number of sergeants and captains retired, thrusting the younger generation into positions only some of them were ready to assume.

"Everything he's said up until the Michael Tanksley coming back part makes me think he murdered Tanksley forty-one years ago," Parsons said firmly.

"That's well and good, but I think a psychologist might disagree, and I mean no disrespect, Sheriff."

"I called in some arrangements to confirm what I already believe through DNA tomorrow morning."

St. Amand looked surprised.

"They answered on a Sunday?"

"That's why you're surprised?"

"Mostly. I guess I'm also wondering if we still have a DNA match from four decades ago."

"We do. I'm taking Nichols to a lab in Bloomington when they open in the morning."

"What's the rush?" St. Amand questioned.

"Because I want the sample shipped first thing tomorrow morning. Tanksley's homicide is linked to what we've had the past three days, and this man is the key to the whole thing." Parsons pointed his finger heatedly toward the ground during the last statement. "Keep working him until you've squeezed him for everything. Don't cover the Tanksley back from the dead thing because it softens our case. Just get every fact you can out of him."

"*If* he's telling the truth. You know as well as I do he'll say anything to stay behind bars."

"The man is legitimately scared of something. Keep working him."

St. Amand gave the most enthusiastic nod he could muster before turning to return to the interview room.

Parsons watched his detective insist that Nichols start from the beginning once again, but as the same story began unfolding he decided to get some fresh air. Already into the noon hour, he suspected his day wasn't even close to being over, especially with the last-minute appointment at the lab not happening until seven p.m. when the lab tech became available. At some point he would break away to get some food and beverages for his detective and suspect, but for now he just wanted to step away from the stuffy confines of his office and the county jail.

After checking in with one of his dispatchers who controlled the front door, Parsons walked out of his office area into the large waiting area that allowed access to the jail as well. Once he stepped outside the front doors only a dispatcher could allow him inside by releasing the magnetic lock device with the push of a button. Deputies gained access through the back of the building, interacting with jail officers and dispatchers during their sparse visits. With technology allowing them to type reports from their patrol vehicles, and no stringent requirements to check in before or after their shifts, deputies dropped by less than ever.

That didn't mean Parsons simply let them roam free without checks and balances. GPS in their car laptops monitored the movements of their patrol cars, and he made certain his shift commanders checked on the road deputies a few times each shift.

When he stepped outside, surrounded by overcast skies, Parsons leaned over the blue hand railing atop a multi-tiered ramp that accommodated disabled people. Although he couldn't take credit for building the ramp, he made certain to maintain it as a wounded war veteran. Located on one corner of the Bedford town square, the facility didn't favor a scenic view in any direction. As the sheriff's elbows rested atop the painted railing, he looked across the street, finding a brick building that housed businesses between vacated spells.

To the left he could see the town square, very scenic and historic in nature with its brick and limestone buildings. Down a hill to his right, however, a mix of forgotten industry and small, aging residences lined the streets. Parsons inhaled the fresh air deeply through his nostrils, about to reach for the canister of dip residing in his back pocket when movement across the street, behind the brick building, caught the corner of his eye.

Wondering if he might have someone interested in his day's activities, or planning something far more nefarious, Parsons decided to casually stroll down the concrete ramp while glancing inconspicuously across the street. By the time he reached the sidewalk Parsons could no longer disguise his true purpose for descending the ramp, so he quickly glanced to his left on the one-way street, finding it clear. Assured of his personal safety, Parsons crossed the street, heading directly for the corner that adjoined a shadowy alley.

He instinctively reached for the firearm still holstered at his right side, though he didn't draw it with lazy Sunday traffic a possibility on the street behind him. Quickly but cautiously, Parsons approached the corner of the old building, peering around the bend instead of stepping into the alley. The view from end to end provided no evidence of anyone lurking, though a large industrial trash receptacle needed to be cleared for him to be certain.

Parsons wondered why an abandoned building required a large metal bin, unless new renovations he hadn't heard about were taking place inside. Now he carefully slid the firearm from his holster, since no one from either side of the alley could see his actions in a passing vehicle. As he neared the garbage bin a foul odor entered his nostrils, like rotten, decaying food. He knew the smell a dead body emitted, and this was definitely common decomposing trash of some sort.

Nearing the bin, he hunched over a bit, darting across the receptacle's front only to find no one hiding on the other side. Groaning to himself, Parsons looked at the two large, plastic flaps resting atop the bin, silently daring him to lift them for a peek inside. Swallowing hard, he held his Glock firmly in his right hand, retreating half a step as he lifted the first lid, flipping it upward for a full view inside the entire bin. The smell virtually slapped him in the face as the sight of maggots combined with the resounding buzzing of flies let him know that retrieval of the contents was long overdue. Only a few black garbage bags lined the bottom of the canister, along with some other loose debris, but he knew there wasn't enough time, or space left inside, for someone to be hiding.

He caught the lid with his free hand when it dropped, staring into the bin a few seconds longer. Nothing moved, and though he felt certain he'd spied someone across the street, Parsons questioned the quality of his own eyes with fatigue setting in. Sighing, he let gravity take the lid back to its resting place as he holstered his weapon, taking a slow walk back to his jail. Perhaps the creepy factor of the case seeped into his mind, or the toll of two recent unsolved murders weighed on him, but Parsons suspected he wasn't going to sleep well until he delivered Nichols to the lab in the morning.

Chapter 19

Jean wasn't particularly happy about having her aunt's calling hours on a Sunday evening, but it made the most sense due to timing. Her local relatives decided to wait until more family members could attend from other states, with Sunday being the earliest date possible. A number of her cousins weren't on speaking terms, which made the proceedings feel a bit awkward, but at least no physical altercations broke out.

Looking at her watch, Jean discovered it was past seven o'clock, leaving less than an hour of visitation for Vivian. She stole a glance at the open casket, still amazed the morticians were able to create a look that made Vivian presentable for viewing. For what seemed like the hundredth time Jean saw how the family surrounded the decorative steel burial device with photographs and memorabilia of Vivian's lengthy life. A few poster boards atop tripods displayed her life in photographs at the opposite end of the room while a video montage played on a large screen along a side wall. Strangely, the family had requested the largest of the funeral home's viewing areas, but the attendance felt staggeringly low to Jean. Perhaps her aunt had simply outlived many of her friends, because mostly family members and a few dozen members of the community attended. She also considered the possibility that Vivian hadn't kept many friends, or wasn't entirely well-liked by the community she helped reinvent.

Soft music played in the background with the montage, but Jean's thoughts trained on how much she missed her aunt. She owed more to Vivian than words could express, and she felt an emptiness that came without closure when someone left the physical world. The ink wasn't even dry on the death certificate and already some family members were pushing for the reading of the will. Jean didn't much care what she received because the person who put her aunt in the casket before her remained free.

Keeping her distance from most of the family, Jean found some support in the form of her eighteen-year-old daughter Abigail. Rather than explain the complications involved with family relationships around the time of a loved one's death, Jean decided to play nice with her aunts, uncles, cousins, and anyone else she wasn't fond of during this mourning period. She sensed that Abigail noticed some of the cold shoulders being exchanged, but she wasn't a young adult who pushed her single mother's buttons any longer. Now preparing for college the following fall, she continued to make good grades in school, holding down a part-time job at a local fast food restaurant a few days a week.

The number of visitors had dwindled severely, so Jean stood alone, some distance from the coffin until Abigail left the sofa where she had been visiting with cousins her age. Giving her mother a hug when she approached, Abigail drained any lonely feelings from Jean. Being a single mother wasn't easy, but having a daughter who turned out so well eased the burden.

"Abby, you don't have to stay," Jean said, cupping both of her daughter's hands with her own. "I appreciate you being here for Aunt Vivian."

"I'm here for *you*, Mom," Abigail answered with her easy smile.

Exceptionally pretty as she grew into adulthood, Abigail had attended junior prom with a boy her age, and though they dated for a few months afterwards, she eventually decided work and school were more important. Her blue eyes sparkled, complimenting her infectious smile, and her brown hair reached several inches past her shoulders when she didn't wear it up. Today Abigail wore a black dress to mourn a woman Jean felt reasonably certain she didn't connect with during her young life.

Jean hadn't talked to her daughter much about the brutal way in which Vivian was murdered, mostly because she felt certain rumors were spreading throughout the high school and she didn't want Abigail overwhelmed with fright since the murderer hadn't been caught.

"It's only another forty-five minutes or so," Abigail said, "so I can stick around."

"Okay. I just wanted to make sure you got some rest since you have school tomorrow."

"I'm fine. You need to worry about yourself for a change."

"Maybe someday," Jean answered with a knowing grin.

Jean was about to say something a bit more inspiring to her daughter when she noticed someone familiar, yet entirely unexpected, walking through the room's main entrance. Dressed in a brown suit Jean felt certain he hadn't worn in a number of years, Colby McWilliams looked almost sheepishly around the room for a familiar face. A starched white shirt and blue and gray striped tie were visible under the suit jacket, making him better dressed than some of the night's visitors. The heels of his shined brown cowboy boots were visible at the cuffs of his slacks, indicating his local upbringing.

Jean noticed her family already eyeballing the bearded man as though he might be some vulture there to pick Vivian's bones, or a taxman threatening their inheritance.

Assuming McWilliams came to see her, or at least hoping so, Jean excused herself from Abigail and strode toward the recently familiar man. Upon seeing her McWilliams smiled, though he quickly shielded the emotion, fearing he might appear too lighthearted within a funeral home. As Jean neared the visitor, she felt the eyes of her relatives now narrowing at her, like birds of prey because they didn't recognize this stranger.

When Jean reached the freelance mechanic, they both paused awkwardly a moment, uncertain of the appropriate greeting between recent acquaintances. McWilliams reacted first, extending his hand for a handshake, which Jean accepted. She found his right hand powerful and calloused from his working environment, and his expression a blend of genuine warmth and sympathy. As someone who'd lost important loved ones, McWilliams seemed completely understanding of her plight.

"Thank you for coming," Jean said, barely getting the words out because she couldn't believe he'd taken the time to attend the calling hours.

"My condolences," he offered, bowing his head slightly. "I'm very sorry for your loss."

"Thank you, but you didn't have to come all this way."

"What's a few miles?" he countered, acting the part of a complete gentleman with his attire and softly spoken words.

Jean had never dated anyone she considered a country boy before, though she questioned what she might have overlooked for years. Vivian gave her strict counsel to marry up, which meant playing the field with only qualified candidates during her younger days. Marriage to an educated, well-to-do man left her with a beautiful daughter, though that particular relationship provided lots of headaches and heartache along the way.

She quickly shunned herself for thinking of marriage and affairs of the heart when she barely knew Colby McWilliams. So far as she knew he was simply being kind because her aunt and his adoptive father once shared a business relationship.

Jean led him toward the casket, stealing a glance at her aunt's peaceful repose, even if it was artificial after her brutal slaying. The funeral home had created a white hydrangea corsage large enough to cover both of her hands and the missing fingers. Makeup and a white lace neck scarf disguised any purple hues that lingered from her strangulation, and her skin tone didn't appear pasty or exceedingly forged. Only the top portion of the coffin was open for viewing, and Vivian's white dress felt appropriate to Jean, even if her aunt wasn't a saint in life.

"I feel bad because there are things I would like to have said," she admitted as they both looked at Vivian's body.

"She knows."

"You say that with such assurance."

"I say that as someone with strong faith," McWilliams said earnestly with his soft drawl. "My parents attended church on a regular basis, and my adoptive parents made sure I continued to go on Sundays. When I lost my folks it was devastating, but the idea that I'll see them again after this life has always kept me going."

Jean wasn't sure she shared such a leap of faith. Religion remained a consistent part of her life since childhood, but her practical side kept her from diving into the rabbit hole. She certainly wasn't an atheist, but questions always plagued her when it came to intangible entities.

Even though Lancaster was a former cop, Jean couldn't share his belief that McWilliams might be part of the recent violence sweeping their county.

If the man harbored any ill-will toward the people of his community, he was incredibly effective at hiding it.

"There were lots of things I wanted to say to my parents," McWilliams admitted. "It seemed the older I got, the more I wished they'd been there to teach me, or give me advice. Growing up with older guardians than everyone else made me a bit envious at times, but I came to realize that wasn't very Christian thinking on my part."

"You lost your parents as a kid," Jean said sympathetically. "I think you're entitled to some self-pity and mixed up thoughts."

McWilliams' cheeks flushed a bit from embarrassment.

"I came here for you, and here I am droning on about my past. I'm sorry."

"Don't be. It means a lot to me that you came. My family hasn't been the most supportive, or empathetic, during this entire process."

"I'm sure they loved your aunt in their own way."

Jean provided a sour expression that indicated his words were likely far from the truth, because most of Vivian's own children didn't love her so much as they stayed close for financial support and free babysitting. Granted, Vivian never made it particularly easy to love her unconditionally, but she certainly provided well for her family during her lifetime.

"I'm sorry this happened to you," McWilliams said. "I wouldn't wish that kind of end on my worst enemy."

"The papers didn't reveal the half of it. She suffered so much."

Jean couldn't bring herself to say anything further. Images from the mortuary still haunted her, with Vivian covered only by a sheet, blood still staining parts of her skin. It worried Jean that her fate, anyone's future for that matter, ended on a cold steel slab covered only by a white sheet. It seemed like a bleak, lonely end when she dwelled upon it in earthly terms. She hadn't experienced a revelation, or some sort of miracle in her life, to believe in a greater power as McWilliams did.

In many respects the family was fortunate to have the body released so quickly, but it wasn't like the coroner's office stayed busy in such a small community.

"They'll catch who did it," McWilliams said with confidence and reassurance, touching Jean's shoulder lightly.

Most of the eyes in the room darted in their direction, as though some great scandal had just come to light when in truth she'd barely known this man a day. Even so, he provided more warmth and comfort to her than anyone except her daughter, because the calling hours and the impending funeral were just a prelude to the division of Vivian's estate for them.

"I'm here for another reason," McWilliams confessed, his expression turning a bit more somber. "After your visit yesterday I searched through Henry's old documents, and I think there are some important things you should look at."

Willing to grasp at any possibility, Jean felt a hint of excitement that additional information might benefit the investigation.

"I can call Jeff Lancaster and be there first thing tomorrow."

"I'd rather you didn't bring him along."

Jean knew she looked as puzzled as she felt.

"If that man thinks I'm capable of murder, it's probably best he doesn't step foot on my property again."

Nodding in agreement, Jean understood his position. Lancaster hadn't treated him cordially, even if the former detective provided the service of being blatantly honest.

"I'll see you tomorrow morning. The funeral isn't until noon."

McWilliams nodded with a sheepish grin.

"Then I'll head home and get all of Henry's papers together."

Without another word he turned to walk toward the main door, leaving Jean with her miserable family members, who immediately began whispering amongst themselves. She didn't care to venture what they were discussing, and couldn't be bothered to care at this point. Although she wanted Vivian's will reading over with, it wasn't because she wanted material goods, but rather to rid herself of the jackals who shared her bloodline. Vivian was straightforward with her about family affairs, so Jean already knew she was coming into a few heirlooms, a very small inheritance, and some stocks.

Abigail wasted little time approaching her mother with a rather excitable tiptoed run, evidently very curious about McWilliams. Jean had let her daughter experience what a bastard her father was the hard way, and when Abigail finally realized some hard truths, she pushed her mother to enter the dating scene.

Rather persistently.

"So who was that?" Abigail asked just above a whisper, apparently unconcerned with any family complications.

"He's someone helping with Aunt Vivian's murder."

"You two looked kinda cozy."

"It's nothing like that," Jean insisted.

"I heard you say you're meeting him tomorrow."

Jean remembered being a teenager, realizing her daughter hadn't experienced much of the real world, or long-term relationships. She wasn't in the mood to debate the logistics of her acquaintance to McWilliams, and Abigail wasn't going to drop the subject anytime soon.

"I can't date everyone I meet, Abby," she said firmly. "There's no time for that."

"Because you don't *make* time, Mom. Maybe if you actually went on a date I'd stop hounding you so badly."

"This isn't the time," Jean insisted, her voice just above a whisper. "And even if I wanted to date Mr. McWilliams it wouldn't be appropriate until all of this business is behind us."

Abigail provided a smirk that preluded her words, and what deep down truth her mother fought to avoid admitting.

"So you *would* date Mr. McWilliams if things were different."

One date, Jean thought, not giving her daughter the satisfaction. McWilliams wasn't like any man she dated, before or after the divorce, leaving her curious about the self-professed country boy.

Of course Lancaster was a rural man as well, and she certainly hadn't taken a liking to him or his overbearing police disposition. She hoped and prayed none of Lancaster's fears about McWilliams proved to be accurate.

Chapter 20

Monday, September 24

Unwilling to entrust the task ahead to any of his deputies or jail personnel, Lawrence County Sheriff Steve Parsons donned a clean suit, along with his badge and sidearm, before daylight even broke across Indiana. He planned on being at the lab in Bloomington promptly when they opened at five a.m.

Signing out Nichols from the jail proved little more than a formality since Parsons had made arrangements the previous evening. Instead of using his usual vehicle, the sheriff elected to use a brown sedan from his fleet that contained a cage between the front and back. Given a safety feature that kept an unarmed prisoner from assaulting him, Parsons didn't handcuff Nichols when they left the county jail. As they stepped from the dingy interior of the county building, only a security light broke the darkness of the alley. Cool and crisp, the morning weather allowed the sheriff to see his breath, which he didn't consider possible until October.

Once again, Nichols acted uneasy when they crossed the threshold, looking around like an animal accustomed to being prey.

"Why're you so skittish, Ralph?" Parsons asked while opening the rear door for the prisoner.

"He's out there, Sheriff."

Parsons said nothing, knowing that *someone* dangerous lingered in his county. While that person may have pieced together the conspiracy that involved Vivian Weatherly and her business partners, it seemed unlikely that person knew Nichols carried out a job for them four decades prior. Parsons considered it far less likely anyone aside from his staff knew that Nichols was in custody and confessing to the cold case murder.

Closing the unmarked cruiser's door once Nichols was safely tucked inside, Parsons took out his canister of dip and tapped the flat end against his hand twice before getting a pinch of tobacco to tuck into his lower lip. At such an early hour he needed something to keep him awake, and nicotine seemed like a good substitute for caffeine since he didn't plan on making any stops on the way to Bloomington.

An empty coffee cup sat in the cup holder for use as a spittoon, the coffee already consumed and not enough to fuel the sheriff. He'd spent most of the night tossing and turning in anticipation of the upcoming day's events. Despite serving his country in the most dangerous of ways, and being elected to the second most powerful position in his county, Parsons let nerves get the better of him. Technically the coroner could arrest the sheriff if the need arose, so Parsons always kept his ego in check regarding his extended powers.

He turned the key, firing up the car before carefully backing out of the spot into the alley. Feeling a bit impatient because he needed certain events to fall into place before he could proceed, Parsons couldn't wait to see the lab results. Following the lab test, he planned on holding a press conference to reassure the public that his department was finding answers in one crime that was inexplicably tied to at least one other.

Once Parsons reached the highway he felt a bit more reassured about overcoming the DNA obstacle, leaving him time to focus on the present murders. He wasn't very certain about relying upon Lancaster for further assistance, begrudging himself for having virtually groveled to keep the former detective around. Had he known Lancaster's property tied directly with the murder of Michael Tanksley, Parsons would never have asked his former detective for assistance.

The vehicle's headlights barely pierced the blackness of the night sky and the light of dawn wouldn't emerge for almost another two hours. By then Parsons hoped to be sitting behind his desk making arrangements for a press conference and getting updates from his current detectives about the Weatherly and Stafford murders.

He *needed* updates, because the public wasn't going to stand for the elderly, particularly the pillars of their county, being butchered in their own homes.

Although his people knew some of the business associates who worked with the two murder victims during their heyday, Parsons couldn't narrow down the field effectively until Nichols admitted in a roundabout way just who contracted him. Despite being armed with this knowledge, no local police agency possessed adequate manpower to protect these alleged associates around the clock unless they admitted to guilt in the Tanksley murder.

And none of them were about to confess after four decades, especially with Nichols accepting all of the blame.

"You okay back there, Ralph?" Parsons asked his prisoner before picking up the empty coffee cup to relieve his mouth from the tobacco juice swishing around his lower lip.

No verbal reply was given, but Nichols looked upward briefly, allowing the sheriff to see his worried eyes in the mirror. Now understanding that Nichols believed some form of Michael Tanksley was destined to come for him, Parsons felt a bit uneasy. With Halloween only a month away, and the fall weather beginning to settle in across Southern Indiana, the haunting sentiments felt right at home.

Around ten minutes into the journey, Parsons passed an area where rock faced Highway 37 on either side of the divided four lanes. Back in the late 1960s, when the highway was first being constructed, crews decided to cut through the landscape rather than bypass it. The "rock cuts" resulted in large, visible flakes of siltstone and limestone that occasionally broke apart, falling beside the highway. Millions of years old, the rocks and loose sediment harbored secrets of life that continued to lure scientists through the present day because they once served as the ocean floor.

Unable to stifle a yawn, the sheriff swapped hands atop the steering wheel as a misty gray fog appeared when the car descended into one of the many downhill dips, nearing the Monroe Reservoir exit. The entire journey from Bedford to Bloomington felt somewhat like a roller coaster with all of the ups and downs that accompanied the hilly topography. Parsons figured the fog would disappear momentarily when the car emerged from the depression, but it seemed to grow thicker as he reached a level surface. The hot and cold air often mixed during the morning hours, creating fog in the lower lying areas of the valleys, but Parsons found this weather pattern particularly irksome.

Nichols took notice of the fog as well, his eyes widening in terror as he leaned forward against the divider.

"Oh, no."

"What's wrong with you, Ralph?" Parsons asked with irritability, like a parent scolding a child.

He began slowing the car because visibility dropped as the fog grew in intensity to a level Parsons had never seen on a natural level. Perhaps the fog machines at Lancaster's new park might replicate such an unbearable white cloud, but the sheriff couldn't recall worse visibility while driving along the highway.

"Don't stop," Nichols virtually pleaded through the metal brackets. "That's exactly what he wants. This is what it looked like the morning I killed him!"

"Quit that nonsense, Ralph," Parsons said sternly, shrinking the prisoner back to his seat.

Parsons wasn't sure his words scared the man nearly as much as whatever fantasy ran through his mind about Michael Tanksley returning from the dead for vengeance.

Noticing a fence line along the side of the road for a large property, Parsons decided to pull over until the dense fog subsided. He couldn't see more than twenty feet in front of him, and if an ignorant driver stopped in the wrong place a collision was inevitable. His eyes darted down to the speedometer, lowering from fifty-five miles per hour as he slowly veered the car safely onto the shoulder.

The car had decelerated about halfway when a blur came from the left, emerging from the white mist before striking the car's front bumper with a distinctive thud. Whatever hit the car went barreling forward along the shoulder, rather than finishing its path across the road.

"Holy shit!" Parsons blurted, all professionalism leaving his mind and mouth momentarily.

Thinking he'd hit a deer, the sheriff wanted to assess the damage with minimal delay to his objective. He couldn't afford to miss the set appointment, and turning in any damage for insurance reasons meant calling out the state police to generate a report. Using his own department was unethical and screamed conspiracy to taxpayers, and city police didn't cover the highways, so the state troopers were his only option.

Willing to live with a small ding in the front bumper, Parsons pulled the car to the shoulder as it cut through the pea soup fog.

"Don't do it," Nichols said. "It's a trap."

"And I suppose that was him crashing into the car?"

Nichols aimed his eyes at the floorboard, his voice barely audible as though he'd given up on life entirely.

"It was."

Throwing the car into park, Parsons shut it off, removing the keys from the ignition before looking back at his prisoner.

"I'll lock it, Ralph, if it makes you feel better."

"It doesn't."

Parsons barely heard the man's words as he opened the door, virtually feeling the moisture of the fog brush against his skin. Though he didn't detect much of a breeze, the sheriff's skin tingled from the cold dew clinging to the exposed portions. The air, normally cool and brisk in the morning, felt almost wintery outside the car. He half expected snowflakes to replace the white mist any moment, but nothing changed as Parsons hit the lock button and shut the door behind him.

He hesitated momentarily before walking toward the front of the car, realizing the mist had grown so thick he could barely see a foot ahead of him. For verification he held up his right hand, barely able to see its outline through the white wisps. Deciding that standing beside the highway wasn't a particularly wise move because other drivers wouldn't be able to see ahead of them, he walked briskly toward the front bumper.

"Not bad," he muttered upon assessing the damage.

He surmised the dent, barely larger than a human foot, could likely be restored using modern bodywork that didn't require paint or putty. Not even worth turning in for insurance purposes, the ding still puzzled the sheriff, because he never actually saw what struck the car.

"Tough son-of-a-bitch, whatever it was," he said to himself, deciding to wait for the weather to clear before hitting the road again.

Unable to shake the wonderment of the frigid air around him, Parsons recalled stories of freezing temperatures accompanying beings from the spirit world when they visited. For the first time he questioned whether Nichols had the right idea that Michael Tanksley wasn't at rest, and if so, how did the confessed killer *know* such a fact?

Although the fog barely allowed him to take in the topography around him, the sheriff realized he was at the edge of another rocky formation that loomed overhead. Beside it, however, the landscape descended sharply into a field below, the slope treacherous enough that even kids sledding on winter snow might think twice. A grassy area curved upward behind the limestone, also too steep for people to climb without some assistance. At first Parsons thought the extreme weather might have exaggerated the danger of the slopes, but a closer look revealed that he certainly didn't want to tumble down the slope a mere ten feet removed from the highway.

The breeze picked up in an instant as the sound of rustling leaves reached his ears. Suddenly thinking it prudent to take a slight risk and begin driving again, Parsons started around the car when he thought he heard a car door opening. He stopped midstride to listen more intently as the noise continued, and he realized it wasn't Nichols trying to exit the car, but rather someone violently attempting to get inside.

Standing on the driver's side front of the vehicle, the sheriff heard several thumps, realizing the car was rocking back and forth. He put his hand on the hood for confirmation, and once he felt the vibration his right hand reached to his side, clasping his firearm as he heard what sounded like the bending and tearing of metal. He knew the sound from watching rescue crews use the Jaws of Life to remove entrapped victims from cars, but he felt certain his ears were deceiving him, because even as he rounded the vehicle with his firearm drawn, the fog obscured his vision.

Drawing a nervous breath because he couldn't see two feet in front of him, and now the screams of Ralph Nichols were reaching his ears, Parsons used his left hand to wave the misty fog out of the way as the back door gave way and ripped from its hinges. Barely catching a glimpse of dark, almost mop-like hair, the sheriff took aim with his Glock, but the assailant already had a grip on Nichols and yanked him from the vehicle without hesitation, the broken door lying beside the back tire like part of some discarded wreck.

"Freeze!" Parsons commanded the attacker, his heart virtually pounding through his chest at this point.

Somehow this potential threat had managed to yank a car door from its hinges before grasping Nichols as though the man were a cardboard cutout, giving Parsons good reason to fear for his life.

As though daring him to fire the Glock, the assailant let go of Nichols, who dropped to the ground with a thud, before turning to face the sheriff. Wisps of fog floated through the air, still obscuring his vision, but Parsons was able to see that this intruder was scarred or disfigured somehow. His face wasn't a natural flesh color, appearing almost a deathly light purple in hue. The man's clothes were tattered, and what skin showed through the rips appeared bruised or cut in some way. Fearing this man was high on PCP or some other kind of drug that provided him with temporary incredible strength and prevented him from feeling pain, the sheriff didn't hesitate to fire his sidearm when the attacker began lifting a foot toward him.

Parsons fired two shots center mass, just like the police academy taught him years prior, but his anticipated result didn't happen. He wasn't even sure the mess of a man before him flinched from the two bullets lodged inside his heart, as though he was some invincible killer from a horror movie. Tilting his head slightly to one side, waiting for the man to slump to the ground in a more lifeless state, Parsons could only watch with anticipation until the dead, glassy blue eyes met his own from beneath the black hair.

Chilled to the bone, and not from the climate, Parsons took aim once more, firing five consecutive shots into the unwelcome guest's torso, receiving the same result. Although the sheriff doubted this man was wearing a protective vest, he couldn't fathom any other explanation for the bullets proving ineffective. Positive his gun wasn't loaded with blanks, Parsons watched as the glazed eyes stared through him, and for the first time a downright angry expression formed across the grayish skin.

He heard Nichols whimpering as he desperately clawed the ground, trying to get away from the unexpected violence. Getting behind the unmarked car wasn't nearly enough cover to keep Nichols safe, and the sheriff felt highly inept at keeping his prisoner safe.

Drawing a deep breath, Parsons assumed a shooting stance, raised his firearm a little bit higher, and fired several more shots into the man's head.

He witnessed the holes enter the assailant's cheeks and forehead, causing him to flinch at last. Still, the man did not fall to the ground, nor did any of the fresh wounds appear to bleed. Exasperated, Parsons took half a step back, hoping the mysterious attacker would follow him and forget about Nichols for the time being.

Continuing his string of bad luck, Parsons watched the opposite occur as the stranger turned his attention toward Nichols, who hadn't stopped making noise for one complete second since being dragged from the car. Because he'd left the two extra magazines he sometimes attached to his belt at home, the sheriff lacked extra ammunition once his fifteen rounds were expended.

"Hey!" he yelled, drawing the attention and the ire of the stranger intent on doing harm to Nichols.

Parsons used his last half dozen shots to pepper the chest, neck, and face of the stranger, doing absolutely no guaranteed harm as he became the focus of the attacker's wrath. Hearing the click of his firearm once the last casing ejected, Parsons didn't have a Taser or any kind of club like his road officers. And though he wasn't particularly keen on the idea of hand-to-hand combat with anyone capable of withstanding fifteen slugs, the sheriff saw no other option because he wasn't going to abandon anyone in his custody.

Now certain the assailant wasn't going to deviate from attacking the sheriff who'd interfered one too many times, Parsons decided to use his absolute last line of defense. Although he kept it secret from everyone outside of his family, Parsons had lost his right leg below the knee while deployed overseas. Giving up part of a leg for a medal with a ribbon attached didn't feel like a fair trade, but he never used it as a crutch. He let the rumors run abound throughout his department before, during, and after the election because he didn't want a tainted win based on sympathy or misplaced admiration.

Now, serving as his last line of defense, the prosthetic leg that cupped his knee was easily within reach. Constructed of metal, and covered by synthetic materials, the artificial limb provided the illusion of real flesh. Parsons reached down, removing the artificial limb with practiced ease as the seemingly robotic assailant closed in, prepared to show no mercy to the law enforcing nuisance. Because he never wanted sympathy in life, or at the polls,

Parsons always wore pants and some form of boot throughout the year, even during the hot summer months.

And even when he wore a suit.

At this moment he decided to use the steel toe of his duty boot as a weapon, hoping to save his own life.

He waited until the ominous figure closed in, trying to ignore the glossy, dead-looking eyes while he balanced on his one good leg. Keeping his back against the car for additional support, Parsons lunged forward, timing his swing perfectly as he struck the steel toe against the side of the aggressor's skull. The foul stench he'd come to recognize as the odor that accompanied death overwhelmed his nostrils mid-swing, but the sheriff followed through, striking his intended target. Finally knocking the stranger to the ground, Parsons barely hopped on his left leg to maintain his own balance, hoping he'd bought enough time to escape this lunatic.

"Get in!" he commanded Nichols, who hadn't moved from the back of the car where he continued to whimper.

Still clutching his artificial leg, Parsons leaned against the hood of the car, attempting to replace it when he saw the attacker sit up from a completely prone position, as though possessed and commanded to do so. Very stiff and almost artificial in his movements, the assailant wasn't the least bit slow, despite his awkward body language. Parsons hurried to replace his leg as Nichols dove into the back of the car, but the stranger would not be denied his prize.

"Oh, fuck!" Parsons barely managed to utter as two powerful hands grasped him by the shirt collar, launching him into the front windshield of his own car.

His back and head took the brunt of the impact, dazing the sheriff as he heard and felt the glass giving way behind him. Without ammunition, or the steel inside his artificial limb, Parsons found himself practically defenseless against this monster in human form. Unable to regain his senses, he felt the two cold hands grab him once more, hurling him across the hood of the car and into traffic this time. Hitting the edge of the hood before tumbling over the car kept Parsons from hitting the unforgiving pavement with full impact, though the side of his shaved head struck the surface before he rolled to a stop in the lane closest to his car.

A new danger presented itself when a pair of headlights pierced the fog about fifty yards out, accompanied by the sound of an engine. The oncoming car wasn't driving at breakneck speeds, considering the fog lingered throughout the area, but Parsons was missing half of one leg, slowing him considerably. Only survival instinct kept him from blacking out after his head struck the windshield and the pavement. Bruised and aching all over, he half rolled and half hobbled to the side of the road, reaching the safety of his patrol vehicle as the vehicle passed by, missing him by less than a foot. His mind barely registered the danger, contemplating the hazards of a rematch with the assailant while his body began to betray him, teetering on unconsciousness.

Parsons quickly learned he was in the clear, although he had failed to protect Nichols, and therefore close a cold case four decades old.

His legs felt rubbery beneath him, and as the sheriff put a hand out to steady himself against the car he stumbled to one knee, hearing terrified screams from Nichols growing distant. Incapable of pursuing the assailant or his prisoner, Parsons realized the mysterious person was dragging Nichols to certain death down the ravine. The cold seizing the vicinity, along with the fog, began dissipating all around him, indicating whatever force of nature brought them in the first place was leaving.

Parsons wasn't certain what the attacker was doing to poor Nichols, but it sounded absolutely horrific based on the man's agonized screams. The sheriff attempted to crawl in the direction of the screams, forgoing his own safety momentarily until he remembered the cell phone clipped to his belt. Feeling lightheaded, he pulled the phone from its case, making the somewhat ironic call to 911, knowing whatever personnel arrived would surely assist him. Nichols, however, was lost to the world, and the sheriff who vowed to keep him protected while in custody. His screams grew more distant until some painful, deathly cries were followed by dead silence.

With the bizarre weather now completely gone, Parsons put his right arm forward, willing himself to find Nichols, no matter the man's condition. He saw only flashes of light in his vision, feeling dizzy as though he'd been blindfolded and spun around a dozen times at a party. As the dispatcher answered the phone on the other end, the sheriff went completely limp and the phone dropped to the ground beside his unconscious form.

Chapter 21

Lancaster treated his father and brother to breakfast in Bedford before taking them out to the theme park for a morning tour of the facility during downtime. His mother declined, saying she'd just seen it a month earlier near completion and didn't want to miss setting up her church's tent downtown for the Persimmon Festival. They usually ran a food tent the entire week, raising money for an annual mission trip that went to a chosen parish family.

Somewhat surprised that his father accepted the offer, the theme park owner figured Wyatt Lancaster didn't care much for the setting, but wasn't going to pass up the opportunity to see his two sons simultaneously. With Jeff putting every waking moment into the theme park, when not struggling to avoid his old profession, and David working late hours as an attorney, the sixty-four-year-old farmer valued what time he spent with his boys.

Now taking his annual autumn break from work, David had begun growing a beard in anticipation of hunting season. He still worked cases when necessary, and attended court like always, but his receptionist knew never to schedule new work for him between the Persimmon Festival and the end of October without running it past him first. Working in a small practice allowed for such a flexible schedule, particularly in a small town setting.

Today, as usual, he donned a suit because he never knew when a client or the office might need him. Some calls came unexpectedly, which left him no time to drive home miles into the country for a change of clothes. Leaving a suit at the office permanently sounded like a smart move, but he hadn't gotten around to such small personal details yet.

He had broken away from a large firm several years earlier, making less money each year, but discovering the happiness that came from being around his wife and five children. Despite coming from a more contemporary family in terms of size, David always wanted a large family. His career allowed him to live out the dream that he and his wife shared to raise children and live outside of city limits.

"It doesn't look very ominous during the day," David commented as the three men stood just inside the front gate, viewing the roller coasters and haunted houses that lost their effectiveness when daylight exposed their wood and plaster facades.

"I've got to work on that," Lancaster admitted, knowing his park was going to be open many daylight hours in the future.

Lancaster didn't expect his father, a traditional Christian and farmer, to approve of the business venture, regardless of what he said. Wyatt Lancaster wore thick eyeglasses, maintaining a beard with a few distinct gray stripes that might get him mistaken for someone from an Amish clan if he dressed plainly. Though he sported a somewhat rotund belly from good farm cooking, his hands and arms were thick from decades of labor around the farm before the advent of computerized tractors and automated equipment.

Always one to be outside doing work, Wyatt sold his hardware business shortly after both of his sons were firmly on their own with education and careers. Although it shaped the lives of both men, their father never mentioned missing ownership or the work it entailed.

Only a few workers milled across the vast acreage of the theme park in the form of maintenance and security personnel. Fortunately, a hefty portion of the land was already cleared of trees, large rocks, and other vegetation from the years the land spent growing vegetables for farmers on land contracts. Lancaster knew his father would have loved to work on such flat, plentiful farmland, but his own farm was miles away, closer to Mitchell than Bedford.

"Care to go through one of the haunted houses, Dad?" Lancaster asked his father. "Or maybe ride a coaster?"

The elder Lancaster chuckled.

"No thanks, son. I could use a restroom though, if you have one handy."

After taking a brief look around, Lancaster pointed his father in the correct direction.

"Around the bend and to the left."

Wyatt Lancaster gave a nod and began sauntering in the appropriate direction. Both brothers waited until their father disappeared from view before conversing.

"I looked up those items you gave me," David said with a rather disappointed expression.

"No luck?"

"On the contrary, I found exactly what I think you were looking for, but I'm concerned that you shouldn't be butting into this stuff. You've got a business to run, because you *gave up* playing detective, remember?"

"Is that sagely advice for my well-being, or because you're worried about having to go back to a big firm again?"

Lancaster retained his brother's services for a flat, fairly substantial salary that provided David with some breathing room that normally did not accompany a downsize in firms. He trusted his older brother implicitly, and David had remained a constant presence at his side throughout the purchase of the land and the subsequent construction of the theme park. He never truly asked for anything during the process, so Lancaster wanted to make it up to the entire family by rewarding his brother.

"It's for your own good. Sticking your nose in this stuff isn't going to endear you to the town elders."

"They're getting bumped off in case you hadn't noticed. I'm pretty sure living a few more years beats the alternative. Now tell me what you found before Dad gets back."

David sighed, knowing his recommendations were often futile when it came to his younger brother.

"Here are the five names of the people who actually purchased this land forty-one years ago."

David handed him a list, and the names matched the five people he discovered through Jean's research. This didn't come as a surprise to him, but when Lancaster received the documentation of every person or company to own the land before him, he discovered a corporation of some sort purchased the land shortly after Michael Tanksley's death. No individual names were provided, so he asked his brother to ferret out the identities of those people on some official documentation.

"You can't protect them, if that's what you're after," David stated. "That's a job for the police."

"The same police who sat by and watched two people get dissected by this madman? I'm not feeling overly trusting of my former colleagues at the moment."

David's eyes narrowed, indicating he really didn't want his younger brother to pursue any part of this new discovery.

"What are you going to do? Hire private security for everyone left on that list?"

"I don't owe these people anything," Lancaster admitted, "and they're probably paying for some sins they committed in the past, but maybe, just maybe, I could find out who's behind all of this because someone keeps fucking with my theme park."

"And you could also get innocent people killed. It's not worth it."

Lancaster hadn't decided which course of action to take just yet, but at least he possessed accurate facts to help him choose. His brother continued to wear a grave expression, as though something else weighed on his mind.

"What else did you find?"

"It may be nothing."

"And it may be important."

David looked to the ground as though trying to figure out the best way to break the news to his brother.

"That Michael Tanksley guy," David began with a level of hesitation, scuffing the bottom of his shoe against the ground as he lightly kicked the concrete.

"What about him?"

"He's buried in the Mitchell cemetery."

"Okay," Lancaster said slowly, unsure of where the conversation was heading.

"Well, he wasn't always buried there."

Lancaster closed his eyes, figuring exactly what his brother was going to say next. He inhaled a deep breath through his nose, just waiting for the words to punch him in the guts.

"When he died, he requested a burial on the family property, and you know what that means."

Understanding, Lancaster gave a slow nod.

"When the property was purchased by that group, *those* five people," David said, pointing to the list, "they had the body unearthed and moved to Mitchell Cemetery."

Technically called Mitchell City Cemetery, the resting place for the deceased mainly occupied a hilly field between two roads, seated in close proximity to a small shopping plaza. Lancaster knew it all too well.

"Do you have the plot location?" he asked his brother.

"Well, no, but it's just a phone call away."

Brotherly concern crossed David's face again.

"What are you thinking of doing?"

"I'm thinking of visiting the grave site and seeing if I can find any clues. If this is some sort of retaliation for something these five people did, then maybe someone visited the grave before starting on their killing spree."

David's look of disapproval softened, perhaps because their father was returning from the restroom, or maybe he saw the logic in his brother pursuing answers that were basically right in front of him.

"I'll make the call when we're done here," Lancaster informed his brother quietly enough that their father didn't hear. "Maybe I can finally shed some light on what's turned this town upside-down."

"What are you two scheming about?" Wyatt asked his sons, apparently not as hard of hearing as he often led them to believe.

Humble as a man could ever be, he often put down his own intellect, making off the cuff remarks that he was just a dumb old farmhand, or he wasn't smart enough to attend college. His sons both knew those remarks to be completely unfounded. His family couldn't afford to send him to college, not due to lack of financing, but because they *needed* him to run the family business when he reached adulthood. Wyatt's father fell ill, forcing him to take the helm and work their vast acreage rather than hire the work done. He was never afforded the opportunities he provided his two sons, and they appreciated it all the more that their father never harked on his own hardships.

They learned of their father's strict upbringing, and his reluctance to take over and save the family business only through other family members.

"Just a little business," Lancaster answered as neutrally as possible.

"Business my ass. David couldn't keep his voice that low in a library if he tried."

Their father gave a suspicious look, indicating he'd deduced the topic of their conversation.

"Are you still looking into those murders for your old department?" he asked Lancaster with a disapproving look similar to David's.

"I wasn't, but it seems there's a connection to this property."

The elder Lancaster appeared surprised.

"Dad, what do you know about the Michael Tanksley murder?"

Shaking his head, Wyatt didn't seem very comfortable with the question, but he openly tried to recall.

"I don't remember much, except it rocked this community. Tanksley was regarded as an odd duck, but he was still a local. Everyone knew his folks before they died."

"You've pretty much always worked on the farm. Do you remember when they tried to buy this land for the county fairgrounds?"

"That was short-lived, son. It just wasn't for sale."

"Until the last owner died anyway," Lancaster said more bitterly than he intended.

"What are you getting at?" his father asked, placing his hands at his hips.

David had remained strangely quiet, simply glancing between his brother and father, as though waiting to see how this discussion unfolded.

"The more I look into this, the more strange I find it that Michael Tanksley's parents died rather suddenly, Colby McWilliams' parents died rather suddenly, and Tanksley himself was brutally murdered after refusing to sell this very land we're standing on. I just feel as though this whole community buried a deep dark secret two generations ago."

His father now looked befuddled, as though the sequence of events and their ramifications never truly occurred to him. Lancaster felt certain his father knew everything about the area and most local events, so he wondered if his father was attempting to skirt the line of questioning for some reason.

"We were so sure those were unfortunate accidents," he said slowly, outwardly doubting the circumstances surrounding four of the deaths for the first time. "And when nothing ever came of the carnival thing they tried here, we just thought it was bad luck on their part." He paused a moment, looking to the ground before returning his attention to his younger son. "Maybe this place is cursed."

"You of all people don't really believe that, Dad," David finally interjected.

"History says otherwise, David. I *do* remember them trying to import a metal ride from overseas and the ship going down. That was big news. And every single time they tried to reopen this place an accident happened, or some costly repair kept their big rides closed. I remember coming here sometimes on weekends, and it just never felt quite right. Back then I just blamed it on the park being broken down all the time, but now I wonder if there was something more to it."

"What exactly do you mean it didn't feel right?" Lancaster pressed.

Again his father searched for the correct terminology before speaking.

"I guess it felt like we were trespassing, like someone, or some *thing* didn't want us here. It doesn't feel like that now, though, so I guess you're doing something right. Hell, maybe they just had bad maintenance and I just read too much into the problems."

Lancaster didn't feel so assured that his land wasn't tainted. Perhaps some, or all, of the curse that accompanied it departed when Michael Tanksley was laid to rest elsewhere. He was already itching to check on the new grave site for clues, unable to shake the detective part of him. Still, he wanted to show off his new investment just a bit and spend time with his family members.

"Let me give you two a tour before you get scared off," Lancaster said with a chuckle, hoping *his* theme park fared better than its predecessor.

Chapter 22

When Jean pulled into the driveway at Colby McWilliams' house, she didn't see any doors open along the barn, the garage, or the house. She noticed a car and a truck parked in the driveway, but wasn't sure if they belonged to the mechanic or they were some of his projects. Reluctantly stepping from her car, she breathed the clean country air, not smelling gas fumes, trash bins, or grease from the local fast food establishments. Being outside of town felt somewhat liberating, particularly along the scenic route that led to this property.

Dew clung to the shaded blades of grass as the sun hid below the tree line, not yet able to penetrate the natural surroundings. Jean didn't expect to hear much noise from such a serene, picturesque setting, but she began to wonder if McWilliams was awake, or even home. She walked the concrete walkway up to the front door, noticing the yellow Lab hadn't come to greet her like the last time.

Feeling a bit apprehensive, in case McWilliams was sleeping in, she reached her forefinger toward the doorbell when the inside door swung open. McWilliams was already fully dressed in blue jeans and a work shirt, readily smiling when they made eye contact as he pushed the storm door open for her.

"Please, come in."

Walking into the living room, Jean noticed the place a bit more tidied up since her first visit. Certainly not bad for a bachelor pad, she felt certain any dust was now swept away, the coffee table appeared devoid of anything except a few coasters, and a fresh scent that obviously emanated from an air freshener filled the room.

McWilliams offered her a seat, though he remained standing in the center of the living room.

"Can I get you something to drink?"

"No, I'm fine," Jean answered, hoping he hadn't simply invited her over because he was feeling lonely.

She seriously doubted such a shallow motive from McWilliams, but she wasn't completely sure until he walked into the kitchen momentarily. He returned with a manila folder and a rather aged binder. The look on his face indicated he wasn't about to reveal good news, though she couldn't imagine what the man might have discovered in just two days.

"After you stopped by the other day I decided to go through some of Henry's belongings and I found some interesting things."

Based on his apprehension, Jean wondered if he meant atrocious finds.

Instead of handing her the paperwork, McWilliams took the adjacent chair, looking between her and the papers a few seconds before beginning.

"I verified the five people my adoptive father sold that theme park to. Henry left behind a substantial amount of paperwork that his wife never threw away in case someone needed it."

"That will probably match the five names I found in my aunt's files," Jean said, hoping that confirmation might force the police to protect the remaining business associates.

"There's something else," McWilliams added, his worrisome look returning. "I found some sheets from Henry's old ledger that said Michael Tanksley came to visit him and knew what the group was up to."

"Up to?" Jean questioned.

"My cousin said he knew they wanted his property and he was taking steps to ensure that if something happened to him the guilty party wouldn't get away with it. Henry documented practically everything, on and off the record, so it doesn't surprise me that he put this in here. He was a lawyer, so he probably wanted to have this conversation on record so he could remember it later."

"Can I read it?" Jean asked.

"It's kind of weird," McWilliams warned, reluctant to hand it over until she indicated his words weren't enough to deter her.

Jean took the bound journal from him, looking through Henry Cauldwell's handwritten notations that detailed the encounter with Michael Tanksley. She immediately wondered if the entry could be taken at face value since Cauldwell worked for the adversaries Tanksley came to discuss with him.

Once she started reading the entry, Jean believed its authenticity because it sounded too off the wall not to be true. She began questioning Michael Tanksley's sanity because he informed Cauldwell that he knew the group of five intended to murder him for his land. He'd already been approached about selling the land for use as a 4-H hub where the county fair could be held on a permanent basis, rather than in town in temporary tent setups. Expressing his desire to keep the family property his parents fought so vehemently to obtain from the state, Tanksley said if the five conspirators dared murder him that he would have no choice except to enact revenge.

Feeling a bit confused, Jean wondered how a dead man planned to seek vengeance, and why he felt so certain he was going to be murdered for a piece of property, albeit a rather large chunk of land.

Aside from some ominous foreshadowing, the entry revealed very little. Jean still couldn't imagine her aunt and her partners would have anything to do with cold-blooded murder, for land or profit. Perhaps Tanksley, in his delusional state, brought some form of harm to himself by angering the wrong person.

She didn't have the benefit of reading the police report from Tanksley's murder, and Lancaster hadn't been very forthcoming with information when they temporarily teamed up. Any personal investigation on her part certainly felt one-dimensional because Jean didn't possess police resources, even though local agencies appeared powerless to discover who killed Vivian and Charles Stafford. She refused to believe Michael Tanksley set a revenge plot in motion four decades prior, somehow predicting his own death while knowing those responsible.

Even so, Jean couldn't simply dismiss the man's foresight as a major coincidence.

"That entire conversation strikes me as odd," Jean confessed.

"Finding that journal entry got me remembering what was in that trunk inside my barn," McWilliams revealed. "It actually came back to me the same day that you and that rude former cop stopped by."

"And you didn't say anything before?"

"It wouldn't have done any good. They've obviously been gone for a while now."

"What were they?" Jean inquired.

McWilliams sat back in thought momentarily, finally leaning forward when the answer came to him.

"I distinctly remember a tomahawk of some sort in that chest because I found it odd. But my cousin was apparently big on his Native American heritage, slim as it may have been. The other thing was a book of some sort, and I think it had entries from Michael, but I don't remember it looking like a diary."

"Why did you remove them from the chest?" Jean decided to ask, mainly to see if McWilliams deviated from his original answer.

She felt such a move made her no less of a jerk than Lancaster, but her aunt's memory dictated that emotions took a backseat to facts.

"I *didn't* remove them," McWilliams said firmly. "And I don't know when they came up missing. The first time I remember seeing the outline in the trunk was definitely after someone tried breaking into my house."

"You mentioned that the other day," Jean stated. "What kept the thief from getting inside if they really wanted to?"

McWilliams raised a questioning eyebrow.

"I mean to say you live on an isolated road, so what kept the person from just kicking in your door and taking whatever they wanted?"

McWilliams shrugged.

"I assumed the dog might have scared him off. He stays inside when I'm gone because I don't want him running down the road."

Jean hardly considered the yellow Lab an attack dog, much less an effective watchdog. Perhaps the sight of someone kicking in the front door might trigger a more assertive mode within the canine, but she couldn't picture that scenario. If it spied McWilliams in immediate danger the dog would almost certainly risk its life to protect him, but it might not consider defending an empty house worthwhile.

That was assuming the dog was even on the property when the attempted break-in occurred.

Suddenly his revelation didn't seem as groundbreaking as he made it sound at the calling hours. A dozen thoughts flooded Jean's mind, some concerning this man's motives and others about whatever Michael Tanksley attempted to set in motion before his untimely death. His veiled threats might have been ramblings of a mentally unstable man, or something far more nefarious. Jean couldn't imagine what kind of plan took forty-one years to unfold, particularly when it involved revenge. Even worse, she couldn't fathom her aunt being a party to murder over land, no matter how much acreage it involved.

A large, important piece of the puzzle remained unseen, and Jean decided her best chance of finding it was through McWilliams. She didn't share Lancaster's skepticism about the man, hoping her optimism didn't bring harm or ruin to her later.

"You seem a little deep in thought," he said, scattering her thoughts and bringing her back to the present.

"Sorry," Jean said, nervously raising her hands before placing them in her lap.

McWilliams looked at her with his blue eyes, a soft, understanding expression crossing his face.

"Look," he said with a bit of nervousness in his voice, "I know we just met and this past week hasn't been easy for you."

He appeared hesitant about continuing, and Jean had a strange feeling McWilliams wanted to ask her out.

"I'm heading to Nashville on Wednesday to pick up some vintage car parts for a project I'm working on this week," he said almost sheepishly, with a light trembling in his voice that left Jean unable to believe any evil ran through his veins. "It's beautiful up there this time of year, and I was wondering if you might want to make a day of it. If you're free, and I'm not imposing."

He spoke the last part quickly, as though anticipating she might cut him off before he finished.

"Yes," Jean said before she could change her mind. "I'd love to."

"Great," McWilliams said with a genuine, but still somewhat shy smile.

Jean sincerely hoped he was one of the good guys, because she'd met enough pretenders for one lifetime already.

Chapter 23

Deciding he couldn't wait any longer for his brother to make inquiries, Lancaster made a call to the appropriate county department to locate Michael Tanksley's most recent burial plot. He hadn't received a return call before Steve Parsons phoned him from Bloomington Hospital. The sheriff apologized for his earlier actions, and for not trusting in Lancaster's instincts earlier, but he refused to reveal any details. Parsons simply asked Lancaster to meet him at the hospital because he was under observation for concussion symptoms for an undetermined amount of time.

When he first laid eyes on the sheriff, Parsons looked almost completely helpless, wearing a hospital gown while lying atop a sturdy bed. He wore both an identification bracelet and a dismal expression when Lancaster walked into the room until their eyes met. Parsons provided a forced smile that indicated his disproval about staying any length of time in the hospital.

By this time Lancaster knew a few details from the radio news, but their reports were vague. He needed to hear it from the sheriff's mouth to believe what actually happened that morning.

"The media would get a kick out of this," Lancaster joked as he eyed the sheriff from head to toe, smirking all the while.

"They know better than to step in here," Parsons replied sternly. "I'm glad you came, Jeff. And, again, I'm very sorry I doubted you at all."

"Yeah, well, the ties between Michael Tanksley and my property seem to be growing in number."

"Forget about that," Parsons said. "That son-of-a-bitch attacked me in the middle of the highway."

Lancaster felt completely puzzled.

"Nichols?"

Parsons shook his head with an almost dismal shame.

"What I told the state police, and what I will tell the press is *not* what I'm about to tell you. You're the only one getting the entire, unedited truth."

Lancaster couldn't imagine why the sheriff would have to spin different versions of the prisoner transport gone wrong unless something embarrassed him.

The sheriff informed him of Nichols' confession and the events of the past twenty-four hours to prelude the morning's events. It required almost fifteen minutes for Parsons to relay the story of the car ride up to Bloomington because several times he backtracked to add details. Lancaster found most of the tale incredibly difficult to believe, but he knew Steve Parsons wasn't the type of man to dabble in anything that might alter his mindset. He was absolutely focused on getting Nichols tested to prove or disprove the man's guilt in at least one murder.

"What exactly did you tell the state police?" Lancaster asked, curious how the two tales varied.

"A variation where I implied that something hit me in the fog and this guy came out of nowhere to attack me. I implied he was probably on PCP or bath salts."

The sheriff took a deep breath, trying to settle his mind before continuing.

"This guy was scrawny, and practically falling apart, but he threw me like I was a ragdoll. There's no way he was a living human being, and Nichols was terrified the entire trip, like he knew something bad was going to happen."

"What you're suggesting sounds insane," Lancaster felt obligated to point out.

"You wouldn't think so if you'd heard Nichols screaming while he was being dragged away."

"Did they find him?"

"Nichols? They found what's left of him. Take a wild guess how he was killed."

"Something to do with a hatchet?"

Parsons gave a slow, affirmative nod, unable to look Lancaster in the eye.

"A few of the troopers told me he was missing some fingers. And his feet."

Raising an eyebrow in surprise, Lancaster couldn't help but search for a reasonable explanation to each part of the sheriff's story. Fog wasn't common in the area, and to have it blind drivers along Highway 37 didn't seem plausible. He also couldn't imagine Parsons struck a human being with his unmarked car and that person was unfazed enough to attack both him and Nichols. At least the victims certainly shared a connection if Nichols told the sheriff the truth during his confession.

But the elephant in the room continued to cross his mind, forcing him to revisit the issue that seemed by far the most unbelievable.

"Steve, you couldn't have shot him fifteen times," he said, shaking his head negatively. "Fifteen flesh wounds would still kill anyone out of eyesight of a hospital."

Parsons stared without blinking, using a very firm and level voice when he delivered his next words.

"I shot him fifteen times, not once in the legs, not once in the arms, and not once anywhere except his torso and his *fucking* head. Jeff, I can't even remember if that son-of-a-bitch flinched one time when he took a bullet because he just kept coming at me. It sounds crazy, I know, and I'm probably going to get crucified during the investigation, but I swear to God it's the truth."

Lancaster had overheard two of the officers from the scene stating there wasn't any blood near the unmarked car, but plenty of it close to Nichols' body. It didn't sound like the search party made good time finding the remains of Nichols, because the lack of blood and other evidence hindered their search.

"He came at me," Parsons said in a more haunted, distant voice this time, "but it wasn't *me* he was after. I was just something in his way that he didn't have time for."

If the perpetrator was capable of throwing a nearly two-hundred-seventy-pound sheriff across a car's hood, the man certainly could have planted a hatchet in Parsons' skull at will. So many logistical open ends ran through Lancaster's mind, like how someone could have known the sheriff would head that way, how the perpetrator arrived to that spot, how he rammed the sheriff's car without injury, and so much more. Lancaster literally felt his head begin to spin from all of the questions running through it.

"I want to watch your interrogation of Nichols," he finally said, deciding to start closer to the beginning. "When are they letting you out of here?"

"That's debatable," Parsons said, his usual gruff voice returning. "Stop by the office and get whatever you want. I'll call Miranda before you get there."

Lancaster nodded, knowing a few other pressing matters awaited him, including checking a grave site and running a theme park. He hated his sense of responsibility, but he also hated leaving open business unfinished.

He walked out of the room, nearly stopping in his tracks at the sight of a deputy seated across the hall on a waiting bench. Any other deputy wouldn't have bothered him, but Ronnie Qualls remained a thorn in his side, long after the man bedded Lancaster's ex-wife. Not only did he play politics with some certain sleazy individuals, but he tried cozying up to the sheriff whenever possible for perks on the job and in the political arena, which explained his presence in Bloomington.

Word was spreading that he planned to run for a county council seat during the next election to test the salt of his political merit in the public arena.

"Jeff," he said in a bland greeting, attempting to be cordial, despite a lingering coldness between them ever since the affair.

Refusing to even glance the man's way a second time, Lancaster marched down the hall, barely catching Qualls' smirk as the man stood to check in on Parsons. From what Lancaster heard, the sheriff barely acknowledged Qualls, and when the investigations assignment was given to Lancaster instead, it apparently rubbed the man the wrong way.

Just deserts, Lancaster thought all along, appreciating the sheriff and his moral compass.

Just deserts.

Chapter 24

Despite what he said to Parsons, Lancaster didn't feel comfortable entering his old workplace alone. It felt akin to selling a house because he didn't have keys to the front door, or a good reason for stepping foot on the property in the eyes of others. Besides, watching a video of Nichols confessing wasn't going to explain why the man was picked up in dozens of pieces, or how his assailant allegedly took fifteen rounds to the chest and head.

Allegedly in Lancaster's mind, because he still couldn't fathom any living thing absorbing that kind of firepower and surviving.

Choosing a different course of action, he discovered the grave site for Michael Tanksley. He decided to call upon his father, because David was preoccupied with casework and setting up his hunting camp. Wyatt Lancaster worked many odd jobs during his years of farming, one of which was digging graves for the city. Lancaster hoped his father might spot some clues around the grave based on his years of experience around cemeteries.

"I can't believe you dragged me out here for this," his father complained as they walked from the concrete path where Lancaster had parked.

Several such paths crossed through the cemetery, which started at the base of a hill where the older, mossy graves sat near the business district of Mitchell. From there the graves grew more recent until the hill leveled off, entering a newer portion where recent graves and unpurchased plots left a rather vacant field of grass.

"Part of being retired is helping out your kids," Lancaster said, trying to read the tombstones to locate Michael Tanksley's plot.

"I'm not *that* retired. Don't you have lackeys at work you can call for this stuff?"

"I do, but none of them ever dug graves for a living, and I have a feeling this might have been some of your handiwork."

His father grunted, pointing him in the right direction to save them both time.

They arrived at the plot a few seconds later, just barely down the hill and closer to the road where many deceased from the 1970s were buried. Tanksley's body hadn't been relocated very long after his initial burial, which made the plot a logical area in Lancaster's mind. He studied the ground around it momentarily, thinking it didn't seem quite as pristine as the manicured lawn around them.

"Something wrong?" his father asked.

"Doesn't the grass around the headstone look warped?"

"Warped?"

"Not level," Lancaster elaborated, dropping to one knee so he could pat the area, which he immediately found soft and spongy.

It took little more than a gentle push on the area to send some of the grass and dirt inside a recess, which swallowed most of Lancaster's arm before he knew it.

"What the hell?" he asked himself.

"Jeff, there are people pulling into the cemetery," his father said in a hushed, nervous voice, as though the dead might report them to the authorities for grave robbing.

"Well, maybe you should go distract them, Dad," Lancaster suggested, possessing little patience with his father because he felt certain the man was impeding his search.

Exhaling in a huff, Wyatt Lancaster circled the grave as his son widened the hole with a sweep of his right arm, discovering what appeared to be some form of tunnel from beneath the ground.

"What aren't you telling me, Dad?" Lancaster demanded when he studied his father's nervous behavior a moment.

Holding his hands at his waist, Wyatt appeared uneasy about something.

"I dug this grave all those years ago, son. No less than three times the city officials came to me and asked me what I did wrong because this grave was disturbed, like the ground had caved in."

"And you didn't think to tell me this before?"

Wyatt shrugged, exasperated and frustrated beyond words.

"It didn't *matter*, Jeff. That was years ago, and nothing ever came of it."

Lancaster pulled a chunk of soil from within the small tunnel, letting it filter through his fingers to the ground for his father to see.

"It seems to matter now. This little tunnel probably goes straight down to the coffin."

Determined to find out, Lancaster began digging around the edge of the hole, widening it for a better look.

"What are you doing?" his father barked in surprise.

"I need to know if Michael Tanksley is still down there."

"He was down there every other time," his father said, trying to reassure him. "We checked."

"That was years ago, Dad," Lancaster said, abandoning the hole and standing to make a point. "I need to know if he's down there right this second."

"Why?" his father almost pleaded with a tormented look, as though he knew no good would come out of this search either way.

Lancaster decided the truth, because it sounded crazy, wasn't a prudent answer for his father just yet.

"I just do."

Thinking better of the situation, considering residents he knew were driving by the cemetery on a regular basis, Lancaster decided to contact the police and have them examine the plot. If he reported an attempted grave robbery, skipping past certain details, they would have to examine the grave closely. With the tunnel already leading to the coffin, they might be able to skip over certain procedural delays and get to the casket. It wasn't as though they needed family permission to exhume the body because nothing so sacrilegious would ever take place. A simple popping of the lid would suffice to ascertain whether Michael Tanksley remained at eternal rest.

Or not.

As he pulled out his phone to make the call, his father stepped forward, inadvertently finding a second weak point in the plot. Before Lancaster comprehended the scene before him, his father instantly sank three feet into the ground, almost dead center where the casket was presumably lying beneath him.

"Get me out of here!" Wyatt barked fearfully the second his feet hit solid earth, now waist-deep in soil.

Lancaster grabbed his father by both arms, but the earth held his legs like quicksand, refusing to let him out of the awkward snare. Admittedly, he had never seen his father act this squeamish, as though something far more than standing in the cemetery and falling into a small tunnel bothered the man. Over the years his father remained a rock, whether putting his own father in a nursing home, or helping deliver a newborn calf. To see him this shaken left Lancaster a bit unnerved, even as he struggled to pull the larger man back to level ground.

"I'm stuck!" his father said, trying desperately to free his feet from the soil, but more kept falling downward, like a sinkhole devouring more surface material.

Lancaster finally gave a powerful tug with everything his arms could muster, which freed his father from the grave, dropping them both to the ground. Trying to catch his breath momentarily, he watched his father scurry away from the tombstone like a crab before regaining his footing and walking further away. He hadn't seen his father move so nimbly in years, and began wondering what had the older man so spooked.

Deciding to ignore the now gaping hole before Michael Tanksley's tombstone, Lancaster followed his father, who ambled down the hill, taking deep breaths to overcome the scare.

"Dad, what aren't you telling me?"

Instead of answering, his father glared momentarily, as though Lancaster had wronged him somehow simply by bringing him to this cemetery. He felt certain this trip had conjured up bad memories for his father, even if Wyatt Lancaster knew nothing about Michael Tanksley's murder. The entire town had tiptoed around the subject for years, as though speaking the truth might cost one his life.

"You need to stay away from this, Jeff," his father warned, still not answering the question.

"Why?" Lancaster demanded, uncharacteristically raising his voice to his father. "What is so frightening about this *fucking* case that we all have to treat it with kid gloves?"

Wyatt Lancaster looked to him, not with disappointment or anger, but rather helpless exasperation. His eyes looked misty behind the thick spectacles, and Lancaster truly wondered for the first time if his father might pose more of a problem than a solution regarding the larger mystery.

"Did you have anything to do with Michael Tanksley's death?" he asked his father pointblank, rather than ask a dozen more questions that simply led to the one he wanted answered.

"Of course not," Wyatt answered vehemently.

"Then why does all of this have you on edge? You acted like an alligator got hold of your foot at the grave."

"Because Tanksley was insane, son. He put a curse on this whole town, and that's why things began to fall apart."

"Fall apart?"

"You were too young to remember, but that circus, theme park, whatever you want to call it, never had a chance back then. Someone kept sabotaging those rides, and they said it was Tanksley. They imported some ride from overseas and it sank to the bottom of a lake. Tanksley. That lawyer who died in that mysterious car wreck all those years ago. You know, the one that represented the group that owned your land. Tanksley."

Lancaster couldn't believe his ears. One of the most rational men he'd ever known was claiming that a ghost was behind numerous murders and acts of vandalism.

"Dad, you've never been superstitious before. Why on earth would you believe Tanksley could be responsible for any of this when he was killed over forty years ago?"

"You weren't there," Wyatt Lancaster said, obviously shaken by the memory. "That son-of-a-bitch came into the local diner one night and predicted his own murder. He stared each and every one of us in the eye and said we were responsible because the people who wanted his land were going to kill him for it, and we'd done nothing to stop it. His eyes were cold and dark, even for him, and his voice wasn't right, like someone, or something, was talking through him. We all thought he was talking crazy like usual, but he said he'd found a way to come back from the dead and make things right. He said he would never rest until everyone responsible had their own graves in the town cemetery."

"And you believed this?"

"Not at the time, but after his murder, this town was shaken to its core. It wasn't until they bought his land and things started going wrong that we began noticing his predictions coming true."

"Well, of course," Lancaster stated as though the obvious answer should have already struck his father. "Someone who heard one of his rants decided to carry through with the man's promises. He wouldn't have been the only town crazy, Dad."

"And that same person came here and desecrated that grave?" his father asked testily, throwing his arm upward to point toward the grave. "That tunnel has shown up several times, son, and not *once* has it been dug inward."

Lancaster felt his blood boiling. He couldn't believe his own father had hindered his investigation by not telling him about the plot's history, followed by an insane tale about Tanksley swearing revenge before he even died.

"Let's put this to rest right now," he said as he angrily stomped toward the chaotic mess that was Michael Tanksley's plot.

"What are you doing?" Wyatt questioned with a hint of fear, as though the wrong move might add both of them to the dead man's list of those who'd wronged him.

"I'm going to have a look at the motherfucker," Lancaster said, dropping to his knees at the already partially unearthed plot. "Let them arrest me if they want to, but I'm putting this ghost story behind me. All of you townsfolk are driving me crazy with your lack of cooperation and ghost stories."

His father started to utter a protest, but the words never formed more than a grunt as Wyatt Lancaster started to walk away from a deep, primitive fear. Curiosity, however, brought him back as his son dug like a badger at the dirt, throwing more and more of the loose soil atop the grass, complete with earthworms and old, withered chunks of grass.

Considering David worked as a lawyer, neither man truly feared arrest, particularly since Lancaster was working with the sheriff on solving murders directly tied to the Tanksley slaying.

Following the existing tunnel made the dig easy for Lancaster, and all of the dirt felt loose in his hands, as though recently sifted. It certainly didn't feel hard and compacted like one might expect from a gravesite undisturbed for decades.

It required only a few minutes for Lancaster to reach the head of the casket, which he discovered had a gaping hole in it where dirt had consequently filled the inside. He pawed at the dirt, throwing more on the hill behind him as he stood in the narrow six-foot-deep portion of the grave. He discovered much of the upper portion of the casket was already torn apart, and as he removed enough dirt for a closer examination, his mouth fell open. Fully aware of his father's pacing around the plot above him, Lancaster detected the movements stopping as both men stared into the partially unearthed coffin.

A coffin that held no body inside.

"Shit," Lancaster muttered, wondering if the town's hokey superstition might actually hold some merit.

Chapter 25

"Do you two have any idea what kind of trouble you could be in?" David Lancaster asked his father and brother inside the conference room at the theme park. "Desecrating a grave in broad daylight doesn't exactly make either of you pillars of the community, especially if you're looking for good press."

The last part of the lawyer's statement was directed at his brother, who didn't particularly want to hear a lecture about actions he wasn't likely to suffer any consequences for carrying out. What made him more upset with his family members was the fact they had kept secrets about the town and his theme park from him, allowing him to buy into a curse. Even if Michael Tanksley wasn't back from the dead avenging his own murder, the stigma kept locals from fully supporting his endeavor, which filled in some of the blanks for him.

"I tried telling him," Wyatt said to his older son. "It's finally coming for revenge."

"I know," David replied. "God knows I tried talking him out of buying that property."

Lancaster felt his blood begin to boil.

"Why do I feel like everyone knows this backstory except for me?" he demanded. "The two of you are trying to paint me into a corner when it's your fault for not telling me everything."

"Would you have believed us?" his father asked.

Lancaster supposed not, but he still felt betrayed. It wasn't as though Lancaster left town for years and suddenly returned, which meant his father confided in his brother with tales of the past, but not him.

"David, why did you buy into this?" he asked instead. "You're a lawyer, and your kind are usually pretty practical."

"Dad showed me evidence through the years of news articles. I started to realize it couldn't all be a coincidence."

Dropping his face into one hand, Lancaster couldn't look at either one of them. He still felt like important information was missing because the timeline of unusual events held a gaping hole between possible paranormal activity and the recent murders. *If* Michael Tanksley was hell bent on revenge, why would he, or his spirit, wait so long and risk his adversaries dying of natural causes?

Apparently one already had.

"Who else knows about all of this?" he asked, still frustrated by his own family.

"Just the people who witnessed events like I did," Wyatt answered. "And anyone they've told over the years. I think most of us kept it to ourselves, not wanting to admit they were real."

"Why did no one solve Tanksley's murder? Did anyone even try?"

"It's a small town, Jeff. No one dared go against the powers that be, especially with no evidence to support such claims."

"You both fared just fine keeping the town's deep, dark secrets."

"That's not fair," David said adamantly. "Neither of us had the power to bring the story to light, and you didn't exactly break the cold case as a detective."

Their father stepped between them, holding up his large hands.

"Stop," he said calmly. "Bickering isn't going to get us anywhere. We're damn lucky the sheriff intervened and got us out of any hot water."

Lancaster felt fortunate the sheriff answered his phone and insisted his deputies and the Mitchell officers not charge Lancaster or his father because he wanted to talk to them first. With some political finagling Parsons was able to arrange for the grave to be restored and no one to suffer any punishment, despite witnesses filing complaints.

"If what you're telling me is true," Lancaster began, "and Michael Tanksley isn't in that grave because he's out murdering those who wronged him, we need to figure out how to stop him and how he returned from the dead."

"You've got to let nature take its course, Jeff," his father advised.

"It's not in *my* nature, Dad. I can't risk this spilling over and hurting innocent people. Steve Parsons almost got killed this morning just trying to carry out his duties. Hell, I owe it to him to find out who attacked him and killed his suspect."

He knew his family wasn't going to abandon him, but he also knew his father and brother didn't possess the skill set to assist him in such a search. Lancaster didn't personally know anyone who might help him investigate the paranormal aspect of the case. Following the original trail was his best bet, but unfortunately that meant talking to the dead man's last living relative, and their first meeting hadn't gone especially well.

Lancaster had only himself to blame and knew it. His line of questioning set Colby McWilliams against him, and for the life of him, Lancaster still wasn't certain why he pressed the man so hard. Perhaps his earlier lack of suspects prompted him to lash out at McWilliams, and he wasn't convinced the man was completely innocent, but he needed to hash out an apology of sorts before speaking to the man a second time.

"Jeff, I really don't like the idea of you pursuing the truth in these murders," his father stated with grave concern in his eyes. "It's not going to end well for any of these people who brought harm to Tanksley."

"If what you say is true, Dad, I'm no better off holing up here at the theme park. There has to be a reason why decades passed before whoever this is decided to start bumping off senior citizens. Maybe someone found a ledger and used the Michael Tanksley murder as a convenient excuse."

"Why would someone else kill these people?" David questioned. "There's no motive, and you've said it yourself, Tanksley only had one family member in the world."

"Only one that we know about," Lancaster answered. "There are still a lot more questions than answers in this mess, and I intend to uncover the truth."

"Just be careful," Wyatt almost pleaded. "Don't let the mistakes of others get you hurt."

"I will, Dad. The only thing I ask is that you two don't keep any more secrets from me about all of this."

Both of them nodded in understanding.

"If you have questions, I'll do my best to answer them," his father vowed.

"I'm glad, because something tells me this isn't anywhere close to over."

***

Danny Schall wasn't exactly certain why his talents were being wasted following one employee around the theme park. His job grew increasingly difficult because Hank Barwick wasn't supposed to know he was being tailed. Although the mechanic never confronted Schall, it seemed he knew his movements were being watched whenever he came to work. Even if Barwick asked why he was being followed, Schall couldn't readily provide an answer. He believed Lancaster wanted the man protected more than anything else, but a definitive reason was never given.

Today the maintenance chief was working on the mine coaster, which contained four tunnels built from wooden planks on their exteriors. The last of the tunnels carried the roller coaster train upward on a chain lift toward the ride's end. The inside of the tunnel, however, provided lots of scenery for the riders as painted tribesmen shook their mechanical arms at the riders while an ominous voice warned that they were trespassing on sacred grounds. Haunting music played the entire time the voice echoed through the tunnel. It was a play on mining prospectors being attacked by Native Americans a few centuries earlier. All of the Native Americans were adorned with faded war paint, little more than large torso busts set atop pedestals. At the peak of the interior lift hill was a sculpted chief with glowing red eyes that held his hands ominously in the air to strike fear into first-time riders.

At the moment none of these chilling effects were in action, leaving only the creaking of the wood from passing breezes to fill the tunnel.

Barwick worked inside this particular hill, attempting to repair a few of the busts with immobile or slowed arm movements. He had already locked out the loading station to ensure no trains came through, and there was no reason for the power to be on because the park was closed to the public.

After flipping on the work lights, which consisted of six regular bulbs on each side of the tracks, Barwick trudged up the wooden stairs toward the first figure in need of repair. Only a wooden door along the side provided additional light, so Barwick left it open. He never looked back to spy the head of security keeping vigil at the bottom of the hill at a curve alongside the track just before it began its ascent.

Schall knew when he accepted his position that the job wasn't going to be glamorous or high-paying, but he figured it might provide a solid stepping stone if he hated the job. He knew it was a business built from the ground up, and anticipated several issues, but he never expected to be a glorified babysitter for fellow employees. He liked Lancaster well enough, but his boss wasn't forthcoming with information, which Schall would have appreciated from a fellow former cop.

Indiana provided a quieter pace for him after working in Kansas City and visiting St. Louis often. In Missouri distractions seemed abundant, from sporting events to live shows and theme parks.

Established theme parks.

His son and daughter were both attending college in their home state, and he hoped to avoid paying out-of-state tuition the following semester due to his new address. Both were on partial scholarships, and moving them to Indiana schools wasn't going to prove much more economical in the short-term. He had fathered both of them at a young age, but working as a cop matured him quickly, so Schall never felt as though he'd missed out on too much of life's freedom. He always found time to hit the bars with his buddies, or play softball and golf with his department teams. By no means an absentee father, he often watched the kids to give his wife date nights with her friends, or they made their own dates by hiring babysitters in those early years.

One didn't survive twenty-five years of marriage without making numerous concessions.

Finding a solid wooden shelf that housed several props, including a plaster, male Native American holding a spear, Schall took a seat after testing his weight on it. He heard occasional clanking, drilling, and hammering sounds from the tunnel as Barwick set to work, though he kept his eyes on his surroundings.

Most of the grounds beneath and around the ride consisted of mowed grass with occasional shrubs and trees to break up the landscape. Vines grew along some of the overhead planks and their supports during a few of the headchopper areas. Headchoppers are design elements used in roller coasters to give riders the sensation that their head or arms might be struck by the upcoming bar.

Wearing a full suit, Schall didn't feel particularly comfortable because the midafternoon sun left the area warm and muggy. He adjusted the necktie that felt like a constricting snake around his neck as sweat trickled into his white shirt and down the small of his back. When he stood from the shelf a few minutes later to stretch his legs, Schall turned and startled himself when the realistic Native American statue pointed its spear directly at him. He jumped back, taking a deep breath when he realized the prop almost made him reach for his sidearm. Exhaling a sigh, he heard the wooden door from halfway up the tunnel creak and realized he needed to check on Barwick.

Schall initially thought to look around the corner toward the door's exterior side to see if Barwick was stepping outside, but some noises from inside quickly drew his attention. A few random clanks, followed by Barwick crying out in pain, quickened the security director's pace. Schall didn't particularly care if he gave away his position at this point because Barwick's safety was his primary concern.

As he rounded the corner, Schall froze momentarily as he witnessed Barwick being attacked by a man with long, black hair. The attacker had his back to the former cop, but Schall noticed a bloody wound along Barwick's lower back as though the man had been taken by surprise. Weakened by the wound, Barwick had retreated further up the stairs beside the roller coaster tracks, almost to the top. Schall started up the stairway, still unable to see the attacker very well because the man's back was to him.

Grasped in the attacker's right hand was a rather large knife that appeared modern military in make. Blood covered at least one quarter of the blade, and it glistened as light from one of the bulbs struck it. Rather than take a second stab to the back with his slowing pace, Barwick turned to grapple the killer for the weapon. Despite a distinct size advantage, Barwick wasn't nearly as quick, and the blood loss had already sapped his strength.

The attacker struck him in the face before running the knife across the palm of his hand, ensuring he couldn't grab for it again.

"Stop!" Schall shouted as he reached for his Glock, buying time for Barwick to begin a second retreat up the stairs after their eyes met for a split-second.

Never did Schall expect to pull his firearm inside the theme park for a fellow employee being attacked, but Lancaster's fears had just materialized.

Instead of stopping, the attacker, dressed in some form of tattered Native American garb, barely paid the security director any mind with barely a glance over his shoulder. He pursued a now slumping Barwick whose breathing came in heaves as he used the wall to steady his unstable walk up the stairs. Schall pulled the gun from its holster, but didn't dare fire for fear of striking Barwick with a stray round. He could only watch helplessly as the attacker ignored his command completely, spun Barwick around, and launched the knife into the man's stomach within a matter of two seconds.

Doomed the moment the blade pierced his internal organs, Barwick's eyes widened momentarily as blood spurted from his mouth. His eyes then rolled backwards before his body began to fall limp from his injuries.

"No!" Schall screamed, raising his firearm as Barwick slumped to the ground, firing two rounds that missed as the murderer dashed through the opening atop the hill that led back to the station.

Although he knew Barwick was dead, or would be within minutes, Schall ran up the stairs to the man's side. He wanted to chase down the killer and shoot him dead, but the man could choose any direction to run and hide once he cleared the last of the tracks. Schall couldn't even radio for assistance because he was currently the only security member working at the park during the off-day. Dropping to his knees beside Barwick's side, the security director set down the Glock before pulling out his cell phone to dial 911 for assistance.

"Hank," he said, clasping the man's bloody right hand as the phone rang. "Stay with me."

A hardened veteran of medical calls and death scenes, Schall knew no one could save Barwick, but he hoped to get police on scene to catch the man responsible.

Clinging to his last few, precious breaths of life, Barwick used his other hand to clutch Schall's sport coat, trying in vain to speak. Schall wondered what the man had to say, knowing he would be Barwick's only way of communicating any messages to loved ones after the man passed. As the man's grip loosened, falling away as his heart pumped its last few beats, Schall realized too late that Barwick wanted to warn him of impending danger.

As the 911 operator answered, inquiring about the nature of Schall's emergency, he heard the sound of a footstep behind him. Suspecting his worst fear, he swiftly reached for the Glock, but a thin rope of some sort draped around his neck, pulling upward before he gained a full grip on the weapon. He immediately felt his oxygen supply cut off, left with the choice of reaching for the now distanced gun or attempting to free himself from strangulation. Uncertain of where the killer's knife was located, and why the man hadn't used it in the first place, Schall decided to take immediate action.

Getting his feet beneath him, the security director launched the combined weight of his body and that of the killer into the wall directly behind them, drawing a grunt from his assailant. His action loosened the tension on the rope just long enough for Schall to gasp in a life-saving breath. In quick desperation the attacker attempted to regain his grip on the cord, but Schall pulled it away from his neck, feeling the rope slide through the killer's palm, burning it with friction.

A louder, more frustrated yelp came from the assailant as he regained at least a partial grip on the cord. Schall rammed the killer's back once more with force, but the man refused to release his grip on the rope a second time, actually using the momentum from Schall's movements to take them both to the ground.

Refusing to remain in such a precarious position, Schall immediately pulled himself up with the intent of ramming the killer once more, or turning to confront him head on. Immediately after reaching a standing position, Schall felt a hand on his right shoulder push downward while a foot in the back of his knee on the same side sent him crashing to the ground. The killer ensured he wasn't going anywhere this time by placing a knee squarely in the security director's back, leaving him pinned to the ground like an insect on an entomologist's wall. With his strength and size advantage nullified, Schall felt the noose tighten as he grasped with his fingers to gain another precious breath.

He croaked for air as his fingers loosened the rope just long enough for him to suck in another breath. The sound of footsteps thumped in the distance as Schall began seeing stars from a lack of oxygen to the brain. He continued struggling to pull the rope from his throat, but he couldn't even feel his fingers to tell if they were responding to his wishes. On the verge of passing out, where certain death would follow if the killer kept pressure on the rope a minute longer, Schall suddenly felt sweet release as the rope fell slack. His head struck the wood of the stairs as he drew a desperate, long breath. The killer's footsteps headed out the exit tunnel once more as the noise of several people entering through the bottom of the lift hill reached Schall's ears.

His right hand fumbled for the Glock, but he knew he wasn't going to personally catch the killer in his condition. The sound of the operator's voice from his phone reached his ears, but Schall felt like a complete failure because Barwick died on his watch. Even if the killer was caught nothing could bring the man back.

Wrapping his fingers around the firearm, Schall felt hands and arms helping him to his knees as a few other employees rushed to Barwick's side, quickly realizing he was beyond their assistance. Knowing he didn't have time to explain this situation to everyone surrounding him, thankful as he was for their timely arrival, Schall holstered his firearm and scooped up the phone. He took charge of the scene, throwing aside any self-pity once he began conversing with the dispatcher, requesting an ambulance and police assistance to the theme park.

Rubbing the raw skin along his throat, Schall took the time to order the park employees to stay close so no one played hero and chased after the killer. They all listened to his discussion with the dispatcher, quickly understanding the horrific events that claimed Barwick's life. Although he put on a strong front for the employees around him, Schall internally dreaded informing his boss about Barwick's death. He didn't want to leave that to the police, because he felt responsible, and Lancaster already had plenty to worry about.

Schall didn't want to think about the public relations nightmare about to strike the park, because he wanted to find the man responsible for murdering Barwick. If locating that man assisted Lancaster's investigation he considered that a bonus, but either way he wanted to see the responsible party caught. He fingered the fresh gouge along his neck just in case he needed further inspiration, knowing how close he came to joining Barwick.

Chapter 26

Lancaster felt sweat dripping down his neck, into his clean shirt when he approached the crime scene within his own park. Making the situation worse, he saw three marked police cars from his old department, and what he assumed was Steve Parsons' unmarked vehicle. Genuinely glad, but somewhat surprised that the sheriff was cleared for duty and able to personally attend crime scenes, Lancaster didn't want to see the man under such dire circumstances.

The afternoon sun brought about muggy air, but the idea of losing an employee, a man he respected, left him sick to his stomach. He only wished he had trusted Barwick more, even protected the man personally perhaps. Although Lancaster didn't want to believe the maintenance man's death had anything to do with the other three murders, he knew it couldn't be coincidence. It seemed someone wanted the man dead for the sins of his father, and Lancaster wanted to find that person. Even if the killer turned out to be some vengeful, undead version of Michael Tanksley, Lancaster needed to find him and stop him, even it meant burying the man in a concrete tomb or burning him to a crisp.

Drawing closer to the last tunnel of his roller coaster, Lancaster saw a deputy standing outside with a clipboard. Off to one side he saw another deputy and Parsons speaking with Schall, who appeared visibly upset about the entire situation. Lancaster had his own questions for his security director, but those could wait until the murder investigation moved forward.

Knowing everyone at the scene helped Lancaster move past the deputies without incident until he drew near the sheriff. Parsons barely gave him a glance as he continued interviewing Schall, and the glance wasn't particularly friendly.

Once again Lancaster found himself on the wrong end of the murder investigation. While he thought investigating the murders was inconvenient and distracting, being a focus due to numerous happenstances felt even worse.

Standing by, Lancaster listened to the narrative Schall provided, growing less upset with the man with each passing second because he realized his security chief barely survived the incident. Any doubts he harbored about the man's watchful eye or bravery were quickly dispelled when Schall recalled witnessing the murder and how the killer actually came back with the intent of murdering him.

At that point Lancaster's eyes met those of the sheriff because both men shared a thought.

"So you didn't chase after him?" Parsons asked for verification.

"Like I said, I took two shots at him and decided to dial 911 before pursuing him."

Lancaster knew the killer made every effort to avoid Parsons when he stalked Nichols, even though the sheriff could have potentially called for help any second so far as the killer knew. Yet instead of making a quick, clean getaway, the killer tried to strangle Schall after stabbing Barwick through the guts.

Compared to the first three murders, the motive and methods seemed a bit off, as though the killer was rushed. Maybe the location prevented the killer from carrying out his intended plan, but he didn't necessarily have to hunt Barwick at the man's workplace. Lancaster wished he hadn't for a number of reasons, but more importantly, he wished no harm had come to his maintenance chief.

Considering Barwick's size and strength, Lancaster had little doubt the same man who overpowered the sheriff murdered Barwick.

"Did you smell anything strange when the killer got near you?" Parsons asked, drawing raised eyebrows from both Lancaster and Schall.

"The man had a cord around my neck," Schall gave a deadpan reply.

"You would have smelled this without question. An overpowering odor like death."

"No."

Schall appeared to distance himself from the interview temporarily by turning away and strolling a few steps, but Lancaster caught the look of discontent from the sheriff. He knew Parsons detected a pungent odor from the assailant who murdered Nichols, but any number of reasons explained why Schall didn't experience the same phenomena.

"Can I have a minute with him?" he asked the sheriff, who nodded a slow affirmative.

Knowing full well Schall was every bit the hardened veteran police officer he was, Lancaster hadn't come within seconds of dying at any point in his life. He didn't know if Schall needed consolation, but he suspected the man needed a break from incessant questioning to collect his thoughts. For his part, Lancaster felt guilty because he didn't trust completely in Barwick, the man died on his property, and Schall nearly died after risking life and limb to intervene.

Lancaster was about to speak with his employee when Parsons walked hurriedly with a purpose in their direction as though he needed to say or ask something before he forgot it.

"Was there any kind of fog in the area when you were attacked?"

Schall appeared even more confused this time, and even looked to Lancaster as though to ask if the sheriff was in his right frame of mind. Lancaster nodded, indicating he wanted his head of security to answer the question, crazy as it might sound.

"No," Schall answered somewhat testily. "The weather was exactly the same as it is now."

Parsons exhaled heavily through his nose before turning around and returning to his original spot.

"Why the *fuck* haven't you told me about all of this?" Schall demanded under his breath once left alone with his employer.

"You wouldn't believe me if I told you."

"Try me. After nearly meeting my maker I'm pretty much open to anything."

Lancaster felt he owed the man some form of explanation for putting his life in harm's way, but he didn't feel very informed himself.

"Look, I'll tell you everything I know later," he promised Schall. "Right now I just want to give you a break from the questions and make sure you're okay."

"I'm fine," Schall answered, though clearly he wasn't from the droplets of sweat running down his face and a nervous shaking of his hands that indicated he wasn't far enough removed from the situation yet. "I just wish I'd gotten a bigger piece of that bastard."

"You were doing what any of us would've done. I don't blame you for putting the safety of others over chasing that prick."

"But I shouldn't have let him get the jump on me."

Lancaster didn't have any consolation for that statement. It didn't sound like a usual tactic for the killer to worry about anyone other than his intended victims, but the man seemed full of surprises. With only a few potential victims left, Lancaster could predict with fifty percent accuracy where Tanksley, or whoever the killer was, would strike. Ralph Nichols and Hank Barwick were two victims no one really thought about, for different reasons, but the former detective felt obligated to stop the killer after he spilled blood at the theme park.

The way Schall had described the killer's attire didn't entirely match what Parsons said at the hospital. Lancaster thought it extremely odd that *if* Tanksley was the killer he would have a change of wardrobe, or care about it as an undead killing machine with a single purpose. While the man may have possessed a fascination about Native Americans during his life, he was likely buried in a customized suit from the mortuary like everyone else.

God forbid more than one person was active in the murders, he thought. If that were the case, he would place a lot less faith in the theory that Michael Tanksley had returned from the dead. Even if his father and brother were spooked by the local legends, Lancaster found very little validity in them. He felt hot and cold about the subject from one minute to the next, finding evidence that supported either side of the debate. Realistically, however, he felt deep down the possibility of resurrection years after the fact was absolutely impossible.

He felt utterly confused on the subject, particularly since he hadn't personally laid eyes upon this enigma. His mind flashed back to the mysterious ascent on Sidewinder with Barwick where he spotted someone on the ground from almost two-hundred feet above. People looked like ants from that height, so he couldn't recall details, but he remembered that person staring directly at him for what felt like an uncomfortable amount of time.

"You okay, boss?" Schall asked, breaking his trance.

"Yeah. Sorry, Danny."

"Look, I'm going to talk to the sheriff, even though he's weirding me out."

"He just went through something similar to your attack, Danny. He's just trying to compare notes is all."

Schall gave a moody sigh.

"He could've said something."

"He probably didn't want to taint your statement. I know this is a pain in the ass, but maybe I can get him to let someone else take your statement if you're willing to compare notes with him afterwards."

Schall reluctantly nodded.

"If you think it'll help."

"It will. And I'll even sit in. We can't let this guy murder anyone else. Hank didn't deserve this."

Lancaster glanced toward the lower part of the enclosed lift hill where police officers stood watch while the coroner's representatives walked into the entrance to examine the crime scene.

"I'll be back," he said before walking over to the sheriff.

Parsons appeared distraught, at a loss even, for a way to end the madness that encompassed his county over the past week.

"You need to let one of your detectives interview him, Steve."

"I know," Parsons acknowledged, hanging his head as though admitting a fault. "Jeff, I just want to find out how to stop this son-of-a-bitch. Fifteen bullets couldn't put him down, so I'll take any scrap of information I can right now."

"Danny said he'd compare notes with you, but you can't ask him that sort of stuff on the official record. For his sake, and yours, you need to keep your distance from him as a lawman."

Parsons gave a nod, and Lancaster walked away, unable to keep stealing glances at the entrance to the last lift hill.

Helping with the investigation temporarily kept Lancaster from dealing with his own problems, but he still felt immense guilt about Barwick. As both a former deputy and businessman, he considered employees to be part of his extended family. He hired many of them himself, and he wanted them on the ground floor of the theme park, sharing his pride as the business grew.

He felt incredibly helpless at the moment, almost completely vulnerable, because he didn't know where to go next with his dream. People expected the theme park open on Friday, but he wasn't about to put the lives of his employees or park guests at risk.

Schall approached him with a concerned expression.

"Boss, do you want me to tell them you were having me keep an eye on Hank the past few days?"

"Telling them that might make both of us look bad for a few different reasons, Danny. I'd never ask you to lie, but bringing that up will definitely raise some red flags. Personally, I want to find out who did this instead of answering a lot more questions."

"So I'll take that as a no."

"Again, do whatever you feel is right. I'm not going to hold it against you."

He couldn't read Schall's thoughts, but he figured the man feared losing his position if he spoke. Schall looked a bit uncertain as he turned to speak with the authorities, and Lancaster truly didn't care if he told them about monitoring Barwick. Whether Schall kept watch over the maintenance man or not, someone would have killed him and revealing this fact to the sheriff's department only served to have detectives looking at them more closely, rather than searching for Barwick's sadistic killer.

Knowing at least some of Barwick's family remained in the Lawrence County area, Lancaster decided to open the man's personnel file and assist the police with the death notification. He suspected some of the family might hold the man's death against him, and Lancaster really couldn't blame them. If he were on the outside looking in, he might believe the owner of a new, multi-million dollar theme park could have done more to make his investment a safe environment.

After alienating himself from his own family he felt completely alone in the world with a choice.

He could either sulk and watch his life and business suffer, or he could carry out one final task with his former employer and bring a killer to justice. After retrieving the file he planned on getting a stiff drink and taking the night to ponder his immediate future.

Chapter 27

Colby McWilliams put in a full day of work in his garage, taking a minimal break for dinner, which he cooked himself before returning to work on a 1971 Dodge Challenger. A calico mixture of red, black, and primer, the car needed some body work, but at the moment he focused on the motor, rebuilding it completely after tearing it down and finding most of the new parts in local junkyards. Some local business owner who had a good year decided he wanted a car that looked just like his first vehicle in high school, only slightly upgraded.

Around ten o'clock he wiped the grease from his hands with a rag for the last time that evening, shut off the lights, and walked from the garage to his house. Without the porch light turned on, only an overhead light from the garage lit his way across the driveway and the concrete walkway in front of his porch. Yawning as he stepped up on the porch and opened the unlocked front door, McWilliams let the yellow Lab follow him inside where the smell of his dinner still hung in the air.

After his bizarre week he wanted little more than to collapse into bed, but his plans for the following day continued to distract him. For the first time in a long time he was going on a date, informal as it might actually be. He didn't want to wear anything with grease smudges or mud on it, so he headed straight to his bedroom to peruse his closet for respectable clothing. He felt like a high school kid again, trying to pick just the right thing to wear. McWilliams wanted to show he owned more than work clothes and an old suit, but he didn't want to appear too formal either.

After all, this was supposed to be a friendly ride to Nashville, not an actual date.

Rifling through shirts inside his closet, McWilliams tried to find something contemporary that didn't give the wrong impression. He avoided his loud western shirts left over from his line dancing days, setting aside a few earth-colored shirts with minimal or no stripes. He kept telling himself Jean Garrison likely wanted nothing to do with him. Culturally, they came from two different worlds, and from all appearances they didn't have much in common. She remained successful in every facet of her life, and in contrast he had squandered enough of his family legacy that he still worked for a living. Truth be told, he rather enjoyed working with his hands, but wished he made more time for friends like he had in the past.

As he sorted through his blue jeans and pants for the best possible option, his mind wandered to holidays. Often lonely times because none of his family remained, Thanksgiving and Christmas always left him feeling empty. McWilliams was blessed with acquaintances who invited him over for the holidays, but he never felt truly at home with them. In his younger days he considered settling down and raising a family, but time slipped away and he found himself constantly working.

When it came to business he was known as respectable and professional, but his personal life felt like a wreck. Perhaps it stemmed from his parents dying unexpectedly, leaving him alone to face a cruel world, but McWilliams never found a lifestyle that suited him. His childhood friends moved away and he simply fell into the routine left to him from his childhood and teenage years.

The only things he knew that remained familiar.

He pulled a pair of brown cowboy boots from his closet that looked barely worn, and immediately questioned if he should wear dress shoes and khakis instead.

"You're picking up car parts, stupid," he chastised himself aloud, "not going to a business convention."

Because his mind refused to quit spinning, McWilliams decided to take a shower to calm down and relax before focusing on his morning plans. He stripped down before walking into the bathroom to spend the next twenty minutes cleaning the grit and grime from his hands and face. By the time he finished showering the water heater was audibly straining to heat the influx of well water filling its tank. After spending the night in the garage during the damp, cool conditions, McWilliams felt refreshed after the hot shower as he toweled off his face and chest.

He emerged from the bathroom, deciding to put on sweatpants and an old, faded shirt since he was in for the evening. Thoughts of what to wear the next morning suddenly didn't feel as important as he stared into his closet. Already convinced that Lancaster painted a bleak picture of him to Jean, he decided to try being himself in the morning, but felt certain he wasn't going to sleep well. The idea of companionship took him back to a time when high school friends and people he considered family were an essential part of his life.

Ignoring the laid out clothes for the time being, he sauntered out to the kitchen to grab a beer from his refrigerator. Considering he didn't plan to work in the morning, and the trip to Nashville wouldn't require him to be up too early, he figured one beer wouldn't cause any harm. After removing a Michelob from the fridge he twisted the cap and immediately enjoyed a lengthy swallow.

"Ah, the benefits of bein' self-employed," he said, toasting his own statement by raising the beer bottle for another swig.

When he rounded the corner of the kitchen, planning to watch some television to further calm his mind, he noticed something rather odd forming within his living room.

Seeing what looked like smoke swirling from the base of the front door and occupying his residence, McWilliams dropped the beer bottle and stared in awe momentarily. He quickly collected his wits and wondered if he still owned a functioning fire extinguisher, frantically searching for something useful to combat a fire through cabinets and underneath the sink. On the verge of ransacking the storage area under his sink for a bucket, McWilliams reconsidered what he spied in his living room, realizing he never felt heat or saw flames. With his heart already racing, and his breaths coming in heaves, he felt numb to the point that his mind wasn't necessarily occupying his body as he dared peer around the corner a second time.

He hadn't even gained a good vantage point before a discolored hand pierced the foggy substance, clutching him by the throat. His assailant appeared as a vague outline through the substance McWilliams now understood was not smoke. Feeling the fingers reposition for a better grip on his thick neck, McWilliams wriggled away from the danger, instinctively pushing his attacker into the fog from which he came. Considering the front door was inaccessible, he immediately stumbled down the hall with hopes of finding an alternate escape route.

Passing a bathroom and a guest bedroom on the way to a sunken family room at the end of the hall, McWilliams couldn't tell if he was being pursued or not. Feeling certain he would collapse from fear if he stopped for less than a second, he rounded the corner and darted into the large family room that now served as a man cave for him with a big screen television, a pinball machine, a pool table, and surround sound speakers that would be heard throughout the house if not for the noise dampening walls and ceiling within the room.

His adoptive father built the large house, along with the barn, before McWilliams ever came to live with the family. Even after Henry died he bounced around from job to job, but made time to help Lilly keep up the large house, even staying there occasionally because she never touched his room or made him feel unwelcome. Everything the couple owned transferred to McWilliams when they both passed, and he always considered the property his primary home growing up because his parents died so early in his childhood.

Nearly falling down the three stairs that descended into the family room, McWilliams glanced to the backdoor across the room that led to freedom. A cool, ceramic tile floor greeted his sock-covered feet as he nearly slipped and fell. Recovering quickly by sticking out his arms like a tightrope walker, he darted as best he could across the large room, instinctively feeling danger drawing nearer.

A few wooden chairs rested near the exit, so he threw them behind him to delay whatever presence invaded the sanctity of his home to attack him. Without taking the time to look back, McWilliams reached for the doorknob as a powerful hand clasped his shoulder, ripping him away from potential safety. Not only was he yanked away from the great outdoors beyond the door, but the hand clasped him by the collar and threw him across the room toward the stairs he had just descended.

Before he even contemplated reacting, McWilliams saw his assailant dart across the room in a flash. He instinctively threw up his hands to protect himself, but the intruder grasped him by the collar once more, tugging him up the stairs toward an unspecified destination. He reached up to free himself from the powerful grasp, but McWilliams felt a cold, dry hand almost waxy in texture with an unrelenting grip. Unable to scream, he simply uttered frightened groans of protest, trying to release the hold on his shirt, or tear the cloth to free himself. At this point McWilliams might as well have been a mouse in the talons of an experienced falcon regarding his chances of escape.

He felt the stairs bump his tailbone before the familiar walls of the hallway revealed themselves on either side of him. For some reason this trespasser wanted to reach some destination with him, but McWilliams felt certain he was destined to die at the hands of this person as he kicked, scratched, and tugged to no avail.

He knew calling out for help was no help considering his closest neighbor resided half a mile away. No phones, weapons, or makeshift weapons presented themselves as he was dragged down the hallway and through his living room where the fog continued to linger at nearly the same thickness. There was no breaking the powerful grip from his collar, and even as McWilliams dug his fingers into the hands of his assailant he felt certain this person felt no pain whatsoever.

McWilliams watched several rooms pass by until they reached the room beyond the kitchen, separated from the house by a closed door. It once acted as his surrogate father's office, and Lilly never made an effort to alter it. She said there was plenty of house for them to live in without converting the office, and besides, every document from clients and cases was locked in that room. McWilliams agreed, and followed her lead, leaving the lawyer's collection undisturbed for years in case any former client returned for information.

Now the attacker kicked in the door with ease, rather than simply turning the unlocked knob, as though for effect to further intimidate his captive. The air inside the room immediately felt cold to McWilliams, and not just because he kept the climate control inside at a bare minimum. The stale coolness stuck to his skin, permeating it to the point that he shivered involuntarily. He sensed something unnatural might have occurred inside this very room, though he suspected he was about to answer for something Henry might have perpetrated.

McWilliams felt a stronger grip wring his shirt collar as he was dragged into the center of the room and unceremoniously thrown against a wall. Free at last, he started to crabwalk forward but an aged tomahawk, adorned with dirt and streaks of blood blocked his path at eye level. He stopped, swallowed hard, and slowly backed into the spot where he originally came to rest.

For the first time his attacker slowed down and paused momentarily, staring at the wall behind McWilliams while blocking any exit points. McWilliams dared to look up, seeing his assailant from a toddler's point-of-view, studying the wall as though searching for something. Perhaps this strange intruder wasn't a mindless murderer after all, because he could have killed McWilliams without much effort, or even revealing himself.

The strange fog, which made its way through the entire house over the course of a minute or two, now stopped short of entering the room. It lingered at the door momentarily as though waiting for permission to enter before it finally turned tail back to the living room. McWilliams squirmed, wondering if the mysterious intruder harbored supernatural powers over the environment, because the mist certainly didn't appear naturally occurring.

When his gaze returned to his assailant, McWilliams noticed the man's right hand tighten around the handle of the tomahawk as though intending to use it. He tried to shuffle to his left, out of harm's way, but the hatchet hurled downward, sticking into the wall inches from his skull. After the weapon was pried from the wall the man switched it to his left hand, freeing his right hand to cup McWilliams' bearded face. McWilliams struggled to get free from the grip until he realized only enough pressure was being applied to keep him in place. He stopped resisting long enough for his blue eyes to steal a glance upward that showed him the intruder found what he was looking for along the wall.

Only a few powerful swings from the bladed weapon were required to remove the wood panel covering the wall and the drywall resting behind it. Chips of wood and chunks from the inner building materials rained down on McWilliams until the hand let go of his face. Somehow, instinctively, he knew this person never truly meant him harm, and that this visit was the delivery of some sort of message. McWilliams looked up as the hatchet switched back to the right hand before the visitor swung it into the wall, planting it firmly just inches above McWilliams' head, causing him to shudder momentarily as the strangely-dressed, reeking individual slowly dropped to both knees before him, almost as though surrendering.

Or at least offering peace after such an unexpected and aggressive intrusion.

For the first time McWilliams took a long hard look at the intruder, realizing an unbelievable truth about the man's identity.

"Michael," he said just above a whisper, recognizing the face from old family photos, even if the eyes were a pale ghostly blue.

Somehow four decades hadn't deteriorated his features beyond recognition. What should have looked like mummified skin atop browned bones was actually very human in form. The skin was dry and tanned, but still highly pliable as though he'd been dead a year instead of forty-one. Likewise his eyes appeared to retain some form of moisture, although moderately glazed over, with black streaks intermittently crossing the pupils. They were a haunting form of pale blue, flickering intermittently with recognition as though he remained torn between this physical world and whatever followed. Strangely, his clothes weren't shredded by insects or earthly decay, although their odor reminded McWilliams of used gym clothes left in a locker for months, if not years. He felt certain this was his long dead cousin, somehow returned from eternal slumber and alive, at least in some capacity, before him.

The cloudy eyes seemed to recognize the family connection when McWilliams spoke his cousin's name, but Tanksley already knew their relationship. He appeared with a purpose, which McWilliams figured he was about to learn now that he knew the truth. So many questions still ran through his mind, but he wanted to know why his cousin died some forty-one years prior, and why his body wasn't at rest.

Perhaps because they shared no other living family Tanksley chose to visit him, but McWilliams found the timing odd. If his cousin maintained free will from the great beyond, why had he waited so long to make contact? As though sensing that very question, Tanksley stood above his cousin once more, staring at the fresh hole in the wall before slowing raising his arm and a mummified finger toward the opening. McWilliams slowly regained his footing, following the finger into the dark opening where he could see an object hidden within the recesses of the drywall, as though purposely hidden there a long time ago.

McWilliams started to reach for what looked like a small metal lockbox as his eyes adjusted to the darkness, but a cold snap passed through him that caused him to shudder. He turned to look at his cousin, but no one else remained inside the room. Pulling himself to his feet he dashed for the front door, finding no sign of his deceased cousin. It took only seconds for him to reach the front door where no fog, no footprints, and barely any sign that anyone ever violated his privacy remained.

He breathed in the cool evening air at the threshold, exhaled heavily, and decided to see what secrets awaited him in Henry's old office.

Chapter 28

Lancaster wished he had never agreed to assist his old department with the murder case because his perfectionist nature wasn't about to let him opt out now. Just as he had built his theme park with every detail as he imagined it on paper, he now felt obligated to see this one last case to the end.

Even if that meant conferring with some rather unconventional sources.

He journeyed to Orange County, one county south of his home, where a casino had recently been built. The casino saved two historic hotels in the area, and basically brought a much needed economic boost to Orange County. Lancaster knew his theme park and the casino would unintentionally assist one another as two of the larger area draws, but right now his immediate goal stemmed from the murder case.

After pulling into the parking lot behind the historic West Baden Springs Hotel, Lancaster walked along the mildly descending sidewalk to the valet area. Two sets of sliding double glass doors glided aside when he set off the motion sensor, gaining him entry to one of the most beautiful interior views he'd ever seen. Although this wasn't the first time Lancaster had stepped foot inside the old building, he remained equally impressed every time he laid eyes on the round atrium nearly the length of a football field.

Skylights built into the dome above the atrium flooded the area with natural light during the day, providing natural warmth within the common area that few other public buildings could match. Six stories tall, the main portion of the building was completely round with rooms along an inner and an outer ring that shared a central hallway. Manicured gardens and floors covered with tiny ceramic tiles that numbered in the thousands were just a few of the tasteful touches done nearly a century prior. Although Lancaster shared several values with Paul Clouse, the hotel's owner, he made the trek to see someone entirely different.

Most of the offices appeared to be located on the ground floor, but hotels always had basements and other floors where personnel might be housed. Lancaster decided to avoid any wasting of time by heading straight to the check-in desk where a young woman greeted him with a smile.

"How may I help you today, sir?" she inquired.

"I'm looking for Craig Jennings. I wasn't sure which office was his."

Lancaster spoke the words in such a way that he implied a friendship with Jennings that frankly did not exist. Jennings worked as the head of security at the hotel, and the two only met one time before the theme park opened.

The young lady pointed out the direction since the hotel's hallways were circular.

"His office is the third door on the left."

"Thank you," Lancaster said with a nod before heading into the carpeted hallway.

He passed a coffee shop and a conference room before approaching several glass doors obscured by draperies. Lancaster could see all of the rooms were lit from within, so he rapped his knuckles against the first of the doors before popping it open for a look inside, as though Jennings might escape through a window to elude him. Although he suspected the man wasn't going to be thrilled about seeing him again, Lancaster realized he was acting overzealously about finding the security director.

Chalking it up to desperation, he found a rather stunned security director seated behind a desk, looking up from a computer and several monitors fed by various security cameras.

"Can I help you?" Jennings asked, not recognizing Lancaster immediately.

His brown eyes narrowed as a scowl crossed his face, indicating he remembered the man standing at his office door.

"It's too late if you're here to offer me a job," Jennings grumbled, returning his attention to one of the monitors.

"I actually need your help," Lancaster said humbly, though recalling a few reasons why he didn't pick Jennings to head his security force out of a dozen perspective candidates.

Jennings appeared intrigued by the plea, though wary at the same time.

"I know you've had some strange occurrences down here, and I think what I'm looking into may be similar."

"Stop right there," Jennings said, holding up a hand. "I can't talk about any of that."

"Then maybe I should talk to your boss about how you applied for a position at my theme park. Your loyalty might *really* come into question."

Jennings didn't appear the least bit interested in holding a conversation with Lancaster now, but during the interview process he had hinted about hidden dangers that came with his current position. And though the press could never provide definitive answers regarding the unusual activities around the hotel, they hinted that the supernatural or occult could be a factor.

"Let's go for a walk," Jennings finally said testily.

***

After a walk halfway around the rounded hotel, Jennings pushed on a metal door that revealed a set of descending stairs to the basement area. Fully carpeted and equipped with state-of-the-art electronics for any presentation within its four conference rooms, the basement provided an area free from distractions and the fun activities just one floor above.

Lancaster gauged the security director as a man in his mid to late-forties who wasn't entirely qualified for his position. Considering Jennings worked as a shop teacher before suddenly heading up a security force comprised of teenagers and college student interns, something didn't add up.

Left with just a fringe of brown, graying hair, Jennings sported a thick goatee that displayed more gray than original color. He wore khaki slacks with dress shoes and a polo shirt that displayed the resort's emblem embroidered along the left side of the chest. Although Jennings did not openly carry a firearm, he had informed Lancaster during the interview process at the theme park that he maintained reserve police status locally and possessed a lifetime gun permit.

None of the conference rooms appeared to be used at the moment, considering it was the middle of the week, so Jennings chose a room containing a dozen seats. He motioned for Lancaster to enter first, shutting the door behind them with a rather irritated look crossing his face.

"I don't know exactly what you think I can tell you," Jennings began, remaining in a standing position even as Lancaster drew a seat, "but I can't talk about certain things that have happened down here."

"Some kind of secrecy clause?" Lancaster asked, though he really didn't want details about their dealings around the hotel.

"Something like that."

Lancaster folded his arms, staring intently at Jennings, who didn't appear especially comfortable. Perhaps he lacked the stomach to ask Lancaster to leave, but it seemed more plausible that the security director wanted to hear him out. Experiencing something unusual, supernatural perhaps, wasn't something most human beings ever came close to, so if Lancaster's plight was at all similar the two might have something to discuss, even if the details remained unspoken.

"When you came to the interview I had a gut feeling you were trying to escape your current position," Lancaster said straightforwardly. "Am I on the right track?"

"My current position hasn't exactly been everything I expected, I'll admit, but I shouldn't have interviewed for your spot."

"I'm not here to rough up your reputation, but based on your past employment, I think we both know you weren't exactly groomed for police work. Your former principal gave you high marks as a shop teacher though."

Jennings forced an insincere grin.

"For someone wanting my help you aren't exactly endearing yourself to me."

"Sorry," Lancaster said. "My point is I think Mr. Clouse gave you a position here to keep you quiet about certain events. A bribe, if you will."

Jennings started to interject but Lancaster held up a foreboding hand.

"While I don't care about those particular events, or the details that go with them, I want your unbiased opinion about some murders I'm dealing with and a rather unique element that I think may be responsible for these murders."

"I'm listening," Jennings said, finally taking a seat and folding his hands atop the conference table.

Lancaster spent the better part of twenty minutes explaining the murders and the odd occurrences that he said defied explanation. Jennings listened intently, perking up at the notion that someone from beyond the grave might somehow be involved.

When he finally finished the tale Lancaster studied the security director momentarily as the man fidgeted with his hands before nervously cupping his jaw. It seemed Jennings wasn't entirely certain whether to believe him or not, but something in the unsolved murders and the possibly supernatural involvement shook him.

"I hope you aren't making any of this up," Jennings finally said with a hard stare.

"Not a word of it."

"Fine," Jennings said, finally conceding a bit. "Show me something that proves something about what you're saying. I can't just take your word on all of this."

Lancaster activated his phone and showed the security director photos within his smart phone of the empty grave and the tombstone above it.

"A lot of this is circumstantial or supernatural events that have been relayed to me. These people aren't crazy, and I know I've seen some very odd things this past week. I'm begging you to tell me *something* about what I'm dealing with."

Jennings inhaled deeply through his nose, contemplating how much he dared speak of the strange events surrounding the old hotel.

"I can't give you details, and I can't tell you exactly how I know about such things, but it sounds to me like you're dealing with some form of a curse."

"A curse?" Lancaster asked, wondering if the man was completely misleading him after he just surrendered critical information about local murders.

"It's not like the movies where someone is murdered and comes back to haunt people until their murder is solved," Jennings began to explain, animating the words with his hands, "but sometimes people can make a deal."

"A *deal*? You're not making any sense."

"Have you ever heard of cursed objects?"

"No."

"They are earthly objects that have a curse placed on them, supposedly by the devil himself. And these curses come in all shapes and forms."

Lancaster struggled to wrap his head around this foreign concept being thrown at him. Believing Michael Tanksley was back from the dead was one notion he'd almost grown to accept, but having religion added to the mix placed a bridge before him that he couldn't mentally cross.

"I can't fathom that my killer made some deal with the devil before he died to avenge his own foreseeable murder."

"You said it yourself that he dabbled in Native American rituals. They see death a lot differently than we do, so is it *that* inconceivable that he may have carried out some ritual to enact revenge? Maybe he was duped, or maybe he fully perpetrated the act, but it doesn't sound like any living person I know of could do the things you say your killer is doing."

Lancaster agreed with that point, but didn't see himself any closer to stopping the killer, regardless of whether it was Tanksley or not.

"If this is the work of some curse, can I stop it?"

"You're treading in dangerous territory. But if you intend to stop it, you need to find its origin. If this guy was really and truly dead, and just now came back, that means someone *else* is pulling the strings."

Finally Lancaster gained an answer that made some sense. While that explained the time lapse between Tanksley's death and his sudden return, it failed to provide any clarity about who might want to bring him back.

He had an idea where to look next for answers concerning that line of questioning.

"I thought you were running a theme park," Jennings noted. "Didn't you quit your police job?"

"I did, but it didn't quit me. Guess you could call it a cold case that needed finishing."

"Look, you can go on thinking I'm some kind of glorified babysitter, or whatever, but I can count three different times I've almost died since I got involved in this business. And those are just the ones I *know* of."

Lancaster softened a little.

"I just didn't think you were a good fit for my theme park. I wasn't trying to be rude, but the job calls for a little more experience."

"And I'm just saying if you're dealing with a cursed object, this could very well be your last case if you aren't careful. These things, and the people who use them, aren't anything to scoff at. They are fanatical, and they don't give two shits about killing you or me to get what they want."

"I appreciate you being so candid, considering you don't owe me anything."

"I dare say things worked out best for everyone involved," Jennings said earnestly. "You aren't completely wrong about how I came to get my position, but they've treated me very well here, and I can't imagine working anywhere else now that the worst is behind us."

"You say that like it's a guarantee."

"Let's just say all of the trouble has been laid to rest down here."

Lancaster grinned, catching Jennings' meaning, particularly since the man delivered the line with a stone cold expression.

"And there is one other thing," the security man said, keeping Lancaster's attention. "If you're dealing with a cursed object, they cannot be destroyed. You can't burn them, crush them, or shred them."

"They're around forever?" Lancaster asked with surprise.

"Yes. The best you can do is hide them incredibly well. To the best of my knowledge these are created through some kind of pact with the devil. Maybe your guy got tricked, or maybe he knew what he was doing all along. If you can't destroy the cursed object, maybe you can find a way to destroy or lock away the other source of your problem."

"How do you know all of this?"

"Let's call it mandatory research."

Lancaster got the impression the man carried out his own research in the name of self-preservation. He was trying to think of an appropriate way to excuse himself when a quick knock came at the door and a husky man in a dark suit stuck his head inside.

"You available?" the man asked Jennings, giving Lancaster a polite, but quick nod.

"I am now, Todd," Jennings said as both he and Lancaster stood.

They shook hands, giving one another cagy looks to ensure their words never left the small conference room.

"Hope I was of some help," Jennings said sincerely.

"Me too. Thank you."

Lancaster watched as Jennings exited with the man he assumed was a security detail or bodyguard of some sort. Despite the new information laid at his feet, Lancaster felt daring enough to confront the killer in person.

And he had a very dangerous idea about where to find Michael Tanksley.

Chapter 29

Jean pulled into the driveway of Colby McWilliams' home in the morning as they had agreed. She didn't particularly want him visiting her residence quite yet, though she still instinctively trusted him. Traveling an hour to Nashville, Indiana provided her with plenty of time to assess his character and possibly obtain some answers.

She couldn't turn off the shrewd businesslike nature that her Aunt Vivian had instilled upon her since childhood.

Dew covered the grass in the front yard, much like it had during her initial visit to the property. A light fog hovered in the lower valley down the hill from the backyard, typical during fall mornings in the Southern Indiana counties. She stepped from her car expecting the yellow Lab to appear from its usual leisure spot in the yard, or from within the old barn. Hesitating only momentarily to wait for the dog, Jean continued toward the house after her presence went undetected.

Jean halted abruptly when she saw the storm door swinging open halfway, thrashing against the retention chain that had somehow gotten partially wrapped around itself. At first she thought perhaps McWilliams left the door as an open invitation for her, but she peered around the frame, seeing that the front door was also open with some strange black markings near the doorknob.

At first they looked like footprints, leading Jean to think someone might have kicked in the door, but as she drew closer the marks appeared more like soot or some form of smoke damage. The storm door continued to swing open as far as its leash allowed, making a metallic clanging sound every few seconds that unnerved her slightly.

"Hello?" she called, holding the storm door steady as she slipped inside, finding an even more disturbing sight that caused her to reach for her cell phone.

It looked as though a tornado had passed through the house with papers strewn everywhere, books lying face down, and a few pieces of furniture overturned. Jean clutched her cell phone, deciding to look for evidence of actual foul play before dialing 911 for the police. Swallowing hard, she treaded lightly through the living room, looking down a mostly clear hallway to her left. Deciding to press on to the kitchen, she found more loose papers on the floor, and an open door to another room beyond the dining area.

Her heart raced as she began to wonder if McWilliams was alive, unconscious, lying in a ditch somewhere, or chopped into little pieces. Signs pointed to an intrusion of some sort, and possibly something far more sinister. Based on her one visit to the property she couldn't fathom the mechanic making enemies, or attracting nefarious types to his house. Still, the dog and McWilliams weren't anywhere to be found, so she slid the activation bar on her cell phone, fully prepared to call for assistance.

Closing her eyes with a bit of trepidation, she decided to check the room beyond the kitchen first, drawing in a deep, nervous breath.

Every fiber of her being screamed for her to do the sensible thing and run outside before calling for help. Jean didn't watch many scary movies, but she knew she didn't want to be the female character too dumb to run while she had the chance. The flip side was being the brave character that faced down whatever danger potentially awaited her.

Jean pressed forward, finding a set of knives atop the kitchen counter on her way through. She grabbed the largest of the bunch, setting her purse on the floor so she held the phone in one hand and the knife in the other. Firmly deciding that she was only checking the last room before taking action, Jean picked up her pace and walked into the old study.

Quite possibly far more ransacked than the rest of the house, the study looked as though burglars had gone through every square inch of the room. Loose papers covered the floor like water after a small flood, not leaving any clue about what the floor looked like beneath. Cardboard storage boxes were overturned and empty, an old computer appeared sideways atop a sturdy wooden desk, and several holes lined the wall beside the desk. Jean couldn't fathom what had occurred in the overnight at this house, or if she wanted to find McWilliams at this point. She envisioned him bloodied and battered at best, and Jean had experienced enough death and loss the past week.

The room smelled stale, as though it hadn't been open in years. A damp chill hung in the room, unlike the rest of the house, causing her to wonder if the room harbored some kind of secret that caused McWilliams to seal it. If she believed in ghosts, Jean might have thought it haunted by some lingering spirit that couldn't pass into the afterlife.

Seeing nothing that answered her pertinent questions, she decided to get somewhere safe to place a call. Replacing the knife to its spot in the kitchen, Jean reached for the pepper spray in her purse instead, figuring a quick shot to the eyes was easier than plunging a knife into an intruder *if* she managed to catch one by surprise.

It suddenly dawned on her that perhaps calling McWilliams was smarter than calling 911 hastily, considering his cell phone number was in her phone. Making her way back to the living room, she found the number and tapped the send button on her phone. She received half a ring before the line went straight to his voicemail, leaving her even more concerned.

Looking toward the ceiling, Jean questioned her own sanity for not running from the house and phoning the police. She supposed she needed some form of proof of something more than a highly messy house to ensure she wasn't that nuisance caller police detested. With this thought she started down the hall to investigate further, clutching the pepper spray. She had to imagine no intruders lingered because there were no vehicles outside and the closest neighbor was half a mile down the road. She prayed McWilliams wasn't home when the figurative twister tore through the house.

Jean was about to call out again when she neared a bathroom with a light on and a shower fan running. She crept up toward the room until she noticed a bedroom virtually across the hall that distracted her a split-second. This brief window allowed someone to touch her arm, and instinctively she feistily pulled her arm back and sprayed her assailant with the pepper spray before stealing a glance. He cried out in pain as she finally let loose with an involuntary shriek as her back smacked the wall on the opposite side of the hallway.

Immediately realizing her mistake, she saw McWilliams covering his eyes with both hands, trying to battle past the pain. He was wearing blue jeans with a shirt draped over his shoulder, as though in the middle of getting himself ready for the day. She felt like a complete heel as he groaned in agony, considering this was likely his first experience receiving defensive cocktails in the face.

"I'm so sorry!" she repeated three or four times in a row, pleading for his forgiveness.

Jean rushed into the bathroom and grabbed a large towel, soaking it with water before bringing it to McWilliams.

"Here," she said, holding the towel before him. "Put this to your eyes."

McWilliams continued to groan, but he didn't seem upset with Jean for spraying him, as though larger worries plagued him, or he half expected to be assaulted.

"Get me some running water," he said, holding out his hand for her to guide him.

Leading him into the bathroom, Jean turned on the sink, stepping aside so McWilliams could splash the water into his eyes for some relief.

Jean knew water only helped so much, and time typically proved more valuable in overcoming the effects.

"Oh my God, I'm so sorry," Jean said with sincerity. "The door was open, and when I came inside and saw the mess I thought the worst."

McWilliams took in several deep breaths as he flushed his eyes, trying like hell not to groan. Jean could only guess the agony she caused him because he kept sniffling and breathing awkwardly, trying to act tough on her account.

It took several minutes for the water to begin clearing the chemical from his eyes well enough for him to open them and regain control of his senses. Jean led him to the living room as he threw his shirt on and began buttoning it, attempting to remain modest. His eyes were bloodshot with red circles around them, looking nothing like a lack of sleep, or the results of a fistfight. No, the chemicals left their own distinctive pattern on skin and blue eyes.

"This isn't how I pictured the day going," McWilliams admitted slowly, trying to joke although little humor accompanied his voice.

"Some first non-date, huh?"

McWilliams forced a grin at her words, since they had tried to avoid making this anything close to a formal outing.

Jean still felt terrible about injuring him, but the mess all around her reared its ugly head as a reminder of her initial concern. She drew a deep breath through her nose, looked to McWilliams who continued to rub his eyes with an extremely damp cloth, and decided she couldn't avoid the elephant in the room any longer.

"Colby, what happened here?"

McWilliams dotted his eyes momentarily, obviously stalling for time to conjure up an appropriate answer. Jean already suspected she wasn't about to get the entire truth from him based on his elusive actions so far.

"Most of this is from me," he said with an air of defeat in his voice. "I had a visitor last night from my past, and I needed to find something in a bad way."

"Visitor?"

"You wouldn't believe me if I told you. I still can't believe it myself."

McWilliams appeared despondent as he stood momentarily to fetch something from the kitchen. He returned with a small metal box in one hand that looked as though it had survived a number of natural elements, though it suffered some wear. A few distinctive dents and rust spots gave the box some character, but it wasn't until McWilliams carefully cracked it open like a carton of eggs that Jean grew intrigued.

Inside the box rested a rectangular object shrouded in what appeared to be a very dated plastic bag. Sealed along one edge, the bag looked cloudy and weakened from years of suffering the same fate as the box. McWilliams patted the top of the bag, creating a crinkling noise as though he wasn't sure whether to open the bag or not.

"What I read last night in this journal explains practically everything, including what happened to your aunt," McWilliams stated slowly, treading carefully.

"And why wouldn't I believe it?" Jean asked, suddenly curious about McWilliams and his motives, trying to read him.

"Because this journal was written by my adoptive father, and if what he said is true, my cousin is out there seeking revenge."

"But isn't your cousin-"

"Yes. And if I don't find the object I was looking for last night, a lot more people may die."

Chapter 30

When Lancaster pulled up to the sheriff's department, he found four news vans parked across the street, because Parsons wasn't about to allow them near the building. Four murders within a week made for good media coverage, and Lancaster felt fortunate they weren't knocking down the doors of his theme park and condemning him. For the sheriff's part, he'd been cooperative and provided press releases, but he wasn't about to let them interfere with his deputies, inmates, and the general public that visited his facility.

Groaning under his breath, Lancaster decided to avoid the media circus altogether. Instead of stopping his truck in one of the front parking spaces and potentially drawing attention to himself, he circled the block to the back of the large facility, finding the sheriff's unmarked sedan present. Lancaster decided to park in one of the marked spots reserved for deputies instead of making another pass. While he might have overstepped his bounds somewhat, Lancaster knew most deputies were out patrolling this time of day, and he still technically worked for the sheriff.

He hoped the keypad code hadn't been changed since his departure, and it hadn't he quickly discovered, because no one had likely thought to make an appointment with the security company. Everything about the past week surely rocked the department and left Parsons in a foul mood, barking orders for his people to find the party responsible for four murders.

Lancaster made his way up the stairs without encountering another soul. When he finally entered the common area of the sheriff's department, he saw one deputy duck into a room with paperwork in hand, possibly preparing to testify in court. Several phone lines were ringing and the sheriff's personal assistant was probably about to pull her hair out from dealing with so much public inquiry and input.

Without delay he walked into Parsons' office, causing the sheriff to hold up his index finger as he attempted to finish with a phone call. Lancaster wasn't immediately certain whom the man was speaking to, but he sensed it was someone important like the mayor, the governor, or someone with clout. Parsons used the word "sir" quite often during this conversation, and Lancaster couldn't remember him using it very often previously, unless speaking to current or former military personnel.

He noticed the sheriff had shaved his mustache from a horseshoe shape to a more conventional style, apparently foregoing the charity event in lieu of having to give press conferences in front of state and national media sources.

"Sounds like you've got problems of your own," Lancaster said when Parsons finally hung up the phone.

"I'm hoping you're here with good news."

"No, and based on all of your friends pitching tents out front, I'm guessing you haven't satisfied their curiosity?"

"Fuck them," Parsons said, toying with his canister of chewing tobacco momentarily before tapping it on the desk. "So why are you here if you don't have news?"

"Because I think I know how to stop our killer before he gets the next victim."

Parsons eyed him cautiously, as though sensing a trap within this idea about to be pitched his way. For his part, Lancaster couldn't deny that although his idea was sure to lead them to Michael Tanksley, a high degree of danger was involved.

"I'm listening," the sheriff grumbled.

"We know who Vivian Weatherly and Charles Stafford partnered with back in the day, Steve. That never changed. I'm suggesting we keep an eye on Barbara Lewis and Cat Summers around the clock until this is resolved."

"Fuck," Parsons muttered, dragging out the word as he stared at his desk. "I barely survived transporting a prisoner, and I don't have much interest in facing that motherfucker again, Jeff."

"So we just let two elderly ladies get hacked to pieces?"

Parsons didn't take very kindly to the implication that he was going to stand idly by for that particular chain of events to unfold. A scowl formed on his face and he openly fought to keep from standing and going nose to nose with his former deputy.

"You didn't fire fifteen shots into that son-of-a-bitch and watch him keep coming," the sheriff said.

"That doesn't mean I don't believe you."

"And if bullets don't put a dent in him, how do you propose we stop him?"

"Creatively. A machete, a flamethrower, I don't care. But if you want to find him, that's where to look, because last I checked he wasn't lying in his coffin."

"You know if I assign any of the boys to guard these women that they'll underestimate what they're up against. I can't tell them the truth because they'll think I'm bat shit crazy, and if I don't, I'm doing them a disservice by putting them in harm's way."

"Look, my park opens in two days and I'm willing to take some shifts."

"You're still opening this weekend after everything that's happened?"

"What choice do I have?" Lancaster countered. "I've sunk almost every cent I have into this place and I need it to succeed. And like it or not, something has to be done to protect the last of Vivian Weatherly's group."

Parsons groaned, dropping his head into an open palm momentarily as he weighed his options.

"Okay," he finally said. "Catherine Summers lives in the assisted living community at the edge of town. Barbara Lewis still lives along Highway 60 towards Spring Mill. I think she has adult grandchildren that check in on her from time to time. I can't have you watching either of them in any official capacity, though. I'll figure out something with overtime to get both places covered."

"So I'm good enough to consult but not protect civilians or stop a killer?"

"Jeff, you *are* a civilian. I can't have you acting in an *official* capacity. Period."

Lancaster understood from the sheriff's tone that acting in an unofficial capacity wasn't off the table. Between operating the theme park and keeping watch over the last two possible targets for Michael Tanksley, he expected to have a virtually sleepless week.

He briefly considered telling Parsons what he'd learned from Craig Jennings in Orange County, but he figured the sheriff already knew something unnatural kept Michael Tanksley from dying a second time. Besides, Lancaster possessed no real proof that a cursed object or any other supernatural force was behind the dead man's reemergence.

Of course he couldn't provide any logical explanation either.

"Was there anything else?" Parsons asked, popping open his can of chew and letting the fragrance of wintergreen linger in the air before popping a pinch into his bottom lip.

"No. I'm going to take a run at Tanksley's cousin again. Oh, and can you see if we did any reports at the guy's residence the past few years?"

"Should be easy enough."

Lancaster jotted down the address along with the name Colby McWilliams to make the sheriff's search easier. He shoved the slip of paper across the desk toward the sheriff, who used a piece of tape to stick it to his computer monitor as a perpetual reminder.

"I'll check on it right after I have a chat with my *buddies* out front."

Lancaster gave a courtesy nod as he turned for the door.

"And for the record I've got plenty to keep me occupied. Take care, Steve."

Chapter 31

When McWilliams initially suggested Jean read the journal on their way to Nashville, she considered it a sound idea considering the thickness of the book. Almost an hour into their journey, however, she discovered the entries weren't as numerous as she anticipated and the content wasn't anything like she expected. The journal raised as many questions as it answered, and now she was almost to their destination, virtually a captive in the passenger's seat with McWilliams driving a late model truck that she found strangely comfortable since she wasn't accustomed to riding in trucks.

She felt her head spinning and her mind virtually numb as she tried to grasp the outlandish concepts this attorney, a man who in fact worked for her aunt regularly prior to his death, put to paper.

Because she couldn't fathom some of the words the first time through, she found herself rereading some of the important passages a second, and sometimes a third time. Jean understood why McWilliams might be upset, though she wasn't sure if he believed the tale within the journal, or if he shared her sentiment that his adoptive father might have actually been insane.

Perhaps because she wanted to see someone pay for the heinous murder of her aunt, Jean refused to even acknowledge the possibility that the journal held a dark truth, but it required a giant leap of faith.

According to Cauldwell, he actually met with Michael Tanksley over a period of two months before the man was murdered. Although Cauldwell worked for Vivian Weatherly and most of her associates, he made a name for himself winning the case in which Tanksley received land from the State of Indiana. It was the only settlement the state ever made in any case claiming Native American rights.

Cauldwell speculated that perhaps Vivian hired him for some insight on Tanksley, eventually discovering that she wanted him to approach the man about appropriating the land above market value for a business venture.

When that meeting failed to budge Tanksley from his property, even with great financial incentive, Vivian asked Cauldwell to try at a later date. Cauldwell wrote that he attempted to use his influence as a family friend, truly believing the money was more than enough to help Tanksley relocate to a very nice home wherever he wanted. Again, Tanksley refused the money, and for his part Cauldwell was relieved that Vivian and her group did not ask him to broker any further talks between them and Michael Tanksley.

Much to his dismay, however, they used the junior partner in his firm, Terrence Newsome, to begin harassing Tanksley on a regular basis. Although Cauldwell didn't appreciate his actions, or Vivian's for making him carry out her dirty work, Cauldwell didn't want to lose his clients. Cauldwell overheard parts of conversations between Newsome and Vivian's people, and he understood how badly they wanted the land. They were careful never to mention exactly *why* they wanted the land, even to Newsome, but Cauldwell knew that local farmland was available at fair market value.

No, he decided, they wanted this for something much bigger, and much more unique.

"They're going to kill me," Tanksley said when he visited the law firm one day when Cauldwell was the only one present during a lunch hour.

"Excuse me?" Cauldwell asked, looking up from some paperwork.

"Your clients are going to murder me," Tanksley said, pounding his fist atop one of the few cleared areas of the desk.

"Why would you ever think that?" Cauldwell asked, knowing which clients Tanksley was talking about immediately.

He stood to look Tanksley in the eyes.

"Your lackey has been dropping subtle threats because I won't budge on the land."

"Newsome?"

Tanksley nodded.

"I'm not going to tell you how to live your life, and I know how much that land means to you, Mike, but their offer could buy you a lot of happiness somewhere else."

"My parents are gone, Henry. This land is the only thing I have left of them and their legacy. Vivian Weatherly and her people aren't going to strong-arm me away from it."

"I still don't see where this is coming from," Cauldwell insisted. "They're businesspeople, not monsters."

"They won't do it themselves," Tanksley said angrily. "That's why I've taken steps to make sure they can't get away with it."

"Mike, what have you done?"

Two months passed before Michael Tanksley was found murdered on his own land. Jean found little distinction between the journal and the events publically revealed by the police some four decades earlier. She hadn't thought much about the writing so far except that Tanksley appeared paranoid in every conceivable way. What came next, however, threw her for a complete loop.

Cauldwell revealed that he was left a three-page note that felt more like an instruction manual by Tanksley. The dead man never retained anyone else as an attorney, so police turned over the remainders of his estate to Cauldwell once they combed through everything for useful evidence. Technically everything the man owned went to the one remaining member of his family, but Colby McWilliams was too young to receive money and any family heirlooms. Cauldwell took it upon himself to set up a trust fund for the remainder of the estate, although his land was the only thing of value that Tanksley owned.

Eventually Cauldwell donated Tanksley's clothes and what few belongings the man kept at his isolated home to a Christian store affiliated with a local church. For weeks after that he tried to avoid the subject altogether, believing it too painful to dwell on Tanksley when in truth, at least in his written words, he grew to believe Tanksley indeed predicted his own murder.

With no proof, Cauldwell wrote that he dared not talk to the police because he wasn't certain how far the conspiracy traveled. Instead, he decided to go through the remainder of Tanksley's belongings, particularly some items mentioned in the victim's lengthy note. Only a few medium boxes remained from the man's estate, which the lawyer purposely avoided while trying to sort out his own thoughts about the murder.

Finding it difficult to believe that Tanksley accurately predicted his own death, which the man indeed had done, Cauldwell absolutely couldn't fathom an instruction manual that the man guaranteed would enact revenge would work. After reading it for the third time while sitting in his favorite chair, the attorney felt certain Michael Tanksley wasn't in his right mind when he died, or during the weeks leading up to his untimely death. Most townspeople and anyone within the county who knew the man already thought he wasn't right in the head. No one lived off the land that didn't have to, and no one passed up good money for farmland. Those facts, coupled with Tanksley's obsession with the Native American lifestyle, made him a weird hermit.

Just before his death he told Cauldwell he wanted to legally change his name to Ahtunowhiho. Reluctantly, Cauldwell asked his client why he wanted the change and what exactly the name meant because it sounded Native American when Tanksley spoke it. He made a note that the man often used words familiar to Cheyenne and Shawnee Indians, using their style of accent when he spoke them. Cauldwell wondered whether he had ever actually met authentic Native Americans, or he just copied the accent from movies he'd seen.

"The name means 'one who lives below,'" Tanksley informed him, a look of borderline disgust crossing his face that he even needed to elaborate.

"Why, Michael?" Cauldwell asked with a sigh, hating that every meeting with the man drew him deeper into the crazed mechanisms of the man's psyche.

With probably the most grim and serious face Tanksley had ever produced, the man leaned forward, intimidating the lawyer slightly.

"Because I want those motherfuckers to know that when I'm gone it won't be over."

At this point Cauldwell didn't fear for the man's safety so much as his mental well-being. He began to wonder if the hermit might plan some kind of preemptive strike against those he felt certain were going to claim his life. Cauldwell knew these people wanted that land, but they were doing every legal action possible to try purchasing it from him.

They were businesspeople, not *murderers*.

It wasn't until after Tanksley's murder that Cauldwell began to reflect heavily on these conversations. Soon the weight of holding Michael Tanksley's estate in his hands became too much as Vivian Weatherly and her group began inquiring heavily about purchasing the land. In the attorney's mind all of the events were connected and with only one heir left to claim Tanksley's land and possessions, he feared for the safety of a young Colby McWilliams. Riddled with guilt, he eventually sold them the land for the highest offer they ever provided Tanksley to secure his adopted son's future. Not one fiber of his being felt justified or fair when he carried out the deal and signed dozens of documents that changed ownership of the property. He just kept telling himself that placing Tanksley's last living relative in danger failed to honor the man's memory.

"I just can't believe this," Jean said from the passenger's seat, seeing the early fall colors as they drew near the tourist town of Nashville.

"It would've been difficult for me if not for my visit from beyond the grave," McWilliams admitted.

Jean genuinely felt conflicted by the words written in the journal, having no reason to think of Henry Cauldwell as a ranting lunatic, but finding even less credence in the notion of her aunt killing someone over property. Considering the land never amounted to anything until Jeff Lancaster purchased it, she failed to see adequate motive.

"Why would my aunt have any part in the murder of Michael Tanksley when she never developed the land for any practical use?"

"Keep reading," McWilliams urged. "Henry covers pretty much everything."

"I don't know that I can," Jean said, her head beginning to ache from so many unbelievable thoughts swimming through it. "Maybe you should give me the *Reader's Digest* version of the story."

"We're almost to my parts stop," McWilliams said. "If you want to read a little more I can fill you in about the rest when we stop for lunch."

Jean didn't feel particularly hungry, but she wanted to remain in public places while they discussed the matter at hand. Technically she had agreed to spend time with McWilliams in Nashville, but she really didn't think he'd hold her to it after dropping such a bombshell that morning. She fully believed the man had suffered some trauma, but she wasn't sure how much of his story she believed. Although he possessed absolutely no reason she could think of to lie about the events he'd experienced or read, she still couldn't bring herself to believe Michael Tanksley wasn't buried six feet under dirt and sod.

She was able to read a little bit more while McWilliams stopped to pick up his parts from a mechanic just outside of town. Although the shop wasn't anything fancy, the mechanic had a large, two-door pole barn on the property serving as a garage, and a fairly new sign out front indicating that "Thompson Auto Body" was indeed open for business.

After watching McWilliams interact with the mechanic momentarily before paying him, Jean sighed and went back to reading the journal as the two men loaded the parts in the back of the truck.

According to Cauldwell, Vivian and her group indeed tried to make the land into a permanent carnival, or theme park, rather than using the property for the county fair and 4-H grounds as they originally stated they would. Cauldwell seemed to think the popular opinion of politics getting in the way of business was unfounded, and the group never had any intention of using the ground for anything other than their own original business.

Her stomach twisted and writhed because her mind couldn't decide whether this attorney whom her aunt often retained was being deceitful or her aunt was something more sinister than a shrewd businesswoman. It made little sense for Cauldwell to stow a journal inside a wall if he was writing fiction, but everything she knew about the ledger came from McWilliams.

Who to trust?

The writing carried on with more detail about what Cauldwell considered a conspiracy to murder Tanksley for his land. Jean skimmed through these passages until she reached the part where the attorney uncovered a strange book and a few pages of instructions about what to do with the old, leather bound book. Cauldwell said the instructions were for him to visit the grave site of Tanksley, open the book, and watch what happened before reading the inside of the book.

Admittedly, life got in the way and the lawyer forgot about the book and the vague instructions for several months before a guilty conscience got the better of him.

It wasn't until after dinner one evening that he got around to visiting the cemetery near downtown Mitchell. With the sun beginning to set and the seasonal fall weather making it brisk outside, he parked near the tombstone, finding the area around it fully set, as though the sod had never been disturbed. He hadn't paid the grave site a visit since the funeral at the original site, partly because taking care of Tanksley's affairs proved somewhat difficult, but also because he kept forgetting the book. The man was insistent that he follow the directions, and who was Cauldwell to deny a murdered man his final wish?

McWilliams opened the door, disrupting Jean's reading momentarily as he slid into the driver's seat. She studied him to see if the man appeared capable of creating such an elaborate hoax, seeing no difference between now and the day she first met him with Jeff Lancaster at her side. If McWilliams concocted the journal, she couldn't think of a reason why other than to cover up the murders of Vivian and her old business partners. Jean didn't think of a ghost story as a very convincing alibi, and she thought McWilliams would have to be completely insane or delusional to draw attention to himself when no one would ever consider him a suspect in the first place.

"Getting anywhere with the reading?" he asked as he started the truck.

"It's been, um, interesting."

McWilliams smirked, indicting he understood her reluctance to believe the story.

"I can't even explain what barged into my house last night, Jean. He was my cousin, but he wasn't the person in our family photos."

Jean couldn't detect any insincerity or dishonesty in his words, which left her wondering if he imagined something or misinterpreted what he saw.

"I just don't understand how your cousin could visit you in any form," she dared say, trying to receive more details about the encounter.

When McWilliams spoke of the encounter during the drive he gave vague clues and acted as though he was on the verge of giving a major revelation before pulling back. Jean wanted to know exactly how a man dead over four decades came to visit him at all short of being a hologram.

"You haven't read far enough," McWilliams said, looking to the floorboard as though some internal conflict kept him from speaking the words himself.

"Your adoptive father just decided to visit the grave with the book he found."

"Ah," McWilliams said with a spark of realization. "You're right to the part that explains everything and still leaves you asking a hundred questions. Let's grab lunch downtown since we're here, and I'll tell you exactly what I saw last night, and why I *believe* what Henry wrote down in that book."

Jean agreed, since anywhere downtown in the small shopping town of Nashville was public. Some businesses had migrated to a newer outlet mall the past few years after local landlords decided to hike the lease rates, but a decent variety of shops and eateries remained. Normally she loved spending a relaxing day downtown, hitting the stores for personal finds and early Christmas gifts, but today was supposed to be an informal date. Instead it felt more like a misadventure.

Chapter 32

While her mother dealt with several issues in Nashville, Abigail Garrison finished putting several books in her locker before heading toward the cafeteria for lunch. Unfortunately for her the administration decided to suspend off-campus lunches just before her senior year, so Abigail was relegated to the cafeteria with freshmen and middle school kids alike. While upperclassmen weren't thrilled about the decision, local businesses lost considerable income when the school system decided the liability was too great to let students drive around town for an hour.

Now two months into the school year, Abigail was resigned to her lunch situation, though still slightly bitter the administration couldn't wait until after *her* senior year. Most of the younger students had already dashed ahead to the cafeteria but Abigail wasn't in a hurry. She hoped one of her friends might join up with her because they had classes on the second level and it took them longer to put away their materials.

Her past week hadn't exactly gone splendidly with the death of her mother's great-aunt. Instead of preparing for local festivities and hanging out with her friends, Abigail attended a funeral and stayed with her mother more than usual. Sometimes it felt like just the two of them against the world, so Abigail made certain her mother was okay before resuming normal teenage activities.

She still had plenty of senior year left before summer and college, so she considered staying home more often a small sacrifice. It still bothered her that the police hadn't found Vivian's killer, and if they discovered any leads they weren't sharing with the public, or even her family. She hadn't known Vivian very well because of the significant age difference, but she felt positive the woman didn't deserve to be tortured and killed.

Such thoughts made Abigail shudder because she worried about the remainder of her family. She wished her mother hadn't thrown herself directly in the middle of this mystery. With the funeral over, Abigail just wanted to escape the town and the annual event that most teenagers outgrew quickly. She wished she could take her mother away from everything for a while and return to a halfway normal life once the police captured the murderer.

The hallway appeared unusually empty as Abigail walked toward the cafeteria, hearing and seeing nothing ahead of her. Most kids rushed there for lunch to get seated and hold conversations with their friends about classes and their lives outside of school. Abigail saw little need to scurry except that teachers would write her up if they saw her roaming the halls without a pass.

When she walked past the girls' bathroom a hand reached out from the door, groping her hair and startling her as she released a brief shriek.

Abigail turned, finding her friend Cassie Dunbar standing inside the alcove beside the bathroom door with a smirk.

"I totally got you," she said, bursting into laughter.

"You *bitch*," Abigail replied firmly, though letting a smile slip past her façade after a few seconds. "Why would you do that?"

"Girl, you've been on edge lately. Lighten up a little."

Abigail and Cassie had been best friends since the first grade, with only a few interruptions to their friendship over the years. Summer camp separation, an argument over which of them deserved John Tomlinson as a boyfriend, and an out-of-state summer trip for Cassie to stay with her grandmother in Vermont were the only bumps in the road and the girls easily survived those.

Their lives took somewhat different directions, with Abigail finding interest in horses and country life that her mother afforded her through hard work. Cassie dreamed of living in the big city, perhaps moving to California for college, even though her parents couldn't afford it. She dreamed bigger than her lifestyle allowed, not that her parents didn't work hard and provide for her, but her dreams as an only child were lavish.

And sometimes she put her own needs and wants ahead of others.

"Cassie, you know my mom's aunt was just murdered. It hasn't been an easy week."

"An aunt you barely knew," Cassie said as they sauntered in the direction of the cafeteria. "I feel for your mom, but you need a distraction, girlfriend."

Abigail sighed, taking a risk by stopping in the middle of the hallway. For a change it was devoid of teachers, students, and even custodians, giving them a rare peaceful moment to converse.

"I'm *not* going to the Persimmon Festival to see people I see every day, Cass."

"And I'm not talking about the lame-ass Festival. We're going to that new theme park on Friday night."

Abigail leaned against the wall, shaking her head.

"My Mom will never let me go. She's all worked up, and I think she hates the guy who owns the place for some reason."

"Then you tell her you're going to the Festival with me. Girl, it'll all work out."

"I don't like lying to her, especially this week of all weeks. And she shouldn't be by herself this weekend."

"Those are weak excuses, Abby. You're going to the theme park, end of story."

"But-"

"No. No 'buts' this time. You need a break, I'm buying your ticket, and you have no excuses not to go."

Abigail found herself running low on excuses, so she simply smiled, giving in to her friend's charismatic nature.

"We are going to have *so* much fun, Abs, that you're going to forget all about your shitty week," Cassie promised. "Now let's go get you some nourishment before you fall over."

Although she hated the thought of disappointing her mother during such a time of need, Abigail felt thankful for a friend like Cassie who provided timely escapes from reality. Perhaps a brief trip to the theme park was just what she needed to forget her woes for a while.

***

When Jean finally regained her composure and thought about the journey with McWilliams she realized the man had gone out of his way to dress
nicely, even after she doused him with pepper spray. He wore a pressed but-
ton-up shirt, new blue jeans, and brown cowboy boots that looked freshly
polished. During the ride north she occasionally caught a whiff of his cologne, which helped mask the scent of the pepper spray. She would've needed to be blind not to notice his interest in her, which openly made it difficult
for him to tell her the truth about his cousin.

Or at least what he perceived as the truth.

With the sun peeking through a batch of fluffy clouds, they were able
to sit on the patio of a small Nashville restaurant and order lunch while
conversing. Set on the outskirts of the main shopping area where most of
the shops were clustered, the restaurant offered Italian, American, and some
Mexican cuisine. McWilliams ordered a pasta dish, which he seemed reluctant about doing, as though he were more of a burrito kind of guy. Jean wondered if he was trying to impress her, but she followed her instincts, ordering
a small salad with some Garmugia soup that came out looking somewhat
like a vegetable-laden stew. She gave the restaurant credit for trying to intro-
duce culture to the layman customer, though she envisioned the cook being
a part-time college student following a printed recipe.

Unfortunately the pictures within the elegant menus made the dishes
look far superior to the actual product. Jean took solace in the fact that
her companion made for good company, despite the dire circumstances he
brought to her attention.

"So what happens at the end of the journal?" she asked him about halfway through her soup.

Avoiding the subject altogether, the two made small talk before and after
the ordering process. Time allowed Jean to become more objective, and curious, about the events surrounding her aunt and McWilliams' cousin. Both
of them were children when the events surrounding Michael Tanksley's
murder occurred, and she wondered how well they *really* knew the adults
who shaped their lives.

"Where are you again?" McWilliams asked, his fork full of pasta coated
with Alfredo sauce.

"The part where Henry visits the grave of your cousin after avoiding it for months."

"Ah," McWilliams said with a look of apprehension, as though it might be difficult for him to verbally explain the tale.

He set the fork down in a deliberate way before looking Jean directly in the eyes.

"He opened the strange book that my cousin left for him while he stood over the grave as he was instructed."

"And?" Jean questioned somewhat apprehensively, already suspecting what the next information had to be.

"Henry wrote that my cousin rose from the grave right before his very eyes."

"He did, did he?" Jean asked, fighting to curb her skepticism although it was about to boil over from her internal monologue.

McWilliams looked torn between trying to appease her by debunking the tale and siding with the man who raised him. Jean suspected he wasn't sure exactly what to believe, wavering in his opinions much like she was beginning to. He could have easily called off the trip to Nashville if he wanted to avoid such an awkward situation, though she felt he was genuinely shaken up about something and forgot entirely about their plans. Whether that something was his cousin visiting him from the grave or some elaborate hoax had yet to be discovered. Jean just wasn't sure what to believe at this point.

She still believed Jeff Lancaster was incorrect in his assessment that McWilliams harbored any ill-will toward the senior citizens of Lawrence County.

Both of them finished their lunch with just a few words between them. For his part, McWilliams looked almost ashamed for dragging Jean to Nashville, and into his personal problems.

"Are you going to be okay?" she finally asked him with genuine concern.

"I really think you need to finish reading that on the way back, whether you believe it or not," he answered gently, but adamantly. "It's hard telling what happened in 1971, but I don't think Henry had any reason to lie. He just wasn't that kind of man."

But he *was* a lawyer, Jean thought, refusing to let go of her cynicism.

"I'll read it," she promised before swabbing her mouth with a cloth napkin, "but I have to admit it reads something like a fiction novel. And it's just as difficult to believe without some kind of proof."

A realization struck McWilliams like a hammer because he looked her directly in the eyes as his frown slowly reversed positioning.

"What is it?" she asked.

"I keep a security camera mounted on the security light that overlooks my entire yard," he said. "It never even dawned on me this morning to review the footage since nothing was stolen and I wasn't going to call the cops. Maybe it caught something that shows him coming onto my property last night."

Jean wasn't excited about seeing their time together reach a sudden end, but at the same time she wanted definitive proof of something so she could either befriend McWilliams or steer clear of him in the future. She hated that she couldn't make up her mind whether to trust him or not. Instinct told her the man was harmless and a sweet country boy at heart, but her reasoning, a trait bestowed upon her by her Aunt Vivian, told her to listen to logic and know none of this could be true.

A week ago she never would have thought someone could chop her aunt into pieces, yet that scenario had come to pass.

When the waitress passed through the outdoor seating area Jean asked for the check, insisting that she pay since McWilliams was kind enough to drive, even after she assaulted him with pepper spray.

She felt a bit disappointed that their informal date turned out to be little more than a trip to Nashville to pick up parts and grab lunch, but she hoped for something more formal if McWilliams could prove he wasn't involved in any nefarious activities.

At the moment, however, she simply wanted to see how the journal ended and if the self-employed mechanic could indeed prove some of the strange occurrences from the previous night in fact happened as he stated.

Chapter 33

Jean found her mind oblivious to the return trip, occasionally looking up to see glimpses of the same fall colors in their infancy, or registering whatever country song played softly through the speakers in the truck. Unfortunately the drive home didn't seem nearly as long because she finished the journal about halfway there. Even so, she couldn't bring herself to talk about the events that transpired in the journal with McWilliams. Although the last portion of the writing didn't equal the quantity of the first half, it exceeded it in action and pertinent information.

If one chose to believe the written words.

Henry Cauldwell wrote that when he visited the grave and opened the book he began rereading the sheets of paper that accompanied the book to make certain he followed the man's last living wishes perfectly. Almost like a prophet, Tanksley had apparently predicted his own death and the events that followed, but as the attorney read through the instructional papers he began to question the man's sanity more than ever.

While the sheets were bizarre, the wording inside the book proved far more insane. They spoke about things to do once Tanksley rose from the grave and began enacting his revenge and how best to time his attacks on those who wronged him. Cauldwell couldn't believe one single word, thinking the man had completely lost his mind before his death. Only in the Bible had the lawyer read about someone rising from the grave, and these words seemed completely blasphemous by comparison.

As he stood reading the words about how he needed to shut down Tanksley's revenge from the grave every so often to preserve the man's body, Cauldwell shook his head. According to the dead man's words, only by closing the book and sealing it with blood, any human blood, along the crest and clasp combination would Tanksley find his way back to the grave and rest until the book was reopened.

"This is complete nonsense," Cauldwell muttered as he slammed the book shut, taking a deep breath to compose himself before deciding if he wanted to leave or say a prayer for his deceased client.

Before a decision came to him, several consecutive thumps reached his ears, like someone ramming a shoulder against a wall in an attempt to breach it. He looked around, thinking someone was carrying out cemetery maintenance at a strange hour of the day, considering the sun was setting in the distance. Not one person or vehicle was visible within the cemetery, and no vehicles were traveling along the three roads surrounding the sacred land. Cauldwell considered the remote possibility of an earthquake striking his home state, but those only made the news about once every decade or two.

Clutching the book close to his chest, the attorney surveyed the area around him, finally noticing movement from the dirt atop the recent grave. He absentmindedly stumbled backwards a step, his eyes never once blinking or looking away from the dirt that moved as though a cluster of ants were tunneling just beneath the surface. When several discolored fingers broke through the sod and wriggled, Cauldwell felt certain he was about to awake from a hellish nightmare.

He wanted to continue stepping away from the grave, but curiosity overrode his sense of self-preservation momentarily. In absolute horror, with the realization of what he had accidentally unleashed, Cauldwell watched the dirt and grass fall apart as more of the man buried six feet under began to surface. First a forearm, then the shoulder and torso began to emerge, showing discoloration that ranged from human flesh to a reddish purple color in the areas of skin not covered by clothing.

Little of the cloth had actually deteriorated over the past few months since the murder, but some of the suit appeared tattered as though clawed at by animals.

Or perhaps someone who detested the idea of wearing a suit in death when he never wore one in life shredded it in anger on his way out of the coffin. Suits were for businesspeople who took advantage of others, stealing their money, ruining their lives, and occasionally murdering them for profit.

Cauldwell knew without a doubt, even before Michael Tanksley emerged completely from the earth that the scene before him was no hoax or illusion. Like an earthworm tunneling effortlessly through the dirt, the reanimated man rose from the grave with utter poise, not staggering or hunched over like some movie zombie. No, this man emerged with a purpose, rising slowly and purposefully from the ground, eventually standing on the ground before his tombstone, taking a moment to look behind him at the fresh carving with his name and dates before turning to lock his pale blue eyes upon the only man who helped him in life, put his affairs in order, and inadvertently brought him back.

Shaking like a leaf, fearful of what Tanksley might do with his second chance at life, Cauldwell continued clutching the book, which the undead man eyed only a few seconds with virtual indifference. Standing as erect as a statue, Tanksley wore a look of purpose upon his face, as though he knew exactly what needed to be done. He showed no hint of anger or violence toward the attorney, though he didn't seem thankful for his freedom either. It went unsaid that he believed the man owed him this courtesy, even if it was accomplished through some measure of deception by preying upon Cauldwell's guilty conscience.

He wanted to speak, to say something enlightening, or ask the man to let their town maintain its peace, but his throat felt as dry as sandpaper. Cauldwell could only watch helplessly as Tanksley dashed from the scene, his posterior completely exposed because of the slit along the pants and sport coat of the suit.

"Thank God it was getting dark outside," the attorney later jotted in his notes after the shock of the scene washed over him.

Jean continued to read the remainder of the journal, discovering that Cauldwell learned that he indeed needed to drip blood into the cursed book's lock area to force Tanksley to return to his grave, per the man's instructions. He claimed to have done so on a few occasions, each time debating whether or not to set the deceased man free again. During the few times he set Tanksley free from the bonds of death, the man caused destruction and misery for the people he believed murdered him by ruining their fairgrounds and quite possibly sinking a ship in the Great Lakes that contained a roller coaster purchased overseas. Cauldwell hadn't thought much about it until he read something in the local newspaper about the group's disappointment that rough waters claimed the ship and cost the group significant money on an uninsured venture.

Twice he wrote that he saw Tanksley return to his grave site shortly after a blood sacrifice was given to the book from the attorney's own hands with a knife. Both times the man wore the Native American garb more suited to his lifestyle toward the end of his life. The second time Cauldwell said Tanksley brought a tomahawk with him, though he wondered where the man found any of the items.

"Why would you believe any of this?" Jean finally asked from the passenger's seat as they turned onto the road that led back to the mechanic's house.

"Before last night, I would have thought Henry was a lunatic myself," McWilliams admitted. "But there are newspaper clippings that match the events he talks about in there."

"Henry could have based his journal *on* those clippings to make it look like they matched."

"And he could've been telling the truth. Someone stole items from my house. What if one of those things was that book he mentions?"

Jean felt frustrated from trying to explain all of the holes in Cauldwell's explanation to this kind man, thinking him naïve for believing any of his surrogate father's tale. She believed she might have better luck talking to Lancaster, though she had nothing to offer the former detective in his investigation. She certainly didn't think of McWilliams as a murderer, and no real clues about Vivian's killer presented themselves, leaving her stuck.

"I know you don't believe any of this," McWilliams said after a silent minute, sounding deflated, "but it's all coming together for me. I just hope my security camera picked up something from last night to help prove what happened."

Saying nothing, Jean doubted anything could sway her opinion. Absolutely every shred of evidence so far felt circumstantial and without merit, and it was going to require more than words for her to believe Michael Tanksley walked among them.

When they finally pulled into the driveway she considered finding a reason to excuse herself quickly to avoid watching the video. What started as an innocent unofficial date earlier in the week snowballed into a complete mess the moment she hit McWilliams with pepper spray that morning.

"After those things were stolen from the barn I did some repair work for a guy and he repaid me with a security system," McWilliams said, slowly releasing his seatbelt. "I'm not sure I ever looked at it again after he showed me how it worked, but I'll give it a try."

Jean figured a few more minutes wouldn't kill her, and once all supernatural theories were disproven she could move on with her life and wait for the authorities so solve Vivian's murder.

Happy as ever, the yellow Lab ran up to them with its tail wagging. Jean felt certain if there was such a thing as a smiling dog, this was it. Perhaps it dropped all defenses when it spied its master, but the dog appeared perpetually joyous, making her question if it would actually bark at or defend against intruders.

Apparently not, she assumed, if someone stole items from one or more of the buildings behind the man's house.

McWilliams unlocked his front door, completely ignoring the parts he'd picked up in Nashville for the moment. After holding the door open for Jean, he led the way to a spare bedroom with a computer table that held a very basic piece of hardware with a faceplate that resembled a disc player. Beside it sat a monitor that showed a live feed of the activities transpiring outside in front of the house and along the main garage where people either parked or drove further back.

"It's been a while since he installed this," McWilliams confessed. "And I wasn't really paying very good attention when he explained it to me. Truth be told, I wanted security after my stuff was took, but I was doing the guy a favor, too."

Jean watched him fumble through the dials and knobs momentarily, studying the machine while he toyed with it. She saw a button that indicated it gave different viewpoints when pushed, but McWilliams said there was only one camera installed. It took a minute, but he finally figured out how to rewind the footage. What started out as a slow rewind gained momentum when he turned the knob backwards some more. Every so often he stopped to check on the recorded time stamp until he drew closer to the time in question.

"Here," he finally said, stopping the process during the evening hours the previous night.

Jean stared intently, barely able to see much because the property was lit by a single overhead light in the driveway at night, and the camera was mounted a distance away for a wide-angle view. Both waited about half a minute before the video started to grow distorted with interference, almost like television stations before the digital age ensured clearer pictures and practically did away with antennas mounted outside of houses.

Practically nothing was visible between the low lighting and the interference until a haze began to put a stranglehold on the entire screen. Slowly, like puffs of smoke, a cloud entered from the left edge of the monitor until it began filling the driveway and the front of the house.

"What is that?" Jean questioned.

"Fog," McWilliams answered without falter. "This is about the time I noticed it."

While the sight provided some credibility to the man's story, Jean knew it wasn't going to reveal much from outside when everything McWilliams claimed happened to him occurred within the residence. Suddenly she noticed a shape making its way through the haze without any hesitation or concern, as though it knew exactly where it was going and the forces of nature weren't an impediment. The dark shape, the size of a human being, crossed the driveway and the sidewalk to the front door, occasionally disappearing into the fog as it stalked forward.

"I just wish there was something more," McWilliams said, sensing her doubts.

"What is that?" she asked, pointing to the button that indicated it might change the screen to something else.

McWilliams gave a curious grunt and tapped the button, which changed the view from a single camera outdoors to four simultaneous views both inside and outside the house.

"What in the hell?" he questioned aloud, obviously convinced the outside wide-angle view was the only camera his customer installed.

A second outside view from above the garage gave a more detailed view of the driveway, one inside view watched over the kitchen from the corner of the living room, and another was located at the opposite end of the hallway, close to the room where the security recording equipment was located.

McWilliams pressed a button to pause all four screens simultaneously before bolting from his chair to have a look in the hallway.

"I was positive he just installed the one camera," he said adamantly. "I know it's wireless, but I've never even noticed anything else around here."

Jean wondered if the man may have installed additional cameras for his own reasons, or if McWilliams truly didn't listen to the explanation of how the system worked. Either way the man provided him with a truly remarkable setup at what sounded like a very even barter. Joining him in the hallway, Jean noticed a black dot about the size of an average spider a few feet above them on a dark wall where it seemed to blend in well. After the break-in, McWilliams likely had little cause to use the security cameras for anything until now, so he probably didn't check the man's handiwork. The mechanic seemed to throw himself into his work on a daily basis, which meant he seldom left the confines of his property to leave himself vulnerable to trespassers.

McWilliams looked somewhat disappointed at the discovery of the additional camera, which Jean imagined was more embarrassment than anger at the installer.

Without a word he returned to the security camera and waited for Jean before continuing the video saga. She watched the replay, occasionally glancing downward to see his reaction to it as the footage showed a figure emerge from the misty substance and stalk McWilliams before catching him outside of the hallway camera's view and dragging him down the hallway as he vehemently fought to escape. Jean sucked in a breath and held it instinctively, as though this ghastly figure might come through the screen for her. Her muscles tensed and she couldn't breathe or blink at the thought of the strong mechanic being helplessly dragged like a child against his will.

When the hallway camera began losing track of the scuffle, the living room camera picked up the action, showing McWilliams being yanked toward the kitchen area and beyond. The last visible frame showed his feet disappearing at the far end of the kitchen as though he might never reappear again.

Everything about the video footage confirmed what McWilliams reluctantly shared with her that morning. The timestamp, the details McWilliams provided, and the upheaval done at the home left little doubt that the man was indeed telling the truth. Jean felt like her world was crashing down around her, and that her aunt, the woman she admired so much during her adolescence, brought death upon herself and her associates.

"I'm so sorry," she said just above a whisper to McWilliams, who turned to her with an expression that displayed complete forgiveness.

He forced a grin, despite the dire circumstances that kept them together over the course of half a day.

"Don't be. I'm just sorry this happened to you and your family. If I'd have known sooner I would have tried to stop it."

"I'm not sure there's much you could've done."

"Maybe not. But someone has that book and we need to find them before they do more damage."

Jean felt completely helpless. She and McWilliams weren't detectives, or capable of defending themselves in the scrap that would likely ensue from a citizen's arrest. And besides, they still had no idea who trespassed on his property and stole the book and possibly other items in the first place.

"Have you followed up on the theft report that you filed when your stuff came up missing?" she inquired.

"Not recently."

"Maybe it's time we paid the sheriff a visit and checked up on that, and on my aunt's murder."

Although Jean had an idea exactly what happened to Vivian, she wanted to know what the police thought. She doubted Lancaster possessed any notion of the truth, and she didn't particularly want to speak with him ever again if she could help it. Perhaps she felt biased, but she thought the man was too preoccupied with his new business to put forth much of an effort looking for a murderer who targeted their town elders.

No, she decided, if she wanted answers she needed to take matters into her own hands as Vivian would have done. Perhaps the woman wasn't always correct or moral in her business decisions, but she did get results.

And Jean planned to see her own results very soon.

Chapter 34

Friday, September 28

When Friday afternoon arrived, Jeff Lancaster felt completely exhausted.

After spending the two previous days doing his best to guard two senior citizens from harm he returned to his place of business for the grand opening. Not only had his efforts of guarding two former community leaders in the town gone unappreciated because they were done in secret, but the current city council and mayor were irritated with him opening his theme park during the usually busy weekend where people flocked to the Persimmon Festival in town, spending their hard earned money on rides and food. Both newspapers and television stations covered Barwick's murder, but didn't put much focus on it like they had with the murders of elderly statesmen. Lancaster was irritated because he considered Barwick a friend who deserved much better in death, but relieved at the same time because the press hadn't blacklisted his park.

Parsons kept his end of the bargain, sending what manpower he could spare out to watch the two elderly ladies who still lived nearby. He even worked some shifts personally, undoubtedly disappointed that his shifts were so quiet. If someone dared target the last two business associates of Vivian Weatherly, it would certainly give the police a fighting chance if they were present to confront the killer.

Lancaster found the sheriff's unmarked sedan parked beside his personal space in the employee parking lot when he pulled behind Hallowed

Grounds. Stepping from his truck, he warily eyed Parsons, who leaned against the front fender with his arms folded.

"What brings you out here, Steve?" he asked, pulling a leather briefcase from the passenger's seat before closing the door.

"Jean Garrison and Colby McWilliams paid me a visit a few days ago."

"So?" Lancaster asked as he started walking toward the employee entrance with the sheriff in tow.

He still couldn't believe he *owned* a place with employee parking and entrances.

"They were asking some tough questions, so I talked to them personally."

"Tough questions about what?"

"About Vivian's murder, and about the break-in at Colby's place. I was going to let them talk to the deputy who responded to the break-in, but decided to handle it myself."

Lancaster stopped, and the sheriff came to a halt as well with a grim look scrawled across his face. He'd asked Parsons which deputy responded to the theft a while back and never received a response.

"Qualls responded to the theft on the McWilliams property."

Lancaster groaned audibly and took up a stiff walk toward the entrance door.

"Fuck that fucker."

"I've already talked to him," Parsons said quickly as both stopped about twenty paces short of the entrance. "He said he didn't remember anything unusual."

"Because he's so well-known for telling the truth and not fucking his coworkers' wives."

Parsons shook his head.

"Look, I'm not defending his character. But if he says he didn't find any evidence during the break-in, I'm inclined to think he's telling the truth. How many times have you and I worked burglaries and found nothing useful?"

The sheriff wasn't telling him anything he didn't already know. Police didn't waste time or resources dusting for fingerprints after a burglary, and seldom were there witnesses who saw anything. Thieves didn't break into places during times when witnesses might spot them. It required a security system, a lucky break with a witness, or being caught in the act to convict such sneaky criminals.

"Did those two have anything useful to add?" Lancaster inquired.

"Not really, but I felt like they weren't telling me something."

"Think they saw something *unusual* like we did?"

"I don't know. Maybe. They seemed to be getting along rather well since you introduced them. And that woman doesn't like you very well."

Lancaster grunted. He felt she hindered his approach to solving the murder, fixated on the fact that her aunt couldn't be anything less than a saint. He already knew her group got things done and built up their little town at the expense of other residents. Perhaps his money came from some good fortune, but at least he came into it honestly. Lancaster worked diligently before becoming wealthy and hadn't given up his work ethic as of yet.

He wondered, however, what drove Jean Garrison to McWilliams, considering they approached the man as a potential suspect.

Both he and the sheriff walked to the entrance door before Lancaster turned to his former boss.

"I'm absolutely exhausted, Steve," he admitted. "I feel like the last two days have been for nothing."

Parsons looked to the ground momentarily.

"I know. I've been burning the candle at both ends the past two nights and there hasn't been one sign of our dead man anywhere. I've got one of my guys at each of the locations right now, just in case he shows up."

Lancaster noticed the sheriff looked fatigued, his eyes encircled by dark rings and his face a bit pale. Even his posture looked somewhat slumped, as though he could barely hold himself upright.

"I know you've got a business to run, so I'll leave you be," Parsons said. "I appreciate all of your help, but maybe this guy is in the wind."

"Or buried somewhere else," Lancaster suggested pessimistically.

"Good luck tonight, Jeff," Parsons said before taking his leave.

Lancaster knew from an online search of the weather, all of the local publicity, and his own expenditures in advertising that the park was poised to draw guests and make significant money. He hoped so, because most of his winnings were already spent in creating the hybrid of wood, steel, and concrete that replaced a deteriorating field.

Chapter 35

Abigail hated lying to her mother, especially since her mother was paranoid about her even leaving the house. Technically she didn't lie, since she told her mother she was going downtown to the Persimmon Festival with friends and they did drive by the annual event. Compared to what other kids her age did when they left the friendly confines of their homes, going to a theme park wasn't particularly dangerous or unhealthy.

Her guilt subsided when she and a few of her friends entered the front gate of the new theme park, hearing screams from nearby roller coaster riders. It was nearly seven, growing dark outside, and the inside of Hallowed Grounds was absolutely filled with fog produced by numerous machines. Abigail could barely see a few feet in front of her as they stepped inside while the machines were discharging fog simultaneously from all sides.

Immediately her heart began racing because this theme park was indeed thrilling. People in costume chased guests through the main fairway, the enticing aromas of pizza, hot dogs, and walking tacos filled the air, and the clicks and clacks of roller coasters in motion reached her ears. Something told her the transformation that made a vacant field into a modern business wasn't the least bit in vain. Even her mother wouldn't be able to defy such a fact, even if she hated the horror genre, and disliked the man who owned the theme park.

"This is incredible!" Abigail told Cassie as they virtually skipped along the main drag. "What should we do first?"

Cassie had already snatched a foldout guide from the park entrance, which mapped every ride, eatery, and haunted house inside the facility.

"I want to ride something," Cassie insisted, leading the way toward the new metal Sidewinder roller coaster.

Waiting for the ride required less than twenty minutes and the anticipation grew with each set of cars returning to the station. Abigail had never ridden a roller coaster of this size and speed, which caused her blood pressure to rise as the moment of truth drew near. She wasn't going to say anything and let Cassie down, but she began to wonder if she really wanted to go through with the ride. She hadn't given it much thought until they were within a few turns of getting locked into their seats.

Her stomach felt like a washcloth being wrung over a sink when their train drew into the station, and she swallowed hard. She kept telling herself to get over it, even though she felt dizzy from thinking about traveling so high. A practical nature inherited from her mother told her such rides were regulated and nothing could possibly go wrong, but she also felt certain her mother would never give a roller coaster a second look. Cassie practically jumped up and down with excitement, so Abigail put aside any thoughts of backing out and followed her friend through the opening metal gates and took the seat on the right. She had her seatbelt buckled before the ride attendant came to check both their seatbelts and their lap bar restraints.

After a few words from one of the attendants over a wireless microphone trying to raise their excitement about the ride, they were moving forward and eventually up a very steep incline. Abigail sucked in a few deep breaths and kept trying to close her eyes, but the temptation to look got the better of her after a few seconds every time. Each time she glanced down the buildings and landscape grew smaller, from life-sized to doll houses, and finally to miniature replica scale. She looked up just in time to see the crest of the hill and a tiny windmill attached on her side of the roller coaster that indicated wind direction as it moved slightly to the left or right each time the breeze caught it.

Before she knew it they were careening toward the ground at almost eighty miles per hour at an eighty degree drop. She might have thought she was going to die if her thoughts could have caught up with the roller coaster. The next two minutes were exceptionally clear to her as they traveled up and down hills and made two ninety degree banks that put the train on its side for a few brief seconds each time. Near the end, almost wishing the ride had gone upside-down, Abigail entered the last hill a believer that she was going to ride this beast of a roller coaster many more times during the following summer before she left for college. Any lingering doubts about the ride she harbored were left at the bottom of the first hill, because she was sold on leisurely adventure.

Both she and Cassie exited the ride with a skip in their walk, ready to tackle whatever activity they deemed worthy and nearby.

"That was awesome!" she exclaimed to her friend.

"I know! We need to do it again later!"

"What's next on the map?"

Cassie opened the map and they saw several eateries and a haunted attraction nearby. Although Halloween was a month away, they decided it might be fun for some scares on the ground to recuperate. The attraction, Cut Throat Cove, promised the theme of a pirate hideout where trespassers were anything but welcome. Anxious to try their first haunted house on the premises, the girls walked at a hurried pace through the growing crowd of teenagers and families who appeared equally excited about seeing the theme park from end to end.

***

Lancaster chose to carry out some meeting and greeting near the front gates of the park, despite the fact he was about the only park employee not in costume. Practically every other employee in the open, mingling with the crowd, wore some sort of Halloween costume. Many were adorned with blood or torn flesh, some appearing very professionally done because they looked authentic. Lancaster spared little expense, hiring a few very skilled costume designers and special effects people from the Indianapolis area. The old adage about making a first impression continually ran through his mind, and he didn't want reviewers and fans telling people his park was a bust in its inaugural fall season.

People didn't seem to know him, or care that a man dressed in a polo shirt and khakis was present, so he decided to go behind the scenes. He wasn't offended that people didn't recognize him, particularly since his purpose for standing near the front gates was to make certain guests enjoyed themselves from the start.

Moments after slipping behind the employee gate he was met by Schall just outside the main offices, who wore an unwaveringly serious expression. Wearing a full suit and his black, shined cowboy boots, the security chief gave an air of unrest, as though he expected something bad to happen at the park. Based on the past week, it didn't take a detective to figure the run of bad luck wasn't going to stop on its own.

Lancaster wanted to place some kind of memorial in the park for Hank Barwick, whose death remained fresh in their minds. He wasn't going to rush the dedication like some kind of media sideshow, so he decided to wait and ponder the best way to honor the man in the offseason. He considered it more important to bring the murderer to justice before making such crucial decisions, particularly to keep his remaining employees feeling safe and secure.

"Any issues, Danny?" Lancaster asked his head of security.

"No. Everything seems to be running smoothly. I've got absolutely everyone working tonight, so hopefully we can spot any trouble."

"How are you holding up?"

"I'm still here, boss," Schall answered, holding the door open for Lancaster as they entered the park offices.

To call them corporate offices still felt a bit foreign to the new theme park owner, much like the aspect of owning a theme park. He supposed ownership compared to almost any other business in many aspects, but very few people in the world could say they owned acreage that beheld roller coasters and amusement rides.

"I feel like such an asshole for not checking on you more after Hank's death. They probably asked you a thousand questions."

"You've been busy helping them solve these murders, so I don't blame you. I'm a big boy, and I haven't been away from the game that long. I can handle a few questions. Just wish I could've done more to help Hank that day."

Me too, Lancaster thought, though he didn't want to utter such potentially insulting words in front of the man he entrusted his theme park to. It seemed everyone had confronted this ghostly killer except him, but he found it difficult not to believe he would put a few bullets center mass in the murderer and down him for good.

Standing at the threshold of desks and offices, neither man seemed to have business to carry out within the offices, which begged the question why they even stepped inside.

"You staying until close?" Schall inquired.

"I plan to. Looks like we've got a nice crowd out there. God, I just hope we make enough this month to pay the utility bills over the winter."

"I think you'll be covered," Schall said with a confident smirk. "It was ingenious of you not to offer a season pass for the fall."

Lancaster shook his head.

"That was self-preservation for my sanity more than anything. We would've needed more payroll just to process passes, and I need those people working elsewhere in the park. For a month of operation that just didn't seem prudent."

Schall gave a strange look that indicated he didn't believe his employer.

"What is it?" Lancaster asked.

"Despite what you say, I think you're a big softy who cares about all of us. I've never felt like part of a family at a workplace until I came to work for you and moved here. There's no way I believe you base your decisions on money alone, boss."

"I don't, Daniel. But if you start spreading rumors that I'm a big softy, I may have to look for a new security director."

Lancaster spoke in such a way that Schall knew he was joking, and both men let their guard down momentarily with coy grins. As former cops, they knew the front they put on in front of others was often just that, because deep down they shared the same worries and family problems as everyone else at Hallowed Grounds.

"I'd better get to it," Schall finally said, leaning toward the door. "Should I expect to see you mingling amongst the guests tonight?"

"I doubt you'll see me in costume scaring them, so that's a safe assumption."

Schall chuckled as he opened the door to depart the offices, leaving Lancaster alone with his thoughts as the crowd noise drifted in through the closing door. He worried about the safety of his guests, but every available security guard was within the park's walls, and every eatery and attraction had adequate employees to discourage any deviant behavior. Still, Lancaster wanted to contribute to the enforcement of park policies rather than react to any problems.

Making the decision to walk to his office, Lancaster unlocked the door and walked to a small safe mounted into the wall behind his desk. He felt a bit cliché, like some lawman who couldn't let his former calling go as he opened the safe and pulled out a Smith & Wesson .45 caliber semi-automatic compact that once served as his off-duty weapon. He now left it at the park for emergencies since he retained the same reserve officer powers he garnered for Schall. Already seated within a conceal holster, the firearm tucked nicely into his pants, and he pulled the tails of his shirt out from his pants to hide the gun from sight.

He almost wished he had hired local police to moonlight as security for the opening weekend, considering a killer remained on the loose, but they were preoccupied. Those who didn't hate him for opening a business that conflicted with the beloved Persimmon Festival were probably already working overtime downtown or on the road. Considering the killer's targets of choice, he doubted Hallowed Grounds was in much danger unless the remaining town elders connected with Vivian Weatherly decided to pay a visit.

He began to question whether watching over the two remaining women connected to Vivian Weatherly had paid any dividends. Yes, they remained safe and alive, but the sheriff's department couldn't stand watch over them forever, and the killer would eventually strike regardless of who was present. Considering he absorbed semi-automatic rounds and tossed Parsons like the man was little more than a child, the killer didn't seem to have much to fear.

Taking a deep breath, Lancaster decided to focus on keeping his investment and his employees safe through the opening night. For years he dreamed about what the grand opening at his park might feel like, never dreaming it would be marred by violence and local homicides. Having no control over the events surrounding the murders at the moment, he decided to make the most of the evening as he walked to the main door, ready to mingle and hopefully keep his firearm tucked safely away.

Chapter 36

Abigail followed Cassie into Cut Throat Cove when their turn finally came, after waiting close to ten minutes in line. The host beside the entrance let people go in groups of two to six people at a time, explaining the rules each time that anyone they encountered inside would not touch them, and they were not to touch those people in return. It seemed each of the haunted attractions housed paid actors who popped up or jumped out to scare guests, and even chased them because the girls had witnessed another group leaving another attraction getting chased by someone with a fake chainsaw down the concrete path.

Compared to some of the other haunted attractions this one didn't have much of a line, which made Abigail wonder if fewer actors awaited them inside. Perhaps it lacked in animatronics or scenery, or guests just hadn't made their way to it yet. For some reason there seemed to be a delay between the group of four that entered the attraction a few minutes earlier and the two friends. Abigail checked her phone because her conscience nagged at her about not disclosing the entire truth to her mother.

Seeing no missed calls or text messages she looked up to see Cassie staring at her with a disapproving look.

"Quit being such a Girl Scout," she chastised.

"I can't help it," Abigail said, hating the idea of any action on her part cracking the foundation of the bond she shared with her mother.

"We'll ride a few more things and get out of here if that's what you want."

Cassie said exactly what Abigail wanted to hear, but she didn't want to seem like an uncool prude of a friend and agree immediately.

"We still haven't seen half of this place," she said. "We have to stay and ride everything."

Riding everything felt practically impossible as the crowd grew within the confines of the park. It seemed darkness drew even more people inside, so she hoped Cassie might grow bored of waiting extensively for everything and ask to leave.

In the meantime the attendant before them finally got clearance on her portable radio to let the next group inside. To the surprise of both girls, she let them enter by themselves because the group behind them appeared rather large. They giggled to themselves as they brushed past the dingy cloth covering the opening as part of the constructed set.

When the cloth fell back into place behind them, the girls were immediately encompassed by darkness. Minimal lighting existed ahead in the form of reddish lightbulbs and black lights. Abigail tried to guide herself by feel along the walls, which were also covered by thick cloth to obscure any light and provide a creepy vibe. Cassie led the way less than a foot in front of her and Abigail couldn't even see her silhouette through the darkness. Any lighting ahead of them was recessed in the floor, or mounted so low that it did little more than serve as a guide, telling them which way to go next.

A piece of wood clacked suddenly against the wall to their right, startling them both and causing Abigail to give a brief shriek before regaining her composure.

Just ahead to the left the girls noticed red lighting, possibly meant to imitate fire except that it didn't blink or flicker. When they drew closer Abigail noticed it highlighted a portion of the wall recessed behind a barricade made of wood or bamboo, with an island feel about it. Abigail couldn't see anything of note behind the partition, so she drew closer for a look, wondering why it was highlighted at all. Perhaps one of their props hadn't arrived in time for assembly and display within the attraction.

She was about to turn away when a loud hissing noise from the highlighted area caused her to turn around. What appeared to be a solid wall behind the barricade was actually a well-disguised curtain that didn't move until an animatronic pirate sprung forward from the alcove and surprised them with a diabolical laugh. Wearing dark, traditional garb, the pirate held a sword and uttered some kind of warning about them trespassing on his island and hunting for his treasure, but they were the ones being hunted.

A musty odor lingered throughout the attraction, which certainly had to be intentional considering the entire theme park wasn't past the grand opening phase. While the light of day would certainly make the interior look more like a maze within a large conference room draped in cloth, the low lighting did wonders for the authenticity of a dark, dank cave. Every turn ahead of them was blind, offering some new and mysterious scare, whether from mechanical devices or hired actors. Abigail and Cassie suffered several more of these frights around the next few bends until they entered a narrow, almost completely dark hallway. Only a dim light embedded within the floor ahead offered any kind of navigation to them.

Abigail wondered why another group hadn't caught up to them yet, remembering that there weren't many people in line for this haunted house. Also, they had entered a rounded hub that offered them seven doors in addition to the one they had just passed. After picking an incorrect door and walking about a dozen paces to a dead end, the girls guessed correctly the second time. Perhaps the group behind them wasn't so fortunate, still trapped in a number of hallways that went nowhere.

When they reached the end of the hallway the girls were greeted with more wooden boards clacking and the loud noise of something metal being dropped onto an object that sounded metallic. With Cassie clutching her shoulders, Abigail rounded the next corner, finding yet another dim hallway with a foggy substance slowly floating across from right to left, disrupting a dim light at the end of the hallway. She thought it looked a bit like clouds crossing the moon, stealing what little light the distant orb offered during the overnight hours.

She took a few steps forward, trying to feel for a wall on either side of her, but for some reason this hallway seemed wider. Though signs forbid flashlights and other glowing objects inside the haunted attractions she wished she'd broken the rules.

Rather unexpectedly a figure suddenly crossed before them, stopping between them and the source of light. He stood there momentarily, saying nothing, silhouetted by the light behind him and embraced by the misty substance hanging in the air. Based on the shape of his attire Abigail thought he was another pirate actor, but she didn't get to study him before he continued his walk, as though exiting stage left to duck to another part of the attraction behind the scenes.

Ready to push forward and get through the attraction, Abigail grabbed Cassie's arm and pulled her along through the lingering artificial fog to a more open area that mimicked a campfire on a beach where pirates might linger after a hard day at sea. Sounds of ocean water lapping against the sandy shore filled the room, providing a sense that this room was the finale of the entire trek. A treasure chest barely showed in the far corner due to the low lighting, and she felt certain surprises awaited them as they crossed the room almost directly through the middle where rails on either side kept them on a strict path. Several additional props came into view, like discarded swashbuckling swords and gold bullion scattered across the sandy-looking flooring.

Nearing the end of the directed walk Abigail felt resistance from Cassie so she pulled a little harder on her friend's arm until Cassie pulled away completely, speaking a few muffled words.

"Cassie," she said with an annoyed sigh as she turned around. "Come on."

When she turned her around her eyes caught a glimpse of steel, almost like a dim camera flash going off within the dim atmosphere. Unable to see Cassie, who should have been mere feet from her, Abigail groped in the darkness for her friend as she heard a thump followed by several footsteps running away outside of the allotted walkway. Confused, she started back the way she came, stumbling over something solid on the path almost immediately. Hearing a moan from below, Abigail knelt down to find her friend lying on the ground and as her hand patted Cassie she felt something moist smear her palm.

"Cassie! Talk to me!" she demanded, feeling certain the warm liquid could only be blood.

For a few seconds her friend moaned weakly, so Abigail continued to determine what happened without regard for her own safety.

"He stabbed me," Cassie said between labored breaths as Abigail found the shoulder wound and began applying pressure.

"Help!" she screamed for anyone in the vicinity of their location. "Someone help us, please!"

Praying the employees didn't think they were pulling some kind of prank, Abigail called for help a few more times, varying her wordage as she continued to curb the bleeding.

"Hang in there, Cass," she said to her friend, wondering why anyone would randomly attack her friend in a theme park attraction.

Chapter 37

Seated on a comfortable outdoor chair on the deck behind his chalet, Jack Carmichael inhaled deeply on a cigar as he stared out at the gentle waters of the Monroe Reservoir.

The sound of a motorized boat circling the lake diminished as the owner decided to take it toward its home pier for docking. Barely visible in the dying daylight, the water provided tranquility at dusk and dawn for the retired lawman. In a few months he planned to head south to Florida to snowbird for the winter with his wife. Tonight she was playing cards with her friends somewhere in Bloomington, not due to return for another hour or so.

Despite the fact that his three children and five grandchildren remained in the tristate area, Carmichael would happily have moved south if his wife had been more agreeable with the idea. A lengthy career, partly in the private sector, provided more than simple financial stability for the couple over the years. Not quite seventy years old, he didn't miss the years of protecting a public that didn't always like cops, or rich snobs that often treated their protectors no better than their gardeners.

Standing from the comfort of the outdoor seat, Carmichael inhaled deeply on the cigar one last time before casting the stub out to the lake. After a few health scares on his part, his wife hated him keeping the habit, so he discarded the evidence before spraying his clothes with a scented spray and using a breath mint. He took a moment to lean on the railing, looking out to the lake as he reflected on how lucky his life turned out. Of course he made tough choices, some of which weren't seated on the moral high ground, throughout his decades of service.

He did the best he could for his own family, occasionally bending the laws he swore to protect. Even so, he never killed anyone, or even drew his firearm in honest fear for his life in all those years. Opportunities to earn more money at the expense of higher risks came his way, but he passed them all by, knowing that such work often led to an early grave one way or another.

A few frogs croaked in the distance, though late September in Southern Indiana often meant frogs and turtles were getting close to planning their winter hibernation. Pesky bugs finally thinned out as the temperatures fell a little each day, and most people took their boats out only on weekends, preparing to winterize them before the holiday season. Much like the birds and any other nearby creature, Carmichael began to sense the time for his own migration south, away from the temperamental winters of Indiana. Sometimes barely a few snowflakes visited the entire winter, and other times feet of snow came at the worst of times to small towns inadequately equipped to plow more than a few inches at time.

About to head indoors, Carmichael felt a large drop of wetness smack his forearm. He immediately looked down, expecting to find the moist droppings from a bird resting on his skin because the sky remained cloudless above him. Instead he found a large raindrop, which he began to dismiss as a fluke when another one struck his neck, then another landed on his other arm. Feeling certain he was witnessing some miracle of nature, Carmichael looked upward, finding not even a speck of a cloud above. When he looked down, however, he noticed a low-lying fog creeping across the top of the lake, but only in his vicinity. Before it reached any neighboring houses, or covered much distance further out on the water it appeared to thin out considerably.

"What the hell?" he muttered to himself, wondering what kind of bizarre weather pattern reached his little neck of the woods.

Strangely, the spatters of rain reminded him of a particular morning when he reached the most prolific crime scene of his career. He watched as the mist before him dissipated into thin air while a few more droplets tapped his exposed skin. That particular morning started with him finding a body in a desolate part of the county, triggering a series of events that forever changed his life. Halloween was a month away, but the hardened lawman felt his skin crawl as though something purely unnatural invaded his property. He couldn't explain the paranoia specifically, wondering if the deaths of some town elders in Mitchell subconsciously worried him. Carmichael hadn't stepped foot in the town for almost a decade, knowing nothing except bad memories and broken relationships awaited him there.

Still nearly six feet in height, age and a few health problems slowed him down, but he remained strong enough to push mow his own yard and chop wood for what little bit of cooler season he remained in Indiana. Carmichael walked daily, staying active and following his doctor's advice. He also kept several firearms throughout the house for self-defense because he made a number of enemies during his years of service. Some people disliked him for putting them in prison, and others remained who might seek revenge over business dealings.

Deciding to close up the chalet for the night, Carmichael turned from the edge of the deck to see someone standing inside the middle of his living room, staring directly at him. Little more than a silhouette, the figure stood unmoving as though entitled somehow to be in that exact spot. Carmichael instinctively reached to his right hip, finding no firearm present, yet unwilling to yield to someone trespassing on his property.

Slowly stepping closer to the sliding glass door, he studied the man standing before him, trying to determine whether or not the intruder was armed.

"Who the fuck are you?" he asked, stepping slowly towards the door, his eyes intently looking for details while he bought some time.

Only a single lamp was turned on within the living room, so Carmichael couldn't see very much until he reached the doorway, and even then it appeared the man inside his home was wearing mostly tan garb. The face was obscured by dark hair and the man never moved an inch from his rigid stance.

"You're not scaring me," Carmichael said, inwardly harboring concern for his own well-being. "Make your move."

Given the chance to flee or step inside where several weapons awaited him if he could reach them, the former lawman chose the second option. As he stepped a bit closer, however, he noticed several turquoise adornments along the chest of the outfit that appeared Native American. His mind immediately went back to an event he investigated some four decades earlier, easily the most heinous murder he ever witnessed. The subsequent investigation changed his life in several ways as he wrestled with several moral decisions over the years. He finally put them to bed, but here they were staring him in the face because someone knew and wanted to remind him of his sins.

"You're not going to get me," he stated with more conviction than he felt. "Not like the others."

Sidestepping in the direction of a shield and two crossed swords above his fireplace mantle, he kept his eyes fixated on the figure. It remained in the same spot, turning only to keep tabs on his movements through the stringy hair. Carmichael thought the tribal clothing looked as though it had been distressed on purpose, or looted from some collection that hadn't been properly maintained.

Knowing he needed to make a move before the intruder figured out his endgame, Carmichael dodged a few pieces of furniture and snatched one of the swords from the collectible centerpiece. Intentionally piecing them together so they made for emergency weaponry, Carmichael also took the liberty of having them sharpened. He drew one from the metal clips holding it in place before the intruder even made a step, thinking the potential assailant might flee, or make his move, but instead he simply stood there.

"Don't you move," Carmichael growled, holding the sword like a baseball bat, close to his right shoulder as a defensive weapon.

When the figure finally raised his right hand, he didn't make an aggressive move, but instead used dingy fingers to brush the hair aside from his forehead. Striking, pale blue eyes that looked like stained glass with sunlight behind them stared directly at the former sheriff, sending shivers down his spine because he knew this was no hoax. Every bit of this man's skin appeared shriveled, dry, and leathery with age beyond what any Hollywood makeup team could replicate. The smell that accompanied the clothes and an aged but preserved body smelled tenfold mustier than anything Carmichael ever recalled unearthing.

"It can't be you," he muttered in a raspy voice, unwilling to believe his eyes because accepting the truth meant accepting the fate of Vivian Weatherly and her business partners.

A glistening piece of steel caught his eye as the mysterious figure produced a tomahawk from his right shirt sleeve, that slid down perfectly from hours of practice or some form of black magic. It looked as sharp as the sword Carmichael held, only lighter and easier to swing. Knowing he couldn't wait to be attacked, the retired lawman stepped forward and swung the sword as ferociously as he'd swung any object in years. It struck its mark along the neck, completely severing the head from the torso as both fell in opposite directions to the floor where they landed with separate thumps.

Carmichael immediately breathed a sigh of relief, letting the tip of the sword fall straight down where it pierced the hardwood flooring of the living room. He didn't care so long as the monster from his nightmares didn't get to chop him into pieces with that glorified hatchet. Letting the sword fall completely to the ground, he grabbed the fireplace mantle for support, breathing in gasps as his heart pounded inside his chest from being closer to death than ever before.

As he leaned on the mantle for support he debated whether to call 911 or try dumping the body into the lake. The last thing he needed was a barrage of questions after the media circus surrounding the Tanksley murder began to surface with the deaths in Lawrence County. It took years for the local and national press to finally leave it alone, and now it reared its ugly head once again.

Along with its pale blue eyes.

Carmichael closed his own eyes momentarily, trying to shake loose the haunting image of Michael Tanksley from the past and just a minute prior. Taking a deep breath through his nostrils, Carmichael felt his heartbeat slow enough that he decided to open his eyes and deal with the situation at hand.

The first image he saw was the large shield that helped hold the pair of swords, and in its silver reflection Carmichael noticed movement behind him that looked like someone standing up in the center of his living room. Unbelieving, he whirled to find the man he just beheaded cupping the back of his undead skull and his chin with each hand, adjusting the fit atop his neck as he replaced his own head.

"Impossible," Carmichael stammered, understanding now that his own doom was imminent.

Once Tanksley moved his hands away from his head, he tilted his head and neck in two distinct directions as though adjusting the fit with both eyes closed. Carmichael trembled, wanting to reach for the second sword even though he knew his action was in vain. He simply watched as Tanksley stood still only for a second or two before his pale eyes popped opened and he charged forward with ill intent.

Pale blue eyes were the last thing Jack Carmichael was meant to see in life as he screamed for help that wasn't coming.

***

Lancaster heard the radio traffic on his portable radio immediately after the attack in Cut Throat Cove occurred. He ordered that the attraction be shut down immediately and that the security force seal all exits. After bypassing the entrance of the attraction and running inside to find all of the lights turned on, he made his way to the scene of the attack where park medics worked on the victim and her injured shoulder.

Danny Schall stood nearby and questioned a teenage girl, so Lancaster stepped forward, attempting to assess the situation. From what he overheard it sounded like two friends were going through the attraction by themselves when the one was attacked. Both girls kept trying to talk to one another, their friendship readily obvious through their open concern. Lying on the ground, the victim complained of pain to her shoulder as the medics reassured her everything would be fine. They applied some gauze to her wound and began wrapping it, and from his personal first responder training Lancaster sensed the wound wasn't near any vital organs. He felt as though someone chose to target him and the theme park because he investigated the local murders, as though they wanted his attention.

Noticing his head of security was nearly finished speaking with the sole witness, Lancaster stepped forward.

"What the hell happened?"

Schall moved away from the girl and talked to his employer just above a whisper so others did not hear what he said.

"This girl and her friend were walking through the haunt when someone attacked her friend from behind. She never got a look at the guy and we have all of the exits sealed, but I think the guy is already long gone."

Feeling absolutely frustrated, Lancaster could hardly afford another publicity nightmare, and worse, he didn't want some lunatic attacking his employees and guests at every turn.

"You're positive he isn't still inside the building?" he asked.

"My team has been through almost every square inch and we haven't found anyone out of place. Of course we don't know exactly who we're looking for either."

"Talk to the girl and see if she remembers anything else. I'll call the police and start checking the surveillance footage from this building. Keep me posted, Danny."

"Will do, boss. And I've already called for the authorities."

"Okay. Good."

Lancaster would have stayed if he thought the girl was in mortal danger, or there was a good chance the attacker remained in the building. No, he decided, the person behind this was likely the same person who attacked Hank Barwick, and possibly the figure that mysteriously showed up when the Sidewinder ride ascended the lift hill before the park opened. As he walked toward the main offices he began to question whether these attacks were directly related to the other murders. Aside from being on the site where Michael Tanksley was brutally murdered, his theme park had nothing to do with what Vivian Weatherly's group carried out some four decades earlier.

"Maybe that's enough," he decided aloud as he reached the main offices, opening the door and showing himself back to the security area where no less than twenty monitors provided live feeds throughout the park.

Nearly one-hundred cameras watched over the park and inside every attraction to ensure guest safety and keep Lancaster from getting sued. One of his security guards, Mike Holden, often manned the security footage because he was attentive and adept at using the technology. Holden often called other guards about issues he spotted before they became major problems.

"Mike, I need to you check any and all footage from around the Cut Throat Cove attraction," Lancaster said as he slid into the seat beside his security guard.

"I heard the radio traffic," Holden replied, his eyes not yielding from the monitors mounted just above him, all right beside one another at slightly varying angles like the eyes of a fly. "I took the liberty of checking all of the footage from around the building and inside, and think I might have found something."

"Let's see it," Lancaster said calmly, though anxious to see what his attentive guard might have discovered.

Not quite thirty years of age, Holden worked as a reserve for several police departments but never quite seemed able to join any of them full-time for some reason. He looked almost boyish with a smooth face and some lingering freckles, keeping himself in very good physical condition for any departmental physical agility tests he might need to pass. Lancaster wondered if the young man was assertive enough in public, which might have been what held him back on department tests. Regardless, he was perfect for the job he currently held, which prompted Lancaster to give him a raise before the park even opened.

"I didn't notice anything at first," Holden admitted, "because I think the guy was in disguise the entire time and I wrote him off as part of the acting crew inside."

With a steady, practiced hand, Holden worked his way through some footage that showed a man dressed in what appeared to be some kind of odd costume that looked something like a scarecrow. The material looked similar to bags once used to hold grain for wholesale, very pliable and bland in color. He also wore a mask that covered his entire face, except for his eyes, and with the camera so distant there was little chance of seeing any details. He also wore some kind of black hat, rather large in nature, that could easily have been mistaken for a pirate hat from a distance. Lancaster didn't blame Holden one bit for overlooking this man if he saw him during the live feed.

"He enters the ride at this time," Holden said, pointing out the time stamped on the screen when the man walked into the haunted attraction. "He's there about ten minutes, and then we see him leaving out the same way."

Lancaster made a mental note of the second time stamp, irritated that his prime suspect entered and exited through a route behind the attraction reserved for employees. He seriously doubted the costumed person worked for him, so he continued to watch, his eyes fixated as Holden switched camera views as flawlessly as real time to follow the suspect.

"He heads toward the employee parking lot," Holden noted.

Knowing the employee parking lot wasn't far from the highway, and a clever person might park just outside of the lot to avoid camera detection and identification of their car or license plate, Lancaster hatched an idea.

"I'm heading to the lot," he informed Holden. "Let me know where he goes as far as you can see him on Channel B."

Holden seemed to understand what his employer had in mind with a nod. Channel B kept them off the main channel where other security personnel were trying to communicate about the incident.

"Will do. Be careful, sir."

Armed with his sidearm and the portable radio he took from the office earlier, Lancaster left the offices and made a dash for the employee parking lot, able to avoid guests by taking routes behind the scenes. He seriously doubted he was going to catch the assailant, knowing he was more than ten minutes behind the footage. Fortunately the parking lot wasn't far from the offices, constructed there intentionally to keep his employees safe all of the time and dry during rainy and snowy days. He envisioned a skeleton crew to run the park during the off-season, selling season passes and answering questions on the phone or via e-mail.

He passed through a metal gate that required an employee badge for entry into the park. Further down was the entrance for vendors, repair people, and any other outside contractors who were granted access to the park, watched by a security person at all times. As he reached the nearest edge of the parking lot his radio squawked beside him before Holden's voice came over the air. Lancaster plucked the device from his belt, holding it up to his ear to ensure he didn't miss a word.

"Sir, he continues to walk through the entire parking lot, parallel to the highway in an easterly direction to the very last that I can see."

"Thanks, Mike."

Lancaster clipped the radio to his belt before picking up his pace, practically sprinting to the far edge of the parking lot. When he passed the last parked car he looked straight ahead, finding only a field that needed a mowing in a bad way. He found no vehicles parked beyond the lot, but due to the tall grass he immediately spotted a path where the attacker had walked, following it diagonally toward the highway where he harbored little doubt a car had been parked alongside the road, far from any cameras.

"Fuck," he muttered when he reached the spot where the vehicle in question left indentations in the grass, but no tire tracks or any useful evidence.

He called Holden and ordered him to store every bit of the footage throughout the park for the hour during the attack. Although he doubted anything new and useful was going to show up, Lancaster wanted to cooperate with the local and state police in every way possible. He also wanted to find the person responsible for attacking people inside his theme park and put two bullets in his chest.

Chapter 38

It required several hours for Lancaster to deal with the police and family members of the two girls, including Jean Garrison. She provided him with an additional headache he didn't need, though she was openly displeased with her daughter for going to the theme park instead of the Persimmon Festival.

He let Schall handle much of the dealings with the police while he personally handled the press. They proved to be less intrusive than he expected, but Lancaster still had to avoid a lot of questions by providing generic answers because technically everything was still under investigation. In the end he opted to leave the park open the entire time because footage showed the assailant leaving the premises, and the police presence quickly thickened, discouraging any criminal behavior on the grounds.

Cut Throat Cove was shut down, and the employees reassigned to other attractions after they were questioned by police and park security. Lancaster couldn't settle down during any of the investigation, his mind racing for answers and any open ends he hadn't investigated personally. It occurred to him that he had yet to speak with Ronnie Qualls, the current love interest of his ex-wife, and former colleague when Lancaster worked for the county.

Perhaps he put that avenue in the back of his mind for a reason, personally disgusted by both of them, despite Candice's infidelity contributing to his lottery win in a strange karmic sort of way.

Unsure of what assignment Qualls currently held with the sheriff's department, Lancaster decided to call Steve Parsons to find out. He also wanted the sheriff to order Qualls to speak with him so there was no unclear communication that Qualls was *required* to cooperate with the man who personally detested him.

As deputies and state troopers began leaving the park, their interviews mostly wrapped up, Lancaster stood outside the offices to call Parsons on his cell phone. He heard the shouts and screams of park guests having a good time, likely oblivious to the earlier attack on one of their own. He prayed he wasn't making a mistake by leaving the park open as the phone rang in his ear after pressing a button to call the sheriff.

"Parsons," the sheriff answered somewhat hastily, as though he hadn't bothered to check his Caller ID.

"It's Lancaster."

"What can I do for you, Jeff? It's been a rather busy night."

"I'm surprised you weren't at the park tonight, considering what happened."

Lancaster heard the sheriff address someone outside of their phone call before returning to the conversation.

"Sorry about that. I'm actually in Bloomington where there was another murder tonight."

"What do you mean by 'another'? Similar to the ones we've had around here?"

"No. *Exactly* like those. Jack Carmichael, the guy who held my position years ago, was killed tonight. His wife came home and found him dead in their living room, his fingers all chopped off presumably before a hatchet found its way into his skull."

Lancaster looked skyward, taking a deep breath as he tried to wrap his mind around the events of the evening.

"Someone was attacked at my park tonight, Steve. Is there any chance the same person was responsible for both attacks?"

"Not unless they have superhuman speed. I got the call about your incident, and it's probably within the hour that Carmichael was murdered."

"Why him?" Lancaster questioned. "We were so sure the two women were the last two targets."

Once more Parsons spoke to someone outside of their conversation before returning.

"People always speculated that Carmichael was a yes-man for Vivian Weatherly and her group, always doing their dirty work. Sometimes that meant kicking people off their property when they weren't ripe for eviction yet, and apparently it might have meant covering up a murder, or at least ignoring what little evidence existed."

"Something about all of this isn't adding up," Lancaster deduced. "Are we looking at some kind of murder team?"

"Well, your victim was barely wounded from my understanding," Parsons countered. "How do we know it wasn't some kind of sick prank?"

"We don't, but someone has trespassed on my property with bad intent three times now."

"Look, I hate to cut you off, but I need to help these guys with their investigation up here. They were kind enough to invite me up for a look."

Lancaster looked ahead, seeing the artificial fog creep through the fence line that separated the employee area from the main park. It stayed low to the ground, creeping in his direction with nowhere else left to go.

"I need a quick favor, Steve," he insisted. "Call or text Qualls and order him to meet me here at the park."

"I'm not even sure he's on duty."

"I don't care. His theft report is one of the last few loose ends I have in this investigation and I have a few questions for him."

"You sure this isn't personal?"

"I'm positive. Just get him over here. Please."

Parsons chuckled.

"You got it. I'll call him right now."

"Thank you."

Lancaster shut his phone and listened to the activity around the park, happy for the most part how things turned out on opening night. Except for the attack the evening proved successful in virtually every facet. His primary concern remained just how far people would travel to visit a theme park that essentially catered to teens and adults because of the haunted theme.

He wasn't opposed to creating an area for children, or making a more family-friendly portion of the park one day. For now he simply wanted to enjoy his dream without having to worry about some lunatic trying to dismantle his reputation by attacking guests.

Turning around, he decided to wait for his former colleague inside the offices, hoping the sheriff followed through with his promise.

***

Parsons eventually sent him a text message to inform him that Qualls was on the way, so Lancaster settled in behind his desk to conduct some paperwork while he waited. He put in a call to the security guards out front and back to let him know when the deputy arrived. It stood to reason Qualls was driving a marked police car since he was still in the patrol division, or an unmarked sedan if he was temporarily on some special assignment.

Schall walked into his office without knocking since the door was open. Lancaster considered his chief of security a fellow veteran police officer and treated him as such. The two worked well together, and Lancaster felt fortunate the former Kansas City officer didn't have his throat slit by the coward who murdered Hank Barwick. Such attacks were the work of terrorists, Lancaster believed, knowing only people with agendas didn't show their faces when carrying out such acts.

"What's the word?" Lancaster inquired.

"The girl is on her way to the hospital, no leads on the attacker through security footage or otherwise, and Jean Garrison hates you with a passion."

"No surprise there."

Taking a seat, on the other side of the desk, Schall put one booted foot over his knee, wincing as though his feet needed a rest from so much walking.

"I'm heading to the hospital momentarily," he announced, rotating the foot without removing the cowboy boot as though trying to massage some feeling into it. "The cops are doing their own thing, so I thought I'd check on the girl and do some damage control."

"Sounds good. I'm working on my own lead as soon as he gets here."

Schall raised a curious eyebrow, lowering his foot to the ground with a slight thud.

"It's a long story," Lancaster said with an airy wave of his hand. "And it probably won't amount to anything."

Standing to leave, Schall turned as Ronnie Qualls stepped foot inside the door, glancing at Lancaster before studying the security director a bit more thoroughly, as though curious whether Lancaster lured him there with nefarious intentions. Returning the favor, Schall stared at him momentarily before looking to his employer as though asking if his services were required before leaving for the hospital.

"I'm good, Danny," Lancaster assured his security chief.

Schall squeezed past the uniformed deputy as Qualls stepped inside, eyeing Schall as he left before turning a sour gaze upon Lancaster.

"What could you possibly want from me at this late hour?" Qualls asked, not sugarcoating his words in the least bit of civility.

Dressed in a full county uniform, Qualls wasn't the most likeable person when Lancaster worked with him, and things between them certainly went south when the man slept with his then wife Candice. Perhaps she thought Qualls was an upgrade, being a few years younger than her husband, slender and good-looking with dark hair. Perhaps the icing on the cake was the family money Qualls came into, always buying a new car or boat, often taking distant vacations that looked good in his social media accounts.

She couldn't have known that her greed would bite her in the ass the day the divorce papers were signed and Lancaster officially became a single man. He hadn't really spoken to either of them any more than necessary since the divorce, but he knew neither of them liked the fact that he won the lottery and left his job.

Neither of them could afford to quit the working life, so he hoped they were miserable together, having to work for their counterfeit happiness.

"I need to know what you found when you investigated a break-in at Colby McWilliams' place."

Qualls eyeballed him momentarily before a sly grin crossed his lips.

"You already got my report from Parsons. What else do you want from me?"

Just the testy tone of the deputy's voice satisfied Lancaster, but he hadn't summoned the deputy for personal gratification.

"I just want to know what you remember seeing when you were there. Anything seem out of place to you?"

"Not really. Someone tried to break into his place. I did a report. End of story."

Qualls tilted his head slightly, as though evaluating Lancaster's interest in the theft.

"What about that report could possibly interest you in the slightest?"

Now a game of cat and mouse ensued with neither man wanting to divulge information to assist the other.

"What I want to know is if anything was taken from the property."

"No. Someone tried prying the front door to the house open and they didn't get the job done."

"And the chest?"

"What chest?" Qualls asked suspiciously.

"The one in the barn."

Lancaster knew the investigating officer would likely have no idea about the chest, or the barn, since the theft of the items from the chest occurred later in all likelihood.

Qualls took just a second too long to answer, as though deliberating about something. His lips revealed the slightest of smirks, a move similar to what he did when he knew he was getting away with something.

Like screwing a fellow deputy's wife.

People like Qualls always considered themselves smarter than everyone else, and above other people, Lancaster deduced years prior. The man's arrogance, however, gave him away in key situations when he didn't even realize it.

"What the fuck are you getting at?" Qualls asked, trying too hard to avoid giving telltale signs or emotions. "I didn't go in the barn, or the garage, or beyond the living room inside the house. I simply did my job and left."

Lancaster wondered why he'd struck such a nerve, and why even Qualls, a man who hated him, hadn't been compliant sooner so he could leave the theme park. For some reason it seemed he wanted to play a psychological game with Lancaster, as though he felt he needed to prove something. Although the signs were subtle, Lancaster instinctively felt his former colleague was trying to pull something over on him.

"The reason I originally wanted to talk to you was because I considered Colby McWilliams a person of interest in the first two murders. Since you talked to him while he was under duress I wanted your take on him."

Qualls visually relaxed once Lancaster acted less adversarial towards him.

"He was obviously upset someone tried to break into his place, but I didn't see any cracks in his psyche if that's what you're after."

Even though Lancaster no longer considered McWilliams a viable suspect, he wanted to lure Qualls into a superficial sense of trust.

"But he lives out there alone. You don't think he could've leafed through some his cousin's things and realized the man got railroaded all those years ago?"

"It's possible, but again he never said anything about missing things while I was out there. If you want to build a case against him I'm no help to you."

Lancaster still couldn't pinpoint it, but Qualls was still a bit uneasy at the moment after being so cocky after he stole Candice away. It might have been easy to figure the man was intimidated standing within the grand company Lancaster built from the ground up, but Qualls came from money so he wasn't about to give Lancaster any satisfaction in that department.

Finally when Qualls shifted his stance Lancaster noticed something the man had quite possibly been trying to conceal the entire time. Along the palm of his right hand a reddish streak appeared so well that it could have been fresh. The light caught the injury and provided a glare because it looked as though a salve might have been applied to ease the pain or expedite the healing process. Lancaster knew in police work gloves could easily have been used a majority of the time to mask the injury from fellow deputies.

"We about done here?" the deputy asked, growing impatient and openly not certain whether his wound went unnoticed.

Lancaster had only a second to decide how he wanted to play this out before Qualls automatically suspected his secret was compromised.

"Did you get into a scuffle with a perp?" Lancaster asked, immediately regretting his decision to give away his advantage as the words spilled out and he glanced at the injured extremity.

"No," the deputy answered, quickly shielding the hand from view. "Accident at home."

He said it quickly enough that virtually anyone else would have believed him, but Lancaster knew the man and his temperament well enough to avoid falling for his lies.

Both stood there awkwardly a moment, each suspecting that the other knew what each one of them tried so desperately to keep secret.

"I think I'm good here," Lancaster said easily, trying to be casual and put Qualls at ease again. "Thanks for stopping by."

Qualls twisted his face into an uncertain sneer before turning to leave, giving one last uncertain glance back as he crossed the threshold. Lancaster wanted to call his security people immediately to run through the security footage again. He dismissed the thought immediately because they didn't know how Qualls walked, and for that matter he barely knew the man when they were amicable at work. Adrenalin coursed through his body, feeling certain that he had a confession without any spoken or written words validating his belief.

Knowing he had no hard evidence against Qualls for conjuring a dead man to carry out murders, he wondered if the deputy had caused the problems at his park. Snatching his car keys from his pocket, Lancaster decided he needed to take care of some personal business before he pursued more evidence against Qualls. He needed to talk to Parsons, and perhaps Colby McWilliams one more time if the man would give him the time of day. Suddenly his perspective was entirely turned around, and proof wasn't going to come from conventional means.

Before he did anything else, however, Lancaster needed to ensure the man who raised him wasn't in danger, and possibly ask him some hard questions in the process.

Chapter 39

When he pulled up to the farmhouse where his parents lived, Lancaster noticed another vehicle in the driveway. He was surprised to find anyone still awake considering it was an hour before midnight and his parents usually turned in early. For some reason his brother was visiting, and both David and Wyatt Lancaster were enjoying beers on the front porch, swaying to and fro in rocking chairs.

"Nice to see you two all comfy," Lancaster said as he approached. "You know, most families come and support their loved ones when they open a new business."

"But most people open restaurants or beauty salons," Wyatt noted. "Not haunted theme parks."

"I'm surprised you can walk with all the money you probably raked in," David said, offering him an unopened beer, which Lancaster accepted. "You spoiled us with the behind-the-scenes tour, so we didn't feel a need to attend the madhouse during the evening hours."

"We had a good night overall," Lancaster admitted, though he couldn't hide the concern from his family.

"Something happen?" David inquired.

"Yes, something did. We had a guest attacked by some nutcase tonight."

"What happened?" Wyatt asked.

Lancaster briefly explained the situation, ensuring them the teenage girl was doing fine at the hospital according to the latest update from Schall.

Following their usual custom, the three men sat in silence momentarily, drinking beer and staring out at the stars. Far from buildings and smog that obscured the night sky, all three enjoyed country life, though the sons tended to be drawn to the towns and cities more so than their father. Lancaster hoped his brother would leave shortly so he could have a private word with their father, but it appeared no one was leaving the serenity around them anytime soon.

"Mom in bed?" Lancaster inquired.

"Yeah, but she's probably reading or watching one of her late shows."

"Dad, did you know Jack Carmichael?" Lancaster decided to ask, rather than dive headfirst into the line of questioning he memorized to ask his father.

"Wasn't he sheriff some years ago?"

"Quite a few years ago. In fact, he was sheriff when Michael Tanksley was murdered."

His father shot him a hardened look that indicated he didn't want to stroll down memory lane again.

"I told you before that I had nothing to do with that group back then."

"Jack Carmichael wasn't just murdered tonight, Dad. His fingers were chopped off one by one and he suffered before the killer finally put him out of his misery. I have a feeling he had nothing to do with the murder of Michael Tanksley, directly anyway, but someone thinks he's guilty by association."

"What exactly is this all about?" David asked, somewhat perplexed.

"Your brother thinks I conspired with a group of sinister businesspeople forty years ago to cover up a crime."

"I never said that, Dad!" Lancaster interjected. "But if you had *anything* to do with those people you need to tell me so I can try and protect you."

"There's no protecting anyone from their reckoning," Wyatt stated flatly. "And I think you're coming to realize that."

"What the hell is going on here?" David asked, still confused by the exchange. "You should never have taken that last case, Jeff, because it's going to your head. Dad had nothing to do with those people."

"You wouldn't say I'm crazy if you'd seen the things I've seen this past week, Dave."

"I don't know where you got the notion that I had anything to do with these people, Jeff, but I *didn't*," his father assured him.

Lancaster sat quietly a moment, simply wanting to keep his bloodline safe, even if he couldn't protect his theme park family.

"I wouldn't have thought Jack Carmichael was a target before tonight," he admitted. "I just wanted to make sure you weren't trying to protect me when you said you had no dealings with Vivian Weatherly and her people."

Wyatt shook his head negatively.

"I was barely out of high school and working wherever I could to make a buck, son. Those people weren't going to give an old farm boy like me a second glance. And even if I did dig the man's grave, I don't think anyone comes after people for that."

"You both sound like you're talking crazy," David stated. "If Michael Tanksley really did come back from the grave, how could he cover so much ground in such a short time?"

Both his brother and father looked away from him to the ground, unwilling to dive deeper into the rabbit hole.

"I don't believe this," David said. "I'll give you the fact that this entire week has been bizarre, but one man, even undead at that, can't run around half the state committing murders and take time to pop up at your theme park to wave hello, Jeff."

"I think he has help, or someone is controlling him," Lancaster answered.

His brother eyed him suspiciously.

"You know something more, don't you? Why else would you stop out here so late?"

"I think the person who's been visiting my park and attacking people is human. And I think he might have found the cursed thing that brings Michael Tanksley back."

"In a sharing mood?" his brother pressed.

"No. Not until I have more proof."

In truth Lancaster couldn't take *any* chance of Qualls' possible involvement slipping out.

"This is no time for secrets, Jeff. You've basically got a half dozen people dead within the last week and you're not even officially investigating the thing. If you can't talk to your family, who can you tell?"

"Dave, I'm not telling anyone until I get more proof. How did we get off the subject anyway? I came out here to make sure Dad wasn't in danger like the former sheriff."

Lancaster's brother openly disliked being left in the dark regarding suspects. Accustomed to knowing everything before heading into court, he sometimes forgot that life outside the courtroom worked differently.

"You know what, I'm going home where maybe I can sleep this off and pretend this conversation never happened," Dave said, standing before throwing his arms in the air.

"Be careful," Wyatt said evenly, obviously considering his oldest son steady enough to drive home or he would have said something more.

David threw up another frustrated hand as he walked away, sighing and muttering under his breath.

"You probably shouldn't have started that conversation in front of him," Wyatt said a few minutes later as both men watched the taillights of David's car fade down the road.

"My brother being pissed at me is the least of my worries," Lancaster admitted. "I need to put an end to this, Dad, and at least in part I think I know how to do it."

"How's that?"

"Don't worry about it. If my hunch is correct, I might actually get this whole mess under control tomorrow."

Wyatt smirked cautiously.

"Well I wish you luck then. And rest assured, son, I had no dealings with those people back then, or ever."

Lancaster nodded, finally believing his father. He only stayed a few more minutes before excusing himself, giving his father a quick hug, and heading home to plan his next move.

Chapter 40

After an overnight that consisted of very little sleep, Lancaster awoke with a cloudy mind, wondering if he truly caught clues that Qualls might be involved with the murders, or if he simply wanted the man to be capable of such evil. He showered, dressed in slacks and a white dress shirt complete with tie, and black shoes. Although he needed to carry out some errands in the morning, he fully expected to wind up at the theme park by noon.

He fed the dogs before walking outside to a dawn that had already evaporated the dew from the ground and provided warmth enough for most people to don shorts. A reddish glow along the horizon indicated the impending rise of the sun, ordinarily a beautiful sight that Lancaster might take a few seconds to admire. Today, however, his attitude was all business with no time for dawdling or small talk.

Easily remembering the route to Colby McWilliams' house, he drove along the highway before turning onto a more rural highway, followed by some county roads. He wondered how the man kept so busy with mechanic work when he lived so far from the two largest towns in the county, but people apparently liked his work and his prices.

When he pulled into the driveway he spied even more vehicles than the last time he visited. He questioned whether business was booming, or if McWilliams had recently busied himself with matters that kept him from his occupation. Suspecting he wasn't about to be welcomed with open arms,

Lancaster pulled into the driveway before shutting off his truck. He opened the door, finding no yellow Lab to greet him, no open door along the front, and the sun barely shining over the horizon at this point. McWilliams struck him as a morning person, so he didn't expect to awaken the man from a deep sleep if he knocked at the front door.

A moment later he indeed knocked on the front door and it took about a minute for someone to answer. Lancaster found the mechanic on the other side, dressed in sweatpants and an old T-shirt with a rather unhappy look upon his face when he saw the former detective standing on his front landing. In the background Lancaster spied Jean Garrison dressed in a robe a few sizes too large for her, and obviously borrowed as she clutched it shut over her chest.

"Can I help you?" McWilliams asked grumpily, not bothering to fake any friendly formalities or open the storm door.

"I'm glad you're both here," Lancaster said, "and I want to start by apologizing to both of you for the way I acted before."

McWilliams finally opened the second door, waving Lancaster inside. It took a few minutes as they both left to make themselves presentable down the hall, and not one word was spoken in the meantime. Lancaster took a seat in the living room, noticing the house wasn't as neat and organized as before. Some minor damage looked to have cropped up along a few walls, which he stood to examine as McWilliams returned in blue jeans and a work shirt.

"Did you have another intruder?" Lancaster asked with genuine concern.

"You could say that."

Lancaster returned to the nearby chair as McWilliams sat on one end of his loveseat. They sat silently a moment as Jean continued to dress down the hallway.

"It's not what you think," McWilliams finally said as though a guilty conscience had gotten the better of him. "Jean and her daughter both spent the night last night after the attack at your park."

"I don't blame them. And for the record, I wasn't thinking anything. It was kind of you to take them in."

"Please tell me you're close to catching whoever's behind all of this."

"That's actually what I came to talk to you about. I've come to the conclusion that your cousin is behind at least a few of the murders."

Lancaster watched for a reaction and when he saw McWilliams breathe a sigh of relief knowing someone else finally knew the truth Lancaster suspected he was justified in most of his conclusions.

"He attacked me earlier this week," McWilliams admitted.

"Why didn't you tell anyone?"

"Who the hell would believe me? The only evidence I had was grainy footage from the security cameras."

"You have footage?" Lancaster asked, feeling excited about the prospect of closing the case that much sooner.

"He has more than that," Jean said as she entered the room wearing her normal attire. "His cousin pointed him in the right direction."

"What does she mean?" Lancaster asked.

McWilliams stood to retrieve the manifesto his adopted father left hidden inside the home so many years earlier.

"This pretty much explains everything about my cousin and how he's back with us," McWilliams said as he handed it to Lancaster. "Maybe you can help us fill in some of the blanks after you read it."

Thumbing through the notes, Lancaster figured he was in for a lengthy read that might have saved some lives had it been recovered sooner.

***

Wyatt Lancaster started at the crack of dawn, examining hay in one of his fields that he had cut the previous evening. Riding his John Deere tractor along the field to work on some of his equipment beside the road, he found the hay satisfactory. It amazed him that things hadn't changed much over the years. Sure, tractors replaced horses at some point, but farmers still cut hay, raked hay, and finally baled hay, all with different machines behind the tractor. He already had some high school kids lined up to put the bales on the wagon that afternoon for some tax-free cash. They were kids or grandkids of fellow farmers he trusted, so they were certainly reliable farmhands.

Dressed in bib overalls with a red short-sleeved shirt and old work boots, he didn't plan on baling hay until later. He brought a thick canvas work jacket in case he needed to fix something underneath the baler he'd left inside the fence line the previous evening. Despite being a veteran on the farm, he didn't like getting poison ivy or itchy skin from hay bristles scratching his skin any more than non-farmers.

While no part of readying hay went quickly, baling proved the most taxing because the tractor required a slow, steady hand and sometimes ran out of twine. In the old days the twine sometimes balled up and failed to properly wrap the hay, or twisted within the machine. Synthetic twine eventually replaced its cotton predecessor, eliminating such problems. Over the years he witnessed a few advents on the farm, but more in the tractors and construction equipment used in fields. Most upgrades simply provided comfort, but some came about in the name of safety, and he often thought the government stuck its nose in a little too often.

With light rain possible that afternoon, Wyatt wanted to get the bales ready for the boys who still had school, but he needed to wait for the morning dew to evaporate. Even the Persimmon Festival didn't provide reason enough to move the school's fall break from the middle of October. He hoped the boys didn't waste time driving to his property, because wet bales created double the work and effort after any decent storm.

Dismounting from his tractor near a corner of the field beside the county road, Wyatt needed to make certain the baler remained in good working order. He didn't want to get halfway done with the job only to have a piece of equipment break. Experience had taught him to start the job with preventative maintenance rather than battle any surprises and the elements halfway through.

Walking to the back of the baler he flipped open a compartment lid for a peek inside to find the twine sufficient for the work ahead. As he closed the lid, prepared to check the belts, grease the bearings, and clear the chute, the sound of a car approaching reached his ears, which wasn't common along his road. He glanced over when he heard the car slowing, figuring someone needed directions, instead finding a marked county squad car pulling beside the opposite side of the fence.

He watched as a uniformed deputy stepped from the car, his heart immediately racing because he feared terrible news about his youngest son. Wishing Jeff had never chosen to help investigate murders best left in the past, Wyatt took a deep breath and closed his eyes momentarily before walking toward the deputy, saying a silent prayer all the way.

"Mr. Lancaster?" the deputy asked.

"Yes."

"Can you step over here with me please?"

Wyatt wasn't certain he recognized the deputy among the handful of officers he'd met through his son. Complying, yet still nervous he was about to hear heartbreaking news, he felt his mind and body disconnect somewhat, as though slipping into shock to shield him from incredible grief. He walked to a nearby opening in the fence and crossed over, taking his time to avoid whatever inevitable fate awaited him.

"Is this about my son?" he asked when he neared the squad car.

Instead of answering the deputy gave him a furrowed eyebrow, indicating his confusion. Confused now himself, Wyatt looked at the man's uniform nameplate, finding the name familiar as the clouds broke within his mind.

Qualls.

When Wyatt lifted his head he noticed the deputy's expression wasn't particularly friendly because he knew the realization that the farmer reached.

"You're that punk who slept with my son's slut wife."

"And you're under arrest for the murders of Vivian Weatherly, Charles Stafford, Ralph Nichols, Pete Thompson, and Hank Barwick."

Wyatt stumbled backwards a few steps, recognizing all of the names, knowing he was not responsible for harming a one of them. He reached into his overalls for his cell phone, prepared to call his son for assistance but Qualls knocked it out of his hand.

"You're not here on official business," Wyatt stated. "Leave now and I won't press charges."

"How is it going to look when you confess all of your murderous activities to me and make me kill you in self-defense when you try to overpower me?" Qualls asked, reaching for his gun.

"Pretty damn suspicious, I'd imagine," Wyatt answered sternly. "I don't know why you're trying to pin any of this on me when the real culprit is running free."

"If you're going to continue to resist arrest I'm going to have to put you down, Mr. Lancaster."

Wyatt didn't know why Qualls wanted to target him, other than to make Jeff look bad in the public eye. He and Candice were always infuriated that Jeff won the lottery when the ink from the divorce papers wasn't even dry. If this was a legitimate arrest situation no deputy would come to the farm alone, without backup, to carry out an arrest. Knowing his rights, and feeling positive Qualls had no legal reason to detain him, Wyatt reached down for his cell phone to place a call to one of his sons.

Without warning he felt his body stiffen like a board as he lost all motor skills. Unable to move, though completely aware of his surroundings, Wyatt collapsed in a heap to the ground atop the prickly hay. Instead of a gun Qualls used a Taser on him, leaving him helpless to whatever fate awaited him. He began to realize that Qualls wasn't out to frame him, or simply make Jeff's life miserable. The man wanted at least one of them dead, and he likely had something to do with the recent murders, whether he carried them out or covered up evidence.

"Don't you worry, Mr. Lancaster," Qualls said bitterly as he slapped handcuffs on the older man behind his back. "Soon this will all be over and there'll only be a few more funerals in Lawrence County this month."

Wyatt couldn't regain any use of his muscles during the time it took for him to be restrained. Nearly half a minute later when he thought he might be able to move again Qualls hit the trigger on the Taser and shot nearly 55,000 volts into his system a second time. He groaned inwardly because he felt positive no utterances escape his mouth. Wyatt didn't want his life to end at the hands of the creep who stole his son's wife, but he remained helpless as Qualls heaved him over his shoulder like a grain sack before dumping him unceremoniously into the squad car's trunk.

"Keep quiet back here or you'll start losing loved ones," Qualls warned once Wyatt made eye contact with him.

As a precaution Qualls used some kind of coiled cloth to gag Wyatt because any kind of tape wouldn't stick properly against the man's thick beard. Wyatt tried to object through the gag, his mind racing for a way to escape this new predicament, but Qualls shot him a hateful glare before slamming the trunk down. Left in complete darkness, and restrained to the point that he could barely move, Wyatt required a small miracle to save his life.

Chapter 41

After a lengthy read and some discussion with both Jean and McWilliams, Lancaster decided the trio was on the same page at long last.

He now understood that some sort of book brought Tanksley back from the dead, but wondered if Qualls actually possessed the book or just played into the first few murders. Obviously he wanted to cause Lancaster grief and cause Hallowed Grounds to fail, but the depths of his treachery were undetermined. He thought back to the discussion with Craig Jennings at the hotel in West Baden Springs, knowing the book might very well be the type of cursed object the man told him about.

For his part, Lancaster left nothing on the table. Ignoring his standard moral code and penchant for following police procedure, he revealed everything he knew from the investigations and every observation he made at his theme park. He also told them he believed Ronnie Qualls was involved in some of the crimes, if not the very reason Michael Tanksley was freed from his coffin in the first place.

"What do we do now?" McWilliams asked once everyone was up to speed.

Jean's daughter emerged from a bedroom only to get herself a glass of water before retreating to the privacy of the other room.

Lancaster's instinct was to give the rational response that they were citizens and had no business risking their lives in the gory mess. He immediately realized that his credentials were no higher than theirs, so he simply conceded to accept whatever help they were willing to give.

"The problem is anticipating who your cousin might attack next," he said, looking to McWilliams. "Now the wildcard is Qualls, and he isn't going to be easy to track. The patrol cars now have laptops in them for writing reports, and with that a mapping system that includes GPS. I could ask the sheriff to track Qualls for me because if any of us try it he'll surely notice."

"Can you trust the sheriff?" Jean asked.

"I can trust him, but he tends to get overzealous sometimes. I'm worried if I tell him all of this he'll want to confront Qualls, which won't do us any good, and might put him in danger."

"It beats seeing someone else cut into pieces," Jean offered, her look quite serious.

Lancaster shrugged, unable to deny the statement.

"I might have an idea that circumvents a few of our problems," he said as a thought entered his mind. "If I can get one of those computers we could track Qualls ourselves because all logged in cars can always see one another."

"And if he logs out?" McWilliams asked.

"We're screwed."

"What if we could locate that book?" Jean inquired.

"We could stop this once and for all," McWilliams said, finishing Jean's thought.

Lancaster shook his head negatively.

"Qualls isn't going to leave it lying around. He'll keep it around him at all times if he's the one who has it. If I knew for sure he had it I would hold him at gunpoint until he produced it."

"That wouldn't hold up in court," McWilliams said with a forced grin.

"No, but it would put an end to this."

Lancaster wondered if the book worked as the paperwork stated, and if Tanksley retained much of his conscious decision-making ability. He obviously took a detour to visit his cousin and reveal the nature of the curse, but why? Doing so provided McWilliams with the ability to potentially stop him from a situation he designed. Perhaps deep down he wanted to be stopped, or maybe he simply wanted his story to be told to and understood by his last remaining family member.

He was about to suggest a course of action when his phone rang. His mother never called him at such an early hour, but today she did, causing him concern. In the back of his mind Lancaster had worried about his entire family since the beginning of the investigation, so he couldn't simply ignore the call.

"Excuse me," he said to both McWilliams and Jean before stepping aside.

He slid the bar on his phone's screen to answer it.

"Mom?"

"Jeff, your father went to work in the fields this morning and now he isn't there."

"Isn't there?"

"He didn't come up for breakfast or coffee like usual. I went down there to check, but he isn't in the field, and he isn't in the barn. I tried calling his phones, but he didn't answer either one. And his work jacket was still near the tractor."

"I can be right there."

"One more thing, Jeff. A county police car slowed down near the house about half an hour ago. Would he have gone somewhere with one of your old friends?"

Lancaster painfully closed his eyes, groaning inwardly as he began to picture exactly what happened to his father.

"I'll be right over, Mom. Stay put and keep the doors locked."

"Jeff, what's happening?"

"Just stay put."

He ended the call before turning to Jean and McWilliams, finding each of them wearing very concerned expressions.

"You should go visit your cousin's grave and see if it's undisturbed," Lancaster said as calmly as possible. "If it's intact, just keep an eye on it from a distance. I'll be in touch shortly."

"Is everything okay?" Jean asked.

"I'm about to find out. I'll catch up with both of you later."

Lancaster bolted through the front door, hoping he wasn't too late to stop Qualls from harming his father. He felt like such a fool for revealing too much to the man the prior evening, and for not taking action to stop Qualls with any means necessary. Now he was already a step or two behind what-ever sinister plan the man conjured up to make his life a living hell.

∗∗∗

When he pulled beside the tractor nearly fifteen minutes later, Lancaster surveyed the area, finding an area along the road where a car had parked recently. He found his father's work jacket beneath the tractor, and after a minute or two of searching he found his father's phone in the cut hay, which still stood about a foot off the ground. His father possessed a personal phone and a business phone, which were both typically on his person at all times throughout the day.

Flipping open this older style phone, Lancaster decided the contacts list indicated it was used for business purposes. He had bought his parents new phones for Christmas the previous year so he could keep them in his net-work and track them a bit easier since they were getting older but insisted upon being independent in every way.

Thinking much like a police officer at all times, he managed to put an app in each of their phones that allowed him to track their phones with his own at any time. The app was meant to assist hunters who lost their phones in the woods, or parents who wanted to know their kids weren't visiting dan-gerous places. Nothing guaranteed the app wouldn't be used for malicious reasons like jealous lovers stalking their significant others, but Lancaster harbored no ill intent when he decided to keep tabs on his parents if an emergency arose.

Holding the phone out in front of him, he knew calling his father wasn't a good option if Qualls held him captive. He also couldn't call Qualls with-out alerting the man to the fact that he knew his father was missing. Pulling out his own phone, he activated the app and entered his father's phone num-ber as the one to track. It immediately provided results with a large map that gradually grew more detailed as it closed inward. For a few seconds the red dot that indicated the specific location of the phone didn't move, causing Lancaster paralyzing fear that he was too late.

His heart skipped a beat and his eyes didn't blink until he saw the red dot begin to move along one of the county roads just outside of Mitchell.

Turning to get to his truck and begin a pursuit, Lancaster nearly bowled over his own mother who had come down to the field against his advice.

"What's happening?" Donna Lancaster asked of her son, the concern readily apparent in her eyes.

Her dark hair was passed on to her younger son, and her body remained toned from years of work on the farm that included typical indoor chores in addition to running a tractor and dealing with unruly animals from time to time. Wearing blue jeans and a flannel shirt to shield her from the gusting winds and the cooler weather following the overcast sky over Indiana, she stood defiantly awaiting an answer.

"I think someone took Dad," Lancaster answered, though he knew he couldn't afford to waste a second.

"Took him?"

"Yes, but I have his location, Mom. I need to get going before anything happens to him."

His mother looked shocked because Wyatt Lancaster had no enemies.

In this case he was simply a pawn used by someone who wanted to torment his son.

"I'm going with you," Donna insisted.

"No, Mom. It's dangerous and I have to move fast. Call David and get him over here."

"But-"

Lancaster shook his head with resolve, indicating he wasn't letting her come with him.

"Call David. I'll let you know when I find Dad."

Just short of pushing past his mother, Lancaster jumped into his truck and took off down the road, hoping he caught up with Qualls before the man carried out an unimaginable act that he could never take back.

In truth a navigator might have kept Lancaster moving faster and more safely while driving, but he wasn't placing his other parent in danger. Experience in a police cruiser taught him to multitask using a computer terminal, talking on the radio or his phone, navigating stop lights and stop signs, and avoiding other motor vehicles. He began to suspect that Qualls might be heading into Mitchell using a route that avoided the highway completely.

Debating whether to call Jean or possibly Parsons, Lancaster suddenly felt paranoid about placing a call from his phone as though he might disrupt the app tracking his father. He knew technology didn't fail so easily, but felt as though taking his eyes off the ever changing map on his phone might cause the trail to grow cold.

When he finally turned onto a county road that wouldn't provide any turning options for a few miles he called the sheriff's cell phone.

"Parsons," the sheriff answered after a few rings.

"Steve, I need a big favor."

"What now?" the sheriff asked with a tone that indicated he was somewhat preoccupied.

"I need you to call Qualls to the station."

"Why?"

Lancaster felt an internal conflict about how much to reveal to the sheriff. Telling details took up too much time, so he decided to skirt full disclosure for the time being.

"You can't keep up this feud with him, Jeff," Parsons lectured. "It's not healthy."

"This is business, Steve."

"Why do you want to meet with him this time?"

"I don't want to meet with him. I just need to pinpoint his exact location and if he's there with you I'll know. He can't know I asked you this favor."

Momentary silence followed by a brief sigh let Lancaster know that Parsons wasn't particularly happy about being used.

"What did he do, Jeff?" he finally demanded more than asked.

Lancaster wasn't about to delay rescuing his father any longer. He needed to end the call.

"Please, Steve. Just call him in and make up some reason. I'll explain later."

When Parsons replied he didn't sound happy, but he seemed to understand Lancaster wasn't lying about the urgency of the situation. The sheriff needed to remain committed to someone he considered an ally who might potentially fund his campaign heavily during the next election, so he wasn't about to deny Lancaster.

"Fine. I'll call him in."

"Thank you," Lancaster said before severing the call.

He stared at the phone's map, drawing closer to the signal, hoping it continued moving. As long as the red dot migrated in any direction there was a good chance his father remained alive.

***

Immediately after Lancaster left his house, McWilliams and Jean headed to the cemetery in his older truck, hoping to remain undetected and have a nice tall vantage point from the old blue Ford. Two roads ran past the cemetery on either side, both well-traveled even in the early morning hours, so McWilliams chose to park on the top of the hill for a good look downward into the rest of the cemetery.

On the initial pass driving uphill, McWilliams took a long look at his cousin's grave, believing he saw an object lying on the sod in front of the grave marker. Atop the hill he saw the back of the stone, unable to tell if the object remained or blew away. He sat in the driver's seat after shutting down the truck in silence, simply staring ahead as though blinking might cause him to miss something around the grave.

Apparently thinking similarly, Jean said nothing as she shifted her position in the passenger's seat, trying to get comfortable for what could be extended surveillance of the cemetery. McWilliams glanced her way occasionally, thinking back to how she told her daughter to remain where they had spent the night. She didn't want to take any chances of someone finding Abigail, particularly if a rogue deputy was responsible for the assaults at Hallowed Grounds. Of course Qualls knew where McWilliams lived, but she doubted the deputy was about to go anywhere near the house if he wanted to establish an alibi.

"We could have avoided all of this if I had just looked through my cousin's belongings years ago."

"You can't blame yourself," Jean said, patting his hand with hers.

"It is my fault," McWilliams continued. "I was so consumed with going out and partying back then."

"You were a teenager. We all ran around with friends back then."

McWilliams groaned.

"But I didn't grow out of it soon enough. When Henry died I just used that as an excuse to stay away from home even more when Lilly needed me around more than ever. Those are days I'm not proud of."

"You weren't their natural son and your parents died when you were a kid. No one blames you for being a little wayward, Colby."

"I know, but I wish I would've put more effort into learning about my family. For years I was scared to look at my lineage because I didn't see the use in it. I'm the last of my line at this point."

"Be that as it may, what could you have done if you found the book and the paperwork earlier?"

"I could've hidden them long enough to see that these people my cousin is hunting died of natural causes instead of getting hacked to pieces. It still boggles my mind that he took time away from his objective to pay me a visit. Why do you suppose he did that?"

Jean sat silently a moment, contemplating the question.

"Maybe he had a change of heart, or he wants you to stop him. Did he even know you when he was alive?"

"I don't think we ever met," McWilliams said slowly, unable to recall ever seeing his cousin in person.

He wasn't even sure his parents mentioned the man, as though he was considered the black sheep of the family with his awkward hermit ways.

Both McWilliams and Jean stared down to the marked grave, seeing the sky grow gloomier instead of the sun taking center stage as it did most mornings. Townsfolk hated rain during the Persimmon Festival week, particularly during the last day when the parade capped off the festival in the afternoon. Following the parade, rides and food stands opened as people saw old friends who came in for the weekend, listened to the main stage band in the evening, and discovered some overnight magic when their streets were cleared by sunrise.

Any steady rain threatened to severely hamper any business and fun along the downtown streets.

As the wind picked up McWilliams saw a piece of paper tumble away from his cousin's grave. It appeared partially crumpled as though read and discarded, making him wonder if it was the same debris he noticed while driving up to their current location. Aside from the single piece of litter the graveyard appeared pristine, and considering it took so long for the piece of paper to move he believed it wasn't just coincidence.

"I need to go check that out," he said to Jean.

"Check what out?"

"There was a piece of paper or something on my cousin's grave when we pulled up and now it's blowing away. There ain't no way it doesn't mean nothing."

Jean gave him a confused look, as though still trying to straighten out the double negatives used in his sentence or decide what he saw that she did not. McWilliams didn't take any chances of the paper blowing into the street and out of reach as he opened the truck door and marched down to the grave. He didn't hear her follow, and it took less than half a minute for him to navigate the downward slope to the tombstone. By this time the paper rested a few grave markers away, but he noticed a stake planted in the sod atop Tanksley's grave as though someone had left a note there on purpose.

His feet felt unsteady as he drew near the gravestone, and he discovered why as he steadied himself and looked down. He found the sod loose, with small dirt piles clumped near the tombstone, just like Lancaster described about his experience at the grave when Tanksley's body was missing. McWilliams suspected his cousin had left the premises sometime during the overnight when no one took notice. He swallowed hard, still finding his cousin's resurrection a difficult reality to accept.

Looking around, wondering if someone was monitoring his activities, McWilliams walked over to the crumpled piece of paper, scooping it up. He saw nothing out of the ordinary around him, so he unfolded the note and read the brief message as his heartbeat immediately elevated and he regretted not checking the note sooner.

Dashing up the hill toward his truck, McWilliams hoped he wasn't too late to stop his cousin from being someone's pawn and doing more regrettable deeds.

Chapter 42

Ronnie Qualls knew the time to complete his makeshift plan was limited, so he decided to use the one scapegoat he originally set free to take the fall once again.

Abducting Lancaster's father wasn't a good idea under the best of plans, considering the former detective knew enough of the truth to come after Qualls. Legally there wasn't much he or Parsons could ever do, but Qualls didn't believe Lancaster was above vigilante justice for the wrongs done to him, his park employees, and guests. What started as a simple plan to give Lancaster bad publicity went wayward when Hank Barwick fought back, forcing his slaying in a form of self-defense.

Qualls used restraint with the teenager on Friday night, providing her with just enough of a superficial wound to make the park appear unsafe.

Every other recent act of violence was perpetrated by Michael Tanksley, which left Qualls in the clear so far as the authorities were concerned. No one would believe a man dead forty-one years was capable of enacting revenge from the grave. He wished Tanksley showed less restraint, however, perhaps making some townsfolk and Steve Parsons collateral damage along the way. Qualls had visions of one day running for sheriff, and having Parsons out of the picture might have expedited that dream. Although Qualls wasn't well-liked by many of his colleagues, the public didn't know the details of his indiscretions.

Parked just outside of town along Old Highway 60 where very few cars traveled during the morning hours, he stood outside his patrol car, waiting rather impatiently. An occasional thump emitted from the trunk of his marked vehicle, prompting him to warn his abductee often.

"Keep it down back there or your wife and precious sons will be next," he said this time, which caused the ruckus to cease.

Knowing he could ill afford to shoot Wyatt Lancaster outright, Qualls felt fortunate the Taser worked or he might have been punched out by the larger man. With the older man now subdued and locked safely away, the deputy planned to dispose of him without even getting his own hands dirty, furthering his agenda.

Qualls turned to look when he heard the rustling of leaves behind him. He parked near a tree grove that wasn't within sight of any driveway, giving him a bit more privacy when he saw his invited guest emerge from the woods. Only a few times had he and Michael Tanksley laid eyes upon one another, and it never truly became a comfortable experience for the deputy, even if he did control Tanksley's numerous emergences from the grave.

"About time," Qualls said as the undead man drew near, staring intently as always, never uttering a sound.

Clutching the book in his right hand, he pointed to the trunk with his left.

"I have someone that needs to be disposed of," he said, making his second attempt to give direct orders to the deceased man.

The first time resulted in Qualls sneaking into Hallowed Grounds and attacking Hank Barwick because Tanksley refused to deviate from his own personal agenda to assault innocent people. It seemed he outlined his rules for life after death in such a way that no one except those who wronged him in life would be harmed.

Qualls intended to challenge that notion, even as Tanksley's pale blue eyes stared holes through him at the moment.

After checking to make certain no traffic was coming in either direction, Qualls walked to the back of his squad car and popped the trunk. Tanksley stiffly approached the trunk from the other direction, staring in at a wide-eyed Wyatt Lancaster, who obviously recognized the dead man from their younger days.

His muffled cries couldn't escape the gag around his mouth as his hazel eyes stared unblinking at Tanksley, obviously recollecting their history.

Qualls knew the men were contemporaries back in the day, but wasn't sure of their relationship. Based on Wyatt's reaction, he gathered the two knew one another, or the older man was simply terrified by Tanksley's current appearance.

Qualls held up the cursed book in his right hand and a knife in the other, openly displaying them for Tanksley.

"Take him and string him up at the theme park where you used to live, Michael. I want a public display made of him so they close that place."

Tanksley simply glared back, not moved by the words.

"I want you to hang him from one of those roller coasters there for everyone to see," Qualls continued. "Do it and I'll give you the freedom to finish what you started. If you don't, I'll seal this book with my blood and keep it closed for eternity and you'll never get your revenge."

He started to run the knife down the side of his arm, drawing a thin line of blood as the sharp blade did its work with minimal pain. After switching the book to the other hand, he held it beneath the blood as a stream trickled down his arm, edging closer to the book's clasp. Finally Tanksley stared at something other than the deputy, his deteriorated face drawing close to a concerned expression.

"Even if you wanted to, you couldn't stop me before I sealed this book and put an end to your plans. I want him to suffer and kick for his life from a rope. Do we have an understanding?"

With what little range his dried skin allowed, Tanksley shot a disapproving glare, causing Qualls to back up a few steps. He worried that Tanksley might disobey him, even assault him, but Qualls was facing jail time or the barrel of a gun from Jeff Lancaster. Without much to lose, the deputy needed his amended plan to work. Too much work and risk were already in the rearview mirror to take a cautious approach now. He and Candice hated Lancaster with a passion because they felt the man cheated them somehow when he won the lottery the day the divorce was finalized and got to keep every penny.

Surprising him somewhat, Tanksley begrudgingly reached inside the trunk and scooped out Wyatt Lancaster, throwing the large man over his shoulder with ease. Wyatt kicked and screamed the entire time, his sounds not ranging far enough that anyone might hear them and rush to his rescue.

Within seconds Tanksley disappeared into the brush, and Qualls knew it wouldn't take a man who didn't need to breathe, and never felt pain, very long to reach the theme park because he could run continuously. Hearing some vehicles along the parallel highway, the deputy decided to vacate the premises before anyone saw him. He slammed the trunk shut and scurried to the driver's seat, prepared to create an alibi now that Wyatt Lancaster wasn't a factor.

Looking to his phone, he noticed a missed call from the sheriff, wondering what the man wanted this time. Parsons had proven to be a thorn in his side lately, siding with Lancaster on almost every topic, surely wanting a campaign donation from his former employee.

"Fuck you both," Qualls muttered as he called the sheriff's cell phone, turning around to head for the county building where his presence was almost assuredly required.

***

Lancaster felt certain he was about to catch up to the elusive red dot on his phone finder app when it suddenly veered off in a completely unnatural direction that didn't follow any conventional road.

He pulled over to the side of Highway 37 when he saw the red dot parallel to his location, wondering if something had happened to his father's phone, or the app was on the fritz. His heart began to pound at the notion of losing his father after drawing so close to the exact location. He couldn't follow the wooded areas and fields where the red dot now moved at a slower rate, questioning the best course of action.

Life and death decisions came easier as a police officer because they didn't directly involve his loved ones. Right now he *needed* to see his father alive because he felt guilty for not stopping Qualls when the opportunity presented itself. He couldn't have legally kept Qualls in check, but he owed the man some punishment stemming back a few years, so shooting him didn't sound completely out of line.

Lancaster had decided to follow the red dot as best he could from the highway when his cell phone screen changed, alerting him that Colby McWilliams was calling him. He almost refused to answer, again thinking that he might somehow sabotage the app. Deciding he couldn't afford to miss any piece of information, he clicked the green button on his screen to answer the call.

"What do you have, Colby?"

"We found a note on my cousin's grave that said for him to meet with someone on Old Highway 60."

"For your cousin to meet someone?" Lancaster asked for clarification.

"Yes. So we went out there and arrived just in time to see a county police car driving away."

"Did Qualls see you?" Lancaster inquired, piecing together the scenario.

"Seriously doubtful. He's driving towards Bedford now."

"You're *following* him?"

"From a distance."

Lancaster took a few seconds to collect his thoughts, drawing a deep breath.

"Where exactly are you right now?"

"Passing the couple of closed gas stations just past the Kettle Kitchen on 37."

Lancaster knew the area wasn't even within a few miles of his red dot's location on the map. He suspected Parsons had indeed summoned Qualls to the station, which likely meant Qualls removed his father from the squad car. What he couldn't understand was how his father was moving at such a fast clip through wooded areas and cornfields.

"I think he's going to the sheriff's office, Colby, so keep a very safe distance and see if you can follow him from there."

"Will do. What are you going to do?"

"My father disappeared from his farm this morning and my mother saw a squad car slowly pass the house. So I'm following my father's cell phone signal. At least I hope I am. Give me a call if you see anything new."

"Okay."

Lancaster ended the call, returning the screen to the phone finder. Present once again, the red dot had made some progress heading in a northerly direction. Getting his truck back on the road, Lancaster continued to track the app, pulling over occasionally so he didn't get rear-ended on the highway for driving far too slowly.

He followed the signal for another fifteen minutes, drawing closer to the intersecting highways close to the area that McWilliams called him from while tracking Qualls. Pulling into the parking lot of the first abandoned gas station he reached, Lancaster watched as the red dot drew near Highway 50, which ran east and west compared to Highway 37, which ran north and south. He was about to pull his truck to the stoplight and head down Highway 50, anxious to see if he found his father, or at least a clue, but as he waited at the red light the dot suddenly disappeared.

Lancaster stared into his phone, unwilling to believe the screen momentarily. He tapped the phone a few times, hoping it was a refresh error, or perhaps the signal hit some interference, but his phone sent him a message that the signal to his father's phone was lost.

"No," he said, repeating the word about a half dozen times as he tried to restart the app, receiving a honk from a car behind him as the light turned green. "Fuck!"

Lancaster stomped on the gas and crossed the intersection to get onto Highway 50, hoping to reestablish a signal or draw close to its last location. Strangely the route took him in the direction of his residence and his theme park, but he couldn't imagine why his father would head there when other populated areas were much closer. Lancaster began to wonder if his father was acting on free will, or if Qualls had handed him over to someone else. For all he knew the phone was now attached to a wild animal, sending him on a wild goose chase.

Since his phone provided no further benefit to him, Lancaster called his head of security, wanting no one inside his park in case Qualls or the man's possible mystery partner ended up traveling there. He needed the ability to take whatever measures felt necessary to keep his family and employees safe. Currently driving a bit too fast, he stared down at his phone-finding app, trying to compare his position to the last known red dot blip.

"Schall," the security director answered after a few rings.

"Danny, it's Jeff. I need you to clear everyone out of the park right now."

"We open in two hours, boss. Can I ask what's going on?"

"Sorry, Danny. I need everyone out and no one else getting in."

"So, you want me to stand guard at the gates?"

"No. Just lock up everything, put a sign up, and get out of there until I call you."

"A sign? Saying what?"

"Just say we're closed until further notice."

A few seconds passed without a word from Schall, and Lancaster felt certain the man regretted ever taking the security job. Lancaster didn't blame him one bit, but he wasn't about to endanger the man by leaving him alone at Hallowed Grounds. Either Qualls or Michael Tanksley had almost ended his life once, and Lancaster didn't want more blood on his hands.

"Just make the announcement and wait for my call to reopen the park," Lancaster ordered Schall for his own good. "I'll let you know more when I find out."

"Okay," Schall replied, though his tone sounded disgruntled at best. "I'll take care of it."

Lancaster wanted to fill his security director in about the potential danger, but lacked the time and patience at the moment. He was nearly to the spot where the red dot disappeared, so he began to slow down and look to his left for any activity, either by human foot or an off-road vehicle of some sort.

He wished he still possessed a marked police car. Flipping on the overhead lights and forcing people to slow down and watch around them would keep him safer and allow him to search uninterrupted. Creeping along the road in his truck only served to have people glare at him or honk their horns.

Before he got too far into looking roadside for clues his phone sounded with a ding to indicate an incoming text message. He looked down to see that McWilliams had sent a text message informing him that Qualls was back on the road and heading south out of Bedford.

Finding a rural driveway that wasn't presently occupied, Lancaster pulled in before taking up his phone and tracing where the red dot's blips had been before they disappeared. The app let him see a figurative trail, and he scrolled up and down the map using his finger on the touchscreen to take a guess at where the red dot was heading. He noticed the dot never deviated from a particular direction, even though it meant the phone was carried through rugged terrain.

"No," he muttered when the screen revealed his worst fear.

He already knew the destination couldn't possibly be anywhere else except his theme park, but Lancaster wondered just how much danger his father was in, and if he possessed the ability to save him.

Now within a few miles of his theme park, Lancaster decided to stall his arrival a few minutes to give Schall time enough to evacuate the staff. Anticipation caused his stomach to ache as though it was tied in knots and he desperately wanted to find his father. While he waited beside the highway, he decided to step out and look for clues where the electronic trail went cold. He crossed the road as the sun fought to be seen one last time through the darkening clouds with a storm front blowing from the southwest.

He walked about fifty feet parallel to a shallow ditch, looking for footprints or evidence of any recent human presence. Thanks to the last rays of sunlight he spotted a glimmering gray object about another thirty feet up the road. Breaking into a quick jog, Lancaster made it to the metal and plastic device within seconds as a few heavy raindrops assaulted his arms from above, indicating the powerful weather quickly circling the area. Kneeling down, he found the shattered remains of a cell phone, wondering if the unprotected device was dislodged from his father's clothing or discovered by a sinister party.

Scooping up the phone he looked in the direction of his park, wondering what horrors awaited him once he walked inside.

Chapter 43

Jean couldn't muster the enthusiasm McWilliams displayed as they continued to tail Qualls south on Highway 37 after his fifteen minute stop at the sheriff's office. She absolutely wanted justice for her aunt and the others now that she understood a living human being was truly behind the scheme, but she wasn't eager to confront Qualls. She was hardly a match for a trained police officer, and though McWilliams was physically up to the challenge and owned firearms, he wasn't expertly practiced in shooting.

She wasn't even certain the man carried any firearms with him, but she wasn't about to inquire as they followed the squad car from a safe distance. Qualls neared the intersection at Highway 50 and turned on his turn signal, prompting Jean to guess where he might be heading. The deputy likely wanted to see if his plan unfolded according to his design, and the only way to know was to visit Hallowed Grounds.

McWilliams pressed harder on the gas, prompting her to take hold of his free hand. He took time to notice her action wasn't panic, but rather a delicate reminder to follow more subtly, so he eased back on the acceleration.

When they made the turn both noticed that Qualls and his car were nowhere in sight. Jean looked to her left, knowing the gas station at the corner was the only immediate turn, but found no brown and tan marked car in sight.

"He must've sped up bigtime," McWilliams commented, starting to press down on the accelerator again.

It required only a matter of seconds for him to reach a speed in excess of the posted speed limit and pass a few driveways. Able to see the road ahead of them for nearly half a mile, Jean wondered if Qualls had spotted them and attempted to distance himself from them, or if he cleverly chose a spot to pull off the road that concealed his vehicle.

As though reading her mind, McWilliams seemed to reach the same conclusion, slowing down at the best possible hiding spot for miles.

The Lawrence County Fairgrounds.

After a slight uphill drive a few buildings emerged and Jean knew driving further into the grounds only led to more buildings, stalls, and potential hiding spots. She also knew that deputies worked security on the grounds during the county fair, meaning they knew every inch of the property intimately.

"This isn't a good idea," Jean said as they reached the main building atop the hill.

McWilliams nervously licked his lips, looking around the open fields and parking areas atop the hill. Most of the buildings and activities were further back, and a long walk or reasonable drive away.

"Maybe we should get back on the road," he said slowly, as though the concept of hidden dangers just occurred to him.

McWilliams circled the main building to get them back to the main road they had just used to enter from the highway. He took a final look in both directions before pulling forward and heading west on Highway 50 toward the theme park.

Jean personally felt they were walking into a trap if Qualls pulled into the fairgrounds and waited for them. If he had continued west as they were now doing only one logical destination awaited him. Still, she continued to look from side to side in case he pulled off the side of the road somewhere. For all she knew Qualls never even noticed them following him to the county building and all through town to the highway. Perhaps he simply wanted to see the fruits of his labor, and complete whatever evil intentions he had planned for Wyatt Lancaster.

Hallowed Grounds sat on property that once grew corn and hosted a failed festival, making it easy to spot along a highway of otherwise residential farming grounds. McWilliams drove considerably slower, being cautious now that he had no idea where Qualls might have gone. Even if he drove directly to the park the man certainly wasn't going to enter through the front entrance. Surely he would find a hiding spot nearby that allowed him to sneak into the park as he'd likely done a few times before.

Not even half a mile from the theme park Jean looked out her side of the truck, spying a brown car pulling down a dirt road of some sort.

"Slow down!" she yelled, causing McWilliams to tap the brakes a little hard, sending them both lurching forward as Jean continued to watch the car to her right being swallowed by the woods. "I think that was him," she added, pointing to the dirt path where she noticed the vehicle.

McWilliams made a complete U-turn in the middle of the highway before slowly making his way down the dirt road that seemed like an access road of some sort, and not a formal driveway. Perhaps an entry to a hunting spot, or a path that allowed for farm equipment to access a field, the road quickly became encumbered by darkness as trees and their thick branches cut off the graying sky.

Jean saw him reach for the switch that controlled the headlights and immediately change his mind, even as the wooded area became darker with each foot they traveled. Only specks of daylight pierced the trees, providing just enough light to make the area look like the latter portion of dusk.

She couldn't recall seeing such dense trees except when she and her family visited their summer retreat in Ohio. Well away from any towns or main roads, the camp required miles of driving along barely visible beaten down roads that gave the family vehicle a jolt whenever the tires hit a deep enough hole. Now a different kind of danger potentially awaited them within the dark area, though a glimpse of light finally emerged ahead of them through an open yellow, metal farm gate.

McWilliams drove them through the open gate and into a wider clearing that provided just slightly more light. The skies above grew more gray and dreary as thunder grumbled in the distance. Jean felt a chill run through her body as they both spied the marked squad car just ahead of them, parked at one edge of the clearing even though the road continued ahead. She saw McWilliams stiffen at the sight of the car, though he decided to slow down and pull behind the vehicle.

"What are you doing?" Jean virtually demanded, thinking he might have lost his mind.

"I'm going to ask for directions in case he doesn't already think we're following him."

"That's going to look weird considering we're a quarter of a mile in woods," Jean argued, her internal danger detector already reading in the red.

"Too late now," McWilliams said as he opened his door to step outside.

Jean watched him slowly approach the police cruiser, obviously seeing something she couldn't from her vantage point. His head reared back momentarily as though the sight of something stunned him. Turning to her, he gave a shrug that indicated no one was present inside the marked car.

"No!" Jean screamed as someone quickly emerged from the woods dressed in some kind of leather pelts that appeared Native American. The man wore face paint or a mask so she couldn't clearly see his face, but he went straight for McWilliams aggressively.

Her warning temporarily saved McWilliams as he turned in time to confront the disguised man, clutching the man's arms to struggle over what looked like a large knife to Jean. She opened the truck door, determined to help McWilliams if she could, but both men fought for the weapon, rolling over the hood of the squad car and out of sight.

Running to the front of the truck she heard both men grunting and groaning from behind the car for nearly half a minute until she heard a yelp of pain that sounded like McWilliams.

"Colby?" she cried out, taking a half step forward.

Thinking better of her situation, she stayed back a few seconds, giving her a better chance to defend herself or run in a number of directions. Behind her was the road that led to the highway, but it was shrouded by darkness and trees. She didn't know what lie ahead of her when the path continued, but to her left was an opening that obviously led into a much better lighted area.

She heard another agonized cry, but this one sounded muffled, as though someone were trying to stifle the sound, or might be losing consciousness. Taking a nervous step forward, she felt her heart pounding in her chest because this was no longer a spy game. Even though she couldn't prove it ironclad, she now knew Qualls was behind much of the death and destruction over the past week. Living to tell anyone the tale, however, might prove more difficult than she ever anticipated.

About to head back to the truck to grab her phone and can of mace, Jean was taken by surprise when the mysterious attacker popped up from behind the car. Having no idea whether or not McWilliams survived the attack, she knew her best course of action was to lead the disguised figure away from the area, so she darted to her left toward the clearing.

And the chase began.

Chapter 44

Lancaster pulled up to the employee gate of his park, finding Schall there making certain no one else entered after ushering everyone else off the property. Stepping from his truck, he shook hands with his security director, seeing a hint of distrust and uncertainty in the man's eyes. If Lancaster had to guess, he felt the man was hurt more by his employer not putting complete faith in him and telling the full truth than he was by the recent attacks.

"I'm sorry about all of this, Danny," Lancaster said. "Thank you for taking care of things."

"You're welcome. Boss, I can stick around if you want-"

"No, Danny. Thank you, but there's something I need to deal with before I can let other people in here."

Schall nodded.

"Everyone is out. I put signs at the entrance gates, and everyone here said they were just a phone call away when you need them."

"Good. Hopefully that's soon."

"Boss, I'm just a phone call away if you need anything here, too. Even if it's off the books."

Lancaster forced a grin, catching the hint that Schall was willing to use some not so ethical methods of dealing with the problems surrounding the park.

"I appreciate it, but you've already done enough. I'll call you when I'm done here, Danny."

Schall nodded before getting into his sedan to leave the park in Lancaster's hands.

"I'll call if I survive this," Lancaster muttered, watching his security chief turn left to head back to Highway 37.

Returning to his truck, Lancaster used his personal keycard to get the large front gate to slide open for him. Only department managers had such access because they were scheduled to work through the winter and always arrived before other employees to open the front gate and other areas of the park.

Driving through the gate, he began looking around, wondering if he could spot his father, or anyone, while driving. Although a quicker method of searching the park, driving didn't give him views into and beside every building. Having help certainly would have made the search quicker, but he wasn't risking lives or scaring off Qualls, or whoever was transporting his father at this point.

He questioned whether Qualls had made a deal with Tanksley, or why the undead man would even listen to the deputy. Sure, Qualls possessed the book that controlled Tanksley, but the murdered man had never seemed too concerned about his returns from the grave in the past.

"Of course," Lancaster said aloud, knowing Tanksley's time to enact his revenge was running out. He had already missed an opportunity to murder Hank Barwick's father, and the two remaining women weren't going to live forever.

Praying his father was telling the truth when he claimed he had no connection to Vivian Weatherly and her group, Lancaster drove onward, searching left and right for any clues.

He worried that Qualls wanted to make a major production of some kind in the park to further embarrass him, and to set him up somehow. Knowing Qualls, getting the park shut down and causing public humiliation to Lancaster wasn't going to suffice. Lancaster felt certain their business wasn't going to conclude until one of them lay dead somewhere in the park.

Driving past several restroom buildings, Lancaster reached a fork in the road where he could either continue into the main portion of the park or take the utility roads behind the scenes. He decided to take the hidden roads, figuring someone might sneak through there rather than brazenly walk or drive in the open.

Very few trees existed on the property when he purchased it, so he purchased several saplings and some larger trees to give the property character. A few were already beginning to show the changing colors in their leaves when he passed them, desperately looking out the side window for something much more important.

Most theme parks showed off with skylines consisting of their roller coasters and taller rides, but Lancaster hadn't expanded to that point yet. Much of his park was near the ground with numerous haunted houses that took place inside, outside, or both, and mazes that were entirely inside so they ran during any conditions. He passed several such buildings, carefully examining every side possible without taking time to exit the truck.

His phone rang beside him and he chose to ignore it, purely determined to find his father. He couldn't face his mother again without knowing his father's whereabouts, feeling partially responsible for Qualls targeting the man.

Taking a left bend in the road, Lancaster saw the lift hill of his mine coaster in the distance, about to begin panning left and right again when something caught his attention. An object appeared out of place, dangling from the main hill of the ride, swaying in the breeze as raindrops began to fall heavier on his windshield.

Caught between stopping and turning away, or facing the potential horror that awaited him, Lancaster slowly drove forward, not sure he wanted to face the ominous truth as he began realizing the object swinging from a rope, from *his* roller coaster, was about the size of a human body.

"No," he muttered under his breath when he drew close to the object, beginning to realize exactly what his eyes were spying.

He stopped just short of the roller coaster, stepping from his truck as the rain cut loose, instantly soaking him. Realizing the horrific scene before him, Lancaster dropped to his knees, unable to look away from the sight above him as the rope made an eerie creaking sound. Overhead, dangling like an insect caught in a cobweb, Wyatt Lancaster showed no signs of life as his glasses were missing from his face and his head was lying limply to one side. With his hands at his side, the older man swayed to and fro as his son felt lost to the world, his dreams crashing around him because of one jealous deputy who thought stealing his wife wasn't punishment enough.

Lancaster clenched his fists, determined to find Qualls and take his life, even if such an act meant throwing away his own future. He wanted to get up and overturn every inch of the park in search of the bastard, but his own sorrow kept him planted in the same spot, wondering how to deal with such heartbreak.

***

To say Danny Schall underestimated his duties when taking the security director position would be a drastic understatement.

He expected to deal with unruly kids or the occasional intoxicated adult, but nearly getting strangled days before the park officially opened seemed unrealistic. Even in Kansas City he only faced life and death scenarios a few times during the twenty year span he worked as a police officer. Granted, four of those years were spent doing administrative duties which sometimes felt as hazardous when he was the mouthpiece for the department, often confronted by hostile groups.

Unfortunately he found himself in a portion of Indiana that didn't have good factory jobs or much in the way of private security. He liked Lancaster as a boss, but wasn't sure how much longer he wanted his job if it meant being excluded by the man and targeted by strangers. Schall remained a fixture at the park throughout the construction phases, finding no trouble except for the occasional snooping reporter or amateur photographer who wanted to sneak in for some pictures of the work.

Now driving home in the pouring rain like a scolded dog being sent outside from the house, Schall hoped Lancaster found what he was looking for and settled the bizarre business once and for all.

Shortly after leaving the park Schall was forced to pull over beside the road as the rain mercilessly pounded everything beneath it. Only now did he dare drive forward again, glancing to his left by happenstance to see someone running through a fenced in field that adjoined the theme park property. Technically Lancaster owned the property, and the access road that led off Highway 50 and into the field, but it had yet to be developed.

"Son of a bitch," Schall said under his breath, wondering what kind of loon dared trespass on Lancaster's land during a thunderstorm.

He flipped on his turn signal and turned left onto the access road, which led to the field, or went further up to the back of the theme park where large security gates kept people from entering. If people were crafty, however, they could enter the park through the edge of the field and slip past the minimal security measures left in place at the moment.

His headlights guided him into the first opening as his mind raced for ways to catch up to the person running in the field to his left. Any thoughts of continuing the hunt came to a screeching halt, however, as he noticed an old Ford truck and a marked county police vehicle parked within the clearing. Wondering if someone was running from a deputy, he stepped from his sedan, immediately pelted by rain that made its way through the trees and their changing leaves.

Schall groaned, figuring his suit now required dry cleaning once it dried out. He hated paying the service because he didn't have a connection who hooked him up with a good price since the move east. Knowing he dared not drive into the field, he briefly considered calling the police, but figured a deputy was somewhere on the premises, possibly dealing with a traffic stop gone bad where the offender was fleeing to avoid an outstanding warrant.

Figuring the action was beyond the clearing, Schall started to reach for his door handle to place a call or drive forward when he heard a groan from behind the squad car.

"What the hell?" he questioned aloud, suddenly believing the situation was far more serious than his original assessment.

***

Jean raced through the field until she came across the borders of Hallowed Grounds, which were mesh wire fences about ten feet high directly in front of her and wood panel borders further down in either direction that measured closer to twenty feet.

"Shit," she said, glancing behind her to find no one chasing her in the field of tan straw.

McWilliams fought valiantly, injuring his attacker with some kind of wound to the foot that caused the disguised man to limp heavily into the field after Jean. She thought she saw blood stemming from the fresh wound, but wasn't able to ascertain details while fleeing for her life.

Most of the straw reached her waist, so she wasn't certain that Qualls, or whoever wore the Native American garb, wasn't simply lying low and waiting to strike. Grabbing hold of the mesh fence, she began to climb, seeing no other quick path to safety. It took her about a minute, but she reached the top of the fence and swung her leg over to cross to the other side. She had just started to descend from the top of the fence when she saw someone coming her way from a distance.

Panicking immediately, she dropped to the ground and felt a sharp pain as she twisted her left ankle. Knowing her stalker could see her through the fence, she quickly regained her footing and hobbled into the park before he reached the fence line. Another one of her quick glances back had revealed the man holding a knife covered in blood, and she certainly didn't want to feel the blade sink into her innards.

At long last the rain began to subside, but Jean was soaked and the clothes that stuck to her skin only served to slow her down. She hobbled along, looking for any signs of life in a theme park that was advertised to have an incredible grand opening weekend since late August. It took her a few minutes to reach a concrete path, the first sign she neared civilization, but even with buildings in earshot and one of the roller coasters looming in the distance, she saw absolutely no people.

She wanted to scream out for help, but knew that might draw the attacker closer to her, so she continued onward, hoping to find a park employee.

Beginning to feel like she'd entered a ghost town, Jean noticed no rides were running, no sounds of guests enjoying themselves reached her ears, and she didn't even see any lights turned on despite the deluge that just engulfed the park. Her ankle began to swell and throb as though her foot might forcefully explode out of her shoe, but Jean had no choice except to press onward. Numerous hiding spots presented themselves, but she didn't want to play the victim and wait to be found. She needed to find help for herself, and call the police if it wasn't too late to save McWilliams.

Deciding to remain closer to the buildings and off the main pathways when possible, Jean navigated the park with apprehension, wondering if something caused a delay in the park's daily operation. She questioned why no maintenance people or security guards were visible anywhere within the grounds. Stumbling along, she used the occasional bathroom facility or haunted house building for support to take some weight off the injured ankle.

Although the rain had tapered off, the wind continued to gust through the open areas of the park, impeding her progress. Fighting to keep her eyes open, she pressed forward, inching closer to the roller coaster she spied from a distance shortly after jumping the fence. For a moment excitement coursed through her body like lightning when she thought she spotted someone working near the top of the roller coaster, but as she picked up her anguished pace Jean quickly realized the optical illusion wasn't a person working, but something far more disheartening.

At first she wanted to believe the object hanging from the roller coaster was some kind of prop in the spirit of Halloween and the theme park itself. As she drew closer, however, her eyes didn't blink or look away from the object and she began to realize the heft of it, and how little it swung outward, indicated the body was legitimate.

"No," Jean said as she continued to virtually sleepwalk forward, barely noticing someone on the path in front of her.

A few seconds later it registered that someone ahead of her on both knees stared upward. Either the killer remained to admire his work, or more than likely Lancaster had found his father in a compromised state. Once she felt certain it was Lancaster she dashed forward as quickly as her injury allowed, to solicit his help. He never moved, even as she drew near, her footsteps piercing the sounds of wind and distant thunder, easily heard by anyone halfway alert.

"Jeff," she said, placing both hands on his shoulders as she knelt down next to him, his eyes unwavering from the horrific scene above.

Jean glanced upward, seeing Wyatt Lancaster's work boots dangling at the ends of his legs. Not until they swayed to one side did she see the remainder of the man, his hands and face pale, his head flaccid to one side, barely bobbing despite the weather moving his body. His customary eyeglasses weren't present, but she knew the man well enough from town events over the years to identify him. A synthetic rope, possibly one used by maintenance personnel to carry out their inspection duties from above, was wrapped around the man's neck, though she couldn't see a knot from her perspective.

"He's gone," Lancaster muttered, not even recognizing the person now beside him because he never turned to look.

He's in shock, Jean thought, wondering if she could get him back to her in time to save both of their lives with a dangerous Qualls in the vicinity. Surely the deputy was looking for any way to wrap up any loose ends and explain his way out of the situation later. Jean prayed McWilliams wasn't dead, and she wanted to get back to him and her phone, particularly if Lancaster didn't snap out of his unresponsive state quickly.

"Jeff, Qualls is on the loose. He's coming this way."

Lancaster muttered something inaudible and she tried shaking him, but he simply groaned and looked down to the concrete beneath him. Taking a nervous look around, Jean found her worst fear coming up from behind. Not even a hundred yards down the concrete path she eyed the same disguised assailant coming her way with a knife clutched in his right hand. Upon spying her, Qualls picked up his pace despite the leg injury, forcing Jean to make a life or death decision in mere seconds.

Chapter 45

Schall searched around the patrol car and almost immediately found an injured bearded man on the other side, lying on the ground with an obvious wound to the left side of his stomach. Taking off his sport coat, the security director used it to begin applying pressure to the bleeding gash. By no means an expert about anatomy, he seemed to recall from his first responder training that wounds along the sides such as this didn't become life-threatening until the patient lost sufficient amounts of blood.

"Talk to me, buddy," Schall encouraged the man, who struggled to take in deep breaths and focus his eyes on much of anything. "Who did this to you?"

"Book," the man said a few seconds later when his blue eyes finally looked to his best chance at survival.

"Book?" Schall questioned. "Here, hold this," he said, helping the injured man hold the folded up sport coat against his wound before standing to call 911.

Once a dispatcher answered, he spent about two minutes answering questions and providing his location for true first responders before telling the dispatcher he needed to go to attend to the injured man. The dispatcher encouraged him to stay on the line, but he insisted he needed to go and ended the call, knowing he could call back if the medics struggled to find the unusual location. The dispatcher also promised to send police, who would likely arrive more quickly.

Kneeling down beside the man, Schall helped apply pressure on the wound once again, finding the man more lucid this time.

"I need you to see if you can find an old book in that car," the man said nodding toward the marked squad car.

"You've got better things to worry about," Schall replied.

"It's a matter of life and death," the man insisted.

Figuring there was no harm in a quick sweep of the vehicle, Schall stood and tried the driver's side front door, finding it locked. He knew many cops with take home vehicles often sawed off a key that they left in the ignition for quick starting of the car, keeping the remote entry key with them.

"Do you have the keys?" Schall asked of the man.

"No. He's the one who did this to me. He's the one who's been causing all of the problems at the theme park."

Schall believed the words as soon as they left the man's mouth because it all began to make sense to him. He knew tensions were high between his employer and at least one of his former colleagues, and rumors spread through the theme park like wildfire.

"He went toward the park," the man continued, though it obviously pained him to speak. "He's after someone. I *need* that book to stop something bad from happening."

Schall immediately thought of his boss staying behind at the park, possibly having no idea of the danger heading directly for him. Torn between helping this man, searching for a book, or running to the aid of his employer, he decided to try all three at once. While he called Lancaster's cell phone, Schall drew his own sidearm and held it at the base of the window, firing once as the glass shattered upon impact from the bullet. He waited a few seconds until reaching Lancaster's voicemail on the other end before reaching inside the car and pressing a button that unlocked every door. He quickly swept through the vehicle, covering the glove box, under the seats, above the visors, and in the center console storage area, finding nothing.

He was about to give up his search completely when the man, determined as hell despite his injuries, called to him.

"The trunk."

Schall reluctantly decided to continue the search only because the injured man wasn't losing consciousness.

"What's your name, buddy?" he asked as he reached into the glove compartment to press the trunk release button.

"Colby."

"What's so important about this book, Colby?"

"You wouldn't believe me if I told you."

Thinking he was more open-minded than ever at the moment, Schall decided not to press about the book as he exited the car and lifted the trunk. Inside he found tactical gear, a shotgun, boxes of ammunition, and a few cardboard boxes containing random items and some paperwork. He quickly shuffled through the boxes, finding nothing that even resembled a book, before lifting the boxes and the gear to discover an old, dusty book with a red cover and a gold-colored hasp that made it look like a diary. This book, however, wasn't some run-of-the-mill journal picked up at a dollar store. Heavy, thick, and durable, the book felt as though it couldn't be damaged, and the hasp was thick, indicating anyone without the key wasn't allowed access.

Schall pulled the hasp aside, opening the book as he carried it over to the injured man to help calm him.

"Here," he said, handing the book over, finding the man openly relieved as he closed the two covers together.

"What's your last name, Colby?" Schall asked, trying to make conversation as he watched the man peel back the sport coat from his bloody wound.

"McWilliams."

At first Schall thought McWilliams wanted to assess the wound's damage, but he completely removed the makeshift dressing from his abdomen area, reaching down there with his right hand while the other held the book.

He slid his right hand partially into the wound, drawing out some blood as his body stiffened from the pain. Schall started to intervene, believing the man wanted to hurt himself.

"Don't," McWilliams barked, rubbing the blood onto the book's gold hasp.

Schall decided to disobey and restrain the man with any means necessary until he saw the hasp literally soak in the blood like a sponge until it disappeared. It was like some kind of time lapse where the blood dried up, except it vanished, as though swallowed by the hasp and the book.

"Dear God," Schall muttered.

"I've done what I needed to," McWilliams said. "You should help the others."

"I can't just bail on you."

"My phone is in the truck. Get it for me and I can call 911 if the ambulance doesn't show soon."

Feeling as though he might be abandoning McWilliams and every oath he'd ever taken as a police officer, Schall decided to get the man's phone and head back to the theme park. He wasn't about to cut through an uncut field when driving there and entering the main gate with his electronic key allowed him to cover more ground along the theme park in his car.

He quickly retrieved the phone and handed it to McWilliams, hearing the first sirens in the distance.

"If they drive by, you call 911 and tell them where we are," Schall ordered, figuring the local man knew the roads far better than he did.

"Promise," McWilliams said weakly, still clutching the book close to his chest.

Schall made sure the sport coat was packed tightly against the wound before heading to his car to see if he could catch up with Lancaster and the other two unknown people before it proved too late.

Watching the security director drive off, McWilliams looked at the book, barely feeling the constant stinging of the wound Qualls gave him. And though he sealed the book to ensure his cousin didn't run off to murder his last two enemies in cold blood, McWilliams began to wonder if the little remaining conscience in Michael Tanksley might prove the only thing capable of stopping Qualls. No one except Jean knew where the man was heading, and he could certainly leave a bloody trail in his wake if no one stopped him.

Hearing the sirens draw closer, McWilliams closed his eyes, contemplating whether he could trust his cousin based on their one brief, albeit somewhat violent encounter. He felt the pain nagging along his left side as his body began to grow cold from internal blood loss. Making his decision, he prayed everyone inside the theme park survived the ordeal and Qualls eventually got what was coming to him.

***

Within the recesses of his mind Lancaster knew he committed several mistakes that brought him to this point. He regretted not discovering his arch enemy was behind his theme park's woes earlier, he admonished himself for not believing McWilliams sooner, and his biggest regret at the moment was not bringing a firearm with him when he left the house that morning.

"You two have caused me a great deal of trouble," Qualls said as he removed the painted mask from his face, aiming a semi-automatic pistol between Lancaster and Jean. "But now all of this ends."

"I can't imagine what kind of cover story explains any of this," Lancaster said defiantly now that he'd regained all of his wits.

He did his best to step in front of Jean to shield her, knowing she tried to get him out of harm's way by sticking around. She didn't deserve to die, but Lancaster didn't possess the means to protect either of them at the moment. He knew reaching for his cell phone couldn't be hidden from view at the moment, so he decided not to attempt any such move.

Water still dripped from his clothing as he stared at Qualls, who didn't seem the least bit concerned about revealing his identity.

"You won't get away with this, Ronnie," Lancaster stated, knowing security cameras covered virtually every square foot of his park, including the areas where guests weren't allowed.

"I don't think it'll be a problem," Qualls replied confidently, producing a keycard from within his disguise. "I lifted this from one of your employees a few days ago. Although it didn't grant me access to the security footage room, it did allow me to shut down all of the power to your park."

He waved a hand airily to show that no lights were on around them.

"Guess the storm conveniently knocked out the power while you two met an unfortunate end, so no one will ever really know what happened."

"Why my father?" Lancaster felt compelled to ask, even if he was about to share his father's fate.

"That was part of my plan," Qualls said, his face turning stone cold. "The evidence was going to show that you and your father had a big argument, either here or at your house, and there was going to be a shootout that killed both of you. That didn't exactly work out when Nancy Drew and her boyfriend decided to follow me to Bedford and back, so I guess the story is going to have to change a little."

"Parsons knows you're up to something," Lancaster said. "You're not going to get away with this."

"Even if the sheriff were smart enough to piece this together, what could he do? There won't be any physical evidence linking me to any of this. Tanksley followed my orders and strung up your dad, so there's nothing stopping me from finishing this."

"Asshole," Lancaster sputtered, stepping forward angrily.

Qualls flashed the gun at him, stopping Lancaster who still instinctively needed to protect Jean as long as possible. His mind raced for a way out of the situation, but they couldn't outrun bullets, and help wasn't coming because he'd done precisely what Qualls wanted him to do by sending every employee home.

"Your theme park will fall into ruin, and when it goes to auction Candice and I will be there to swoop it up."

"So she knows about all of this?"

Qualls produced a smile that showed he found a sick enjoyment in every aspect of his plan.

"Are you kidding me?" Qualls said with a chuckle. "It was *her* idea, Jeff, once I found that book at the mechanic's place. Of course I've had to modify a few things after you basically gave yourself away last night."

Holding up his injured hand for Lancaster to see, the former police officer knew he'd accidentally tipped his hand the previous evening.

"I did my best to keep it from you, but you always were good at spotting details, Jeff. I took your pops as collateral, but decided my new plan worked a little bit better. People have seen you arguing with your dad about his involvement, or lack thereof, with Vivian Weatherly's group. All of the recent events tie back to our senior citizens, and who's to say otherwise?"

Qualls shrugged confidently as though no one would ever look past the surface of his imperfect plan.

"I'll be around to help fill in the blanks, and Parsons will appreciate me, or he'll have to meet an unfortunate end, too. You think I could be sheriff and run this place at the same time?"

Qualls asked the question with the intention of infuriating Lancaster, which worked all too well.

"This would look a lot better if I were able to stab you both," Qualls admitted, "so I could pin it on the same person who terrorized your park and killed your maintenance guy."

"He had a name," Lancaster said, finding the callous nature of even his worst enemy unbearable.

"It wasn't personal with that guy, but it *would* feel so nice to feel the knife twisting around in your guts, Jeff. The others were just business, but I'd feel some satisfaction watching the life fade from your eyes."

"Haven't you done enough already?" Jean asked sternly, starting to step around Lancaster until he blocked the path, keeping her in a safer position.

Qualls shook his head negatively.

"I can't be finished until everyone who can testify against me is in the same place as your aunt."

Lancaster remembered exactly why he couldn't stand Qualls. The man went out of his way to irritate every living person, which begged the question why he wanted to ever be a cop. Likely the thought of asserting his authority upon everyone else was the only thing in life that brought him happiness.

He turned to whisper some last minute instructions to Jean, knowing neither of them was going to survive this ordeal short of a miracle.

"When I charge him, run."

Jean gave him a disheartened look, knowing she couldn't run nearly fast enough with a bum ankle. Lancaster wasn't about to stand around to be shot down in cold blood, and Qualls looked as though his trigger finger was itching to shoot.

Lancaster was poised to charge the deputy when the sound of a vehicle reached his ears, drawing closer by the second. Perplexed, he looked over Qualls' shoulder as the deputy turned to see a dark sedan approaching along one of the employee area roads. He suspected the driver was Schall, but he had no earthly idea why the security director returned to the park.

"Go!" he said just above a whisper to Jean, pointing in the safest direction while Qualls turned to see the vehicle barreling directly at him, eventually taking aim with his pistol.

When he realized the sedan wasn't going to stop, Qualls fired two shots directly into the windshield. Hoping Schall wasn't hit by either bullet, Lancaster charged the deputy as planned, watching Qualls turn around too late as the theme park owner tackled him to the ground, able to swing the man's arms and the gun away from his face or chest. During the course of his actions he saw the sedan swerve toward a fence before the impact of the car with one of the fence's support beams reached his ears. Knowing he didn't have time to realign his body to make a play for the gun, Lancaster thrust his right elbow into Qualls' face, stunning him and immediately drawing blood from his nose.

Far from being in the clear, Lancaster clasped both of the man's wrists in an effort to wrestle the gun away from him, or at least get it clear so only fists were involved in their skirmish. It took every ounce of mental restraint not to blindly attack Qualls with every appendage, but instead calculate how he wanted to attack the man so he didn't end up shot.

Qualls kneed him in the groin, but doing his best to ignore the pain Lancaster thrust his forehead against the deputy's skull, drawing a pained groan. Adrenalin alone kept him from feeling any pain as he continued to manipulate his fingers into better position to grasp the gun. Both struggled to aim the barrel of the gun away from their bodies and Lancaster forced his thumb into position against the magazine release, pressing it inward to drop the magazine out of the gun along with every bullet save the one he assumed Qualls had chambered and ready.

Both men continued to try twisting and turning the firearm toward the other man, but both had their elbows locked and the gun wasn't moving in either direction. Forced into a race of strength and stamina, where the first man to fatigue or flinch was doomed, Lancaster's ears barely registered a car door opening or shutting in the distance before footsteps came running in his direction.

Had the footsteps not been produced by cowboy boots, Lancaster might not have heard them at all over the breathing and grunting exchanged between him and Qualls during their struggle. Suddenly he realized Schall had survived gunfire and the car crash, now running to assist his employer. Lancaster also felt a presence on his right side, which surely had to be Jean returning to help him as well. A growing look of panic and desperation crossed Qualls' face as he realized three people were ganging up on him. He threw elbows and every body part possible to free himself from Lancaster's weight and the arms reaching in to snatch the firearm. Jean gave a cry as she was knocked away by a thrown elbow, barely able to keep her footing in the first place as she landed hard on the ground.

Feeling his grip grow less secure on the gun, Lancaster tried aiming it away from all parties involved, which meant directly in front of him where no one was standing. Qualls would have none of it, and with his hand still in control of the grip he aimed toward Schall and pulled the trigger, using the sole bullet to strike the security director, who fell like a dropped grain sack onto the ground. Lancaster thought he saw Schall's head fling back, praying his security director wasn't hurt badly as he glanced to ascertain details.

Unable to see exactly where Schall was struck from just the quick turn, Lancaster left himself open to attack from Qualls, who struck him in the side of the jaw with gun's barrel, knocking him back. Now he and Jean were in exactly the same position as a minute prior because Qualls scrambled to regain the magazine with its extra ammunition. Lancaster dove for the magazine simultaneously, but proved a split-second too late as Qualls swiped up the metal object, slid it into the gun, and racked the slide to chamber a round with practiced efficiency.

Wiping his bloodied nose clean with the sleeve of his disguise, Qualls appeared disgusted and furious. Lancaster had little doubt the man was about to shoot them without another word, wondering if Schall's firearm was along his right hip in its usual spot. With no cover, diving for the weapon was pure suicide for Lancaster, but he didn't want to be shot down in the middle of his own theme park without at least trying. If he knew for certain his head of security were dead he might have tried diving beneath his corpse for use as a human shield, but he owed Schall a better fate than that.

"Time to join your dad," Qualls said bitterly as he raised the firearm, not seeing the saving grace that Lancaster noticed standing behind the disgraced deputy.

"I don't think so," Lancaster said, looking to Jean, who wore an expression of complete shock as she laid eyes on Michael Tanksley in person for the first time.

"What?" Qualls asked with a confused look as Tanksley stood ominously behind him, having appeared like an apparition from out of nowhere.

Lancaster instinctively knew why the man returned from wherever he'd gone, and although he laid eyes on Tanksley for the first time personally, he saw the resemblance between the living corpse and Colby McWilliams. Suddenly he felt no fear of dying because he believed Tanksley returned from the grave to avenge his own death and right a few other wrongs. Somehow the undead man knew locations, events, and people he should have had no right to know after forty plus years in the ground.

By the time Qualls realized someone, or something, stood behind him it was too late. With ferocity and quickness unparalleled by any living person Lancaster could ever recall witnessing, Tanksley wrapped his arms around Qualls' neck and jaw like striking serpents, snapping the man's neck before he could even turn around. Lancaster took a step back upon seeing the unfeeling, murderous nature of the undead man. With no cursed book present to use as leverage, Qualls couldn't threaten the man he should never have dared taunt in the first place.

The deputy's body landed awkwardly on the concrete walkway with both arms spread outward in unnatural positions. In every conceivable way his death appeared undignified, as though Tanksley wanted him treated like everyone else on his hit list. Tanksley looked down at his handiwork for only a second before he turned to retreat back to wherever he resided when he wasn't in his proper burial site.

"Wait," Lancaster dared say, stopping Tanksley dead in his tracks.

As though very perturbed about being spoken to he stood completely still a few seconds before slowly and ominously turning to the man who addressed him. His ghostly eyes shifted upward from the ground to meet Lancaster's gaze, so intensely pale that Lancaster questioned how the man could even see.

"My father," Lancaster said, finding time to reel at the loss of the man who raised him once more. "Why?"

Tanksley looked between Lancaster and his father, who continued to swing above them in the breeze as the sun began peeking out from the clouds at long last. After looking back to Lancaster, Tanksley provided the slightest lip movement that could only be categorized as a grin before he scaled one of the roller coaster's beams to the top where he proceeded to pull Wyatt Lancaster upward by the rope, noose and all, over the course of a few seconds with uncanny strength that obviously accompanied his cursed state. Lancaster watched with stunned awe as he slung the senior Lancaster over his shoulder and descended the same wooden beam with ease, like some kind of insect maneuvering across a stick.

Jean, still undergoing her own internal conflicts, limped over to take Lancaster's side, possibly believing they were stuck in some kind of dream. Both watched as Tanksley carefully laid Wyatt Lancaster at their feet, took a few steps back from the senior citizen and snapped his fingers.

Wyatt's eyes snapped open from whatever trance Tanksley had placed him in, looking wildly around to take in his surroundings. Lancaster dropped to his knees to give his father a hug, not even questioning how the man wasn't dead. Jean walked behind the Lancaster reunion to check on Schall a few feet away. Lancaster quickly discovered that the rope used to string up his father was not a noose, but rather a constructed body harness that supported the tall man around his waistline and under his armpits so no pressure was actually placed upon his throat.

Lancaster looked up to express some thanks to Tanksley, or asked a question that would surely be met with silence, but the shadowy man was already gone.

"I thought you were dead," Lancaster admitted to his father.

"So did I," his father admitted with a quivering voice, finding his eyeglasses in the front pocket of his overalls, quickly replacing them. "Qualls ordered him to string me up, but I guess he never technically told him to kill me."

Lancaster helped his father begin the process of undoing the harness, which meant removing the straps to the man's overalls and his shirt. Assured his father could manage the rest of the feat himself, Lancaster stood and walked over to Jean, who knelt beside Schall. She held the man's right hand, looking down at him with admiration and concern. As Lancaster examined the man's body he noticed a very small pool of blood near the man's head, indicating the bullet had found its intended mark, despite his best efforts to prevent it.

Kneeling down along the other side of Schall, Lancaster supported his own weight with one arm while using his two primary fingers on his other arm to check for a pulse along the man's carotid artery.

"I wish you wouldn't do that," Schall said the moment the fingers pressed against the neck skin, startling both Lancaster and Jean.

"Fuck! You scared me, Danny!" Lancaster exclaimed, rearing back from his security director momentarily. "Where did he get you?"

Schall struggled to sit up, feeling the right side of his head where the blood originated, finding the spot as he pulled away a palm full of blood.

"He must've grazed my skull because I've got a killer headache," Schall said with a groan before glancing over to Quall's body. "Please tell me he's dead."

"He is," Jean assured him before her look changed to a mix of terror and guilt. "Oh my God, we've got to check on Colby!"

Schall swayed back and forth momentarily after sitting up, so he intentionally fell back to the ground to avoid losing consciousness again.

"If you're talking about the guy next to the truck and the police car, the ambulance probably got to him about five or ten minutes ago," Schall said through the pain, his eyes blinking like mad. "Is it just me or did someone just turn on the lights?"

Lancaster gave an exhaled sigh of relief that everyone survived the incident in decent health, although he shared concerns about McWilliams.

"Sit tight, Danny," he said, tapping the man on the chest. "I'll get some help out here."

"I want a raise, boss," Schall said groggily with a groan.

Lancaster grinned, finding his father had managed to undo the rope harness and replace his shirt. He plucked his phone from his back pocket and dialed 911, figuring all of them were bound to visit the hospital for various reasons. There wasn't a good way to explain any of what happened, and no one would believe the truth, but the four of them didn't have the time to create a unified tale. If Parsons conducted the investigation with his inside knowledge, things might go more smoothly than if the state police took over. Looking to the dead deputy only a few feet away, Lancaster suspected the troopers would *have* to take the lead.

Either way the worst was behind him, and he hoped the rest of the fall season proved uneventful as he moved forward with his business and appreciated his family more than ever.

Epilogue

Saturday, April 13

Lancaster stood in the local cemetery just after nine in the morning to pay his respects on the same day his theme park opened for the season, albeit weekends only until school let out in June. Warm and sunny, but not yet muggy and hot like the summer months in Southern Indiana, the day felt perfect for a theme park opening.

He looked at the grave marker that provided the birth and death dates for Michael Tanksley, who had been relocated one last time. The move allowed another family to purchase a plot beside their loved ones, but also placed Tanksley next to a grave marked for Colby McWilliams, his last surviving relative.

Bowing his head, Lancaster felt that things had died down the last six months from the bizarre events that took over local, state, and even national headlines for a while. No one except his ex-wife likely missed Qualls, and the entire affair was left unsolved in the eyes of the state police because none of the survivors actually killed the man. So far as the troopers knew a mysterious person still at large killed the deputy and saved the day.

Schall had quickly recovered from his wounds and remained at his post in the theme park throughout the winter and into the spring. Lancaster indeed gave the man a raise, and they spoke at length about the entire ordeal, even the supernatural parts, creating a bond of trust between them at last. The two barely spoke about the events of the fall after clearing the air, and Schall continued to carry the guilt of Hank Barwick's death with him, though he didn't speak about it. He kept an obituary of the man on his desk, along with a few others from Kansas City, serving as reminders of those he lost far too soon.

Parsons continued his duties as sheriff and tried to help smooth the investigation over with the state police. Because he knew the truth and didn't want panic spreading through his county, he blamed much of the death and destruction on Qualls. Although Qualls proved a black eye for the sheriff's department, it was easier to believe one man went berserk than a supernatural curse brought Michael Tanksley back from the dead.

People in the town of Mitchell still talked, however, and the few times Lancaster visited the library, the red-headed librarian always looked at him as though she knew something more occurred than the media stated. He couldn't avoid questions whenever he spoke in public, whether at a press conference or visiting a school to promote Hallowed Grounds.

He supposed he might have named his theme park a little differently had he known the true nature of how the land ended up in his hands.

"You look deep in thought," a male voice said from beside him as he looked between the two tombstones atop the hill in the newer section of the cemetery.

"Good to see you, Colby," Lancaster said, shaking the man's hand as McWilliams looked at the updated grave marker for his cousin.

"I appreciate you buying that for him," McWilliams said genuinely. "And for covering the expenses of relocating him."

"My pleasure. I see you went the pre-planning route with your stone while we were doing all of this."

McWilliams gave a crooked grin.

"After my brush with death I kinda think of every day as borrowed time."

Lancaster owed McWilliams a debt of gratitude for deciding to reopen the book after sealing it the previous fall. By his own rules, Tanksley was required to return to the grave each time the book was sealed with a blood sacrifice. If not for McWilliams changing his mind, Qualls could easily have gotten away with a triple homicide.

"How are things with you and Jean?" Lancaster inquired.

McWilliams nodded toward his truck parked on the concrete path beside the cemetery. Jean sat in the passenger's seat and provided a wave when Lancaster looked her way.

"I think I'm going to pop the question soon," McWilliams confessed in a whisper as he leaned inward.

"Congratulations."

"Save that 'til I get the answer."

Lancaster chuckled.

"So I hear you're open for business today," McWilliams stated.

"Yeah. The park is poised to do pretty well. I'll open some more rides next year if we can draw enough revenue."

"Hope my cousin doesn't plan any surprise visits."

"Me too."

Knowing how handy McWilliams was with all kinds of machinery, Lancaster had offered him a position at the theme park, which the man declined, saying he wasn't especially fond of heights.

"You know that job offer still stands anytime you want a steady gig," he said. "We can keep you close to the ground if that's what it takes."

McWilliams gave a sheepish grin.

"Maybe marriage will make an honest man out of me and I'll have to take you up on that. I'd better pull my weight or she won't be very happy with me."

Lancaster once went out of his way to make a marriage work, taking overtime hours and providing a nicer house, vehicle, and lifestyle for his wife. It turned out he was simply giving her more time to betray him, though it seemed karma eventually gave them both what they deserved.

"Well, I'd better get going," McWilliams said as the two men shook hands. "Thanks again for everything."

"Anytime. Good luck popping the question."

McWilliams held his forefinger up to his lips as he walked away, silently asking Lancaster to keep his secret.

Lately Lancaster had kept several secrets, mainly all to himself. His smile quickly faded as he watched the mechanic open the door to his truck.

By the time he got to search the area where McWilliams was attacked by Qualls the previous fall he couldn't find the old book. It didn't take long to discover that it was confiscated with dozens of items as evidence by the state police. Lancaster used an old connection from the Bloomington post to locate and retrieve the book for him with the agreement that his friend would get some security hours at the theme park throughout the year. Almost immediately the book was forgotten by authorities because it was never truly considered evidence, so no one missed it. It seemed everyone who read it dismissed it as a work of fiction, or some deranged journal that shouldn't have been lumped in with *real* evidence.

Lancaster wasted no time giving the cursed book a blood sacrifice after he received it, effectively placing Michael Tanksley in his rightful place, six feet under his tombstone. Looking at the palm of his hand, long since healed from that cut, Lancaster felt fortunate Tanksley hadn't targeted anyone else during his brief stint of freedom the previous September.

He originally intended to simply keep the book tucked away in a safe place so no one accidentally set Michael Tanksley free ever again. The two women, and whomever else he might want to enact revenge upon, were safe to live out their natural lives.

Things changed, however, when McWilliams regained full health and talked about moving his cousin's burial spot because people flocked to it over the winter after hearing various tales. Some of the urban legends were actually true, but most were farfetched and hoaxes used by locals to draw tourists to their town. Even in his latest death Tanksley continued to be used and abused by the town he once called home.

Lancaster walked away from the graves to his truck, opening the door to see the old book lying atop the passenger's seat. He slid inside, thinking back to how he acquired the book and how a winter of planning and solitude changed his view about a few things.

What McWilliams didn't know was that his cousin's grave was currently empty. Lancaster volunteered to finance the relocation of the plot intentionally, knowing supervision of the project would be minimal at best. His notion proved correct, and he barely felt guilty, or the least bit worried when he removed the well-preserved body from the old, damaged coffin with the verbal commitment that he would place it inside the newly-purchased coffin personally.

His word didn't hold true for one of the first times in his life, and early that morning he placed a rather large canvas bag inside Candice Fenton's large house that she and Ronnie Qualls shared until his untimely death.

Breaking into the house felt like child's play, and leaving the canvas bag in the center of the downstairs where she would immediately see it when she returned home from work seemed appropriate.

He wanted her to know.

Lancaster forgave infidelity, likely taking more of the blame for their marital problems than he ever should have, giving her cheating, stealing ass more than she deserved in the settlement. So many facts never came out until later, and his fellow deputies who knew about the affair kept everything from him. No one wanted to be that work friend who informed a colleague their spouse was committing the ultimate marital sin.

No, he decided, he wanted Candice to know that *he* knew she tried to murder him along with Qualls and an unwitting Michael Tanksley. Legally, he couldn't pursue her because no evidence pointed to her involvement with the murders or the theme park mishaps the previous fall. Lancaster held the verbal confession from Qualls in the recesses of his mind, admitting her involvement, but without Qualls alive to testify, the words meant little to nothing.

Candice crushed Lancaster when she divorced him, and when he finally got back on his feet, secure and happy with his life, she and her lover tried to take his life for no reasons other than jealousy and spite.

Unforgiveable, he thought.

Closing his eyes, he imagined her coming home to find the canvas bag in the middle of her house. Terrified, she would unzip the bag slowly, first struck by the odor of a body dead several times over, turning away from the disgusting smell. Her attention would then be transfixed until she revealed every last detail of his grayish skin and the Native American garb. Fear would overtake her as she froze in place, unsure of whether to run or zip the bag shut and plan to hide it. Then those pale blue eyes would pop open, surprising her and sending sheer terror up and down her spine until

Tanksley stood from the bag and looked down upon her like a judge about to convict a defendant to death.

Lancaster hoped she would quiver in fear and plead in vain for her life, only to have him raise his tomahawk and swiftly bring it down, lodging it in the center of her forehead. Sitting in his truck, he took a deep breath through his nose with his eyes still closed, questioning whether he wanted to go that far to ensure Candice never conspired against him again.

It seemed a safe bet that her days of collusion were over, and she was happy to move on with what little material worth Qualls left her, but Lancaster didn't want to feel unsafe again, and he wasn't sure his message alone was enough.

Opening his eyes, he stared at the book beside him for nearly a minute without blinking. Since Lancaster sealed it with his own blood the previous fall the book had remained shut, keeping the world safe from Michael Tanksley. A simple undoing of the hasp, followed by breaking the blood seal as one opened the book summoned Tanksley to life once again.

Either way Lancaster felt safe from prosecution based on past precedents in the town of Mitchell, knowing Parsons wouldn't open a case against him. Lancaster had deniable plausibility for the body not being inside the coffin, and no physical evidence linked him to Candice's residence. He made certain no one saw him near the place when he parked, entered, or left, and he was able to get in without damaging the door or its frame. Again, nothing could link him to a body being discovered inside her residence, if anyone even bothered to question him.

His conscience weighed on him a little bit, because he wasn't sure he wanted to stoop to the level that she and Qualls had regarding him. True, it felt like poetic justice, but even if he wasn't personally the one lodging a hatchet in his ex-wife's skull he still felt responsible. He thought about the harm done to people he cared about, both physically and psychologically the past fall. Never again did he want to see those people jeopardized, and he wasn't sure that *hoping* Candice simply lived out her life, carrying her secrets to the grave, was enough.

Lancaster looked at his watch.

9:28 a.m.

Starting his truck, he realized the choice didn't need to be made for nearly another seven hours. Putting the truck into drive, he started out of the cemetery, anxious to see how people reacted to the theme park opening again after its successful fall season. A number of decisions awaited him, and some of those could wait because Lancaster had a theme park to run.